SHANE AND THE HITWOMAN

BOB MAYER

SHANE AND THE HITWOMAN

By

BOB MAYER

Dedicated To Jennifer Crusie without whom this book wouldn't exist. And who taught me a thing or two or three about the craft and art of writing. Nothing but good times ahead.

SHANE'S WORDS OF WISDOM #1

Murphy's Law: What can go wrong, will go wrong.
Shane's addendum: And it will always be worse than you can imagine.

No one knows who Murphy was. Agnes told me he's apocryphal. I looked that up and I must disagree based on first-hand experience; which is the purpose of this official log of lessons learned in my career, written under protest.

Murphy was most correct even if he is a myth. As noted, it generally doesn't just go wrong, but terribly wrong.

Further research reveals a Scottish poet verifying Murphy, who I suspect was Irish, but close enough, with: *"The best laid schemes o' mice an' men, gang aft-a-gley. An' leave us nought be grief and pain, for promised joy."*

I'm not gonna argue with a guy who wears a skirt and speaks like that.

PS: After I showed her the poem, Agnes told me I'm a contrarian. I have to disagree with her on that.

PPS: But don't tell her that. That means you, Carpenter. I'm only writing this because you ordered me to.

PPPS: Hey. Carpenter. My official protest is noted in this log in case you missed it. Which I know you didn't.

TUESDAY AFTERNOON

S hane lay in cold slush, in Glacier National Park, peering through the scope of the sniper rifle. He centered the crosshairs on the woman approaching on an eerily silent snowmobile, riding the contraption between the trees like a ghostly electric horseman of the apocalypse. The thick barrel rested on a bipod; half buried in snow, propped up by rocks buried underneath, the butt plate tight against his shoulder.

The snowmobiler stopped two hundred meters away. The driver, like Shane, was dressed in over-whites and wore a pack. There was also a big knife, more a sword, strapped to the outside of the pack. The driver stood and pulled down her parka hood, revealing short red, mussed hair, and pixie features. Her eyes were hidden by Maui Jim sunglasses. She couldn't have been taller than five and a half feet and slender. She pantomimed, one hand pointing over her shoulder at her back and then the other up.

"Cute," Shane muttered. He stood and waved at the fellow operative from the Organization, a covert government agency.

She accelerated toward him at what he considered an unsafe speed, flaring to a halt four feet away in a spray of slush that almost, but didn't, reach him

"I'm your backup, Phoebe," she announced as she turned off the snowmobile.

"Yeah, I got that," Shane said. "I told Cleaner to have you stand by and wait for my call."

"I was never a good bench warmer," Phoebe replied. "Put me in, coach."

"What sport?"

"Checkers."

"Funny," Shane said. "Not. What's your name?"

"Phoebe. And you're Shane. Did you pick that? I wanted Cassandra, but Carpenter vetoed that as being too long."

"What's with the snowmobile?" Shane asked. "Electric? I didn't know they made those."

"The marvels of modern technology," Phoebe said. "Who knows what they'll come up with next? I hear someone's working on a device to send messages long distances through a wire."

Shane sighed. "How did you find me?"

"This is around where I figured you'd be after Cleaner told me where he dropped you off." She was referring to the third operative who did exactly what his title said: cleaned up after people like Shane and Phoebe did their job.

"I'm ten klicks from there," Shane pointed out.

"I can read a map. This is where you'd be. Why walk when you can ride?"

"Going to ride up there?" Shane pointed at a steep snow-covered ridgeline. It was late Spring, but it would be a while before the higher elevations were clear of their white covering. The target was on the other side.

"Valid point. But I rode it here. How long did it take you to trek it?"

"I enjoy taking in nature's bounty."

"Sure." Phoebe indicated the long .50 caliber Barrett M82 sniper rifle leaning against the tree. "Want me to be your spotter?"

"No."

"Okay." She folded her arms, waiting.

Carpenter had always been Shane's backup on wet work. And Carpenter, their boss, had sent her. Shane didn't know what to make of it. The Cleaner was on station and had picked Shane up from the airport and driven him to a spot ten kilometers away.

"Take the snowmobile and cover the road east out of the target zone," Shane ordered.

"I won't be able to provide direct support for you from the east," Phoebe said. "I'll also won't be able to provide observation."

"But you will be able to give me a warning when the people meeting are arriving along the only road. I'll be above and out of sight. Is that a sword on your back?"

"Men always think things are longer than they are," Phoebe said. "A katana is a sword. This is a wakizashi."

"Right," Shane said, having his doubts about Carpenter's decision-making. "Cover the east road."

TWENTY-FOUR HOURS LATER, the small earplug crackled with sound as Phoebe reported: "Pickup truck inbound. One occupant. Cases in the rear. He's from the militia, not the buyers. Over."

"Roger," Shane said as he checked the laser range finder once more, because tectonic plates are always moving. One thousand, four hundred and twenty-three meters.

He was on the tip of an outcrop on a mountainside overlooking a gravel parking lot for a trailhead in the National Park where intelligence indicated the meeting was to take place. Four minutes after Phoebe's message, he saw the pickup truck. It halted and a guy dressed in woodland camouflage exited, looking around nervously.

In front of Shane's position, the steep drop was covered with pristine snow. His old tracks coming in from a narrow ledge to the left, after climbing over the ridgeline from behind, had been washed out by a light snowfall the previous night, which was fortuitous and therefore worried Shane who was not a fan of good fortune. Therefore, he had strung fishing line mid-calf high on the ledge behind his position, eight feet away, one end fixed under a rock, the other to the cinch on the right ankle of his white snow pants. It was late in the day and the sun was dipping in the west, foretelling freezing temperatures tonight. Last night had been miserable, but that was the price to be paid for being secure. It always paid to be the first one to a deadly party.

The seller was comfortably within the stated range of the big rifle, although Shane had beat that range when the situation required it, because it was a guideline, not an absolute.

However, both sides, seller and buyer of weapons, were the mission's goal. The guy below, dressed in summer camo which clashed with the late season snow, was a local militia member who hung out at a compound with others of his ilk, so he could be found any time. However, local authorities, and even the Feds, were loath to go into the heavily armed militia compound, and were mimicking the three monkeys—seeing and hearing no evil and certainly not saying anything about it publicly. Until the militia did something really bad, it was no harm, no foul. Nobody wanted a Ruby Ridge repeat.

It was whoever the guy was selling the cases in the back of his truck to that was the key to this misery. There were quite a few cargo boxes and several were rather large which didn't bode well. Phoebe would alert him to the buyer's approach.

Shane was surprised when his secure phone buzzed with an incoming message. There were only four people who permanently had the number, and one temporary for mission, so it had to be important. It used to be three permanent, one of whom, since deleted, had been his former boss, whom his colleague Carpenter had replaced, but Shane had expanded his horizons since settling in with Agnes at Two Rivers for the past eight months. He was becoming downright sociable and had almost doubled his circle. But he still hated phones.

He gently unzipped the pocket, no Velcro for him as it made noise, and pulled it out, expecting a change or update from Carpenter.

It wasn't Carpenter. Shane squinted, trying to read the long message, but it was impossible with the screen turned to almost black. For a moment he wondered if he was getting old and needed reading glasses. He gently let the stock of the weapon down, making sure the heavy rifle didn't sink in the snow. He curled into a fetal position and pulled the over-white parka hood up, the phone just inches from his face. He cinched the hood tight so no light would escape. He turned up the illumination, noting that his hand was shaking from the cold ever so slightly. He was getting soft.

It was from Agnes and for the briefest of moments his pulse quickened in fear. They had a rule about communicating when he was on a job and this had to be an emergency.

I'M GOING TO PARIS!
THEY WANT ME TO LEAVE RIGHT AWAY!!

The tension went out of Shane as relief washed through him. He continued reading.

YOU NEED TO COME HOME AS SOON AS YOU CAN!!!
I LEAVE TOMORROW MORNING!!!!
PUBLISHER ALREADY BOOKED MY FLIGHT!!!!!

Paris. *Crap*, Shane thought. It had been something lurking out there, a slim possibility, a long shot. But it appeared the tectonic plates had moved. He was happy for Agnes getting the opportunity that caused her to type all caps and exclamation points that increased with every sentence.

He squinted at a new message.

Wedding party confirmed earlier today
Lisa Livia coming to help

And Joey will do cooking
But I'm doing most now
Weekend all taken care of

Double-crap. Shane dreaded hosting the wedding at Two Rivers this weekend without Agnes' steady hand and expertise.

Prescient as always, a new text vibrated onto the screen.

Based on my questionnaire
It will be small group
Wedding will be no problem

"Ha, humor," Shane murmured.

Agnes was so optimistic. He'd tried explaining Murphy's Law to her, but she'd said he was too much of a downer, which was strange for a woman who talked to her shrink in her own head and sometimes out loud when she thought Shane wasn't in earshot. Shane sometimes wondered if there was a real Doctor Garvin since Agnes claimed she'd finished therapy. On the plus side, it had been a long time, eight months to be exact, since Agnes had hit anyone with a frying pan, so he'd take a fictional Doctor Garvin. Still, she had a point. How hard can a small wedding be when there are no mobsters or homicidal grandmothers of the bride involved?

Shane waited a moment to see if there was anything further, but that seemed to be it. He turned the screen down and put it back in the pocket, making sure the zipper was secure. There was nothing he could object to, nor did he have any base from which to do so. Agnes going to Paris paled in comparison with him, here in Montana, working for Carpenter.

Death does not wait on Agnes and Paris.

He resumed the position, placed the stock against his shoulder and peered through the sight. The wanna-be tough guy was gone, but the pickup was still there. Then Shane spotted the man in camouflage. He was lying on the gravel next to the truck, his heat signature already cooling, which was ominous because there'd been no sound of gunfire. And no radio message from Phoebe about the buyers inbound. Shane shifted slightly and checked the truck bed. The cases were gone. That was fast.

Murphy's Law.

Before he could expand his search, he felt a slight tug on his ankle.

Shane's addendum.

He dropped the Barrett, spinning onto his back and reaching for the pistol in the thigh holster. The movement allowed the round aimed at his head to punch a hole in the snow, close enough to be too close. The sound of the gun firing was low, meaning a suppressor.

Shane jerked his pistol out, thumbing off the safety as he brought it up, toward the huge, dark silhouette rushing toward him. The tip of a boot knocked it out of his hand, sending it flying into the void. Shane's off hand was already grasping for his knife, while he scrambled backward with his feet in the snow, trying to put distance between him and the towering assailant.

Shane went over the edge of the hide spot. A muzzle flash partly blinded him and a round punch into his chest with the force of a baseball bat swung at full strength. His vision blurred and the wind was knocked out of his lungs. A second shot followed, hitting just a few inches from the first, amplifying the pain and accelerating Shane as he dropped out of sight of the attacker.

Shane went airborne off the cliff, trailing a thin tendril of broken fishing line. Then he hit the slope, his over-white parka acting as a sled.

Really? Shane thought, his eyes blurred as he struggled to get his breath as he plowed downhill and finally came to a halt. His chest radiated pain. Shane stared upward, trying to focus his vision, drawing some air, taking scant comfort from the fact that he was in a blind spot from whomever had shot him. Every breath was agony, but as the sky gradually coalesced, he noted that the evening sky this far from civilization was really pretty. Add in the fact he was breathing and he was downright upbeat about being alive.

. . .

PHOEBE TILTED her head as she heard a faint sound in the distance, in the direction of the target zone. A very slight whine.

"Shit," she said, then keyed the radio.

"A helicopter is cranking in the target zone," she warned Shane. "Over."

The whine grew louder as the engines got up to speed.

When there was no response, Phoebe repeated.

"I say again. A helicopter is starting in the target zone."

Phoebe turned on the snowmobile, feeling the electric power throb through the machine. She rolled the throttle and accelerated out of the grove of trees where she'd hidden. She was on the road in thirty seconds, following the single set of tire tracks made by the seller's truck.

The thump of blades joined the sound of the engines. She still had a hill between her and the target zone. She could tell by the sound the helicopter was taking off. By the time she rounded the hill and could see the parking lot, the chopper was nothing but a dark spot in the distance.

She pulled up next to the body lying next to the pickup truck. The cargo bed was empty.

Shane's weak voice came through the earplug. "One target is down. I heard a helicopter. Over."

Heard? Phoebe thought. *How come he hadn't seen it?* She looked up at the ridge where Shane had positioned himself.

"I need extraction," Shane said. "Over."

"Where are you? Over."

"Below the ridge. Someone shot me. Over."

Phoebe got off the snowmobile and checked to make sure the body was a corpse. The left eye was gone, just a black hole. She hadn't heard a shot. Nor had she heard the one Shane said he'd experienced. Professionals.

Except Shane was still breathing. So.

"Turn on your beacon," she told Shane.

SHANE LAY in the deep snow at the base of the ridge. Four feet of powder had broken his fall, but prevented him from seeing the helicopter take off and pretty much everything else. He fumbled with his vest, and turned on the electronic beacon.

He struggled to get upright, but his feet sank deeper into the powder. And his chest *really* hurt. He lay back into the cocoon of snow, which was actually kind of comfortable; except it was cold and his chest was on fire.

He heard a snowmobile crunching over the snow which meant she was close. It stopped thirty feet away and Phoebe put on snowshoes. She came flitting over the snow, like a winter sprite.

"Isn't this a fine pickle you've gotten yourself into, old timer," she said as she stopped in front of Shane. It was not a question.

"The seller is in the parking lot," Shane said, as he sat up, trying to hide any expression of pain; and irritation at 'old timer'.

"I know," Phoebe said. "Small caliber to the eye. That was a professional. I called Cleaner in to do his thing. Where were you shot?" She tossed him a set of snowshoes.

"My vest. I'm fine," Shane said.

"Sure. Looks like it." She looked about as he struggled to put the snowshoes on. "They were here before us."

"Duh," Shane muttered.

"Surveillance," Phoebe said. "Two shooters at least. A helicopter under a camo net close by. Pretty sophisticated."

"I'll put it all in the after-action report," Shane said. "Right now, I need to get home."

"Why?"

"There's a wedding," Shane said as he put them on.

"You're getting married?" she asked. "What are you doing lying out here in the snow then?"

"I'm not getting married," Shane said. "I have to put one on."

"You're a wedding planner?" Phoebe nodded. "That explains this." She pointed toward the snowmobile. "Come on. I'll give you a ride. Unless you want to walk and enjoy nature?"

Shane trudged behind her toward the vehicle.

Agnes was going to Paris.

Fuck.

SHANE'S WORDS OF WISDOM #2

There are two types of soldier: The steely-eyed killer and the beady-eyed minion.
Shane's Addendum: Never trust first appearances.

At first glance, the two are hard to tell apart.
The first is the person you want backing you up in a tough spot.
The other will get you killed or, worse, accidentally shoot you in the back while panicking.
It is only in moments of crisis that the differences between the two can easily be discerned.

THURSDAY MORNING

Shane stood in the Savannah Airport, on the wrong side of security given he didn't have a ticket, and miserably tried to estimate how he was going to survive the next week as Agnes turned one last time and blew him a kiss. He returned the gesture, feeling awkward since it was attention-getting, verboten in his line of work, and then she was gone, boarding the plane which would whisk her away to Paris.

Whisk. Damn Paris. Agnes said it would take her career to another level to be on panels with the other great chefs who'd been invited. There'd been a last-minute cancellation and Agnes had been invited as a replacement. Her publisher was paying her way and it was the opportunity of a lifetime, at least that's what she'd said when he'd gotten home. The possibility of another book. Who was he to argue with that?

His chest was sore from the final hug. The two large bruises that merged into one yellowish black mess on his chest had required no explaining because he'd gotten back from Montana early this morning and hadn't shared a proper sendoff with Agnes so she hadn't seen it. Optimistically, he'd be healed when he properly welcomed her home. If not, he'd need a good cover story. He'd ask Carpenter, because Carpenter supplied the best cover stories, but as quickly realized that Carpenter would advise him to tell the truth, it was always easier in this kind of situation, so Shane shelved that idea. After all, it was Carpenter who'd gotten him shot.

Sort of.

He was extremely lucky ribs hadn't been broken and the second shot had been a couple inches from the first. Best estimate was the shooter had been firing subsonic 9mm, which helped. Anything bigger and/or faster and they would have gone through the ballistic armor plate instead of cracking it.

In the warm glow after living through the first bloody wedding together at Two Rivers eight months ago, Shane had said he'd quit the business. Actually, it had been before the wedding, but just after he'd learned his parents had been murdered by Don Fortunato and then Joey and Frankie Fortunato, Lisa Livia's father, had gunned down the Don and his consigliere. Agnes had been so overjoyed he was still alive (and he'd been kind of glad about it, too) and wrapped her arms around him, that, well, a man might not be thinking too clearly and say anything.

A lot had happened on that day of blessed nuptials.

But then Carpenter had taken over the Organization, and he'd needed help, and Shane was his best, and while Agnes understood loyalty, it became a subject-non-grata between them. In Shane's defense, the Agnes glow had been pretty bright right after surviving that wedding, which had involved a high body count including the traitorous boss Carpenter replaced and two boats sunk. A man couldn't be blamed for speaking hastily and without much fore-thought, especially when he was in Agnes' embrace.

His melancholia and scheming and weak justifying were inter-rupted by his phone buzzing. He glanced at the screen and wasn't surprised to see JOEY followed by a text message:

WE GOT PROBLEMS

Agnes' plane is still boarding and already? Reluctantly, Shane turned away and headed for the exit. He noticed one of the TSA people shadowing him. He'd used one of his many classified government I.D.s to get through security with Agnes, the one that said he was a top-level CIA operative with a clearance straight to the heavens, but that didn't mean the TSA was asleep. Shane gave the poorly paid security people some credit for keeping tabs on him. Or the TSA was bored and wanted to see what Mister Secret Agent Man was up to. In reality, Shane worked for the Organization, which did the covert work the CIA couldn't touch and the FBI didn't want to, which he supposed made him Mister Super-Secret Agent Man. Right now, he felt like Mister Very-Sore-Not-Looking-Forward-To-A-Wedding-Sad-Dude-Who'd-Screwed-The-Pooch-On-His-Last-Mission. He glanced back as the boarding gate shut and wondered who was going to keep tabs on him without Agnes?

He checked the monitor as he walked by, but the flight number he, and the contingent from Two Rivers was supposed to meet, wasn't listed, which was probably Joey's problem. Shane exited through security, where Joey, Lisa Livia and Garth 'Three Wheels' Thibault awaited. Three Wheels held a cardboard sign torn off a box with ANDOVER PARTY written in barely legible magic marker that had begun to dry out around the V, Lisa Livia was crying, and Joey looked perturbed.

The weekend was going to be hell.

Joey, the wizened old man who looked exactly like the ex-mobster he was, wore his usual black pants and red shirt, while Three Wheels was a pale imitation, younger, taller and skinnier, with black jeans and a pink shirt that used to be white; mismatched laundry in the Thibault double-wide even with all the upgrades from his share of the Fortunato loot. It was hard to believe Garth was a millionaire since he'd gotten his deceased father's share of the five million from a long-ago job his old man had been in on with Joey and Lisa Livia's father. Shane had told Garth to stay low about spending it and he had a feeling Three Wheels had taken that to mean burying the money in the swamp somewhere. He hoped it was in a waterproof container.

Lisa Livia was gathering attention from appreciative men with her glossy brown hair, sharp features, mouth etched neon red, and body encased in a T-shirt emblazoned with NO across the chest, Capri pants and precariously high heels. Shane had followed the succinct written advice and not asked what the question was. Her olive skin glowed; life in the islands was good for her. That, and her mother being in prison for trying to kill Agnes. It's the little things in life that make all the difference. Shane was surprised no intrepid man had stepped up to offer to wipe away her tears; of course, that might get someone cut and there was the t-shirt's explicit message.

Shane decided to tackle the problems from least to greatest, since he was discombobulated by Agnes' departure.

"Garth," he said to the young man. "Is that the way you usually greet incoming wedding parties?"

Three Wheels shifted his feet and looked down. "Miss Agnes, usually she types big letters on the eye-pad and gives it to me. But I left the eye-pad back at the big house."

Shane tried not to call him Three Wheels, although everyone did, because the kid's kin had come up with the moniker as a slam since his grandfather, a getaway driver who'd done some jobs with Joey back in the day, had been known as Four Wheels, now deceased via Brenda Dupres' baby blue Cadillac, and his cousin, now deceased indirectly via Agnes' frying pan when he'd come to kidnap her old hound-dog Rhett (long story there), had been known as Two Wheels because of his motorcycle. Three Wheels was in reference to Garth falling off his tricycle as a kid.

Families can be hell, but Garth was a survivor.

"Andova," Shane said. "A-N-D-O-V-A." He sighed. "But they'll figure it out and I doubt they'll be hard to miss, if they ever get here."

Wedding parties were usually easy to spot. Large, often drunk, and either laughing or grim, depending on how everyone felt about the coming nuptials. Sometimes half and half. However, Agnes had texted this one would be small and quiet. Shane frowned and was tempted to check the texts to see if she'd really written quiet or was he hoping?

He and Agnes, mostly her, had hosted seven weddings at Two Rivers over the past eight months and Shane dreaded each one, especially this, since Agnes wasn't going to be here. But Lisa Livia was, so Shane turned to her.

"What's with the tears?"

"I'm gonna miss her," Lisa Livia said.

"We all are," Shane said. "You don't see me crying."

"Yeah, but what's really bumming me is why am *I* not going to Paris with her?"

"You don't cook, you don't have an international food column, and you don't have a book out on it," Shane said, noting that Joey was twitchy.

"There's more to Paris than cooking," Lisa Livia said. "There's love. Wild passionate love."

Shane raised an eyebrow.

Lisa Livia hurriedly covered herself. "Not for Agnes, I mean. But things have been boring in that area. For me, that is."

"You saw Carpenter not long ago," Shane noted.

"Carpenter and I are not a thing," Lisa Livia said. She saw his new look. "We ended it the last time we saw each other. He's married to his job, like you are." She caught herself again. "Were. He's in a relationship with his office which, I think is even worse than another woman. I'd rather be ignored for a person."

"But you just were with him," Shane said.

Lisa Livia snorted. "*Just with him*'? Men have no sense of time when it comes to important things. It's been over *six* months. That's not *just* in any woman's vocabulary. It's half a year, Shane. Even when

I was with him, he was always worried about work. And he didn't tell you, did he? That we're over?"

"Uh. No." *He needs to be worried,* Shane thought, *after last night.*

"See?" Lisa Livia said. "I wasn't important enough to him to tell you."

Shane had no answer to that trap statement. He indicated the cardboard sign. "We got work to do, Lisa Livia. Things aren't going to be boring. We figured this wedding to be easy with Agnes here, but do you see that To Do binder she left us? I appreciate you helping out."

"That's what friends do," Lisa Livia said. "We throw ourselves on grenades for our friends." She frowned. "Not like your friends throw themselves on grenades, I mean not literally. We also turn to our friends to commiserate when a relationship ends. Agnes didn't tell you about me and Carpenter?"

Shane didn't think she had. He was pretty sure he'd have remembered that. "No."

Lisa Livia nodded. "Good. That's a friend. They keep things private. Besides, she figured Carpenter would tell you. But he didn't, did he?"

Shane had already answered that one so he let it slide.

Joey pressed forward, tired of the small talk. "Trouble."

"I got the text," Shane said. "What's the problem?"

Joey nodded at the flight display and then the thick three-ring binder Agnes had entrusted to him before going through security. "I don't see da' number." He squinted at the piece of paper encased in clear plastic. Every page in the binder was inserted in plastic and there were tabs, lots of tabs, with something written on each in Agnes' block writing with alcohol pen. "This is the flight info. But no airline. Just a number. 'Cept no matching number up there."

"Sure we're here on the right day?" Shane asked.

Joey scowled at him. "Agnes wouldn't get the day wrong. Even if she had more important things on her mind. Like Paris." It was obvious the way he said the last word Joey didn't like the destination. He shoved the binder toward Shane. "This ain't my job, *nipote.* I only came along to say goodbye to Agnes. I'm cooking for the wedding; the stuff which Agnes hasn't already gotten done which ain't much, mostly breakfasts, since she was up all night in the kitchen. It's like she don't trust me. Lisa Livia takes care of the wedding stuff. And transportation is his job." He indicated Three Wheels with a mixture of pride and despair, more the latter. When Three Wheels wasn't driving wedding parties, he worked at Joey's diner with results equivalent to the sign's spelling and material and the color of his shirt.

"And she put menus in here for every single meal," Joey groused about the binder, getting to the black heart of his irritation. "Even my breakfasts. As if I don't know what I'm doing? I been serving folks longer than she's been alive. What kind of wedding is this going to be anyway? Where are these people coming from? Did you see what's in the binder?"

All very good questions and Shane wished he'd listened a little closer when Agnes had talked about the upcoming ceremony, but he wasn't sure at times if she was talking to him or Dr. Garvin or herself. During the previous weddings he'd done the grunt work as needed when she told him. Simple stuff like: 'move that' or 'fix this'. He'd never been in on the planning part. Plus, he'd been out of town for the past couple of days. Getting shot, which he considered a credible distraction.

"I even got a book about my cooking," Joey continued his complaining.

"Agnes wrote it," Shane pointed out, referring to *Mob Food*.

"With *my* recipes," Joey said. "Mostly mine. And I'm on the cover."

"Your picture," Shane said. "Not your name."

Joey wasn't done. "Hell, she's in Paris because of *Mob Food*."

"Because she wrote it and because she has a syndicated food column and her publisher wants her to do another book." Shane gave up and turned to Lisa Livia, holding out the binder. "Here."

It was an awfully thick binder for an intimate and small wedding, but then again, Agnes had put it together. The binder she'd compiled for replacing the temporary bridge to Two Rivers had been thicker and there'd been four accompanying tubes of plans for a rather simple bridge. Shane had felt empathy for the poor local guy who'd taken the contract to build it, but he had to admit, it *was* a good bridge when completed. Very sturdy.

Lisa Livia viewed the binder as if it were coated in hemlock. "Agnes and her binders. When did she start doing these again? You shoulda seen the ones she did in school. Even in kindergarten. Scared the teacher."

"She decided to get organized after trusting her ex-fiancee, who shall not be named, and then your mother tried to swindle her out of Two Rivers and Agnes barely escaped with her life," Shane guilted her. "Plus, she's running a business now, which she takes seriously. She said she used to be extraordinarily organized but had fallen out of the habit and she was going to be organized again. When she says she's going to do something, she goes all the way." Which brought back some memories and Shane smiled while Lisa Livia rolled her eyes. Shane noted Lisa Livia hadn't taken the binder. "Come on, LL. Figure out where this plane is."

Lisa Livia grimaced and reluctantly accepted. "Paris," she muttered. "I could be going to Paris. I *should* be going to Paris."

"You're in South Carolina," Shane said. "Get used to the idea."

Shane's secure phone vibrated. Since two of the four who had the number were standing in front of him, he figured it was Agnes sending her love.

"Phone sex already?" Lisa Livia asked. "She hasn't even taken off."

Shane ignored her. It was Carpenter.

Shane walked out of earshot, then took the call. "Yeah?"

"How's Lisa Livia?" Carpenter asked.

"She's crying," Shane replied.

"What did you do?"

"I didn't do nothing," Shane protested, and realizing he'd spent too much time around Joey and Lisa Livia today. "She's upset because Agnes is going to Paris and she isn't. She said there's wild passionate love in Paris."

"It's beautiful there in the spring."

"We've been to Paris," Shane reminded him. "It's not that great."

"We spent most of that mission hiding in the catacombs," Carpenter noted. "And it was winter."

"The stacked skulls were interesting." Shane glanced over at Lisa Livia. "She looks good," he offered.

"She always looks good," Carpenter said.

Shane was worried because Carpenter was chatting and Carpenter didn't do chatter. He waited for the bad news. A few seconds of silence ticked off.

Carpenter finally got to the reason for the call. "The incident site was cleaned up."

"I had to get back here," Shane said, wondering why Carpenter was stating the obvious. "I did debrief before I left."

The Cleaner had taken him from Phoebe's snowmobile to the airport and the Organization plane so he could fly back here at oh-dark-thirty. The Cleaner on each op was #5 on speed-dial and deleted from the phone as soon as the op was over.

"Uh-huh." A short silence. "Someone got behind you," Carpenter said, his voice shifting pitch. It wasn't a question, but an invitation into a touchy topic.

"I was distracted."

"By?"

"Agnes texted me. That's why I had to get back."

Five seconds of encrypted silence was sufficient rebuke. Carpenter then filled him in. "We've got nothing on the buyers, although technically, since they never paid for the goods, they're thieves. As well as killers."

"What did they get?" Shane asked.

"That's what we wanted to find out," Carpenter pointed out the obvious. "You know. By looking in the crates. Most likely, given the data we intercepted and broke down, along with who they were buying from, they contained weapons and demolitions."

"That's not good," Shane said.

"That's why the Organization was involved. That's why *you* were there. We wanted to know who they were and what they're planning."

Two rebukes in one conversation were a record. Lisa Livia was right: responsibility had changed Carpenter. Shane was secretly glad he'd turned down the position; one would think Agnes would have been happy about *that* big decision which allowed him to live at Two Rivers most of the time. "Any line on the buyers from your end?"

"We're working on it."

"I'm going to need a new chest plate for my vest," Shane said, trying to shift the conversation and emphasize the minor detail that he'd been shot. "It's got two dents in it."

Carpenter's voice softened. "How about the dents in you?"

"Sore, but they'll heal. Nothing broken."

"Amateurs," Carpenter said. "If it had been a professional, we wouldn't be talking and your head would be missing pieces and parts."

"The shooter *was* going for head shots," Shane acknowledged as he watched Lisa Livia talking to some frumpy guy in a cheap suit, with an acetate badge around his neck on a lanyard. She was gesturing at the Arriving Flights board. "There was snow. I was on a hillside. I was alerted before they shot. Fishing line to ankle. The first shot was damn close to my head. I was moving fast on my back and downhill so the next rounds hit center of mass. He knew what he was doing. I was lucky."

The suit guy was on his cell phone as Lisa Livia put one hand on her hip and thumped the binder against her thigh. *Better you than me,* Shane thought. Then it occurred to him she might be asking about flights to Paris. Would she take the binder?

"How did they know you were on the mountain in overwatch?" Carpenter asked.

"I walked eight miles to get there. A day early. It snowed the night before so my tracks were covered." *Barefoot and uphill all the way,* Shane thought, feeling like an ancient complaining about how hard it was getting to school in the good old days.

"The shooter came from behind to a hide site," Carpenter repeated. "Logic dictates they knew you were there."

Shane knew Phoebe had also been debriefed. "They were there before us. When did they set the meet?"

"Three days ago."

"So."

"So," Carpenter echoed. "Real professionals. Not other militia or your basement wanna-be terrorist poking their heads up. Besides, if locals had been suspected on both ends, the FBI would have handled it."

"This is not good," Shane said. "And they left by helicopter. Pretty sophisticated."

"It's possible they're terrorists from outside the country and are equipping themselves for an op."

"They wouldn't be from the Middle East or the 'Stan," Shane said. "That militia group is white supremest. They wouldn't deal with darker skins."

"Racism disappears when a lot of green is involved," Carpenter pointed out.

"True," Shane agreed. "The guy who shot me was big, but wearing a balaclava."

Lisa Livia was tapping the binder against her thigh with increasing speed and the guy in the suit was punching in another number as he pointed at the board and shook his head, his face growing redder. Shane half-expected Lisa Livia to grab the lanyard and start choking him.

Maybe the wedding is off-again, Shane hoped.

"Am I distracting you?" Carpenter asked as the silence went a second too long.

"Sorry," Shane said. "We're waiting on a wedding party and Lisa Livia is upset with someone."

"I pity the individual," Carpenter said.

"She said you two are over," Shane said, trying his own distraction.

"What?" Carpenter was confused by the shift.

"Not dating. Over whatever," Shane explained, not quite sure how to describe what the two of them had had.

A few seconds of silence. "We are over. She did mention that if I wasn't going to even consider putting a ring on it, then she wasn't going to act like there was and she didn't want to be exclusive. I had to research the reference. I told her that wasn't something I could do on my end and she said that was that. And that isn't the issue at the moment."

Shane hadn't put a ring on Agnes either, but she hadn't made a big deal or even asked. But she also hadn't brought up not being exclusive. Shane couldn't imagine that for her. Or him. Of course, continuing to do occasional jobs for Carpenter was probably an issue. But Carpenter needed him, at least until he ran the Organization long enough to get a feel for the personnel. Plus, Carpenter was using an analytics program that picked the optimal operatives for various jobs and Shane had come up as number one choice a number of times which was both a compliment and a curse. Apparently being cold in the snow was one of Shane's particular skills. He noted that Carpenter hadn't mentioned Phoebe, which was odd.

Carpenter spoke into the void: "How are you going to pull off a wedding without Agnes?"

"She left a binder. And Lisa Livia is running it. Joey's doing the food. All I have to do is make sure the lights are on and sweep up afterward and turn the lights off."

"Like a cleaner," Carpenter said.

"Without the blood," Shane pointed out.

"Speaking of blood," Carpenter said. "I'm putting a fresh operative on this."

"Does that mean I'm off?" Shane asked.

"You have a wedding," Carpenter said. "Let's say you're on pause for the moment. It worries me they were there before you. Something's wrong about the scenario."

This was another subtle rebuke, taking him off the mission, but Shane was grateful. "Phoebe?" he asked.

"Yes."

Lisa Livia was closer to the airport official, who was both attracted and distracted, but then the guy pointed toward one of the long windows facing the runway.

"Either the buyers are great planners," Carpenter was saying, "or—"

"Uh," Shane interrupted. "Can we finish this in a bit?"

"Something happening?" Carpenter asked.

"I think the wedding party just landed." The guy was still pointing and the look on Lisa Livia's face didn't portend happily ever after. Shane turned his head to see where the finger dictated. "I gotta go. I'll call you later."

CARPENTER HELD the phone for a few seconds, then pushed the off.

Paris? Lisa Livia? He sighed. *If only.* He didn't appreciate that Shane had brought up the relationship being over. That was his fault, but he'd been honest with Lisa-Livia when she'd pressed him for commitment. A man who occupied this office was already committed to something larger than a relationship: the security of the nation and the lives of the operatives.

The walls of his office were bare. No pictures, no windows, just the bland off-white of government paint. There hadn't been any personal knickknacks from his predecessor, Wilson, to clean out. Carpenter ran his hands over his shaved ebony scalp, feeling the familiar, faded scars, hazards of the occupation. Lisa Livia had asked about them, but he'd told her the mission on which they'd accrued was classified. That hadn't helped, but it was the truth.

For the first time it occurred to him that he'd never had a photo of Lisa Livia to brighten up the desktop, since she brightened anything up. Then he realized he didn't have *any* pictures of her. So many years in covert ops where picture taking was a big no-no. He frowned, because she'd gotten irritated when she wanted them to take a selfie and he'd demurred, explaining operational security. OPSEC had become a sore spot. She could make it into a profanity when she said the word. However, he *had* purchased a burner phone and given her the phone number, which was bordering on a violation, although Shane had pointed out that since Carpenter was in charge, the only one who could discipline him, was himself. Still, it had caused Carpenter some restless hours.

Ever since his father died while he was in high school, Carpenter always felt as if he had the old man in his head, constantly critiquing and second-guessing every decision, every action. Years of therapy and meditation had faded the voice, but never eradicated it. One of his early shrinks had told him that was impossible; there are things people carry with them to their grave. Carpenter had privately asked Agnes for help, given how successful Doctor Garvin had been with her anger issues. She'd referred him and Garvin had told him to make the voice an external one, something he could put some distance between. So, Carpenter visualized it as the small ghost of his father standing on his shoulder that only he could hear or see. Right now, the ghost was murmuring about Shane getting shot, a botched mission, the uncertainty of the operation and Carpenter's decision-making. And about the relationship with Lisa Livia being over.

The Organization was headquartered at Fort Meade, Maryland in a small, two-story concrete building with no windows, that had a sign out claiming it was *Facilities Maintenance*. If the Facility was the country, then it was honest. Most of it, including his office, was underground. Fort Meade is the headquarters of the National Security Agency. Thus, secure hard lines allowed the Organization to tap into the most extensive data and surveillance system in the world.

Since he was off the phone, the light above the outside of his door turned from red to green and there was a sharp, but muted, rap of knuckles on steel. Carpenter placed his forefinger on the access pad and the heavy door swung open on hydraulic arms. Wilson had been paranoid, but in the end, it hadn't helped him.

A young, petite woman briskly entered and brought not just a palpable aura of energy, but bright color. Phoebe's fiery red hair, the color of the week, was spiked straight up, adding four inches to her height, stretching her shortness to an artificial, five-eight. She wore a black, one piece skin tight suit with a red blazer. She sported a pair of black rimmed glasses that clashed with the hair and he couldn't recall seeing her wear glasses before. The eyes behind the non-prescription lens were Arctic water deep blue, just before it froze to ice.

"Interesting," Carpenter said, which is what he said every time she had a new color and style. He suspected she'd watched too many episodes of *The Americans*, where the characters drastically changed their look mainly with wigs or hair styles and/or glasses. "But being covert might be difficult."

"It's perfect for that, sir," Phoebe disagreed, "as the hair and glasses are what people notice. Without them, they'll never recognize me twice." Phoebe spoke with a confidence and brashness that Carpenter found amazing from someone so young, but he also valued it. Her name had churned to the top of the analytics readout just below Shane for this operation, so the computer also favored her. "I take the glasses off and flatten and wash out the color in the hair in two minutes. I did that last week when I ditched my date. I excused myself from the table, went to the restroom, turned my coat inside out, took the glasses off, did the hair, slicked it straight back, and walked right past him and out the door. He didn't recognize me."

"Bad date?" Carpenter asked.

"Nah," Phoebe said. "He was all right. I just wanted to see if I could do it."

"But you left him sitting there?" Carpenter asked.

"He's got my number," Phoebe said. "A burner," she added.

"Of course," Carpenter said, wondering if the date would call her again after being left adrift. He had a feeling the guy just might. Phoebe's generation was different. As was Phoebe. Then he wondered, because it was the nature of their business, if the story were even true, not that it mattered. The analytics indicated Phoebe was excellent at deception.

"What do you have on Operation Glacier?" Carpenter asked. It wasn't the most imaginative code name but it's what the computer had spit out.

Phoebe recited: "Victim had two rounds in the head, twenty-two-caliber. A suppressed pistol. Right into the eyeball, so a professional and close range. Our primary took two nine millimeter to the chest, also suppressed, but his vest took the brunt of it; no penetration." She shook her head. "Shane. What kind of cover name for an agent is that?" She pitched her voice to mimic a boy: "'*Shane, come back*'." She shook her head. "Hell, kid, he ain't coming back. He's gut shot. Gonna die in those mountains in great pain. If our Shane hadn't had his vest on, he'd have been in the same situation."

She must rank high in realistic expectations, Carpenter thought. *Probably right up there with Shane's inherent glass half full and that half is poison.*

"I've discussed the issue with the primary," Carpenter said.

"Yes, sir." Phoebe frowned. "It was odd, but fortuitous, that he had a trip wire behind him or else he'd probably have been killed. I wasn't taught that in the Course."

"It's old school when you operate solo."

"I could have been closer," Phoebe said, not complaining, but making a point, "but I was following his instructions."

"I know. But I always gave Shane great latitude when I worked with him. We did a number of missions together."

Phoebe plunged forward without hesitation. "*Shane* was a really good movie. But Alan Ladd was wrong for the part. I liked the Shane on the cover of the paperback; dark, mysterious, dressed in black. Not blonde and wearing buckskins. What kind of gunfighter wears buckskins?

"Anyway," Phoebe said, moving on just as quickly as she'd covered herself, "I called Cleaner after the shooting went down for exfiltration. I picked Shane up and delivered him to Cleaner. I've filed both reports. In essence, it was a mess. What do you want me to do now?"

"Shane's off the operation," Carpenter said. "You're primary. Track down the buyers."

"Yes, sir." Phoebe waited a second, then asked. "Do I have weapons-free?"

"We don't call it that," Carpenter said.

"Okay, sir."

"We call it discretionary latitude," Carpenter said.

"You say tomato, I say tomaato," Phoebe said. Adding: "Sir."

"It's implicit for any operative in the Organization. But the priority is finding out what was in the crates. More importantly: where the buyers are from and what they have planned. Stop them before they do it."

"They had surveillance on the meet beforehand," Phoebe said.

"Is that a statement or question?" Carpenter asked.

"It's the likelihood, sir," Phoebe said. "No one got by me on the road except the seller. Someone must have been there before Shane got in position or else he wouldn't have been spotted. I've checked the imagery. He was in the right place for the mission. He couldn't have been seen from below. I looked from the ground after I got him out."

"True."

"That's actually a positive," Phoebe said. "Given they did the buy with recon in place beforehand, it would be logical we have some time before any op goes down because professionals *will* be methodical about their next step."

"Do you know where you're going to start?"

"At the beginning, sir."

Carpenter waited for edification, but none was forthcoming.

Phoebe started to turn for the door, but paused. "Anything else, sir?"

"That's it."

Phoebe sniffed. "Wilson smoked in here."

When the door shut behind her, Carpenter turned toward the wall on the right as he pressed his hand on a pad underneath the top and his palm print was scanned. A portion of the dull white wall flickered and revealed a six foot by six high-definition display.

"Analytics," Carpenter said. "Operation Glacier. Rerun operative preferences."

This time, given last night, Phoebe's name was at the top of the list. Shane had dropped down to number six, which Carpenter thought was a bit harsh. The computer wasn't factoring in the Agnes variable.

Or maybe it was?

"Records, Phoebe. Official and background check."

A classified cover sheet appeared stamped with all sorts of warnings as if that would stop someone who'd gotten access.

"Advance," Carpenter ordered and he reviewed her file, page by page, trying to reconcile the person described and the woman who'd just left his office. She was a military brat, raised by a single father who'd been in the Air Force. There was no record of who her mother was.

Phoebe had spent a large chunk of her childhood bouncing around Air Force bases in Okinawa, Japan, the Middle East and South Korea. She'd been a brilliant student but also a discipline problem. During her freshman year of high school, she'd been on the gymnastics team and won a regional competition in the all-around, but had not joined the team at the next school she was enrolled in for sophomore year. A footnote indicated that was because the new school hadn't had a program. The travails of a military brat.

Phoebe had studied several martial arts in the various countries but there was no record of her achieving black belt status, which Carpenter knew indicated nothing. A practical person learned what they needed from each discipline and moved on. However, this training clashed with the school discipline issue and was difficult to reconcile.

Her father had died in a munition's accident, aka an explosion, at an air base during her senior year of high school. She'd withdrawn from school, lived in the dojo of one of her sensei for several months, then immediately enlisted in the Army on her eighteenth birthday.

She'd gone to Ranger School, which made her one of a handful of women, graduated, an even smaller group, and been one of the first females assigned to a Ranger Battalion. She'd accomplished a number of deployments with that high-speed Special Operations unit of elite Infantry. Carpenter frowned as he saw a redacted section in the top-secret portion of her official Army file in which she'd served from age 18 to 24. Six years was a lifetime in the Ranger Battalion. Very few lasted that long given the high operational tempo.

What could be hidden in a document that was already top secret? "Clear redaction."

The black rectangles broke apart and the original words appeared. So much for the Top-Secret redaction program the Department of Defense used, Carpenter mused. Phoebe had been nominated for the Distinguished Service Cross, second only to the Medal of Honor, and twice for the Silver Star, for her actions on three separate occasions. The awards had been suppressed by officers higher in the chain of command because she'd been doing missions that weren't officially sanctioned, in a place army personnel weren't supposed to be. At least that was the ostensible reason, but Carpenter knew there was more to it. The Special Operations world had grudgingly allowed women in but that didn't mean they were completely accepted, especially by the older guys, higher in rank. The fact she'd even been nominated by her immediate supervisors spoke volumes.

From her record, it was obvious why she'd been recruited by the Organization. And why she'd left the Army behind, although from the redactions it wasn't clear whether she'd known about the award nominations from her on-the-ground commanders and the denials higher up.

Carpenter shook his head. It took all kinds. "Close." The bland wall returned.

He closed his eyes for a moment and whispered: "Stay centered and true." Then he accessed the file on the next Operation. But, before he started reading, he sniffed. Wilson hadn't been here for over eight months. Carpenter couldn't pick up any trace of cigarette smoke.

"WHO ARE THESE PEOPLE?" Shane demanded of Lisa Livia as they strode from their cars across the tarmac toward the airplane.

On the tail of the plane was a flag Shane had never seen before, although he recognized the French Flag in the upper left quadrant and the Spanish flag in the lower right. The other two quadrants held a coat of arms backdropped against gold in one and the other, magenta. It seemed a bit schizophrenic in terms of symbolism. And colors.

Three Wheels edged the limo closer behind them.

"Agnes didn't tell you?" Lisa Livia asked.

"She might have," Shane allowed. "But. You know."

"You weren't listening."

"They're from some place called Andova. I thought that was in New England."

Lisa Livia was paging through the binder as they walked. "Andova is a country. They're arriving from overseas."

"This part of Andova Airlines? No wonder it wasn't on the arrival's board."

"Airport guy said it's a private plane. That's the biggest damn private plane I've ever seen."

"Airbus 320," Shane said. He halted and put an arm out to keep Lisa Livia from blindly walking in front of the stairs being pushed out to meet the plane as she read the binder. "That flag is kind of nuts. Why aren't they getting married in their own country?"

"I'm sure that's in here," Lisa Livia said, indicating the binder, "but maybe we should worry about not being able to fit a plane load of people in Garth's limo?"

"Agnes wouldn't have missed that," Shane said. He waited a beat. "Would she?"

Lisa Livia turned pages in the binder, holding it open awkwardly in the crook of one arm. "Here it is. Transportation. God, she still writes the way we were taught in Keyes Elementary. Block letters. You'd think—"

"LL. Eye on the target."

Lisa Livia flipped the tab and ran a red fingernail down a plastic-covered page. "Oh, thank you, Agnes. Garth's limo is for the bride and groom. There's a coach bus contracted for the others on the plane, thirteen additional, and Agnes made a note she confirmed it. The bus should be arriving at—" she twisted her wrist, still holding the book, to look at the face of her watch— "now."

"I love you," Shane murmured.

"Thanks," Lisa Livia said, "but it's—"

Shane cut her off. "No, I meant Agnes. Look."

A shuttle bus that could handle two dozen was passing through a gate onto the airfield. Shane straightened his shoulders. "Agnes plans everything. This is going to be all right."

He saw, but ignored Lisa Livia's eye roll, as the plane halted and the engines whined in shutdown. "How many people altogether?"

Lisa Livia found another tab, labeled PERSONNEL. "The wedding is going to be eighteen total." She looked up. "If there's only fifteen people on that plane . . ." Lisa Livia's voice trailed off.

"Names, LL," Shane said. "Bride? Groom?"

Lisa Livia checked the tabs as the stairs were adjusted. "Geez, Shane. You really didn't listen to Agnes, did you? A Marc, with no K but a C, what kind of name is that, Navarro and a Margaurite, more weird spelling, Imbrie."

The door of the plane pulled in and then swung out of the way. The stairs were pushed up against the opening.

"Shane," Joey called out.

Shane looked over his shoulder. "What?"

"It's the cops." Joes held up his phone. "They caught someone trespassing at Two Rivers."

"You got this," Shane told Lisa Livia. "I'm confident Agnes has everything taken care of." He headed toward his black Defender. "Come on," he said to Joey.

"Shane!" Lisa Livia shouted, but he was in the old four-wheel drive truck with Joey before her first curse. "Damn you, Shane. Come back! Shane! Come back!"

As Shane drove away, he spotted a silver-haired older couple appear in the plane's door and they were arguing with an elderly, bald man who sported a distinctive white handlebar mustache. He had a thick, blue baton, eighteen inches long, in his hand.

Parents were the worst at weddings. Shane was content to let Lisa Livia deal with them since his last evaluation had noted he wasn't exactly a people person in terms of conversation and social graces.

Killing them was a completely different matter.

"Hey, Lou," Phoebe said.

The woman surrounded by computer displays peered over her large reading glasses and a smile lit up her face. "Phoe! Oh, my gosh. The hair. Love it, but it's so--" Lou lowered her voice to a whisper-- "daring."

Lou's own hair was blond, long, and shimmering, despite the poor lighting, cascading over her shoulders to flow down her back. Her face was narrow, marred by the over-sized glasses which Phoebe had tried to talk her out of several times, but Lou insisted she needed them since they had a built-in pointer in the frame that acted as a computer mouse. Her pale skin was smooth like perfect ivory. She was tall, as many inches above average as Phoebe was below, and willowy. Her right arm ended above where the elbow would have been, a birth defect that she hadn't let stand in her way. Her voice was a contrast, heavy and husky, and Phoebe could listen to her talk about computers, the weather, or anything, all day long.

Phoebe grabbed a rolling chair from a vacant station and pulled it over to the cubicle. The room had a low ceiling and was claustrophobic. Phoebe figured it was designed that way so the analysts would keep their eyes on the screens. The only light, besides the screens and tiny, focused desk lamps, came from recessed tracks along the top of the walls, reflecting off the dull, white concrete ceiling. Technical Support was deep underground, in what used to be a survival bunker in the optimistic days when it was thought one could live through an all-out nuclear exchange. The air was musty and stale and Phoebe only visited because Lou worked here. Other operatives made their requests remotely. The group's name sounded as if they were the people you called for help booting up your computer and they'd always ask if it was plugged in before going any further. Then tell you to unplug it and plug it back in.

Phoebe gave Lou a hug and passed her a small pewter figurine of a hobbit as she sat down. "Pippin."

"Oh!" Lou blushed. "Thank you so much." She placed it amongst an array of pewter figurines underneath one of the monitors. "You've given me all the hobbits." There was a dragon and a wizard flanking the smaller hobbits.

"You don't have Gollum," Phoebe noted. "He was a hobbit once upon a time. I'll bring him next time."

Lou frowned. "I don't like Gollum."

"He was necessary," Phoebe said. "Remember what Gandalf said."

"I suppose in the long run, he was," Lou allowed. "I didn't know you wore glasses."

"I don't," Phoebe said, taking them off.

"Louise." The man's voice held a tint of reprimand in it. Lou's boss loomed over both women. "What did I tell you about knick-knacks?"

"I'm sorry, Mister Fromm," Lou said.

"They're gifts," Phoebe said. "From me. Besides, studies have determined that a cozy workspace makes for more efficient employees."

"What studies?" Fromm demanded.

Phoebe met his eyes and her voice went cold. "Studies. That I've read."

Fromm shifted his gaze. "Are you here on official business?" he demanded. He wore a three-piece suit a decade out of fashion with a bow tie and his pale skin made it look like this room was his sunny hotspot after arising from his coffin each morning. His receding hairline revealed pale wrinkly skin leading to wisps of gray hair.

"Carpenter sent me," Phoebe said the magic name as she pulled her feet up and spun in the chair, doing a squeaky three-sixty before facing Lou once more. "Needs oil."

"I'll leave you to *business* then," Fromm huffed, before heading off to harass someone else.

"Thanks," Lou whispered, when he was far enough away.

"He's a jerk," Phoebe said. "You're ten times smarter than him."

"He's been around a long time," Lou said.

"I think he died down here years ago, but hasn't realized it," Phoebe said.

"He's not that bad," Lou said, nervously glancing about. "What can I do for you?"

"You had an encrypted intercept three days ago reference Operation Glacier." Phoebe told her the date/time stamp from memory. "What can you tell me about it?"

Lou's left hand floated over the keyboard, which was one of those that looked like an old manual typewriter but without the racket as she barely touched the fine-tuned keys. Each fingernail was painted differently; Lou's indulgence was getting that done weekly. Her fingers moved so fast, Phoebe could barely follow, back and forth, compensating for the missing hand. She shifted her head ever so slightly using the pointer and blinked a fraction of a second longer than usual, to click. It was disorienting, yet addictive to watch. "We locked down the receiver, a guy in Montana—"

Phoebe cut in. "I know where he is now. I need the initiator. Who contacted him?"

"We couldn't lock that down. They used the dark web with a chain of multiple I.P.s, two of which are now offline."

"How'd you break the encryption?" Phoebe asked. She noted that Fromm was watching from his office which was three feet higher in one corner of the room and encased in glass. She wondered if the glass was bulletproof. And if there was a coffin behind his desk.

Lou started speaking technical and Phoebe didn't interrupt although she understood only about half of what was relayed. It might mean something to somebody she talked to down the line, wherever the line went. Right now, she needed to find one end of a thread since the other was dead.

"In essence," Phoebe summarized, when Lou was done, "it was encrypted using a program hacked from the NSA and the NSA had to break their own encryption?"

"Technically correct."

"It's amazing anything gets done," Phoebe said. "Who could have gotten hold of the program?"

Lou shrugged. "A really good hacker."

"The NSA?"

"Okay," Lou amended. "A really, really good hacker with a background in encryption."

"The hacker listed in the file?"

"Possibly."

"Why is this hacker still breathing if we know who it is?" Phoebe thought it seemed like a good mission for 'discretionary latitude'; one she wouldn't mind doing.

"Good question," Lou said. She lowered her voice. "You want my guess?"

"Always."

"My suspicion is that the NSA allowed the program to be stolen since they'd already broken it themselves, making it worthless for their use since they knew if they could break it, someone else would, sooner rather than later."

Lou checked to see if Phoebe was following the twisted logic.

"Makes perfect sense," Phoebe assured her.

"But that's not all," Lou said. "The brilliant part is that the NSA put a backdoor in so they could covertly read and track all the messages people sent thinking they were secure. Encryption is a game of staying one program ahead of the hackers, so the NSA had already moved on but people using it haven't."

Phoebe smiled. "I like that. If it's true, it would restore my faith in our comrades here at Fort Meade. Do we know where this hacker is?"

"Yes. I did some checking after this came through and it was deemed actionable." She crooked her finger and Phoebe leaned forward.

Lou smelled of lavender soap. She whispered a name and location.

"Thanks," Phoebe said as she stood. "Keep up the good fight."

"You too, Phoe."

Fromm was still watching, so Phoebe bent over and kissed Lou full on the lips, slowly running one hand through her long tresses, then headed for the exit.

"WHEN DID XAVIER GET BACK?" Shane asked as he drove the old Land Rover Defender across the new bridge spanning the tidal gully, built to Agnes' exacting specifications. He had a feeling he could drive a tank across it because he'd heard Agnes swearing to the contractor that she would never be without a bridge again, as God was her witness. Of course, one could have driven a tank across the replacement bridge he'd gotten her in the interim since it was designed for a tank, but one can only borrow government equipment that big for so long before it's missed. They passed through the small forest to the house at the end of the peninsula.

Three men were at the edge of the gravel driveway in front of Two

Rivers, two of whom Shane recognized. A rangy older man wearing khaki pants and shirt covered by a fishing vest and his balding head topped with a straw hat. The second was a younger, tanned blond man in a cheap suit, inexpertly holding a large automatic pistol. The man between them was tall, well-built, dark-haired and dressed in mud-smeared black pants and turtleneck. And handcuffed. Most conspicuously, he sported a drooping handlebar mustache which rang a not-so-subtle alarm bell in Shane's mind since it was not fashion-du-jour here in the Low Country, where ZZ-Top beards were more the standard. On the porch of Two Rivers was Rhett, the old hound dog, who let out a single, mournful bark of disapproval every twenty seconds or so from the prone position. Rhett being awake meant he was greatly disturbed by current events. Rhett was in prime position to trip an intruder who took the exact center of the wide front steps. And was blind. And deaf. And couldn't step over the old hound. And who could pass the dog without petting him. Or giving him a treat.

"This week is what I heard," Joey said as Shane parked the Defender next to the unmarked police car. "Hadn't seen him yet. He's been laying low since he snuck back into town with his tail between his legs."

"What happened with him and Evie Keyes?" Shane asked, referring to Xavier's apparent elopement eight months ago with his childhood flame and the richest woman in the town of Keyes. And the mother of Palmer Keyes, who'd married Lisa Livia's daughter Maria at the first wedding Agnes had hosted at Two Rivers.

"Didn't work out, I guess," Joey succinctly summed up. "She's back in her mansion. With her husband who never left it. He stayed put, waiting for the flame to go out. Always thought he just had the name and she had the money and smarts in that marriage, but I might have to refigure that."

"Right," Shane said as they exited. He rarely kept up with the residents of Keyes and their various goings-on, but Joey heard everything at the diner. What he didn't hear, he asked about. Shane suspected when Joey didn't get answers, he made things up.

"Mister Shane," Xavier said in his fine, slow southern drawl. "With my favorite restauranteur, in the diner sub-genre, Joey 'the Gent' Torcelli, formerly of the New York City La Cosa Nostra. Peas in a pod."

"I ain't Sicilian," Joey protested. "And I ain't in the mob. And I own the only diner in town so, yeah, sure, I'm your favorite."

"But you were affiliated with organized crime," Xavier said, "although how organized is open to discussion."

"Live in the here and now," Joey suggested.

"Detective Xavier," Shane said. "And Deputy Hammond."

"*I'm* a Detective," Hammond corrected. "And it's *Mister* Xavier. He's not with the force."

"Right," Shane said. "The cream rises in the Keyes police department." He noted that Xavier's fourteen-foot Boston Whaler was tied up to the Two Rivers dock. "Been fishing?" A six-foot wide pier extended two-hundred and forty feet to a high dock, then a metal gangplank angled down to a floating dock.

"What clue led you to that insightful deduction?" Xavier asked. "I caught myself a large one this time." Xavier indicated the prisoner. "Was out on the wide, calm water enjoying the day amidst the solitude of nature's bounty and heard ol' Rhett barking up a storm and moseyed on over to investigate since that fine ol' hound rarely gets excited. I was worried Miss Agnes might have run into some misfortune. Found this scalawag skulking about. Called it in. Detective Hammond responded with great alacrity, almost as if he weren't far off."

"'Scalawag'?" Joey said. "How was the honeymoon?"

"I've never been married," Xavier responded.

"But you eloped," Joey said.

"I went away," Xavier said. "Now, I'm back." He looked at Shane. "How is Miss Agnes? Is she the right, honorable Mrs. Shane now? You know, I never did catch your last name, despite all the goings-on around here. Or more likely, you be Mister Agnes Crandall?"

"She's always been honorable," Shane said. "And I never threw my name for you to catch."

"I take that as a no," Xavier said, "and that the two of you are living in sin. Obvious and not so obvious sin, that is, given the body count that has accrued on this beautiful land, in the water, and in yonder abode."

The prisoner glanced at Shane and raised an eyebrow, but didn't say anything. He was older than first appearances, around Shane's age.

"I take it you're not Mister Keyes," Shane said.

"Never expected, nor was it possible, since there was already a Mister Keyes," Xavier said.

"So, Evie's back with her husband?" Shane asked. "He's not perturbed over her eight-month absence?"

Xavier didn't reply.

Joey intervened. "Catch the intruder with your fishing pole, Xavier?"

Xavier lifted the right leg of his pants, revealing a snub-nose revolver in an ankle holster.

"Cute," Joey sniffed. "Hard to get to in a hurry."

"I am rarely in a hurry," Xavier said.

"Retired your .357 with the badge?" Joey asked.

Xavier indicated the man in black. "Can we address the issue in hand? Seems Two Rivers attracts all sorts of nefarious characters. Where, may I ask, is the wonderful and delightful Miss Agnes, whom I do not include in the aforementioned nefarious?"

"Paris," Shane said, but he was staring at mustache guy. "Who is he?"

"Paris?" Xavier was impressed. "Did someone sweep her off her feet and take her to City of Lights and bestow upon her the life she deserves? Was she wearing blue when she left?"

"A chef's symposium," Shane said. "What about him?"

"Miss Agnes' cuisine is superb," Xavier said. "I'm glad the international community sees fit to acknowledge that."

"The intruder," Shane repeated.

"He hasn't said a word since I caught him," Xavier said.

"I can hear you," Mustache said with an accent Shane couldn't place. European, not German, one of the Romance languages, which made him think of Agnes flying to Paris at the moment. At least she wasn't here for this, because Shane was pretty sure a trespasser wasn't in the binder.

Hammond tried to be official. "I've searched the suspect, but he has no identification. I read him his rights and he's refused to answer any of my questions."

"I'd refuse too," Joey muttered.

"He's probably here looking for the five million," Hammond said.

"*There is no five million,*" Xavier and Joey said at the same time, then glared at each other.

"You guys should start one of those barbershop quartets," Shane said. "You'd have to find two more balding, old guys, though."

"You ain't funny," Joey groused.

"I concur," Xavier said.

"Thanks," Shane said. "You and Hammond can go now. I'll chat with him."

"And what kind of chat would that be?" Xavier inquired.

"This man was trespassing," Hammond protested.

"He's only trespassing if I say he's trespassing," Shane said.

"You told me you're not Mister Agnes Crandall," Xavier pointed out. "Is your name on the deed of Two Rivers?"

"Yours sure ain't," Joey said to Xavier.

"He's a guest," Shane said. "Your friends just landed at the airport, right?" he asked Mustache.

The man raised an eyebrow as he considered the question, then nodded. "Most correct, sir."

"What guests be these?" Xavier asked.

"For the wedding," Shane said. "This weekend. Being held here. That I'm hosting."

"This fellow sure arrived mighty funny for nuptials," Xavier said, "crawling through the swamp. There are easier ways. I see Miss Agnes has had a mighty fine bridge built."

"One of those games people play before weddings," Shane said.

"Like an escape room except in this case it's to try to get into the venue un-noticed."

Xavier was skeptical, Joey tried to hold back a laugh, but Hammond was totally into it. "That's pretty cool," the young detective said. "I've never heard of that one but it would be fun. Like, hey dude, do you *really* want to get married? Then you have to break into the church, sort of thing."

"This isn't a church," Xavier said.

"You know what I mean," Hammond said.

"I'm afraid, I don't," Xavier said.

"Are you going back on the job?" Joey asked Xavier.

"My reinstatement is on the mayor's desk," Xavier replied. "Most likely already signed."

"Did Jefferson Keyes concur with you being back on the force?" Joey asked. "Since everyone answers to the Keyes' family in this town, including the sheriff."

"Mrs. Keyes is fine with it," Xavier said, rightly pointing where the true power resided.

Hammond didn't look happy hearing that, since it meant he'd be back to deputy and wearing a uniform.

"Criminals everywhere tremble at the thought of you returning to the beat," Joey said.

"Do you?" Xavier responded.

"I'm legit," Joey insisted.

"One could say *you're* trespassing," Shane said to Xavier.

"Citizen's arrest," Xavier blustered. "How is the basement?" he asked, nodding over his shoulder at the house as Rhett gave an irritated bark that indicated he was missing out on some late morning napping. "Built stairs to it? Or close it back up? Or might there be another poor departed soul in it?"

"Time to be going," Shane said.

Xavier was wise enough to know when the cause was lost, a term rarely bandied about in this part of the country. He touched a finger to the tip of his straw hat. "I have no doubt we'll be chatting again soon." He ambled toward the dock and his boat, leaving a flustered Hammond.

"Hit the road," Joey said to the young policeman.

"I heard Miss Lisa Livia is back?" Hammond asked, throwing away what little semblance of professionalism he had. "Is Maria with her? Is she still married?"

"Get lost," Joey snarled.

Hammond uncuffed Mustache and retreated to the Keyes police department only unmarked car, which would soon be Xavier's once more. He spun gravel accelerating toward the very sturdy bridge.

"My deepest appreciation, sir," Mustache said, with a slight bow.

"Sure," Shane said as he did a leg sweep, knocking the intruder to the ground. He put a knee on the man's chest as he efficiently frisked him, revealing a dagger secreted in center of the man's back, the same place Shane carried his. Hammond had learned nothing with his promotion and the time off had dulled Xavier's instincts. Shane appropriated it and got off the man. "Stand."

Shane pointed toward the three-story mansion overlooking the angled junction of the Blood River and the Intracoastal Waterway, which meant it was surrounded by water on three sides. On the distant side of the Intracoastal was a barrier island with mansions that were mostly second homes spaced out on large lots.

A deep gully cut across the grounds, separating Two Rivers from the mainland. It had several of feet of water in it at high tide, along with some deeper pools, and Agnes' bridge was the only means of ingress. Thick woods screened the landward side of Two Rivers with the gravel drive cutting through, a tunnel under the Spanish moss hanging from the trees with the first buds of spring beginning to leaf out. The wedding venue, a restored barn, was nestled in the trees to the Blood River side.

"Walk," Shane ordered.

Eight white columns stood in formation across the front of Two Rivers, flanking the wide, wood staircase. There were wraparound porches on the ground and second levels. Venerable, old oak trees were at each front corner. *I've got a home*, Shane thought, which is what crossed his mind every time he approached the front of Two Rivers. Not that growing up with Joey, living in the back of the diner, hadn't been a home, but as an adult, this was the first time he could allow himself to think, and feel, those words.

He gave Mustache a slight shove in the back to pick up the pace. "Move it." When they reached the porch, he indicated one of the high-backed straw chairs.

Mustache sat and folded his hands in his lap.

Shane pulled the blade half out of the sheath. "A classic. Fairbairn-Sykes."

Mustache twitched a smile. "You appreciate a fine blade."

"Is it an original?" Shane asked.

"Indeed."

"These are hard to come by," Shane said. "Where'd you get it?"

"Traded for it with a British chap."

"SAS carry these," Shane said, referring to the British Special Air Service.

"Do they?"

Shane slid the blade back in hard, with an audible metal on metal. "Small talk's over. Name?"

"Lucien."

Shane held up the knife. "Why didn't you use the dagger?"

"I am not here for violence."

"Why are you here?"

"Reconnaissance."

"For a wedding?" Shane asked.

Lucien didn't reply.

"I saw an older, bald-headed guy with the same kind of mustache at the airport getting off a big purple plane," Shane said.

"That would be the Field Marshal."

"The what?" Shane asked.

"The baton of rank was bequeathed to his distant predecessor by Napoleon and the title has passed down to each man who assumes the office."

Joey perked up. "Napoleon his-self? The guy with the funny hat? What was that about?"

"You still haven't explained what you're doing here," Shane said.

"As I said. Reconnaissance. It's standard."

"Standard for who?" Shane asked.

"I am impressed that your local constabulary is reasonably effective," Lucien said. "It is comforting to know. But the Field Marshal always sends someone ahead. Standard procedure."

"Standard for who?" Joey asked, thoroughly confused, still hung up on the funny hat.

Lucien looked past Shane. "The Field Marshal can explain."

The limousine was crossing the bridge, followed by the bus.

"What kind of wedding is this gonna be?" Joey wondered.

I should have read the binder, Shane thought.

Garth leapt out of the limo and scurried to open the passenger door. As the silver-haired man exited, Garth bowed so low he hit his head on the door handle. The old man extended a hand to a tall, slender, elegant woman his age. A flustered Lisa Livia was next. Shane waited for a bride and groom, but that was the entire contents of the limo.

The bus door swung open and the bald-headed man with the baton came out, followed by eleven more men, of different shapes and sizes but all fit and distinguished by the same handlebar mustache and dressed in dark, well-cut suits. Shane recognized their bearing: professionals.

"This some kind of clown show?" Joey wondered.

"You are in the presence of the Duke and Duchess of Andova," Lucien said as he popped to his feet. "Pay proper respect."

"Right," Shane murmured. *Really should have read that binder.* "They renewing their vows?"

"What?" Lucien was shocked. "They're getting married. What are you speaking of?"

Shane's royalty knowledge was spotty but this didn't make sense. "If they're already the Duke and Duchess aren't they already married? Are they becoming King and Queen?"

Lucien shook his head as if he were in the presence of a complete fool. "They were both married to others, as custom dictates. Dictated, that is. The *other* Duke has passed on and the *other* Duchess was stripped of her title for—" he coughed discreetly into a mud-smeared hand, which he managed to pull off without looking like an idiot— "actions unbecoming the office. And Andova has no king or queen. We alternate our fealty between Spain and France every year. As it has been for centuries ever since Charlemagne, Holy Roman Emperor, signed the Great Charter."

"Right," Shane said. "And the Field Marshal and the other mustache guys?"

"That's the Andovan Army," Lucien said proudly.

"The honor guard?" Shane asked.

"No, that's the entire army. We are also the royal escort. And royal security. And, actually, yes, technically, we are the honor guard. Also, Sacred Protectors of the Statue of Our Lady the Blessed Saint Ingrid. And the Knights Templar of--"

Shane cut off the list of duties. "Right." He looked over at Joey, but his uncle shrugged and spread his hands.

"I'm just cooking," Joey contributed. "Lots of reheating and arranging and serving actually. Unless someone wants some of my Jimbo Marinara? It's so good, it's in a book. The book with my picture on the cover. But it's actually more a gumbo."

The Duke was pointing at them and saying something to the Field Marshal, who was obviously trying to explain. The Duchess was scanning the grounds as if figuring out what it was worth on the open kingdom market.

Lisa Livia used the distraction to run up the steps to Shane, an impressive feat in her heels. "You're not gonna believe this."

"Ahead of you on that," Shane said. "Duke, Duchess, entire Andovan Army."

Lisa Livia was disappointed. "Yeah." She looked at Lucien and her excitement shifted tempo. "And you are?"

"May I join my unit?" Lucien asked Shane.

"Reporting in?" Shane asked, but indicated for him to go.

Lucien took one step, then turned to Lisa Livia, straightened the tips of his mustache as best he could with the slightest of twirls, and gave a formal bow. "M'lady, if you'll excuse me."

Lisa Livia blinked in confusion since she'd never had anyone call her 'M'lady'. "Yeah. Sure. Whatever."

Lucien nodded at her t-shirt. "Is that a definitive no or a conditional one?"

"Depends on who's asking."

"We'll have to address the question at another time." Lucien smiled. "Pardon me." He went down the steps and joined the others.

"He's cute," Lisa Livia noted.

"He's covered in mud," Shane said. "And his mustache is drooping."

"Hmm," Lisa Livia said as she looked over Lucien and the Andovan Army as if she were considering a skirmish, if not a minor battle, with the invading forces, but not in the traditional way. "What was he doing here?"

"Recon," Shane said.

"Of what?"

"The grounds," Shane said. "Armies usually send in recon before they invade."

"It's a wedding," Lisa Livia said. She was already past the recon. "There weren't many people on the plane, but the luggage? They forgot to tell Agnes about that because there's nothing in the binder about luggage. They started unloading stuff you wouldn't believe. Spears and armor and crates and banners and other stuff. Like it's gonna be some Shakespeare play, not a wedding. And the Duchess's luggage? Louis Vuitton. I've never seen that many pieces outside of a store. I'd die for them. Top of the line. She had like, three Vuitton trunks. Can you believe it? Three! And bags I didn't even know Vuitton made. Bags that would look great in Paris."

"South Carolina," Shane reminded her. "Did you get it sorted?"

"That's the funny thing. Agnes had the limo and the bus laid on, but a couple of trucks showed up right after you left. Not in the binder. So the wedding party planned that part ahead on their own."

"Swords? Armor?" Joey asked.

Lisa Livia began. "The guy with the stick—"

"The Field Marshal," Shane said.

"The what?" Lisa Livia didn't pause. "He said the equipment was ceremonial for the wedding. I didn't see anything about that in the binder either." She paused, realizing she'd raced past something. "Why would someone do a recon like that? There're photos of Two Rivers on the web site. And they already signed the contract. Not like they're gonna back out now. Are they?" For some reason she seemed more enthused about the wedding.

"Good question," Shane said. "What's the story with the Duke and the Duchess?"

"It's complicated," Lisa Livia said.

"Is it in the binder?" Shane asked. "A royal wedding? You think that would, like, be important. Something Agnes would have made a point of pointing out before she got on the plane."

"They didn't tell her. She thought this was a small event, eighteen people. That's what she told me."

"Great," Shane said. "They lied."

"No shit," Lisa Livia said.

"Who are the other three?"

"What?"

"I can count."

Lisa Livia held up the binder. "They were asking me a bunch of questions on the way here so I didn't get to read it all. Besides, I don't think the binder actually would have helped that much. There's a lot of stuff they didn't answer on Agnes' questionnaire. It's a really good questionnaire. Really thorough. Agnes on her game, but it doesn't do any good if it isn't completely filled out." She found the right tab. "I brought fourteen. Number fifteen was here crawling around in the mud with his drooping mustache. Sixteen and seventeen are representatives from the French and Spanish embassies. They'll be arriving on Saturday for the wedding."

"The French don't like me," Shane said, more to himself.

"I'm sure they have their reasons," Lisa Livia said.

"You don't want to know why?" Shane was insulted.

"Okay, why?"

"It's classified."

"Killed the prime minister with a spoon, did you?" Lisa Livia asked, putting the binder on her hip and looking at the army gathered around the Duke and Duchess and Field Marshal Domingo as if considering targets.

"Close enough," Shane said. "Number eighteen?"

"I'll ask when I get a chance."

"Where are they staying?"

"Duke and Duchess on the second floor, separate bedrooms, although you'd think they're a little old for that," Lisa Livia said. "The army? In the bedrooms along the barn terrace. I like how Agnes expanded the place and made use of the empty space since last I saw. The upgrades in the barn kitchen are top of the line. I'm glad she could use the money from--" Lisa Livia caught herself before she brought the topic-non-grata of her father's recovered loot, aka the five million that didn't exist.

The Duchess had her hair pulled up tight into a bun and looked like the Keyes' librarian, with the same severe, ascetic, narrow face, who used to shush everyone, even when no one was making a noise, sort of like Rhett barking. Except she'd be the Keyes librarian who'd won the biggest lottery ever given the glittering jewels adorning the necklace she sported, which had to be heavy. Despite that, she stood ramrod straight, ignoring the arguing men. Apparently, Lucien's capture hadn't been in the plan. She wore a long red coat that looked like it cost more than Shane's entire wardrobe and his guns and probably Two Rivers. She stared right at Shane and he felt the power of that gaze. Born to power, used to it.

"By the way, they're upset that Agnes isn't here," Lisa Livia said. "Especially the Duchess."

"*I'm* upset that Agnes isn't here," Shane said. "The Duchess can wait in line."

"I don't think she does lines," Lisa Livia said. "I told her you'd explain why Agnes isn't here."

"Excuse me?" Shane said.

She offered him the binder. "The only princesses I know are mob princesses. This is out of my league."

"On, no, you don't," Shane said, not accepting. "At least you have a league. And she isn't a princess. She's a duchess."

"Whatever," Lisa Livia said.

The Duke and Duchess broke away from the group and strode forward. The Field Marshal assembled his troops in two lines of six each. Shane expected them to do pushups for Lucien screwing up and getting caught.

"Showtime," Lisa Livia whispered. "Do Agnes proud." She prodded him in the back with a long fingernail.

"Welcome to Two Rivers," Shane said as he came down the stairs, trying out his best welcome to Two Rivers smile which seemed to be lacking as the Duchess looked past him to the house, then raked across the grounds.

The Duke turned to his fiancée. "As you expected, my dear?"

My dear didn't seem impressed. "Who are you?" She demanded of Shane. "Where is Miss Agnes Crandall? Your woman told me all would be explained by a Mister Shane."

Shane waited for Lisa Livia to stab the Duchess over 'your woman' but it was an indication of how off-kilter Lisa Livia was that she deferred instead: "*This* is Shane," Lisa Livia said. "He's Agnes' partner. *He'll* explain where Agnes is."

"I adore her column," the Duchess said. "The food was part of the reason we chose this venue."

"She already cooked most of it and left it," Shane said. "And my Uncle Joey—" he turned to indicate, but the old man, who had survived several Mafia wars, had wisely disappeared into the house —"can handle the rest."

"Left the food? Second-hand?" the Duchess appalled. "Frozen?"

"No, it's fresh," Shane said, having no idea if it was or not. "Agnes was up all night, last night, preparing it. She was called away on an emergency early this morning. Completely unexpected. A family emergency. A dire family emergency. A terrible thing. Tragic really. My uncle can handle it. He's actually got a book published about cooking. He's on the cover."

"Hmmph," the Duchess harrumphed with royal contempt.

"My dear," the Duke said. "The grounds. Are they as you anticipated?"

Some of the cold thawed in the Duchess as she grudgingly nodded. "It is charming in that quaint Southern way."

"Which you desired," the Duke said, winking at Shane. He had a trimmed beard, covering a Kirk Douglas chin, and his thick, silver hair was combed straight back. If someone was going to cast a Duke, this was their guy. His three-piece suit was Saville Row, which Shane recognized because he'd taken out a target who'd worn similar and Saville Row suits had been part of the description Carpenter had given him so he'd done the research. There was a gold chain strung across the front of the vest for a pocket watch which might have been too much for someone else but was just right for the Duke. He spoke with a slightly different accent from the Duchess; more Spanish. The Duchess, on the other hand, could have been cast as the ice queen who robbed small children of all their joy while strangling the Grinch beyond hope of redemption while she burned their toys. And kicked the dog with the reindeer headset.

"Don't do that," the Duchess said, having caught the wink, but there was little bite to her reprimand. Her accent had a tint of French in it.

"I see you have Lucien's dagger," the Duke said. "Did he surrender it or did you take it from him?"

"I appropriated it," Shane said. He held it out, hilt leading.

The Duke took it. "Impressive. Lucien is quite skilled with blades, although the sabre is his weapon of choice. He is a champion fencer."

"I prefer forty-five caliber at greater than ten paces," Shane said.

The Duke's eyes narrowed and he nodded. "Of course, you do, Mister Shane."

What the hell did he mean by that? Shane wondered.

The Duke continued. "I prefer the foil. A weapon requiring

different skills than the dagger, sabre, sword or pistol. Precision and on point, literally."

Shane was tired of the lack of being on point. "Why'd you send in a recon?"

"You do not speak to the Duke that way," the Duchess said and Shane wondered if she had a dagger hidden under her coat. Then again, she had an entire army backing her up.

"The Marshal is a cautious man," the Duke said. "He prefers to err in that direction."

"Is there something we should be worried about?" Shane asked.

The Duchess answered. "Of course not. Standard security protocol. I'm weary. Could you show me to my room?" she asked Lisa Livia.

"Certainly. This way, your Duchess." Lisa Livia led the Duchess through the open, carved double front doors into Two Rivers.

Rhett did not bark. Nevertheless, the Duchess gave him a healthy berth.

The Duke stood next to Shane and turned so they were shoulder to shoulder, looking out over the grounds, while the Field Marshal was walking the line, apparently inspecting whether anyone had lost a button on the bus ride over. "Beautiful place. Too bad Miss Agnes isn't here."

"Yeah," Shane agreed. "Too bad. You want to see your room, Duke?"

"Call me Marc."

"Sure, Duke."

Rhett barked.

SHANE'S WORDS OF WISDOM #3

Nothing is impossible to the man who doesn't have to do it.

It's always easier for the person issuing the order to do that, than for the person receiving the order to execute it. The order of magnitude of impossibility goes up the further away the issuer is from the executor.

THURSDAY AFTERNOON

"There are people working in my field," Phoebe said, "who enjoy inflicting pain. I can assure you, I do not. My pleasure derives from the acquisition of knowledge and mission accomplishment. Thus, you do understand that the pain you are experiencing now, is an unnecessary byproduct of what I truly desire?"

The Hacker could only grunt and nod, given Phoebe's right hand, middle knuckle leading, was jammed hard and up into the soft spot just under his sternum. Her left held a silenced pistol, the muzzle inches from his right temple, keeping him from moving away. The suppressor's tip was still warm. Both her hands were gloved.

They were in the office of his penthouse apartment in Manhattan where Phoebe had tracked him down using Lou's intel.

"I'm glad you understand," Phoebe said. "Now. Are you gonna make me happy?"

He nodded again; eyes wide. The eyeballs shifted, taking in the two bodyguards that Phoebe had shot. Phoebe wore the black, one-piece suit, now dust-stained after her shimmy down from the roof and through the air ducts to get to the Hacker's office. The guards had been just outside the door when she'd opened the grate on the far side of the room, leaving it hanging from one connection. She'd dropped to the floor. His yelp of panic at her sudden appearance had brought them rushing in, guns drawn. Both had been dead, each with a bullet in the head, before they realized the threat.

Phoebe withdrew her knuckle slightly, allowing the Hacker to take a semi-breath. "Where's the list of people you sold the program to?"

"'Program'? What—" he didn't get the next word out as she pressed in and up. He gasped in pain.

"I'm on the clock," Phoebe said. "And my shoulder hurts, so I'm kind of irritable at the moment."

"There's no list of—" he stopped as she pressed.

"You're a computer guy," Phoebe said. "A nerd. They always have lists. They can't help themselves. This isn't a guess on my part. I deal in certainties. It's why I never make bets unless I control the outcome. I control the outcome here. Do you understand?"

He nodded.

"I bet you have a list. Can you prove me wrong?"

The Hacker pointed with a shaking finger at a drawer in the antique desk.

"You're not going to try to pull a gun or knife on me, are you?" Phoebe said. "Because, that would be, like, you know, really, really stupid. I *despise* stupid."

He shook his head.

"Go ahead."

The Hacker pulled a silver chain from around his neck and used the ornate key on it to unlock a drawer. He slid it open and retrieved a thumb drive.

Phoebe relaxed the knuckle. "That's everyone?"

A nod.

Phoebe pulled her hand back and took the thumb drive. "I can read it?"

"It's encrypted with the program," the Hacker said, as he gingerly massaged his solar plexus.

"Then my friend can read it to me. I love listening to her. She has a great voice. Sort of Kathleen Turner." Phoebe pocketed the drive. She sniffed. "Did you piss yourself?"

The Hacker gave a slight nod.

Phoebe put the silenced pistol in the open drawer and slid it shut, jerking tight the chain around his neck, almost slamming his head on the desk, so she could lock it. "You shouldn't have shot those two guys."

The Hacker blinked in confusion.

Phoebe ran across the room and leapt up, grabbing the slight lip at the top of the opening. She bent and pulled herself into the vent, feet first, then replaced the grate, taking the time to secure it, thin fingers through the small openings in it and watching the Hacker to see how really stupid he was.

The Hacker hurriedly unlocked the drawer and pulled the gun out, aiming at the vent where Phoebe was just finishing. She stuck her tongue out at him from behind the grate. He pulled the trigger and a blank went off, depositing gunpowder residue on his hand.

Inside the vent, Phoebe popped one shoulder out of joint so she could move in the narrow passageway, and shimmied away, feet first, pushing with her good hand, ignoring the pain.

The Hacker looked at the gun in his ungloved hand as the police pounded on the door.

Really, really stupid, Phoebe thought.

"Is that Rhett?" Carpenter asked over the secure phone as he heard the old bloodhound let out one of his intermittent yelps in the background.

Having done his duty, the dog dropped his heavy head on Shane's right foot and closed his eyes. Shane sat in one of the comfortable chairs Agnes had placed on the high dock. There was a cool breeze coming off the water and other than missing Agnes, a royal wedding to make happen, two painful bruises on his chest, and an increasingly irritated Lisa Livia, it was a beautiful day. Landward, the sun was getting lower in the western horizon, touching the treetops. He checked his watch. Agnes was landing in Paris right about now.

He saw Lisa Livia and the Duchess walking on the flagstone pathway that went from the house through the woods to the barn. Lisa Livia had the binder in one hand, the other gesturing. The Duchess didn't seem impressed. They disappeared into the trees. He noted that one of the Andovan soldiers followed at a discreet distance; the prescribed distance for personal security. He wore the three-piece suit and wraparound sunglasses. Shane squinted. The man had a white wire running from an earpiece into his collar to a radio, like a Secret Service agent. Who was he on a net with and where was the base station? Seemed like overkill but they were a Duke and Duchess and he supposed that made them important to someone.

"Yep, that's old Rhett," Shane confirmed. "He walked out on the dock with me, which is a record movement for him. I don't think he likes the Duchess." *Neither does Lisa Livia*, Shane thought.

"I would imagine he misses Agnes," Carpenter said.

"Him and me, both."

Two large trucks hauling stuff from the airport had arrived not long ago and dropped off at the barn. The sturdy bridge had handled the loads easily. Lisa Livia had understated the amount of gear. Several Andovans were draping red banners with the crest emblazoned all over on the gazebo.

Shane read the crest. "Hey, what does *Virtus Unita Fortior* mean?"

"Why do you assume I know Latin?" Carpenter asked.

"You know everything," Shane said. "Or you know how to know it."

"*United Virtue is Stronger*," Carpenter said. "But it's not because I understand Latin. It was in my research. This is a most curious situation," Carpenter said, which was the equivalent of a normal person screaming fire. "I must admit, like you, I had never heard of Andova. Which isn't surprising since it's one of the smallest countries in the world. In the top twenty; perhaps that would be better phrased as the bottom twenty in terms of size."

"How many tiny countries are there that I've never heard of?"

Carpenter relished dishing out information the way Agnes loved serving food. "You certainly know a few. Vatican City, of course, is the smallest. Then there's Monaco. Some island countries in the Pacific. Actually, there are a surprising number of small, autonomous states. There's even a fellow who took over an abandoned oil rig in the North Sea and—"

"Andova," Shane said.

"Ever hear of Wikipedia, Shane? Googling?"

"I've been busy."

"And I am not?" Carpenter said.

"You like looking stuff up," Shane said.

"That's true," Carpenter relented.

"And you have the best computers," Shane added.

"That is also true, but they're for work." Carpenter pushed on. "Andova is one of the oldest states in Europe. Located in the Pyrenees Mountains between France and Spain. Land mass is a little over two hundred square miles. It was part of the Roman Empire at its height. After Rome fell, it maintained its sovereignty for centuries, despite being caught between two powerful local families, one French, the other Spanish. Each claimed the rightful place on the throne and there was blood spilled for a while. That was solved by a charter written by Charlemagne the Great which alternated rule between the two families every year and gave allegiance to the throne of the country of whichever family whose year it was. It also required they pay an annual tribute to that respective throne."

Shane tried to process that. "You mean one year they're French and the other Spanish?" At least the flag on the plane made sense now.

"Nominally," Carpenter said. "That's why you have a Duke and Duchess, but they never become king and queen. Actually, they have *two* Dukes and Duchesses, one set from each family. Who alternate power annually. It's served to keep Andova neutral during all the wars that have engulfed Europe over the centuries. Neither France or Spain wanted to mess with a good thing. The terrain is fortuitous in that Andova isn't on an invasion route through the Pyrenees."

"Wonder which set of royalty this is?" Shane said. He frowned. "The guy I caught said that each had been married before."

"It is a curious situation," Carpenter said. "I couldn't find anything in a cursory search to explain why this wedding is taking place, why it is being held at Two Rivers, or the current status of the royalty in Andova."

"Isn't that odd?" Shane asked. "I mean, you got the best computers." *And access*, he thought.

"I said 'cursory search'," Carpenter said. "The Organization's computer isn't to be utilized for personal matters. I used my laptop. As you could use yours."

"Right." The Duke and Marshal came out from the trees and went to the lawn near the gazebo. The two Andovans were dressed in one-piece white outfits and had helmets in the crook of their arms. They carried foils, and after bowing to each other, put on the helmets and assumed the position, which Shane had only seen in movies. No wonder they had so much baggage if they carried this stuff. He wondered how much they brought for a trip longer than a weekend.

"They're fencing," Shane said.

"Who?" Carpenter asked.

"The Duke and the Marshal."

"Ah," Carpenter said. "The Field Marshal. He's in command of the Army, which consists of only twelve men, as prescribed by the Great Charter."

"They've all invaded Two Rivers," Shane said. "Who's guarding Andova?"

"Andova is a little Switzerland. They don't do war. The title Field Marshal was given by Napoleon. Some write that because the country has never been to war it was an insult."

Like Three Wheels, Shane thought.

"However," Carpenter continued, "Napoleon gave an actual Marshal's baton to the commander of the Andovan Army, so others write that it was a noble gesture and served a purpose in keeping the balance of power with Spain by acknowledging the Great Charter. A fascinating historical detail."

But Three Wheels was a secret millionaire now, Shane thought, and Two Wheels and Four Wheels were dead, so sometimes it paid to fly under the radar.

"Speaking of Latin," Carpenter said, "do you know what is inscribed on a Napoleonic Field Marshal baton?"

Shane waited for the follow up.

Carpenter, knowing Shane was waiting, gave in. "*Terror belli, decus pacis*, which means '*terror in war, ornament in peace*'."

"Cute," Shane said.

Near the gazebo, the two men went at it and Garth, distracted from whatever he was supposed to be doing, wandered over. The foils riposted and parried. Lucien had also come up to watch, looking spiffy in his suit and clean of mud. His mustache was freshly waxed.

"But it's also likely," Carpenter continued, "that Napoleon got paid off."

"By a tiny country?"

"Did you miss my allusion to Switzerland?" Carpenter said. "The banking and tax laws of Andova have made it a nexus for considerable wealth over the last twelve centuries. The country, of course, takes a taste. As do France and Spain via the yearly switchover."

"Sweet operation," Shane said.

"Indeed. For all involved. A maxim of success is finding a need and filling it and Andova has been doing that for hundreds of years. There's a commonly held myth that Napoleon came up with the idea of giving medals for heroism in combat rather than the common practice at the time of awarding lands and riches. However, it's not true."

Shane knew better than to interrupt when Carpenter went on a historical tangent.

"What Napoleon was a master at doing was using symbols, such as the Marshal baton and medals, which were basically coins with no monetary function. However, those trinkets impressed the masses and became far more valuable than their actual worth, while costing Napoleon nothing of real value."

Shane thought of the medals he'd received while in the army and tried to remember where they were. The foot locker in the back of the diner? He looked up the Intracoastal and there was Xavier in his small boat, to the side of the main channel, making no pretense of hiding what he was doing since he was staring at Two Rivers through powerful binoculars. Shane waved. Xavier did not wave back. But he also didn't give Shane the finger, so he figured they were enjoying a truce.

"How about the Montana thing?" Shane asked.

"There is progress," Carpenter said. "Phoebe is closing on the person who contacted both the buyers and the dead man."

"That's good," Shane said. "Hey. I am sorry about that. I screwed up."

"It happens," Carpenter said. "There's a possibility I'm going to need you to help."

"Lisa Livia and Joey can handle things here," Shane lied. "Whatever you need."

"I fear we might have an infection in the Organization," Carpenter said.

Shane tuned everything out and focused. "Why?"

"We know Wilson was corrupted," Carpenter said. "It's naïve to think it stopped with him. It's likely whoever attacked you in Montana had surveillance there before you arrived, but the question is why? The militia selling the ordnance doesn't employ such caution or expertise. Nor would they have had access to a helicopter."

"You think someone tipped off the buyers that I was there?" Shane frowned. "But you don't know who the buyers are."

"Ostensibly," Carpenter said. "But what if someone *here* does know, but is keeping that to themselves?"

"Who?"

"I'm going to start digging around."

"Be careful."

"That's why I might need your help," Carpenter said. "You're the only person I can trust one hundred percent."

"Whatever you need."

"Good. Stay centered."

LISA LIVIA GUIDED the Duchess through the renovated barn. Multiple sets of tall French doors on both ends and skylights made the interior bright and cheerful. The old wood had been white-washed to add to the brightness. At least Lisa Livia thought so, but the Duchess didn't seem impressed. Lisa Livia figured someone used to a castle wasn't overwhelmed by a building that used to hold cows and their shit. She also figured people used to shit in buckets in castles before they got indoor plumbing so that made her feel a little better.

There was a wide balcony around the large open space with rooms off it where select members of the wedding party stayed; in this case the Andovan Army. Lisa Livia suspected there'd been a lot of hanky-panky, to put it mildly, in those rooms during previous wedding weekends, but for this one, she simply hoped no one got their head chopped off. She'd noticed the distinct lack of bride's maids or even a maid of honor in this group; the testosterone level was through the roof. Which she didn't view as necessarily a bad thing.

There was a large pile of luggage and hard-sided crates piled in the center of the barn, with two soldiers unpacking. It seemed a lot for such a low-key affair and so few people and just a couple of days.

Lisa Livia paused. "What are they wearing?"

The men had on red pantaloons and red shirts with flowing arms under shiny armor breastplates with the Andovan insignia on the chest. They wore crested helmets with red plumes. Lisa Livia was trying to recall where she'd seen similar and then remembered the pictures of the Swiss Guard her aunt had taken when she'd gone to Rome and visited the Vatican on a New Jersey Catholic pilgrimage. The extended family had been trapped for two hours and forced to watch the entire slideshow of the trip. Her aunt had brought back a rusty piece of metal inside a cheap plastic block. She claimed it was a piece of one of the nails from the original cross. It occupied the position of honor on top of the fridge and her aunt had regularly threatened her husband that she'd break it open pound the nail into his head if he didn't shut up.

The two soldiers had set up a rack holding a dozen wicked-looking halberds, essentially long-poled axes, and were now unpacking a copious array of various types of swords.

"The ceremonial uniform of the Royal Honor Guard," the Duchess said.

"Puffy shirts," Lisa Livia said.

"Excuse me?"

"The wedding isn't until Saturday," Lisa Livia pointed out. "Why are they all dressed up?"

"Those two have guard duty."

"For who?" Lisa Livia asked, looking over her shoulder at the guy in his suit who'd been shadowing them.

"Not for who. For what." The Duchess didn't amplify her answer as she walked past the baggage to the far doors which presented a magnificent view of the Blood River, which Lisa Livia pointed out since she didn't think a castle in the mountains had the same. The sluggish water was lined with tidal flats and the trees beyond were festooned with Spanish moss; the low country in all its glory.

For the first time, the Duchess showed a spark, more a tiny sparkle, of interest. "Why is it called the Blood River?"

"There was a battle," Lisa Livia said.

The Duchess arched a narrow eyebrow, a twitch Lisa Livia was growing to hate. "Can you amplify on that?"

I can say it louder, Lisa Livia almost said, then mentally threw herself onto another hand grenade for Agnes. "When this area was first settled, the folks who originally lived here—"

The Duchess interrupted. "I believe they're called Native Americans?"

"Yeah. Them. They didn't care much for the newcomers who—"

"From where in Europe? England? Spain? France? Scotland? Ireland?"

"I got no idea," Lisa Livia said, having not paid that much attention to the local history lessons while spending a portion of her childhood here. "My family came here from Jersey."

"The Channel Island?" the Duchess asked. "English?"

"New Jersey," Lisa Livia clarified. "Anyways. So, there was a fight, blood was spilled and some got in the river."

"I'm sure there's more to the story than that," the Duchess said.

Lisa Livia gripped the binder tighter, red fingernails digging into the plastic. "There were questions that Agnes sent you that you didn't respond to. Do you mind if we cover them now?"

Eyebrow arch. "Reference?"

"The wedding." *Duh.* For a moment, Lisa Livia wondered if she'd said that last out loud, because she was beginning to doubt her own discipline.

"It's a simple enough affair," the Duchess said. "In fact, I don't believe we could have made it any easier."

Lisa Livia indicated two folding chairs near the doors. She didn't wait for the Duchess, but sat down and waited, the binder on her lap. The Duchess stared at the chair with disapproval.

"We're short on thrones at the moment," Lisa Livia said.

There was the slightest hint of a smile on the Duchess' face, but Lisa Livia could have been mistaken. It might have been a grimace.

The Duchess sat ramrod straight and placed her hands on her knees, the better to show off the numerous diamonds and precious stones. "Yes?"

To Lisa Livia, the Duchess was sitting as if she actually had a stick up her butt. Lisa Livia opened the binder to the correct tab. "As I said, you didn't completely fill out the forms Agnes, Miss Agnes that is, sent you."

"I gave sufficient information to accomplish what needs to be done. Besides, our men are doing most of the work."

Lisa Livia thought of her daughter marrying Palmer here and how even her mild-mannered Maria would have skewered anyone who spoke of any wedding so dismissively.

"Well," Lisa Livia said, "you kinda need a preacher for a wedding. Or justice of the peace as we call them here." She tapped the plastic covering the questionnaire with a long, red fingernail. "But you left that blank."

"The Bishop will arrive for the wedding," the Duchess said. She was watching the fingernail, so Lisa Livia kept doing it.

Number eighteen, Lisa Livia thought. "Will I need to find him a place to—"

"He will arrive in time at Two Rivers to do his duty and then he will depart. I do not want him staying any longer than needed. I care not where he stays."

"Not even attending the dinner after?"

"No."

"Oookay," Lisa Livia drew out. "Bishop of what and from where?"

"Of Andova, of course. Ordained by the Pope."

"Okay."

"He is to be treated with all due respect, since he is also a representative of the Spanish government and the Vatican."

Lisa Livia was confused. "Same guy as the Spanish embassy rep coming on Saturday?"

"No. The Bishop is flying in on his jet from Andova and he'll be flying back afterward. The embassy representative will likely be some minor flunky assigned the task."

"Why is this flunky coming then?" Lisa Livia, more out of curiosity. "And the one from the French Embassy?"

"You know nothing of our country, do you?"

Lisa Livia continued tapping the binder. "If you'd have answered more of the questions, I might. I only got here this morning to help out. Family emergency and all that."

That same twitch at the corner of her mouth. "He, or it could be a she, I suppose, given how the world has changed, will also be a minor representative." The Duchess managed to say it as if the world changing had let her down personally. "I believe the closest consulates are in Atlanta."

"Why a minor representative?" Lisa Livia asked.

"As a not-so-subtle rebuke to the marriage."

"France and Spain don't want you to get married?"

"They do not."

"I've heard of in-laws objecting," Lisa Livia said, "but not entire countries."

The Duchess stiffened as she saw something behind Lisa Livia. "Be careful!"

"Yes, Duchess," one of the soldiers responded.

They'd opened a crate and removed an old four-foot-tall statue of a teenage girl, one arm raised up, palm out, the other curled around a young boy, protecting him. The sculpture was faded and it was obviously heavy from the way the two men were moving it. Light glittered off jewels set in a crown on the girl's head.

"Why does she have a crown?" Lisa Livia asked as she peered more closely and had flashbacks of creepy priests and penguin nuns in habits wielding rulers.

"It's not a crown," the Duchess said. "It's a halo."

"But it has jewels."

"Indeed," the Duchess said, without any further explanation. "That will go in the gazebo. The Duke and I will bind ourselves to each other in front of it as per tradition." The Duchess gave a dry chuckle. Or she might have been clearing her throat, it was hard for Lisa Livia to tell. "As each of us did once before."

Lisa Livia figured there was more to that, but the Duchess hadn't been very forthcoming about wedding details so far.

"Who is it supposed to be?" Lisa Livia asked as the two men positioned the statue on a special ark they'd put together from pre-fitted poles and a platform and a bunch of cushions. They lifted it to their shoulders and carried it out of the other end of the barn, heading for the gazebo.

"That is the Statue of Our Lady the Blessed Saint Ingrid."

Lisa Livia was trying to follow. "Saint Ingrid?"

"The patron saint of Andova." The Duchess sighed. "I could tell you the entire story, but let's stick to the blood in the river version?"

Lisa Livia laughed. "Okay, you got me on that one."

"Saint Ingrid was a peasant girl who protected the children of Andova from non-believers a long time ago. She was canonized by the Pope."

"That was nice of her. What happened to Ingrid?"

"She was burned at the stake."

"Ouch."

"Yes. Not quite Joan of Arc, but in the end, the same fate. A martyr."

I can relate, Lisa Livia thought, but did not say out loud. "Who is picking up the Bishop?"

The Duchess shrugged. "I care not."

"Do you have the time his plane will arrive?"

"Lucien would have that information."

"Okay. I'll arrange for Three—Garth, to pick him up and book him a room in town at the Rice Plantation. It's the nicest digs we got in this neck of the woods. Other than here." She returned to the binder. "There's no maid of honor or best man listed?"

"There will be neither."

"Okay. No bride's maids or do some of those guys cross dress?" Lisa Livia felt the drum roll as soon as she said it so she moved on. "How long do you figure this ceremony will last? So, I can give Joey an idea when to start getting ready the various courses for the dinner?"

"It depends how quickly the Bishop speaks. I imagine he will be fast."

"Did you give him any special readings or—"

"He will say the vows, we will repeat them in front of Saint Ingrid, and it will be over."

"Like a tooth being pulled," Lisa Livia murmured.

"What was that?"

"Okay," Lisa Livia said. "I gotta know. Why is this bishop officiating if he isn't happy about the wedding?"

"I've ordered him to."

"Okay. And you didn't want, like, your best friend to be your maid of honor? Family friends to come?"

"I didn't want them exposed to—" the Duchess stopped. "Have I answered enough of your questions? Really. It's a simple event. Given Miss Agnes isn't here, I think we are both somewhat short-changed this weekend, don't you think?"

"But it's your *wedding*," Lisa Livia protested.

"The Duke and I have had royal weddings with all the accompanying pomp and circumstance," the Duchess said. "We don't need to repeat the experience. It's novel and exciting when one is young and naïve. As we get older, we learn the harsh truths of reality."

"Romantic, but yeah, been there," Lisa Livia noted. "My mom wiped out all my savings and my business."

"My husband died," the Duchess said.

"I'm sorry," Lisa Livia said, thinking *you win*.

"Are we done?" The Duchess stood and walked away, her guard following

"I should be in Paris," Lisa Livia muttered.

The Duchess turned. "What was that?"

"Nothing."

Lisa Livia closed the binder and sat alone in the barn. Then she went to the luggage, admiring the Duchess' bags. She noted one of the cases near the swords was partly open. Since she was a Fortunato by blood, curiosity got the better of her and she lifted the top.

"Fuck me to tears," she muttered and quickly shut the lid.

SHANE WAS reluctant to leave the dock, which was an oasis of tranquility. The Duke had given his foil to Lucien, who'd stripped off his jacket and shirt and was dueling his father bare-chested.

"Showoff," Shane muttered.

Rhett rumbled something in his sleep and Shane took it as assent.

Two soldiers in what Shane assumed was their ceremonial garb carried some statue out to the gazebo and put it in the center and were now standing guard, armed with halberds. They had sheathed swords hung on red sashes around their waists. They were surrounded by red hangings. Their armor glittered in the setting sun. Shane wondered what Xavier was making of that, because he wasn't sure himself what it was about.

The Duchess had come out from under the trees with the guard and gone into the house, not bothering to check either the dueling or the statue. He figured she had enough of both back in Andova, because really, what else was there to do in the mountains? Lisa Livia came through the trees on the path, walking with a purpose. Even from this distance, Shane knew she wasn't coming to report all was well in the world and that the Andovan soldiers he couldn't see were sitting in a circle singing kumbaya or knitting a shawl.

Shane got up. "Come on, old grumps," he said to Rhett as he headed shoreward. The old dog gave him the stink-eye and struggled to his paws.

Shane met Lisa Livia between the house and the gazebo. "What's wrong?"

Lisa Livia had been distracted from whatever was perturbing her by the duel. She focused on Lucien as he moved gracefully, parrying his father's thrusts, but never returning them, having worked up a slight sheen of sweat.

Now that he was closer, Shane saw that Lucien had several scars on his muscular torso and not just from the blade. There was a crater outline low on his chest on the right side: bullet wound.

"Lisa Livia?" Shane asked.

She kept staring. "Is *that* the muddy guy?"

"Yeah."

"He cleans up very nicely."

There was a brief pause in the dueling and Lucien turned toward her and raised the hilt of the foil to his chin in salute, then returned to business.

"Lisa Livia," Shane said with a bit more teeth in it. "What's wrong?"

"There's something you have to see," she said.

Shane waited a few seconds. "And that is?"

"Oh, damn it," Lisa Livia said, tearing her gaze from the duel. "Come on." She stalked off and Shane hurried to follow.

Rhett was only halfway down the dock.

They went into the barn and Lisa Livia pointed at a large case. "Look."

Shane opened the top. A row of automatic weapons lay in cradles. Pistols were in their slots; except a dozen were missing. Under the weapons were wooden crates and from the stenciling, Shane knew they held grenades, ammunition, mines, and other tools of war.

"I should have stayed in Montana," Shane said.

"I should be in Paris," Lisa Livia countered.

"Touché," Shane said, perhaps too influenced by the dueling.

PHOEBE DID her best work at night. She ran along the top of a fence, feet nimbly finding purchase through the razor wire uncoiled along it. She moved with the alacrity of a ballet dancer, except a misstep would be worse than a bad performance. The razor wire crowned a fence that was on the top of the ten-story building adjacent to the target's building and she had no idea why someone had put such a fence up here, unless it was to prevent someone from jumping off.

It was dangerous and she was smiling in exhilaration below the night vision goggles that covered her eyes. She felt a twinge of pain in her right calf, but ignored it. She reached where the fence met the corner of the building and her momentum carried her over the ten-foot gap to the target's building, grabbing onto a drainage pipe, while her feet, encased in rubber climbing shoes, splayed on either side, gripping brick. She shimmied up.

She was dressed in her single-piece, very tight, black suit, which Lou had dubbed her 'cat suit' when Phoebe wore it for her one time. She had a small pack cinched to her back and wore black gloves, with a watch cap squishing her hair down. Over the cat suit was a combat vest with a brace of throwing knives in specially sewn slots. There was a strobe light taped tightly to the vest on her off shoulder. She had a pair of special goggles that provided night vision, as well as having other uses. A suppressed pistol was in a thigh holster. On her other hip was a wakizashi, a short sword with an eighteen-inch blade, sheathed for a reverse pull.

Phoebe reached the roof and rolled onto it, popping to her feet. The large square block that housed the machinery for the elevator was directly ahead. She stood still for ten seconds, senses tuned in. Listening. Sniffing. Slowly turning to do a visual three-sixty.

She moved forward, slower, checking for a possible trip wire. She picked the lock and propped the door. She opened it just wide enough for her slender frame to slip inside, the muzzle of the gun leading. The elevator cables stretched down into darkness and weren't moving.

According to the intel decrypted and determined by Lou from the thumb drive, the target owned the entire penthouse floor. It seemed being a bad guy paid well and they liked being on the top floor. Phoebe pulled a roll-n-lock out of her backpack and clamped it onto the cable, adjusting the gauge until it was tight. A loop of nylon extended from it and she put her foot into the stirrup at the bottom. She released tension and slid down the cable, coming to a halt at the first set of doors, one hand tightening the roll-n-lock.

She stepped onto a narrow ledge. The building data she'd studied on the flight in indicated this type of elevator shaft had a door release in the top right. She found it. She drew her wakizashi. Pressed the button and stepped into the penthouse.

A body lay in the vestibule, a large pool of blood beneath it. From the bright red glisten, Phoebe estimated he'd been shot no more than five minutes ago, because blood congeals quickly. The face was turned toward her and there was no doubt it was the target. The eyes were cloudy in death. The source of the blood, and death, was a slashed throat. He wore a bathrobe and there was a gun near his right hand.

Phoebe could smell the blood, an unpleasant coppery odor. She considered the situation for a few moments. It was a professional hit so whoever had done it wouldn't have left valuable intelligence in the apartment, indicating searching would be a waste of time.

However.

Phoebe's nostrils flared. There was the faintest of odors underneath the blood. Tobacco. Phoebe stepped from the nylon loop into the apartment foyer. She moved forward and knelt next to the body, clear of the blood. The throat had been sliced cleanly, not torn. A blade expertly wielded.

Phoebe took a step back. A hallway to the right, lights on. Doors to each side. Ahead, the kitchen. Double doors to the left, slightly ajar. Inviting.

Phoebe remained still. If there was someone inside those double doors, they too were waiting, thinking he, she, whatever asshole was in there, had the advantage.

Patience negated that.

It was the hardest lesson Phoebe had ever learned. From an elder sensei in South Korea who had stood with her on top of a small mountain, while snow fell. They'd both been barefoot, dressed only in their white gis. Doing nothing; just maintaining a kata pose. Not moving at all. For four hours until her shivering became uncontrollable and she'd collapsed. When she got home, she'd told her father she'd had a good day at school.

It wasn't snowing in the foyer. It's the little things in life that were worth appreciating.

Minutes passed. Phoebe's heart rate was normal, her breathing shallow.

The lights went out.

Phoebe dropped to the floor, a split second before there was a muzzle flash from the hallway to the right as the shooter also reacted. Bullets smacked the wall above her. The shooter must have thought he'd scored as he came running down the hall.

The elevator doors behind Phoebe opened with a ding.

"Come on," someone yelled from inside the elevator.

As the shooter sprinted by Phoebe's prone form, she slashed with the wakizashi. She was rewarded with a scream of pain as the blade neatly sliced through the shooter's ankle and he dove forward, minus one foot. His momentum carried him into the elevator.

Phoebe rolled to the side, behind the dead body of the target as the other man in the elevator fired blindly, bullets spraying the foyer, all high. The doors shut.

Phoebe popped to her feet, drawing her pistol. She reached down and picked up the severed foot. She put it in her backpack. Went to the elevator and pressed her ear against, listening. It stopped on the ground floor and went silent.

There were sirens in the distance, rapidly growing louder.

Phoebe opened the elevator doors. She grabbed the roll-n-lock and ascended, muscles straining to pull herself up. She unlocked the device and stowed it. Readied the pistol. She moved out of the partly open door fast, shoulders hunched, half expecting a bullet out of the darkness.

She shimmied over the edge, gripping the drainage pipe and slid down. All the way to street level. She sprinted through the darkness to the waiting van where Cleaner sat in the driver's seat. She got in the back.

She opened the pack and tossed the foot on the passenger seat. "Can Forensic Support learn anything from that?"

Cleaner was unperturbed, indicating he'd seen stranger things. "Blood type. DNA, but that takes time and the person has to be in the database." He smiled. "But it makes identifying whoever owned it easier, if they don't bleed out."

"Yeah, he'll be hopping." Phoebe removed the night vision goggles.

Cleaner started the engine and drove off without further comment as Phoebe pulled the watch cap off and ran her fingers through her hair, half-straightening it, as she thought.

"Airport," she ordered. She shut the divider to the driver's compartment. She hit speed dial one on her secure phone.

It was answered as the second ring started, despite the late hour. "Carpenter."

"The scene was compromised and the target already dead," Phoebe said. "I made contact with two. One is now minus a foot, but they got away."

"Who was the target?" Carpenter asked.

She summarized the situation. "The dead man had purchased the encryption program from the Hacker. He was a lawyer, well known in certain circles for being the middle man on such deals."

Carpenter grasped the situation. "He did the deal for someone else. He was a cut out."

"Yes, sir."

"They know the meet was compromised," Carpenter said. "The buyers are covering their tracks."

"Yes, sir. They were expecting me."

The scrambled signal gently hissed for several seconds. "We have an infection."

"Yes, sir."

"What now on your end?" Carpenter asked.

"I'm going to start at the beginning in the other direction," Phoebe said.

"Which means?"

"Check out the seller. The militia. They aren't professionals. There will be loose ends. There always are with those people. At the very least I'll find out what was sold. That can give me an idea of the target."

"I'll send the latest imagery and intelligence on their compound in Montana. A plane will be waiting for you and a Cleaner will be waiting on the other end so you can get to the target. You'll get a contact text."

"Yes, sir."

A few seconds of silence ticked off, then Carpenter asked. "Any idea who the infection could be?"

"No, sir."

"Keep me updated."

"Yes, sir."

The phone went dead.

Phoebe reached down and her fingers probed the tear in the suit from the razor wire along the outside of the right calf. When she pulled her hand back it was smeared with blood. She licked it off.

"Oops," Phoebe said as she reached for the first aid kit.

FROM THE DARK BACK PORCH, Shane noted that the two guards at the gazebo rotated every couple hours and a variable number of minutes, a smart move. Predictability was the bane of proper security. They had torches lit, flickering in the night and Shane assumed they'd brought those in their baggage since he didn't recall them being stored anywhere at Two Rivers. They also had thin white wires running from ear pieces and he wondered where in that get up their guns were secreted although the halberds were fearsome weapons for close in fighting.

Lisa Livia had filled him in on Our Lady the Blessed Saint Ingrid, which made as much sense as everything else so far. After overseeing a subdued dinner in the barn, Lisa Livia had gone into town, at Shane's suggestion, to stay at the Rice Plantation B & B. She hadn't protested since it would mean she was away from the Duchess with whom she had apparently not bonded over the quality of luggage. She had cast a few glances toward Lucien at dinner but he'd been focused on the food, his father and the Duke and Duchess and had not returned them. Joey and Garth had cleaned up and also headed back to town and the swamp, respectively.

The dinner had been beyond subdued. Shane had felt like he was back in the service as the Andovan army chowed down with little conversation and the Duke and Duchess sat at each end of the table. The meal was one of Agnes' specialties. If the Duchess had chosen this venue because of Agnes, she certainly didn't seem into the food, just pecking away. Of course, she didn't look like she was much into calories at all. Everyone else had paid enough compliments that even Joey had been satisfied and he'd been in a good mood.

Shane did not feel the same. Combining the weapons with Lucien's recon, the implications were worrisome, although Shane didn't think it was directed at him or any of his people. The Andovans were concerned about someone from the outside; the question was: Who? Or was this normal Standing Operating Procedure as Lucien claimed? Shane had spent the last several hours on the porch following Carpenter's advice and doing online research via his laptop.

The light in the kitchen came on, sending long shadows across the porch through the windows and the screen door. Shane closed the laptop, put it on the table, and went inside. The ovens, fridge and sink were along the outer wall along with the windows looking out to the gazebo, dock and intracoastal. A counter with a cooktop ran across the middle of the kitchen and the far wall had cabinets and a marble-topped counter that were original to the house. Rows of pots hung from hooks and there were knives everywhere, which the Duke was admiring. There was a plethora of frying pans, a few too many in Shane's opinion, always unvoiced, of course.

The Duke wore a long, thick robe that was too nice to be called a bathrobe. It was the sort of thing Shane had seen in those old movies Agnes loved to watch. A smoking jacket? Shane would have considered it pretentious and over-the-top, but on the Duke it looked appropriate. All that was missing was the pipe.

"Miss Agnes has excellent taste in blades." He removed one and inspected the edge. "She keeps them sharp."

"She wields a mean frying pan, too," Shane said.

"Excuse me?"

"Can't sleep, Duke?" Shane asked.

"Call me Marc." The Duke went to the fridge and opened it. "I enjoy milk late in the evening. I find it helps my stomach."

"Anxious about the wedding?"

The Duke chuckled as he poured himself a glance. "Not the wedding, no. I've done it before and this will certainly be less strenuous." He held up the milk container to ask if Shane wanted any.

"No, thanks."

The Duke put the container back and took his glass. He walked out onto the deck. "It is peaceful here."

"I'd like it to stay that way," Shane said as the Duke sat in the chair Shane had just spent the last several hours in, with his back to the wall. Shane took the other chair, angling it so that the Duke was to his left and he could observe landward, not optimal but he'd give the Duke the throne. Rhett sleep-grumbled in his dog bed between the chairs.

"Do you have concerns?" the Duke asked.

"I'm concerned about whatever concerns your security people so much they bring military gear to a wedding. Modern weapons. Perhaps you can enlighten me?"

The Duke regarded Shane over the lip of the glass, his eyes glittering in the reflected light. "When did you discover this?"

"Late this afternoon," Shane said.

"But you haven't confronted the Field Marshal about it," the Duke said. "Might I ask why?"

"I've been thinking," Shane said. He indicated the laptop. "And Googling. This is more than a wedding."

"Indeed," the Duke said.

"Why didn't you tell us that?"

"We were hoping, and still expect, that this weekend will go off, as you say in America, without a hitch. Although, strangely, you also call marriage getting hitched, do you not?" When Shane didn't answer, he continued. "Lucien was sent early to check things and now our men are patrolling to ensure the sanctity of the location. Everything is going well."

"So far," Shane said. "You think someone is going to sabotage the marriage?"

"There's a lot at stake," the Duke said. "Some people in our country, and outside of it, are content with the way things have been for centuries and do not want change."

"To the point of violence? Or someone standing up when the preacher asks if there are any objections?"

"I don't believe either will happen," the Duke said. "But the Field Marshal is a cautious man. I follow his lead on security matters."

"The Field Marshal or Lucien?" Shane asked.

The Duke nodded. "You are observant. Lucien runs the day-to-day operations and security. The Field Marshal is getting on in years."

"Anyone specific to be concerned about?" Shane asked.

"Perhaps if you tell me what you know," the Duke said, "I'll fill in the gaps. You've been out here since dinner where it was obvious you were perturbed. The meal, by the way, was excellent. Once more, thanks to Miss Agnes and your Uncle."

"Your guys aren't exactly partying down," Shane said.

"That is not their duty."

Shane indicated the computer. "There are two families that alternate rule of Andova. The country in turn, annually switches allegiance from Spain to France and back. That part is antiquated, since neither of those countries is a monarchy any more. But the switching still has practical implications. One is the annual fee paid to each country. Which runs around a hundred million dollars."

"A bit more than that. Last year we paid France ninety-one million

Euros as per the Great Charter," the Duke said. "It's adjusted annually based on a number of economic factors."

"That's a lot of money," Shane said.

The Duke waved it off. "It's a pittance compared to the wealth Andova takes in."

"Controlled by the Duke and Duchess," Shane said. "In power that year. And now, you and the Duchess want to change that."

"It's *already* changed," the Duke said. "We're just making it formal and permanent." He took a sip of milk and put the glass down next to Shane's laptop. "The Duke of Embrie died three years ago. The Duchess has continued on for her family, which is allied with France. My family is originally from Spain."

"You got divorced last year," Shane said.

"Unfortunately."

"Unprecedented in Andovan history," Shane said.

"Indeed."

"And now you're marrying the head of the other ruling family. Also unprecedented."

"True."

For a guy who was verbose about other things, this topic seemed to require one-word answers.

"Isn't that like crossing the streams in *Ghostbusters*?" Shane asked. "Not supposed to happen?"

The Duke laughed. "What is it? '*It would be bad*'?"

"You've seen the movie," Shane said.

"I believe the film made it to Andova recently," the Duke said.

"If you don't mind me asking," Shane said, not really caring if the Duke minded, "why'd you get divorced? Catholic church and tradition being at odds with it."

"You couldn't find anything about that on-line?" the Duke asked. He picked up the glass of milk and finished it. He dabbed his upper lip with a handkerchief produced from a pocket of the robe.

"No. Which seems kind of strange."

"Our publicity people have a sterling record," the Duke said. "I must remember to commend them on their performance when I get back."

"Their cover-up," Shane corrected.

"Their discretion," the Duke said. "My ex-wife's behavior became erratic and outrageous. There was no recourse but divorce and to remove her from her station."

"She went nuts?"

"Bonkers."

"Is that the technical diagnosis?"

"It's the accurate one," the Duke said.

"In what way?" Shane asked.

"I'd prefer not to get into details," the Duke said.

"Let me see if I got the essence of this," Shane said. "You're Spain."

"Yes."

"And marrying the Duchess unites Spain and France, so to speak."

"No, it gives birth to a truly independent Andova. We will no longer be vassals to *either* country. More importantly, it allows us finally to focus on the people, not ourselves."

"How so?"

"After we marry, the Duchess and I will dissolve the Great Charter. It is well past time. There has been an elected civilian government essentially running the country for over two decades. They could easily find a better use for the transfer fees than France or Spain. But dissolving the Charter requires both families to agree to do so and they never would for centuries. Until us. Now we will be one family."

"Which brings me back to my question," Shane said. "Who are you afraid of and what might they do? Your ex? That makes this more a normal wedding. Sometimes ex's bring shotguns to weddings around here."

"That's Lucien's purview," the Duke said. "Personally, I believe everything will go smoothly."

"How does Spain and France feel about losing the revenue?" Shane asked.

The Duke shrugged. "It is insignificant in the larger scale of things and they value the business that flows through our country to and from theirs, more than the fee."

Shane didn't consider 100 million insignificant, but then again, he drove a twenty-year-old truck.

"You're having the wedding here, in the United States, though," Shane pointed out. "The royal wedding has always been held in the Cathedral of Saint Ingrid in Andova."

"Discretion," the Duke said. "Dissolving the Great Charter is controversial in Andova and—" he stopped as the Duchess spoke up from the doorway to the kitchen, casting a long, albeit narrow, shadow onto the porch.

"We do not have to explain to you," she said. "However, it is standard for our security detail to bring weapons when we travel abroad."

"Seems a bit illegal to do that," Shane said.

"Diplomatic pouch," the Duchess said.

"Pretty big pouches with automatic weapons and demolitions," Shane noted.

"Did you see any customs officials at the airport?" the Duchess asked.

Shane had not considered that. "Don't they have to check your papers at least?" He wasn't quite sure of protocol in this area because he usually entered foreign countries surreptitiously. And exited the same way. And nobody checked his papers when he came back to the States.

"There is an ecosystem that exists," the Duchess explained, "where things like customs officials and official papers are not factors."

They didn't factor in Shane's small ecosystem either, but his was more in the snow and mud while she was talking about one that had jewels and private planes and flew high above the muck. Rhett gave a low rumble as a new voice spoke from the steps leading up to the porch.

"I hope I am not intruding, your Graces," the Field Marshal said. His voice befitted the title, deep and gravelly. He had his baton tucked under one arm. All that was missing was the monocle and he'd be impressive in a game of Risk.

"Mister Shane," the Duchess said, "is wondering about your special items."

The Field Marshal entered the rectangle of light from the open kitchen door, with the Duchess's shadow outlined on his uniform, which Shane had not seen before. Dark blue pants with a hunter green coat festooned with medals and badges. Given the fact Andova never went to war, Shane figured they were an adult version of Boy Scout merit badges; show up to work and get a medal; best shoe-shiner in the army and that sort.

"Standard protocol," the Field Marshal said.

"Right," Shane said.

"Are we done here?" The Duchess demanded. The chill emanating from the doorway was palpable.

"We were just chatting, dear," the Duke said. He stood, glass in hand.

"I'll take that," Shane said.

"It's all right," the Duke said. "I know where the sink is."

He went inside and Shane heard the water run briefly, then the Duke and Duchess speaking in low voices which faded as they left the kitchen and went upstairs.

The Field Marshal was on the porch, so Shane went back out. "Trouble sleeping?"

"I'm on duty," the Field Marshal said. "The Duchess told me that Miss Agnes Crandall had a family emergency. What kind of emergency, if I might ask?"

"You can ask," Shane said. The silence played out.

"Some civilians seeing weapons," the Field Marshal said, "might have called the local constabulary."

"I've seen weapons before," Shane said.

"Yes. You have."

"What's with the mustaches?" Shane asked.

"It's a long story," the Field Marshal began, showing a bit of enthusiasm, but Shane cut him off.

"I'm already bored."

Both men looked down as Rhett moaned in his sleep, his short, chubby legs moving lethargically chasing something in his dream. He must have caught it, or, more likely, it got away, and he gave up, because a few seconds later he was still.

The Field Marshal pulled a pocket watch out of the inside of his dress coat and angled it toward the light. "My time is up."

"Yeah, it is."

"A good evening to you, sir."

"Same."

The Field Marshal marched off toward the barn.

It was after midnight and dawn was approaching for Agnes in Paris. Shane walked to the kitchen door. The comfortable king-sized bed in the top floor bedroom awaited, but he hesitated.

Shane unlocked the door to the steep stairs to the basement. Agnes hadn't known the basement existed when she bought the house and the fatal victim of her frying pan had fallen through the wall into it when he'd come to steal Rhett; more accurately to get the necklace that had been around Rhett's neck. Not anywhere near the Duchess's ecosystem, but it had been worth a pretty penny since it was part of a heist from twenty-five years ago that Joey, Four-Wheels Thibault and Frankie Fortunato had pulled off that had nabbed them the legendary five million.

Agnes avoided the basement and had objected to the stairs being put in, but Shane had pointed out that it was good storage space. For once, the ever-practical Agnes had disagreed, but Shane prevailed, although his real reason, the tunnel that led to the bomb shelter underneath the gazebo, he kept to himself.

Shane picked up the dog bed, wrapping it around Rhett. He grabbed up the heavy Fedex package from the counter. Package in one hand, dog and bed in the other, he went down the stairs. He looked up as the door swung shut and considered re-locking it, but he had dog and package and the Andovan Army on the outer perimeter. He used his elbow to turn on the lights.

The old pool table filled the center. Since Shane was not an aficionado, and no one, not even Carpenter, had a clue how to get the thing out of there without major disassembly, it functioned as a work table. It was solid mahogany and held Shane's tools; his Two Rivers, normal tools which he used when working around the grounds.

A small bar was in the corner. It had been fully stocked when Shane first came down here eight months ago to check that, yes, Two Wheels Thibault was really dead, more from the fall than Agnes' frying pan, although the former had helped precipitate the tumble through the wall above. The wine rack behind the bar was clear of dust, but the slots were empty. Joey had volunteered to take care of the liquor stock and appropriated it. In the corner was a six-foot-tall replica of the Venus de Milo. Carpenter had removed it to work on the mechanism and put it in the kitchen, but Agnes had grown sick of it, so Shane had returned it and hooked it back up.

Shane went to the statue, turned his back to it and used his elbows to press both breasts, releasing counter-weights. Lisa Livia's father had not exactly been a classy guy. A section of paneling next to the wine rack smoothly lifted, revealing a four-foot-wide, by six high, tunnel. Motion detector lights popped on, illuminating the tunnel.

Shane hunched over and walked along the brick-lined passageway until he arrived at a steel vault door. It guarded a Cold War era survival bunker with four-foot thick, steel-reinforced concrete walls. Many years ago, Frankie Fortunato had had it emplaced off a barge by a large crane and then buried, connecting it to the house via the Civil War era escape tunnel.

Shane put down the dog and package. Rhett was snoring, unperturbed and Shane took a moment to envy him. Then he dialed in the combination on the hasp welded to the wheel that opened the door. It clicked open and he pulled the wheel. He opened the heavy door enough that he could get inside. He carried the box and dog inside, putting Rhett down by the entrance.

In the bunker were the tools for Shane's other job, away from Two Rivers. The combat vest he'd worn in Montana hung on a hook. Two small, round holes were on the chest. The ceramic plate inside had been cracked by the rounds. Shane removed the broken plate, opened the Fedex box and pulled out the replacement, kindly sent via Field Support.

He went to the rack of weapons and perused the options. He weighed the Duke and Field Marshal's dismissal of possible trouble against Lucien's recon and the armament in the cases in the barn. He topped that off with the lack of guests other than the entire Andovan army. The result wasn't anywhere near as tasty as what Agnes had stayed up all night preparing for dinner. Shane already had his knife in the scabbard in the sheath in the middle of his back. He decided that for now a pistol would do. He chose the classic .45 M1911 pistol; a bigger round than his attacker had used. Just in case.

Rhett lifted his head and growled, something so rare that Shane immediately racked the pistol.

"Hush," Shane whispered as he aimed the gun at the open space and noted that the motion activated lights had come on.

A voice echoed along the tunnel. "I heard you chamber a round," Lucien called out. "I am not a threat."

Shane waited.

Lucien came inside, hands up. He was dressed in his black outfit, cleaned of mud, with the addition of a sabre in a sheath on his belt on one side and a pistol in a holster on the other. He looked around. "Interesting."

"Rhett doesn't like you," Shane said, lowering the pistol. "He's caught you skulking about twice."

"'Skulking'?" Lucien knelt in front of the dog and scratched behind the old hound's ears, murmuring something in French. Rhett rumbled his pleasure and then rolled on his back, presenting his belly.

"Traitor," Shane said.

Lucien looked up from rubbing Rhett's belly. "The Field Marshal informed me you were inquiring about our weapons?"

"It's not what people usually bring to a wedding. Nor is your outfit. Why are you out and about?"

"Checking on my guards," Lucien said.

"The Field Marshal just did his rounds. He was dressed better."

"I relieved him."

"What's with all his medals?"

"The Field Marshal served in *La Unidad*," Lucien said.

"Spain hasn't been at war in a long time," Shane said. He thought it interesting that Lucien knew he knew that *La Unidad* was Spain's elite naval Special Forces.

Lucien shrugged. "The ETA was active until recently."

"Basque separatists," Shane said.

Lucien nodded. "Special units often do missions far short of official war and never receive publicity, as you know."

"How would I know that?" Shane demanded.

"You know who the ETA was." Lucien indicated the bunker. "Is this a hobby? What I could find of your background indicates service in several elite military units, then it suddenly goes black."

"I retired."

"Certainly," Lucien said. He looked up at the hatch in the ceiling. "I suspect we are directly under the gazebo." It was not a question. "I noticed the outline of an opening in the floor. Very faint, but it is there."

"And you followed me down here?"

"I watched as you spoke to the Duke and the Duchess and then the Field Marshal," Lucien said. "Then you unlocked the door in the kitchen. That door, the basement, the tunnel and this shelter are not on the house plans."

"You checked the house plans," Shane summarized. "And you knew that door in the kitchen was locked because you tested it on your recon. I'm not sure I like any of this."

"It's standard," Lucien said. "The Duke and Duchess are rich. The threat of kidnapping always looms, especially when they are away from Andova. Sixty-six years ago, Francois Embrie, the son of the Duke of Embrie, was abducted while on holiday in Austria. It did not turn out well. That was the Duchess's grandfather. We've been extra-cautious ever since."

"Right," Shane said.

Lucien stood and picked up the shattered armor plate. "An accident?"

"Sure," Shane said.

"They happen," Lucien said.

Rhett rolled back on his ample stomach, closed his eyes, and resumed sleep.

"Is this where the five million was hidden?" Lucien asked.

"There was, and is, no five million."

"Certainly," Lucien said, checking the weapon racks. "Quite an arsenal."

"Ditto for what you have in the barn. You let me take your knife yesterday, didn't you?"

"Why do you say that?"

"The Duke was surprised. And I saw you fencing. It was too easy."

"I told you," Lucien said, "I am not here to fight."

"Where *did* you fight?" Shane asked.

Lucien turned from the long guns and faced Shane. "Excuse me?"

"You have a bullet wound."

Lucien nodded. "Ah. Yes. Africa."

"Andova had a war in Africa?" Shane asked.

"Andova has never had a war," Lucien said. "An accident, as you say. I see you tend toward larger cartridges for both pistol and rifle. Makes sense in this day and age."

"Nice try," Shane said. "Africa? On safari? Something shoot back? I believe shooting unarmed animals for sport isn't sporting."

"French Foreign Legion," Lucien said. "It's a bit of a tradition in our family. We go through selection and training, then do at least one tour in the Legion. On the Spanish side, they go through *La Unidad*."

"Hell of a tradition," Shane said. "The Legion is tough."

"It had its moments of stress," Lucien acknowledged. "Why isn't Miss Agnes here?"

"Family emergency. The Field Marshal asked me that. Why do you care so much?"

"It's an aberration," Lucien said. "I've learned to pay attention to such. And Agnes Crandall doesn't have family."

"She has friends who would die for her," Shane said.

Lucien raised an eyebrow. "Better than family."

"You can leave now," Shane said. "As I said once before, you're trespassing."

"I believe Detective Xavier speculated your name isn't on the deed for Two Rivers," Lucien said. "I know for certain it isn't."

"You need to leave now," Shane said.

Lucien nodded. "As you wish."

As he stepped over Rhett to leave, Shane asked: "You never said anything about getting shot."

Lucien paused and smiled at him. "It hurt."

Then he was gone.

Rhett moaned and his short legs churned briefly as he chased something in his sleep.

"I should be in Paris," Shane said.

SHANE'S WORDS OF WISDOM #4

The latest information hasn't been sent out yet.
Shane's Addendum: And when it is, it's out of date.

Strategic and Tactical Intelligence is always useful on an operation. The problem is, it usually arrives after you need it or learned it the hard way.

FRIDAY EARLY MORNING

It was dark as the Gulfstream descended to the tiny airfield in northwest Montana. The same airfield where 'Come Back' Shane had landed and returned from. Phoebe planned on having better results than the previous operative. She took one last look on the iPad at the most recent satellite imagery of the militia compound, which was essentially a poor man's idea of a training area. Not just poor, but stupid. There was a firing range which was backstopped by a rocky outcropping; Phoebe envisioned numerous ricochets careening all over the place.

There were a half dozen trailers and two cabins scattered around a level clearing in the center of sixty acres. The primary compound was two hundred yards from the gate. Phoebe brought up overlays of other maps, including the bordering National Forest. She had a tentative plan formulated as the plane rolled to a stop. She wore her black cat suit and assorted weaponry and gear. The goggles were pulled up on her forehead.

There'd been some information on the militia members in this local chapter of wanna-be's, which indicated one of them was the real deal: a veteran with combat experience. The rest were playing at being soldiers and the compound seemed more like an Animal House fraternity in the woods.

A truck waited with the local Cleaner. Phoebe exited the plane and walked toward it. A burly, older man with a bushy, white beard got out of the driver's seat. He looked past her, then frowned as the jet's door pulled up and closed.

"Back again?" the Cleaner said. "Just you this time?"

"Do you have what I requested?" Phoebe asked.

"Certain you don't need more?" The Cleaner jerked his thumb toward the surrounding mountains. "These fellows have enough firepower to start World War Three. I brought some additional weapons, just in case. The last operative had himself a mighty big gun."

"And look what happened to him," Phoebe noted. "And the gun."

The Cleaner nodded. "You have a point."

"I'm going to trust everything I requested is in the pack. Unbuckle the bike and roll it out. Darkness-is-a-wasting."

"All right, young miss. How long should I wait before I come get you?"

"I'll call when I'm ready."

"And if you don't call?"

"I'll call," Phoebe said, with a bit of irritation, anxious to be going.

"You know, young miss, I'm not being disrespectful. Part of my job is to make recommendations, that's all. I worry about Operatives when they're in my district. I feel bad about what happened to the last guy."

"He doesn't feel too good either," Phoebe said.

Cleaner opened the back of the truck. An electric motorcycle was winched in place, upright. A backpack was next to it. On top was a bulky, black sweater.

Phoebe climbed inside and lifted up the sweater, questioningly.

"Thought you might get cold, riding," Cleaner said. He unstrapped the motorcycle and rolled it out of the truck as Phoebe undid her belt and looped it, with the sheath over her shoulder so that the wakizashi was angled on her back. She pulled the sweater on over her vest and sword and straddled the motorcycle.

Phoebe looked to the east and sniffed. Dawn was less than an hour away.

"Happy trails," Cleaner said, without the slightest hint of sarcasm.

WEARING ONLY WORKOUT SHORTS, Shane was doing excruciating pushups on the back porch when Lisa Livia walked around the corner. She wore big sunglasses, flip-flops, tight jeans, and a red t-shirt that read:

> *If I Ever Say:*
> *"Do You Want Me To Be Honest?"*
> *Say: "No".*

She had a large bag slung over one shoulder, the top of the binder poking out.

"Carpenter did the same every morning," Lisa Livia said, "which isn't my idea of wake-up fun. I read an article that said my idea uses as many calories, so I don't understand it."

Shane's chest was burning from the blood flowing through the bruises. He lowered himself to the wood deck and then rolled onto his back, trying to moderate his breathing to control the pain. He glanced to the side. Rhett gave him a baleful look. Sunlight slanted through the early morning mist hanging over the water and the air was cool, the humidity low, and it promised to be a beautiful day. Weather-wise, that is.

"What the hell happened to you?" Lisa Livia demanded, staring at the bruises.

"I tripped," Shane lied.

"Over what? A sledgehammer?"

"It's nothing," Shane said as he pulled on a gray t-shirt, which had nothing written on it, which spoke volumes.

"Did Agnes see that?"

"No."

"Does Agnes grow tired of the *'need to know'* and *'it's classified'* shit?" Lisa Livia asked.

"There's a reason for it," Shane said.

"And that is?"

"Operational security and it keeps you safe."

"Damn Opsec. I hate that term."

An uneasy silence lasted a few seconds too long.

"Her majesty awake?" Lisa Livia asked.

"They've been up for an hour," Shane said. "Joey got here before that. He's in the barn serving breakfast."

"I don't think Joey sleeps," Lisa Livia said, heading to the kitchen. "He opens that diner so damn early for the shrimpers. I read the schedule and Joey and I agreed I didn't need to be here for breakfast since he and Garth could handle it. I was just wondering if these people suffered from jet lag and might have slept in. Like normal people. What time is it in Paris now?"

"They're not from Paris," Shane said. "Same time zone, though, Zulu plus one."

"What the hell is Zulu plus one?"

"Greenwich Mean time, plus one hour," Shane explained. "We're Zulu minus five."

"Do you guys ever speak normal? Agnes is eating lunch in Paris," Lisa Livia said. "In Paris." She brushed by him and Rhett. "There better be coffee or I'm gonna get mean."

Shane followed her inside. "Agnes always sets the coffee at night, before we go upstairs to bed. I forgot to do it last night."

Lisa Livia gave a low growl which caused Rhett to lift his head for a moment in concern.

Shane went to the cupboard near the microwave where the coffee usually was, but couldn't find the container that Agnes had bought with *Nectar of the Gods* written on it.

"Agnes has gotten really organized," Lisa Livia said, looking around the kitchen.

"Yeah, but she reorganizes all the time," Shane complained as he searched. "So, where something was, is no longer where it is, so what's the point? Reorganizing negates organizing, don't you think?"

"You're in a bad mood."

"Long night," Shane said, not adding he'd locked the kitchen door to the basement and secured himself in the vault for the night. Just in case. His thin sleeping pad hadn't been as comfortable as Rhett's dog bed. And nothing compared to the big bed on the top floor.

"You heard from Agnes?" Lisa Livia asked.

"We have a rule," Shane said.

"What kind of rule?" Lisa Livia asked as she dropped the bag and binder on the table.

"When one of us is gone, we don't bother the other."

"'Bother'?" Lisa Livia frowned. "That's nuts. Has she ever been gone before?"

"Uh. No."

"So, it's your rule."

Shane remembered the text on the side of the mountain, but didn't explain the danger. "Did Carpenter ever call you?"

"Rarely," Lisa Livia admitted. She thought about it. "Actually, only when it was about when and where we were meeting. He never called just to say hey."

"He never calls me just to say hey either," Shane said.

"It's not the same," Lisa Livia said. "And remember. Carpenter and I are over." She pulled out the container of coffee from a cupboard above the machine.

"That's not where it used to be," Shane complained as he filled the water in the machine.

"She put it in the logical place."

"Right." He inserted the filter and scooped coffee in.

"More," Lisa Livia said.

Shane added another scoop and started it. He sat across from Lisa Livia as she pulled the binder out.

"You know," Lisa Livia said, "Agnes was right about this wedding in one way."

"What's that?"

"It's going to be real simple. We've got pretty much nothing to do today because there's no rehearsal dinner because there's not going to be a rehearsal. According to the Duchess, they've been down this road before, so no biggie. Joey just has to serve the meals Agnes already prepared; lunch and dinner. No bachelorette party because the Duchess is the only woman here. No bachelor party; at least as far as the binder, although who knows what those guys got planned?"

"I don't think the Duke is the partying kind," Shane said.

"Nor the Duchess," Lisa Livia said. "The soldiers, though, seem young and, what's the word? Virile? Manly? Studly?"

"That's three words."

"Maybe they need to let off some steam."

"They're here on a job."

"What job?"

"Security."

"What? Guarding a statue?" Lisa Livia sighed. "I had a dream last night. About being invaded by the Andovan Army. One of them in particular."

Shane closed his eyes. "Lisa Livia."

"Anyway," she said, "they should just make the sign of the cross, say I do, and be done with it."

"Is there *anything* on the schedule for today?" Shane spotted Joey coming back to the house from the direction of the barn dressed in his usual red and black. At the gazebo, the two guards were as still as the statue they guarded. The rising sun glinted off their highly polished armor and the steel of the halberd which seemed as much functional as ceremonial. Shane wondered how that armor would handle a bullet.

Lisa Livia removed her sunglasses and perused the schedule. "Agnes had a boat sightseeing trip of the low country planned, because, you know . . ."

"She's Agnes. She offers that for every wedding."

"Yeah. But the Duchess squelched it. Lost the deposit but that's on the Duke and Duchess. We're just feeding the Army. No special activities at all."

"Is this wedding even going to be legal?" Shane wondered.

Lisa Livia wasn't worried about that. "They got the bishop of Andova, who was sprinkled with holy water by the Pope himself and has his own private jet, so I guess so."

"Since when does a bishop have a private jet?"

"You ever see all the gold stuff in a Catholic Church?" Lisa Livia said. "You see the jewels on that statue out there from their cathedral?"

Shane had not inspected the statue, so he had no comment on that. Lisa Livia wasn't done though.

"I went out with an altar boy a couple of times in eighth grade. He snuck me in the, whatever you call it, vestibule, and they had a freaking walk-in safe in there to hold all the loot. Chalices, crosses, all sorts of shiny things covered with jewels. And this was in Jersey. He had the combination and we fooled around." She sighed. "I think we made it somewhere between first and second base. Is that short stop? But doing it in the church was kinda exciting anyways. Forbidden gold and jewels and all that."

"Lisa Livia," Shane said, pulling her out of the memories. "What about paperwork?"

Lisa Livia checked the tabs "Nothing in here, but I'm sure given how anal they've been about everything else on their end, they've got that covered. Not our problem. We just put on the show. More accurately we let them put on the show."

"The Duchess say anything to you about the Duke's ex?" Shane asked.

Joey came in the door and checked the coffee pot. "What the fuck?"

"I forgot to make it last night," Shane explained once more, "and then I couldn't find the coffee."

"It's right above the pot," Joey said. "Where else would it be?"

"Where it was; where it's been for months," Shane said, but he knew this battle was lost. "Looks like breakfast went off without any gunfire or swordplay."

"Those guys are all right," Joey said. "They like the food."

"Some people are easy to please," Shane said.

Joey scowled. "You talking about me or the boys in the barn?"

Lisa Livia was still on Shane's question. "The Duke's ex? Nope. She's not exactly a fountain of information. Why? What do you know? The Duke say something to you?" She leaned forward in anticipation.

Shane didn't hesitate to shatter her hopes. "He said discretion was the word of the day."

"What day?" Joey asked as he grabbed a mug, still distracted trying to decipher Shane's comment.

"Nothing," Shane said. "What do *you* have to do today, then?" he asked Lisa Livia. "Since Joey took care of breakfast. And lunch and dinner just need reheating."

"I'm going out on the dock and catching some rays," Lisa Livia said. "Looking this good requires a lot of hard work."

"Too much sun causes cancer," the Duchess said from the doorway.

"The blackbird of happiness flutters in," Lisa Livia muttered.

Joey pulled the coffee and poured a cup before it was done, leading to hissing and splattering, which he ignored. He put the pot back. "Want some, m'lady?"

"It's your grace," the Duchess corrected him.

"Your what?" Joey asked.

"My mother died of skin cancer," Lisa Livia said to the Duchess.

Shane and Joey exchanged a look.

The Duchess didn't blink. "I'm sorry to hear that."

"I use sun block," Lisa Livia said. "My tone is naturally dark. I like the feel of sunlight on my skin. It's warm and caressing." She paused a beat. "Hey, your grace. What's it mean when someone is called m'lady?"

"Normally," the Duchess said, "it's the term a servant would use to address a woman of higher standing."

Lisa Livia perked up. "Really? Is Lucien—"

The phone hanging on the wall rang and everyone turned to stare at it. It rang again. The stares shifted to Shane, who couldn't remember the last time he'd answered the home phone because it was never for him and he always let the machine take it if Agnes wasn't around because it recorded messages better than he remembered them.

On the fourth ring, the caller ID reported: '*Maisie Shuttle*'.

"The flowers," Lisa Livia said. "Better pick up."

Ring.

"You've got the binder," Shane said.

"For fucks sake," Lisa Livia said as she got up to answer.

'*Maisie Shuttle*'. Then the answering machine clicked on before Lisa Livia reached the phone, but Shane noted she hadn't moved with any sense of urgency.

A southern voice spoke into the machine. "*Agnes, darling? Helloooo? It's Maisie. Maisie Shuttle.*"

"Christ on a cross," Lisa Livia complained. "How many Maisie's are there in this town?"

"Three," Joey said. "There's—" he stopped as the voice went on.

"*Helloooo? I've got most of the order done, but, I mean, really, Agnes.*" Maisie sounded as if her world were collapsing. "*I've been calling Fedex and they promised me the shipment from Europe will be here today. You know how hard it was to find these, what-do-ya-call 'em?*" There was a pause. "*Corona dee Ray?*"

"Corona del Rey," the Duchess corrected the machine in a low voice.

"*Then I have to do the arrangements. That's a lot of work. I've never seen anything like this. I mean. And so much red. It's not balanced. You can't go all one color. Really, Agnes. I know you didn't do this. Did you? Who are these people?*"

Shane and Joey turned to look at the Duchess while Lisa Livia was checking the binder and found the right tab. She turned heavy, plastic covered pages to FLORAL.

"*Anyway,*" Maisie continued, "*just wanted to let you know that if*

Fedex gets them here today, I'll have the arrangements ready for tomorrow. But I'm gonna be up half the night, you know, and that's going to cost more. You know. Business. Times are tough. Hey, did you hear Xavier is back in town? And miss oh-so-high-and-mighty Evie Keyes is back with her husband? Why she went back to that philandering scum, I've got no idea. Some people, I swear. Anyways. Ta-ta."

The phone clicked off.

Joey laughed. "She's got brass balls saying that about Jefferson Keyes since she was one of those he philandered with. Back in the day."

"Don't forget my stepfather," Lisa Livia said. "And probably my father before that."

"She got around," Joey acknowledged. "But you can't blame a guy. You shoulda seen Maisie back then. She was—" He stopped talking, wilting under the hot glare from Lisa Livia and the icy blast from the Queen of the High Peaks of the Pyrenees.

"I did see her," Lisa Livia said. "Sneaking out the back door one night when mother was in Jersey." She shrugged. "Then again, my mother wasn't exactly easy to be around."

"Flowers?" Shane said, trying to get everyone back on task. "What was she talking about?"

"Wow," Lisa Livia said, looking at a page in the binder. "Check out these arrangements! No wonder Maisie's got her panties in a wad. And she's right. Never seen so much red."

Before anyone else could take a look, the Duchess was at the table, looking over Lisa Livia's shoulder. "Oh!" she exclaimed, putting her hand to her throat which was a seismic reaction for the ice queen.

Shane, Lisa Livia and Joey stared at her. The Duchess blinked hard and swallowed. "I didn't know," she whispered. She turned away and hurried out the back door onto the porch.

Lisa Livia got up. "Fucking Maisie Shuttle and her big mouth," she muttered. "Always causing trouble."

She grabbed her big bag and left a confused Shane and Joey alone in the kitchen. Shane held out his mug and Joey poured him coffee. They went to the table and checked the binder.

"I ain't seen flowers like that," Joey said, "since the funeral for Big Mikey in Kansas City after he got whacked by Louie Six Fingers. Everybody knew Big Mikey was into flowers, so it was more than the usual send-off in terms of arrangements. But this is a lot classier." He remembered for a moment. "Even Louie sent an arrangement. Shaped like a gun, which everyone thought lacked class."

LISA LIVIA FOUND the Duchess on the corner of the porch. She was staring out at the wetlands. There was a sheen in her eyes that she quickly blinked away.

"I'm going out on the dock to relax," Lisa Livia said. "Care to join me?"

The Duchess didn't shift her gaze. "I try to avoid the sun."

No shit, Lisa Livia thought. "There's a big umbrella we can open up. Sometimes dolphins swim by. They can get a little loud and irritating at times with all their noise and screeching, but, you know, they're dolphins. Some say they're smarter than humans."

A muscle twitched on the Duchess' cheek. "It is nice of you to invite me. But it's not necessary or part of your job. I am sorry about your mother."

Lisa Livia laughed. "My mother didn't die of skin cancer. She's locked up in the big house for trying to kill Agnes."

The Duchess blinked. "You lied?"

"Sure. Your grace."

"That was mean," the Duchess said.

"Not really." Lisa Livia slung her bag over her shoulder. "Hey, I'm going out there anyway, so feel free. Whatever."

Lisa Livia headed for the dock. She went ten steps, then turned. "Oh, come on. I'll tell you the full story behind Blood River."

The Duchess descended from the porch and they went side by side onto the long walkway to the high dock. A soldier dressed in his suit appeared out of nowhere and shadowed them, staying a respectful distance behind. He was tall, thin and dark-skinned. He sported the same pointed mustache, but also a beard tinged with gray. He halted two-thirds of the way out on the walkway.

Lisa Livia cranked open the large umbrella, then angled it, providing shade from the rising sun. She maneuvered one of the chairs into the shadow. "There you go. Your grace."

"You say that as an insult so perfectly," the Duchess said, but there was no rancor in her voice. "Well done."

"I've got a lot of practice insulting people," Lisa Livia said as she grabbed one of the lounge chairs and positioned it perpendicular to the rays and to the side of the Duchess. "My father is Frankie Fortunato, who disappeared when I was a kid. I thought he was dead for twenty-five years until he suddenly shows up at my daughter's wedding. My mother is Brenda Dupree, who is in prison for trying to kill Agnes, just before my daughter's wedding. I got excellent genes in the insulting area."

"Is that a truth?" the Duchess asked, squinting at Lisa Livia. "That your mother tried to kill Miss Agnes?"

"Sure. Here." Lisa Livia rummaged in the bag and retrieved a set of big sunglasses. "I always carry extra." She passed them over. They looked like alien bug eyes on the Duchess' narrow face.

"You look good in shades," Lisa Livia said as she spread out a towel on the lounge. "My mother *did* kill Agnes' ex-fiancée, who she was, at the time, married to. It's complicated. But stupid." She shimmied off her t-shirt and jeans, and lay down in her two piece.

"That's a much more interesting story than the Blood River," the Duchess said.

"But as deadly."

"Your daughter's wedding sounds like quite the fiasco."

"It was wonderful," Lisa Livia said. "She married a great guy who she still adores. There were flamingoes. Did you know flamingoes are monogamous and mate for life?"

"I did not know that. Impressive."

"I think, like dolphins, they're smarter than humans too."

"We are a flawed species," the Duchess allowed. "Sun block?" she asked.

Lisa Livia sighed and pulled it out of her bag. As she layered it on, she noted: "My mother would have made a comment about my weight when I took my clothes off. You got kids?"

"Unfortunately, I was unable to conceive with my husband."

"Did you want them?"

Several seconds ticked by. "Although it was expected of my position, I did not."

They were interrupted by the guard coming onto the high dock. "Your Grace, there's a suspicious man in a boat over there, watching through binoculars."

"Oh, that's just Xavier," Lisa Livia said. "He's still trying to figure out the heist my dad and his partners pulled over twenty-five years ago. He's harmless." She smiled up at the guard. "Want to do my back?"

The guard's mouth opened to answer, but no words came forth.

Lisa Livia turned, leaning on her elbow, to give him a better view. "How do you get your mustache so stiff?"

"You may resume your post, Vicente," the Duchess ordered.

"Yes, your Grace."

He hurried away.

"Vicente is a doctor," the Duchess said. "But also a soldier. His father is French, but his mother Algerian. An intriguing combination, as is his professions."

"Can I ask you something, your Grace?" For once, the title was simply part of the sentence.

"Yes?"

"Why'd the floral arrangements upset you? It's obvious you didn't know about them."

"The Duke didn't tell me," the Duchess said. "He must want it to be a surprise."

"I'm sorry we messed that up, then," Lisa Livia said, silently vowing to strangle Maisie tomorrow. *After* she set up the arrangements.

"No," the Duchess said. "It's actually better that I know. It just brought back memories."

"Good ones?"

"It might have overwhelmed me to see them tomorrow. Now, I will be able to show an appropriate amount of public gratitude."

Don't hurt yourself, Lisa Livia thought. "You don't like them?"

"They're fine," the Duchess said in a neutral voice. That seemed to be the extent of the explanation for the Duchess' reaction.

"Why all the red?" Lisa Livia asked. "You got red all over the gazebo and those flower arrangements aren't providing much change."

"The background color for my family flag is magenta and for the Duke's it's gold. Since we're joining together, we're merging the colors, which results in red."

Lisa Livia frowned. "Well, not really, because—" she stopped as the Duchess held up a hand.

"Yes, yes, not exactly. More like amaranth. But it's symbolism. That's important."

Lisa Livia shook her head. "Did you ever see *Game of Thrones*?"

"Excuse me?" the Duchess said.

"Nothing." Lisa Livia decided to go in another direction. "Are the fellows throwing the Duke a bachelor party tonight? Agnes didn't leave any information about that." Lisa Livia reclined. "I could get Joey to help with the planning since they're in a foreign country and all that."

"I very much doubt it," the Duchess said. "I don't anticipate the Duke would appreciate it."

"He's a guy. He'll appreciate it."

The Duchess didn't respond.

"Nothing too crazy," Lisa Livia said, given that the last bachelor party she remembered at Two Rivers had resulted in a dead stripper. They could definitely tone it down from that. "It'll allow him to relax and it would be a surprise, like the flowers. Something he won't expect but nice."

The Duchess didn't take the flower bait. "He's a rather relaxed man," the Duchess said, looking shoreward where the Duke was at the gazebo, chatting with the two guards. "However, a small celebration might be in order. The men love the Duke and I'm sure they'd wish to pay their respects."

Yeah, a bachelor party is all about showing respect, Lisa Livia thought. "I'll talk to the Field Marshal about it. Hook him up with Joey."

The Duchess snorted. "Ricard? He's for show. Lucien runs everything."

"Even better," Lisa Livia said. "Is he married, by the way?"

"Are you looking for a relationship?" the Duchess asked.

Lisa Livia laughed. "Hell, no. I just don't like cheaters."

"Ahh," the Duchess said. "You're talking about a fling."

"I'm considering it," Lisa Livia said, having no idea that she was until she said it.

"Lucien's a devout Catholic," the Duchess said.

"He's saving himself for marriage?"

The Duchess looked at Lisa Livia. "You are very direct."

"Life's too short to be indirect if you want to get to where you're going," Lisa Livia said. "You guys are only going to be here for the weekend. Gotta make hay while the sun is shining."

The Duchess didn't respond.

For a few minutes there was only the sound of low dock creaking up and down in the swell and waves lapping at the pylons.

The Duchess abruptly stood. "I'm going back."

Lisa Livia realized the Duchess hadn't answered her question.

The Duchess walked off, wearing Lisa Livia's spare sunglasses.

It took longer than Phoebe had anticipated to get near the compound. It was off a long dirt road that was off a long potholed paved road that was off a local state highway that was off Interstate 90; altogether fifty miles away from the airport where she'd landed. Phoebe had raced along those roads until she was two miles from the compound, then she'd turned onto a track in the National Forest. The problem was that melting snow had turned the dirt to mud and she was as much brown as black by the time she reached a point on a spur above the compound. She'd chosen the site from the satellite imagery as the most advantageous from which to surveil.

She leaned the motorcycle against a tree and sat down cross-legged as daylight increased. She had the baggy pullover sweater still covering her upper body, appreciating it for the protection from the cold and mud.

Smoke was trickling from the chimney of the cabin and a couple of the militia were gathered around an oil drum which had a nice blaze going. They were dressed in assorted camouflage, most of which didn't match the surrounding terrain, but had probably been on sale at the nearest Army-Navy surplus store or more likely bought off Amazon. There were six men and two women. They were armed, but their weapons were a mixture of types, which meant their ammunition was of various calibers and not compatible, a no-no for any respectable fighting unit. There were several pick-up trucks parked alongside a gaggle of Harley's.

As it grew lighter, Phoebe noticed small pieces of white paper to her right, underneath a fir tree. Further investigation revealed them to be the remains of rolling paper. Phoebe picked up a small piece of brown leaf in a butt and sniffed. Tobacco.

Careless.

Phoebe looked over the camp once more, then put on her helmet , remounted the motorcycle, and twisted the throttle. The engine silently powered up. She slithered downslope through the last of the snow, the slush and the mud, slipping and sliding. She was dripping as she rode into the camp. Because there was no gas motor or exhaust, they didn't hear her coming and she was able to ride up to the group around the barrel fire and brake hard while turning, spraying them with mud.

She dropped the kickstand and dismounted as several weapons were pointed at her.

She pulled off the helmet, revealing smushed reddish-black hair, with some of the dye having washed out. "How ya'll doing?" She had no clue what a Montana backwoods accent was and had debated between Fargo or Redneck, and figured Redneck would be easier to maintain because her father had lived with a woman for a couple of months who had been from some place deep in the old Confederacy. She'd also been one of the nicest of her father's numerous brief live-ins, which wasn't saying much. For some reason, it made that voice easier to access while she focused on the tactical scenario.

"Who the fuck are you?" a fat woman in a black hoodie demanded, while the men were dumbstruck, not sure what to make of Phoebe's unexpected arrival. There were a couple of swastika tattoos visible and Phoebe didn't want to imagine what the jackets covered.

Women were always the most dangerous.

"Anyone seen Jeremy lately?" Phoebe asked.

Glances exchanged but no response.

The fat woman hollered: "Teardrop!" She turned her attention back to Phoebe. "I asked who the fuck are you?" She lifted the hem of the hoodie to display the butt of a pistol.

Phoebe pulled the bulky sweater off, revealing the brace of knives, wakizashi, strobe light and pistol. She settled the goggles on her forehead, even though it was daylight.

Hoodie wasn't impressed as she wrapped sausage sized fingers around the pistol grip, prepared to draw it.

"Calm down, Betty." Standing in the door of a cabin was a lanky man wearing boots, jeans and a lumberjack shirt. He had an M-4 assault rifle loosely held in one hand.

Phoebe gave Teardrop points for not wearing camo. He strolled forward and Phoebe saw where he got his name from: there were two teardrops on his left cheek. She figured it was some sort of prison thing or maybe a gang thing or maybe a militia thing or how many people he'd killed or maybe he liked teardrop tattoos. He also had a barb wire tattoo across his forehead which Phoebe suspected was to keep foreign or blasphemous thoughts from penetrating his brain.

"She asked if any of us seen Jeremy," Betty, aka Hoodie, said.

"I heard," Teardrop said. He nodded. "Nice ride. They say those electric bikes have great torque. Instant power." He shifted his attention to Phoebe. "You're a nice little spinner, ain't you?"

Phoebe sensed Betty coming up behind her, the large presence disturbing the air and bringing with it an odor of sweat, smoke and no showering for far too long. She heard the grunt as Betty pulled the pistol.

Phoebe whirled, drawing the wakizashi from over her shoulder and slicing through Betty's hoodie on her gun arm and parting skin, but not any deeper than a long scratch.

Betty yelped, dropping the gun and Phoebe put the tip of the sword in the soft spot under her chin, at least where the chin should approximately be, because there was a lot of fat. "Betty. You're bothering me. Go away." She reached down and picked up the gun, dropped the magazine, cleared it, and tossed it back to the big woman, who awkwardly caught it.

The sound of rounds being chambered filled the silence as Phoebe was surrounded by a circle of loaded weapons.

"Everybody chill," Teardrop said. "Betty, step back."

Betty did as ordered, glaring at Phoebe.

"Who are you?" Teardrop demanded.

Phoebe faced him as she sheathed the sword. "You know, if anyone starts shooting, it's going to be the worst circle jerk ever. Andrew."

Teardrop's eyes narrowed at his real name.

Phoebe pointed to the hillside. "Someone's been watching your camp. Before me. Before you received the offer for the munitions and weapons. Days before Jeremy went to the meet and disappeared. Andrew."

Teardrop jerked his head toward the cabin. "Come." He held up his hand, palm out to the others. "Everything's all right."

Betty wasn't happy, but the rest lowered their weapons.

Phoebe followed Teardrop into the cabin, which was surprisingly clean but dimly lit.

"Excellent," Phoebe said, noting the lighting.

"What?"

"Nothing. Wanna bet you're gonna do something stupid?"

Teardrop faced her. "Fuck you."

A blaze crackled in a stone fireplace with a thick wooden beam mantle. Above it hung a flintlock long rifle on pegs.

Phoebe pointed at it. "Does it work?"

"Of course. Punch a big hole in whatever I hit with it. Especially little girls."

"You were an 18-Bravo in Special Forces," Phoebe said, referring to the weapons specialist on a Green Beret A-Team.

"You know my name and you know my background," Teardrop said. "Big deal."

"You were rifted from service under a cloud of suspicion over the deaths of three civilians in Afghanistan."

Teardrop sat down at a log table near the fire, indicating for her to sit across from him. He touched his cheek. "One was a supposed civilian. The others were definitely bad guys. Investigator said they'd taken the driver hostage, but that was his tough luck. They were coming toward us. What would you have done?"

"Rules of engagement are for those who've never been engaged," Phoebe said. "That was our mantra."

"What unit?"

"You never heard of us," Phoebe said. "If you did, I'd have to kill you." She said the latter in a flat voice that held no hint of humor.

"Yeah, right, big words," Teardrop said. "You're a fed."

"Not exactly. I'm not here for you. You never heard back from Jeremy."

Teardrop considered the question, then finally said. "No."

"He's dead."

Teardrop didn't seem surprised. "You killed him? Pretty ballsy to ride in here if you did."

"No. I don't have balls nor do I desire them. They get in the way of clear thinking. One of our people was monitoring the meeting. But someone had surveillance on it before we did. Probably the same person who checked out your camp from the ridgeline. They killed your man. The people who didn't pay for their goods. Who were the buyers?"

Teardrop got up and walked to a black coffee pot sitting on a pot belly stove. He used a rag to grab the handle and poured some into a grubby mug. He returned to the table and regarded her over the steam rising from it, forehead furrowed.

Thoughts in the wire, crossed Phoebe's mind, seeing him try sort this out.

He began with: "Anything I say would implicate me in something I know nothing about."

"How do you know it would implicate you, if you know nothing about it?" Phoebe asked. "Don't play stupid. I dislike it. I'm not a cop. I'm not here for you. I want the buyers. You should too, since they killed Jeremy. Or do you guys just play at being bad-asses?"

Teardrop wrapped large hands around the mug.

Phoebe sighed. "When, not if, those people do something very bad, it *will* be on you. Then I will come here and I won't be asking questions."

"Who are you?" Teardrop demanded. "You're getting on my nerves. Lots of big talk from a little girl. I say the word, you never make it out of here alive."

Phoebe held up two fingers. "One. My Organization knows I'm here. Thus, you're screwed coming and going. If I don't show back up, the wrath of vengeance like you've never seen will rain down upon this place. Two. Your premise is faulty. You say the word, whatever one it is, a lot of people die, including you and I've wasted my time. I hate wasting time."

"What organization?" Teardrop demanded.

"Never you mind," Phoebe said, but the accent tripped her up, because that was what her father's girlfriend of the month had scolded her with.

"You wearing a wire?" Teardrop asked as his eyes shifted slightly, looking behind her.

"What did Jeremy take to the meet?"

Phoebe heard the door behind her burst open. With one hand she pulled the goggles down over her eyes and with the other turned on the strobe light on her vest. It pulsed, filling the cabin with blinding light flashing at a frequency that had been designed to initiate seizures in the unprotected.

Teardrop shoved his seat back, trying to cover his eyes, but the chair tipped over and he fell to the floor. Phoebe jumped to her feet and turned while drawing her pistol. Three men and Betty had crowded through the door. The men were disoriented but Betty had her gun trained right at Phoebe.

There was always one in a crowd whose brain was far enough out of the bell curve to not be affected by the strobe.

"Bitch," Betty said. "Drop the gun."

Phoebe was always been appalled when TV shows and movies depicted the infamous 'Mexican Standoff' because it never made sense to her because it was so easily solved since a bullet was faster than a reaction.

Phoebe pulled the trigger and the round hit Betty's hand, tearing into it, splintering the wrist bone and then ricocheting through the forearm along the radius bone and exiting at the elbow. Betty, of course, dropped her gun in the process and screamed in pain.

Phoebe turned off the strobe and gathered guns, ejecting their magazines, clearing the chambers, as the others recovered and Betty cursed. The sound of vomiting provided a chorus to the woman's inventive, profane diatribe.

"No arterial bleeding," Phoebe said to Betty, who had her good hand clamped over her other arm. "You'll be all right." But Betty wouldn't shut up so Phoebe rapped her upside the head with the barrel of one of the appropriated rifles.

Betty collapsed like a sack of flour.

"One of you, bandage her and get her out of here."

Teardrop's hand was shaking as he reached for one of the weapons on the table so Phoebe gave it a love tap with the rifle, the sound of a bone cracking mixing with the last of the retching.

"What the fuck?" Teardrop asked as he cradled the hand. "Get out!" he screamed at the others. "Get out!"

Disarmed and dispirited they trooped out, two of them trying to carry Betty, but a third had to join in to get her weight out the door, one boot dragging on the floor. Phoebe pulled the goggles up on her forehead.

"Told you not to do stupid but I knew you would," Phoebe said as she tossed the rifle onto the table. "It's kind of strange, though, that you only have two teardrop tattoos. Means you know you killed a civilian."

"Fuck you!"

Phoebe closed her eyes briefly in sheer exhaustion from hearing the go-to phrase of the cornered coward. "It's a lose-lose situation, Andrew. Make the best of it. What was sold?"

"Guns. Ammo. Some C-4. Blasting caps. And some weird stuff."

Phoebe perked up at weird. "Elucidate." From the look on his face, that one didn't make it over the wire. "What weird stuff?"

"Swords. Fancy armor. And a dozen of some weird axe on a long pole."

"A halberd," Phoebe said.

"What?"

"You described it accurately," Phoebe allowed. "Halberd is from the old German for *halm*, which is handle, and *barte*, which means axe." She remembered a chilly dojo on Okinawa. "We didn't spend much time on it. Not something one is likely to come across in a modern engagement. Very curious."

Now that he'd crossed the spill-your-guts Rubicon, Teardrop continued. "That weird stuff was in a shipment that Jeremy brought over the border from Canada. It was sealed and bonded, but—" he paused.

"You opened it anyway," Phoebe finished for him.

"Yeah." He frowned, crinkling the wire. "Maybe they got pissed when they saw the boxes had been opened."

"Jeremy was dead the moment he agreed to the deal," Phoebe said, not to reassure, but more thinking out loud. "How much C-4? Type of weapons and number of rounds?"

Teardrop rattled off the numbers. Enough to supply a small group, squad sized, maybe more. Demo that could take out a building or two.

"Why the blade weapons?" Phoebe mused out loud.

"Collectors?"

"Jeremy didn't go through customs with those cases?"

"Nah. I think that's why they approached us."

"Why were those crates sealed and bonded if Jeremy had to sneak it across the border?" Phoebe said, but knew the answer as soon as she asked. "They came to Canada legitimately from overseas. Jeremy was the cut out to get them into the United States un-noticed."

She could tell her musings had left Teardrop behind. "I'd give all this up," Phoebe suggested as she stood. "The clock is ticking. Don't say I didn't warn you."

She walked out. There was no one in sight but she imagined a few weapons were trained on her.

She mounted the bike, put on the sweater and helmet and rolled the throttle. She left the camp via the main gate. She accelerated along the dirt road that ran along the ridgeline. She was trying to unravel the enigma of the packages. The trail was relatively straight and she pushed the bike to the max.

As she approached a sharp curve a mile and a half from camp, she pulled the brake lever and it moved freely. She tapped the foot brake and it too failed.

"Oops," Phoebe said as the motorcycle flew off the edge of the road.

She was airborne and looked down. A cliff face for forty feet, then a steep slope that was a mixture of rocks and trees and rapidly approaching. Phoebe pushed off the motorcycle's pegs, separating from it and tucked herself in tight, as she'd been taught for a parachute tree landing, albeit this time sans the parachute. Fists and elbows together, arms up, turned inward, to cover her face, legs tight, knees slightly bent. She crashed into a pine tree, broke a thick branch with her forearms, bounced off the trunk and finally landed, her legs twisting awkwardly. She rolled through a bush covered with thorns, of course, and stopped, her head bouncing off a rock so hard the helmet cracked and she was knocked out.

SHANE'S WORDS OF WISDOM #5

Pain is weakness leaving the body.
Shane's Addendum: As long as it's someone else.

That's a phrase I heard in many training schools and in various units
I served in.
Sounds great and I'm a big believer in it as long as the person in pain
is someone I don't like.
Otherwise?
Pain is pain.

FRIDAY AFTERNOON

LL

Lisa Livia gently knocked on the door. It was almost noon and she'd searched all over for Lucien, then finally come to the barn. Joey and Garth were downstairs in the open area, setting out lunch for the army. Lisa Livia had taken the outside fire stairs, to the wide balcony, having no desire to trade quips with Joey. She heard the light pad of feet on wood, then the door cracked open and one eye peered out at her.

"Yes?" Lucien asked.

"Did I wake you?"

"No." But the door didn't open any wider.

"May I come in?"

Lucien hesitated.

"Unless I'm disturbing you?" Lisa Livia asked. "Am I disturbing you?"

"I'm not completely dressed," Lucien said.

"You got pants on?"

"Yes."

"Then it's okay," Lisa Livia said, pushing open the door.

Lucien bowed, both to Lisa Livia and the inevitability of her entrance, stepping aside.

"Excuse me," Lucien said as he grabbed for a shirt off a hanger.

"Don't hurry on my account," Lisa Livia said.

Starched uniforms and suits in clear plastic wrappers were hung in the small closet, neatly ordered. There were two starched puffy shirts. A helmet with a red crest was on the shelf. A set of armor was on a mannequin in one corner—which helped explain the amount of luggage, besides the weapons, that is. The bed was made, the corners tucked military tight. A padlocked footlocker was at the foot of the bed. A copy of *Mob Food* was on the night stand; there was one in every room, Two Rivers' version of the Gideon.

Lucien slid the shirt on, but didn't button it. "How may I help, m'lady?"

"Call me Lisa Livia. Or LL. Or you know, whatever you wish. Although, I kinda like m'lady."

Lucien smiled, revealing perfect teeth beneath the waxed mustache.

"Did I interrupt you?" Lisa Livia asked. She held the binder with both hands in front of her chest.

"I was resting," Lucien said.

Lisa Livia looked at the bed, the sheet taut, the blanket tucked. "Where?"

"On the floor," Lucien said, indicating a thin sleeping pad on the far side of the bed.

"You don't do beds?" Lisa Livia asked.

"Beds have their purpose," Lucien said, "but when deployed, I never use one."

"Why?" Lisa Livia asked.

"Beds are soft. We let our guard down in them. And an intruder can find you there. They don't expect you on the floor."

"Right." Lisa Livia leaned back against the dresser. "If you don't sleep in it, then what good is it?"

Lucien walked over to the sleeping pad, reached under, and retrieved a pistol. He slid it into a holster on his belt. "Various things."

"You always hide your gun under where you sleep?" Lisa Livia asked. She still had the binder in front of her.

"Not always." He stepped closer to Lisa Livia, inside her personal space. "What is that smell? It's rather intoxicating."

"Sunscreen."

"Underneath the sunscreen?"

"Me."

"Ah, m'lady." He leaned forward, but the binder was between them. Lisa Livia blindly tried to put it on the dresser behind her, but missed. It thudded to the floor, unnoticed by either of them. His lips were just about to touch hers when his phone chimed. He didn't pull away, but he didn't finish the movement either. Lisa Livia had stopped breathing.

The phone chimed once more, but Lucien remained still. She could feel his breath on her lips. He smelled of, Lisa Livia wasn't quite sure what, but she certainly liked it.

A third chime. With a sigh that Lisa Livia felt, he retreated and snatched the offending device off the nightstand.

"Lucien."

He listened but his eyes were on her. After ten seconds he said: "I'll be there immediately, your Grace."

Damn that bitch, Lisa Livia thought. She wondered if the Duchess knew she were here.

He pushed the off. "I regret that duty calls me," he said to her as he buttoned his shirt.

"Hey, we all gotta do, what we gotta do," Lisa Livia.

"It is most inauspicious timing."

"Yeah. That too."

He walked past her, closer than necessary, a brush of his shirt sleeve lightly against her t-shirt and retrieved a coat from the closet. He slid it on, then went to a nightstand drawer and took out a small radio, putting it in a pocket inside the coat. He threaded the white wire to his ear and emplaced the receiver. He went to the door, then paused.

"Oh, yes. Was there something specific you wanted?"

"There was," Lisa Livia said.

"And that is?"

"Oh." Lisa Livia regrouped. "Two things. Do you guys have a bachelor party laid on for the Duke?"

"We do not," Lucien said.

"I was talking to the Duchess," Lisa Livia said, "and suggested it to her. She didn't think you did or that the Duke would want one, but it's a tradition, and she did say you guys liked the Duke a lot so I was thinking maybe I could talk to Joey and he could like, you know, arrange something here in the barn tonight to show your apprecia-tion." She was babbling and forced herself to stop as Lucien frowned.

"Our duty schedule doesn't give us much free time," he said. Before she could protest, he raised a finger. "But, it is a noble idea. Let me ruminate on it and check with the others."

Lisa Livia tried to remember the last time someone had told her she had a 'noble' idea and drew a blank. "Sure."

"Is that all?"

Lisa Livia almost nodded, but then remembered. "The Bishop."

Lucien grimaced. "What of him?"

"Do you have his arrival information? It's not in the binder." Which reminded her. She bent over and picked it up, feeling his gaze upon her.

"I do."

"Are you guys picking him up? Or I can have Garth do it. Also, do you know where he's staying? I've called and held a room for him in town at the Rice Plantation B&B, since the Duchess told me she doesn't want him staying here."

"She would not want him here," Lucien confirmed.

"Any reason why?"

"He doesn't approve of the marriage," Lucien said.

"Okay."

"But to answer your query, we have made no arrangements for the Bishop. It is thoughtful of you to consider it."

"It's my duty," Lisa Livia said. "I'll arrange pick up if you give me the flight info."

Lucien checked his phone, scrolling. He wrote down the arrival time on a post-it pad on the nightstand and handed the note to her. "He has his own jet. Actually, it's Andova's jet. It's small enough that it can land at the local airport. You can't miss it. Or him."

"Thanks," Lisa Livia said.

Lucien paused and Lisa Livia took half a step toward him. "It would be best if I sent one of my men with whomever picks up the Bishop."

Lisa Livia stopped in her tracks. "Okay."

"Anything else?" Lucien asked, and that was an undercurrent to the question that thrilled Lisa Livia.

"We can finish later," she said.

"I will suffer my duties in the meanwhile," Lucien said. But he paused once more and looked at her in an open way. "You remind me of someone."

"Someone you liked?"

"Very much," Lucien said. Then he was out the door.

Lisa Livia let out a deep breath.

As she left the room, she realized that Carpenter had never let his phone ring more than twice when he was with her. No matter what base they were on.

"HERE'S the flight info for the Bishop," Lisa Livia said as she handed Shane the post-it. She tossed the binder on the kitchen table where it landed with a heavy thud. She went to the cupboard above the coffee pot, moved aside the *Nectar of the Gods* container and retrieved a bottle of Scotch.

"I didn't know that was there," Shane said.

"You didn't know the coffee was either," Lisa Livia noted as she grabbed a shot glass and sat at the table. She poured one and downed it, then refilled.

She caught Shane's glance. "Don't you dare say a word about what time it is."

Shane held up both hands in surrender. "I didn't say anything."

"I saw you look at the clock," Lisa Livia said. "Where're the royals?"

"On the dock," Shane said. "With the Field Marshal. Lucien just joined them."

"Probably planning their next country to invade," Lisa Livia said.

"What's wrong?" Shane asked as he saw Joey and Garth coming back from the barn. There'd been no gunfire so lunch had gone all right, although that didn't rule out swordplay. Shane was beginning to count down the meals until this cluster was over and everyone flew home. And then, Agnes returned and the stars would align and all would be peaceful again.

"Nothing," Lisa Livia snapped, proving that something was indeed wrong. "Oh, yeah. Lucien said he wants to send one of his men with Garth when he picks up the Bishop."

"Why?"

"How the hell do I know?"

Shane decided to avoid venturing deeper into the Lisa Livia fuming ambush and checked the post-it. "They're going to have to leave soon to make it to the airport in time."

Joey came in the door, followed by Garth. Joey saw the bottle, grabbed a shot glass and sat across from her. When Garth reached for a glass, Shane stopped him.

"You've got to make a trip to the airport. And since when do you drink?"

Garth hung his head. "Sorry, Mister Shane."

"He's a man," Joey said as he downed a shot. "He can drink if he wants."

"Not if he's going to drive," Shane said.

"Your old man and I once drove from Jersey to here so shit-faced we didn't remember a single thing," Joey boasted. "Hell, we blew through the tolls on the Jersey Turnpike so fast, the troopers didn't even bother to follow."

"You just said you didn't remember anything," Lisa Livia observed.

"Well, given that example," Shane said, "no. Garth shouldn't drink."

"Hey," Lisa Livia said to Joey. "You need to talk to Lucien about holding a soirée for the Duke tonight."

"'Soiree'?" Joey repeated.

"Sort of a bachelor party," Lisa Livia said, "but no debauching."

"'Debauching'?" Joey said.

"Damn it!" Lisa Livia slammed her glass on the table and stood up. "You men are really getting on my nerves." She stormed out, leaving the binder behind.

"What's wrong with her?" Joey asked. "What did you do?"

"I didn't do nothing," Shane said, but he was eyeing the binder as if Lisa Livia had left behind a ticking time bomb. "There's nothing scheduled today other than meals, right? Just dinner left, right? That's what LL said this morning."

"And I guess I put together some sort of party for the boys." Joey was enthused, mentally spinning his rolodex of seedy strippers. "There's a sweet gal I know at the Peek-A-Boo who does this thing with a flaming sword these guys would like and—"

"No!" Shane said, cutting him off at the debauch pass, pretty certain the Duke wouldn't be into strippers. "How about you return some of that booze you took from the basement? The men can give the Duke a toast or two. Swap war stories. Whatever."

"Ha!" Joey snorted. "They ain't never been to war. I was talking to one of the boys. He said the army ain't ever fought a war."

"That's the best kind of army," Shane said, wondering how many of the Andovans had experience like Lucien and the Field Marshal's? From the way they carried themselves, he suspected they were all combat veterans.

"Who am I picking up?" Garth asked.

"A bishop," Shane said. "And you have to bring one of the soldiers with you. Come to think of it, I'll go too. We'll take my Defender." He pointed at the binder. "Joey, you're in charge here."

Joey looked at the binder as if it were a coiled rattler. "I gotta go to the diner to get the booze."

"You can do that when we get back," Shane said. "Meanwhile, keep an eye on everything."

"Yeah, yeah," Joey said as he poured another shot.

"And easy on that," Shane warned.

Joey shook his head. "Back in the day we'd do shots for breakfast."

"This is a new day," Shane said as he headed out the door with Garth.

"Not likely," Joey muttered into the glass.

PHOEBE DIDN'T IMMEDIATELY OPEN her eyes. She was alive so that was a positive starting point and she took a moment to relish it.

She began with her toes, making slight movements, waiting for pain feedback to indicate how much damage she'd sustained. Left foot. Right foot. Ankles? Knees? A troubling twinge in the right one, but it seemed to work and that was what mattered.

She shifted to her fingers, wrists, elbows and then shoulders. As she tried to move her left one, the pain told her that she'd dislocated it, which wasn't surprising. It had always been weak, popping out at inopportune times ever since the first time she dislocated it sparring in Japan when she was eight and the dojo master had simply popped it back in and told her to continue. It wasn't like she could go home and have her dad take her to sick call; there was always the fear child services might take an interest and misinterpret.

Phoebe opened her eyes. The face shield was cracked. She gingerly turned her head from side to side. The neck seemed fine and there was no sign of anyone on the hillside, not that it was likely.

She sat, then carefully got to her feet, balancing herself against the slope. She took the cracked helmet off. She shuffled toward the nearest tree, her knee signaling perhaps more than a twinge? She slammed her shoulder against the trunk, popping the shoulder back in.

A slower survey showed she was seventy-five feet down a steep hillside that was partially covered in snow. Then there was forty feet of almost vertical cliff to the road she'd flown off of. She'd crashed through the trees so the road above wasn't visible, which also meant the opposite. The motorcycle was ten feet below her, the rear wheel still spinning, the battery powering the engine.

Phoebe carefully made her way to the motorcycle, but it was clear when she got close that it was done for. The front wheel was gone, leaving a bent fork. Phoebe sat in the thin snow and checked the machine. She turned it off. As she suspected, the brake lines were cut. She leaned forward and peered more closely. There was blood smeared on the frame next to where they had been severed.

"Kudos, Betty, you bitch," Phoebe said.

She checked her vest pocket, but one of the branches she'd punched through in her flight had snagged the vest and her phone was gone.

Phoebe looked up.

"Nothing but good times ahead," she whispered.

Then she began the long, arduous climb, but after only a few, choppy steps, her knee buckled and she fell backward, losing what she'd gained and more.

Phoebe lay on her belly and evaluated the challenge. She mentally mapped out a route, bypassing outcroppings and the steepest portions.

"Nothing but *good* times ahead."

She began crawling on her belly up the slope.

"I'm supposed to be the driver," Garth groused from the backseat. "Miss Agnes woulda said take the limo. Even if it's one person. She said appearances are important. Miss Agnes said--"

"Miss Agnes isn't here," Shane cut him off. "And is there a problem with my truck's appearance?" He glanced in the rearview mirror, waiting for a retort, but Garth slumped his head against the side window.

"This is a classic," Vicente said.

He wore his suit and Shane knew he was packing because he'd seen the butt of the pistol in a belt holster when the Andovan soldier got in the passenger side. He was a bit older than the other soldiers, based on the gray in his beard. "Very well maintained for the years that have passed."

"Thanks," Shane said.

He drove along the two-lane road leading to the Keyes airport. On one side were the tidal marshes extending to the Intracoastal waterway. A barrier island was on the opposite side, with a few docks with lifts holding million-dollar boats that rarely ever tasted the water and large mansions that were mostly rich people's second homes that they occasionally inhabited or rented out to vacationers. On the landward side, the marsh merged into swamp, populated with gators, snakes, the Gullah people, and the rest of Garth's relatives.

"About Miss Lisa Livia," Vicente began.

"What about her?" Shane asked.

"She seems very . . . confident."

That was a new one, Shane thought. "She's very capable."

"Her aura is familiar," Vicente said.

"'Aura'?" Shane said.

"I studied holistic medicine for a year in India. The body exhibits a palpable field if one is attuned to perceiving it."

"Right," Shane said.

"I knew a person who exhibited the same as Lisa Livia. Strange, since on the surface her life is so different."

"Different from who?" Shane asked.

Vicente waved it off. "It doesn't matter."

Shane noted a car in the rearview mirror, shadowing them.

"You have someone keeping pace," Vicente said, checking the side mirror.

"Your people?" Shane asked.

"No."

Shane picked a spot where there was some shoulder and pulled off to let it pass, but it stopped behind him.

"Shit, it's the cops," Garth panicked, looking over his shoulder.

"It's just Xavier," Shane said as he recognized the car and driver. He figured Garth's reaction was genetic since the Thibault's relationship with the law had never been good.

"He used to come around all the time," Garth said. "Hassling my dad. He scared me."

"He's the man who has been surveilling Two Rivers from a small boat," Vicente added.

"Xavier can be a pain," Shane acknowledged as he opened the door and stepped out.

Xavier strolled up.

"What's Hammond driving?" Shane asked. "Put him back on his bicycle with training wheels?"

"Your attempts at humor fail to elicit the desired effect," Xavier said, looking past Shane at Garth in the backseat and Vicente in the front. "Who's your friend?"

"You know Garth," Shane said. "He says you used to bother his family when he was growing up. Caused him childhood trauma that he hasn't recovered from."

"I visited his home as much as I did Joey's diner," Xavier said. "Childhood trauma might explain your current state, but I doubt it was due to me."

"I thought you were there for the food," Shane replied.

"That too. I wasn't *bothering* his family. I was keeping an eye on his father who was a known criminal along with most of the clan. That might have given the boy more nightmares than the long arm of the law. As was your uncle, who ran with Four Wheels Thibault."

"Joey reformed. And I've never seen him run."

Xavier ignored. "I know Garth. Who is the other fellow?"

"A member of the wedding party."

"Strange wedding you've got gestating at Two Rivers," Xavier said. "Who are the fancy fellows with spears standing watch at the gazebo?"

"It's a family tradition of the bride and groom," Shane said.

"And they are?" Xavier asked. "I made inquiries and they flew in on a private aircraft to Savannah. A rather large one. From some place in Europe."

"Back on the job?" Shane asked, indicating the car. "Got your tin star? How is Evie doing?"

Xavier walked to the front of the Defender, out of earshot of Vicente and Garth. Shane joined him.

"Why are you jerking my line, son?" Xavier asked.

"Because you got your hook in me," Shane said. "Isn't that the way it works? Or do you just want me to flop over?"

"I don't want this town to turn into the real version of Cabot Cove."

"Where?"

"*Murder She Wrote*?" Xavier said. Seeing that Shane was lost, he amplified. "A television mystery in which an amateur sleuth, a writer, solves murders. Thus, a place where people are dying each week. You'd have thought by the middle of the first season everyone would have seen the writing in blood on the wall and moved elsewhere, given the bad odds."

"You've been gone for eight months," Shane said. "No one was killed in the interim. Nobody is writing a TV show about Keyes, that's for sure. Maybe it has more to do with you than me."

"I spent some of that time trying to learn about you," Xavier said. "You know what I came up with?"

"Nothing."

"Nothing," Xavier echoed. "That worries me more than if I'd found something. That tale you spun me at Maria's wedding and afterward? About working for a special government organization? I couldn't confirm it."

"A *secret* government organization," Shane corrected. "That explains your problem. Do I have to define secret?"

"Do you still soldier on for said organization?"

"It's a secret."

Xavier wasn't ready to quit. "You don't exist in official records. On social media. Anywhere."

"I'm right here," Shane said. "In front of you."

"Everyone has a history," Xavier said.

"What about yours with Evie?" Shane asked.

Xavier leaned against the front of the Defender, age creeping through his professional mask. "Sometimes there's a reason life doesn't play out a certain way. We see the past through rose-colored glasses."

"You got a different pair of glasses than me," Shane said.

"I'm older than you," Xavier said. "Our vision modifies with the years."

"Going blind?"

"No. It's a different perspective."

"What were you seeing with regards to Evie?"

"Why are you so interested in my life, son? You aren't like your uncle, a busybody who sticks his beak into everyone and everything to fill an empty hole in his life. I take you for a serious man." Xavier peered at him keenly. "You've got Miss Agnes, a fine woman, if ever I met one, despite her anger issues and tendency to wield a mean frying pan, albeit in self-defense. What are you worried about?"

"I'm not worried about anything," Shane lied.

"Don't blow smoke at me, son," Xavier said. "I've looked too many shady and not-shady people in the eyes and asked them hard questions. You're sensing unsteady ground beneath your feet at Two Rivers, are you not? Or does it go deeper than that?"

When Shane didn't reply, Xavier nodded as if he already knew the answer. The old detective looked off toward the wetlands. "I've asked Evie to marry me three times. Once, right after high school, when we'd been going steady, behind her parents' backs. They had bigger plans for her and their money. New money. They wanted her to have a name to go with the money. You know how that's received in these parts."

Shane had no idea, but he didn't interrupt.

"The name is important. Some of these folks in Savannah and especially Charleston, act like they came here before our Lord was nailed to the cross. Even here in Keyes, which is so far *North of Broad* we might as well be Yankees. Nothing better than the name of the town to stick on the mailbox." Xavier regrouped and got back on topic. "So, Evie didn't say no that first time, but we both knew she couldn't say yes, and we drifted apart. She ended up with Jefferson Keyes and I went into the military. It was the easiest way to get out of town and try to forget.

"Strange how many important things in our life just occur without any definitive decision. And then I asked a couple of weeks ago. When we left here, we went to what she called her family's hunting cabin. It's a damn mansion in the mountains in North Carolina. I bent my knee to her in the most beautiful spot, just off the Blue Ridge Parkway, where you could see forever. This time she said no; that she couldn't. And we both realized that was that."

"You said three times," Shane noted.

Xavier nodded. "The third was in between, years ago, after we, how shall I say it discreetly? Had illicit relations?" He smiled bitterly. "At the time I thought it a moment's indiscretion where we both gave in to our basic instincts and reminiscences and longings after years apart. Plus, there was a copious amount of champagne. At a Christmas Party at the Country Club. The Keyes' Country Club, of course. But lately, I've wondered."

Xavier fell silent.

"About what?" Shane finally asked.

"Whether it was a spur of the moment thing," Xavier said. "I knew she always wanted a daughter. I'm slow but I'm not dull. In retrospect, perhaps that indiscretion that I always believed happened spontaneously, was something else? Since it was widely announced not long after in the local papers that Mrs. Jefferson Keyes was blessed with child. I can do math."

"You got her pregnant?"

"I don't know. Perhaps she doesn't either."

"How long ago was this?" Shane asked.

"If you're wondering which of her sons it might be, it would be Palmer."

He fell silent and Shane was at a loss how to respond to these revelations.

Xavier continued. "I was naïve enough to imagine I could have a family, ready-made. But Evie has a family. Three sons. A family she's poured the sweat and blood and years into. She's put up with Jefferson and his philandering ways for years. And now she has Palmer with Maria and perhaps grandkids soon. She doesn't want to throw a bomb into their life. So, after she said no for the third time a few weeks ago, I made the mistake of asking about that Christmas party. Said we could do a DNA test.

"That didn't go over well. A schism opened between us, which I suppose meant her decision to return became inevitable. There are words that are said that can't be unsaid. She's back in the life she was born to and made for herself and I'm back here, in my life, asking you, who exactly are you?"

"Why are you so concerned?" Shane asked.

"Something bad is in the wind," Xavier said. "I feel it in my bones."

"Maybe you're just old?" Shane said. "Happens to the best of us. It gets chilly at night this time of year. Wet cold sinks into the bones." He paused. "Anything specific?"

"To begin with, I don't believe your story about that fellow sneaking into Two Rivers being a game. He didn't act like a man who plays games. He seemed quite a serious fellow. Honestly, I didn't catch him as much as he gave himself up to me." Xavier gave a wry smile. "You're worried too, aren't you?"

"My bones ache," Shane admitted and he realized it was true, both literally and figuratively.

"Do you have anything specific?" Xavier asked.

Shane glanced through the windshield. Vicente was watching but his window was up and he couldn't hear what was being said. "The wedding party consists of a Duke and Duchess from a country called Andova. You can Google it. The wedding is causing political problems back home, so they came here."

"Bringing their problems with them?" Xavier asked.

"It's possible," Shane allowed. "So far, everything is fine." *Other than an irritable Lisa Livia*, he thought. *And Agnes in Paris.*

"Serious problems?" Xavier pressed.

Shane thought of the fire power in the barn. "I don't think so, but in any case, they've got the entire Andovan Army with them."

"Spears, armor and all," Xavier said.

"Yeah."

"Are they expecting Vikings to row up the Blood River?"

Shane belatedly realized that Xavier had drawn him in with his revelation about Evie and Palmer.

"We're on top of it," Shane said.

"Certainly," Xavier said, accepting he'd gotten as much as he could for now. "You be safe now, son."

"You too."

Shane watched Xavier walk back to his car and noted the bulge where the .357 nestled in a shoulder holster.

Shane opened the back door. "Garth, you drive."

PHOEBE REACHED the base of the forty-foot cliff, cold, wet and determined. She flexed her injured leg. She struggled to her feet, leaning against the rock wall. Now that she was closer, she could tell it was far from sheer, with numerous nooks, crannies and outcroppings. Not a difficult climb if all her pieces and parts were working; but they weren't.

Phoebe drew the wakizashi. She extended her arms as far as she could above her head and slammed the point into a narrow crevice. Then she pulled herself to the blade. Scrambled with her feet, focusing on the good leg, and secured a perch. She extracted the blade, reached up, and found another place to slide it in.

She focused only on each next move, not the top of the cliff. Several times she had to improvise, one hand on the sword, the other grasping for a hold, feet sliding about, bad knee pulsing in pain.

She wasn't aware of the passage of time, nor did she dwell on the possibility of falling. Inch by inch, foot by foot, she ascended until she was within one move of reaching the ledge. She was breathing hard, one hand on the hilt of the wakizashi, the other clinging with fingertips in a crack in the rock. The toe of her good leg was precariously perched on a knob of rock. Then it slipped off.

Which is when a hand reached down from over the ledge and seized her wrist in a vise-like grip.

"NICE RIDE," Shane said, referring to the Lear. The crossed keys and triple crown insignia of the Catholic church was painted on the tail.

"Andova pays for it," Vicente said. He walked forward and gave a slight bow toward the man coming down the plane's steps.

Shane and Garth were by the Defender, thirty feet from the dual-engine private jet.

The Bishop was a florid-faced, rotund man, wearing a long black cassock with a red cape and a small magenta, circular zucchetto. He looked profoundly unhappy to have arrived. He paused at the bottom of the steps and looked past Vicente at Shane and Garth and then left and right.

"Where is my ride?"

Vicente pointed at the Defender without comment. The Bishop managed to look even more aggrieved, which Shane had not thought possible. "And my luggage?"

A crew member followed the Bishop and went to the cargo hold, opening it. He began removing a number of cases.

"You're here for twenty-four hours, your Excellency," Vicente said. "The Duchess did not believe you would be bringing much."

"The Duchess?" The Bishop said the word with contempt. He folded his arms. "I require treatment equivalent to my position."

Shane was glad Vicente was dealing with this. He'd ruminated on Xavier's revelation the rest of the ride to the airport as Garth drove. With time to think, he wasn't sure it was a true story. He'd hate to have to face the wily old man in an interrogation room.

"You can require it all you want, your Excellency," Vicente said, "but this is what you have. I will have another car sent for your luggage. Bring what is necessary for the ceremony. And remember who pays for your plane."

The Bishop tried to engage Vicente in a stare-down but the soldier turned away and walked to the Defender, opening the back door and waiting.

"Nice guy," Shane said to Vicente. "What's his aura? Darkness with a bad moon rising? What's with the beany hat?"

"It's a zucchetto," Vicente said. "A sign of his station."

"Right," Shane said. "I've got shotgun."

"What?" Vicente said.

Shane indicated the front passenger seat. "I'm riding up front with Garth."

"'Shotgun'? An interesting term," Vicente said, still holding the door open for the Bishop. "It's origin?"

"The man who rode next to the driver of a stagecoach in the old west," Shane explained, "usually carried a shotgun."

"Ah. Fascinating." He raised his voice. "Your Excellency? We will be leaving, with or without you."

PHOEBE WAS LIFTED up and deposited on top of the cliff, but on the way, she jerked the wakizashi out. She rolled away from her temporary rescuer, bringing the weapon up to the ready as she tried to get to her feet, but her knee buckled and she fell.

"Whoa!" Cleaner said. "Take it easy, young miss."

On her knees, she sheathed the blade. Adrenaline ceased pumping and she immediately shivered.

Cleaner picked up a blanket and brought it to her, draping it over her shoulders. "What now, young miss?"

"Could you stop calling me that."

"No disrespect intended," Cleaner said. "Old habit. It's what I call my daughter."

"How old is she?"

"Twenty-eight."

"What does she do?" Phoebe asked as she carefully got to her feet.

"She's a Ranger."

That caught Phoebe's interest. "Really? What battalion?" she asked referring to the three battalions of elite light infantry.

Cleaner shook his head. "Forest Ranger." He indicated the mountains. "National Forest Service."

Working with nature and the birds and the animals and all its splendor day after day, Phoebe thought. *How wonderful. How boring.*

The truck was on the road, the engine running. He indicated the trail through the mud. "Came to check. Saw the single track off the cliff and figured it was you. What happened?"

"Someone cut the brake lines while I wasn't looking."

"Get what you needed?"

"Some."

He indicated the truck. "Need a ride or want to walk?"

"Not funny," Phoebe said. She nodded. "Thanks."

Cleaner smiled. "Easy enough, isn't it? Accepted."

"What's your name?" Phoebe asked.

Cleaner hesitated. "Sam."

"Sam is a good name," Phoebe said. "I'm Phoebe, but you can call me young miss if you want. Either one is fine."

She started to walk toward the van, but had to stop for a moment, to get the knee stable.

Sam scooped her up in his arms and carried her to the truck, setting her inside. "There's a clean sweater."

Phoebe stripped off the torn and dirty one, dropping it to the floor. An identical sweater was folded on the bench next to her. She pulled it on. "You buy these in bulk?"

"My wife knits them," Sam said.

"Oh." Phoebe picked the dirty one off the floor. "Tell her I appreciate it."

"You are welcome."

"Secure phone, Sam?" Phoebe asked.

Sam pulled one out of his pocket and handed it to her. "Airport, young miss?"

Phoebe nodded. She punched #1 in the speed dial as she opened the first aid kit with her other hand, searching for an Ace Wrap, which a medic had once assured her solved every joint injury short of surgery.

SHANE COULD FEEL the chill from the backseat as Garth drove away from the airport. The Bishop had his arms folded across his chest and was glaring. At what or whom, Shane wasn't quite sure. It was pretty much a generic pissed off. Vicente was behind Garth, looking out the window and ignoring the Bishop, his aura peaceful.

But the Bishop's attitude was weighing on Garth, who'd grown up with that in his double-wide and he kept glancing in the rearview mirror at his Excellency.

"Eyes on the road," Shane said to him in a low voice.

"Why did neither the Duke nor Duchess welcome me at the airport?" the Bishop finally asked Vincente.

"Because they're the Duke and Duchess of Andova," Vincente replied.

"Hmmph," the Bishop harrumphed, which Shane graded as

significantly less of one than the Duchess', so he had no doubt she could handle the Bishop.

CARPENTER LISTENED to Phoebe's after-action report without comment, allowing her to tell it her way. Interrupting the flow would derail her train of thought and she might forget to mention some critical piece of information that seemed irrelevant on the surface.

The list of weaponry indicated a significant armed presence and gave a rough idea of the force involved; as Phoebe calculated, about squad sized. But when she described the unique items including halberds, swords, and armor shipped from overseas, he didn't need the computer to make the connection.

The cut brake lines indicated a misstep on Phoebe's part, but her report indicated she was well aware of that. She had, after all, suffered the consequences and had not shied away from admitting her mistake.

"What's your status?" he asked Phoebe when she finished her report.

"I'm fine."

"Good. I'm redirecting you." He issued orders, then hung up. He punched in Shane's number.

GARTH WAS MAKING Shane a bit nuts by scrupulously driving five miles below the speed limit along the coastal road toward Two Rivers and still checking the Bishop in the rearview mirror.

"Xavier isn't going to be sitting here with a speed trap," Shane said to him.

Garth blushed. "I know. It's just—" he paused as Shane's phone buzzed.

Shane saw it was Carpenter. "Yes?"

Carpenter got to the point fast. "Operation Glacier is connected to your current situation somehow. There were weapons and demolitions among the gear taken but also swords, armor, and halberds shipped in from an overseas location to Canada and then smuggled across the border."

Garth was slowing down. Shane looked ahead. They were rounding a bend and a pick-up truck had run off the road into the ditch on the landward side of the road, fifty yards ahead. A man was standing next to it, waving them down.

"Don't stop," Shane ordered Garth.

"What?" Carpenter asked on the phone, confused.

"What?" Garth said, a split second later.

"Keep going," Shane said. "Speed up." The truck was twenty-five yards away. "Out here," he said to Carpenter. He turned the phone off.

"But someone might be hurt," Garth said.

"Go!" Shane shouted.

The waving man realized they were speeding up and jumped out of the road, drawing a submachine gun from under his denim jacket.

"Contact right!" Shane yelled to Vicente who already had his gun at the ready sweeping it across in front of the Bishop with one hand, while shoving his Eminence down with the other.

The gunman aimed at the Defender, but didn't fire. Nor did Shane or Vicente.

"They want the Bishop," Vicente said as Garth sped past.

"You think?" Shane muttered as he twisted in the seat and looked back. Two black SUVs came racing out of a side road from a hide position in the trees, the trail one pausing to pick up the stranded man.

"Faster, Garth."

The Defender was dependable, but speed was not one of its attributes. The SUVs closed the gap quickly. The windows were tinted but Shane had no doubt he and Vicente were heavily outmanned and outgunned.

The lead SUV gave the rear bumper of the Defender a love tap. The backend fishtailed.

"Keep us on the road, Garth," Shane said as he considered tactical options.

"My grandpappy taught me how to drive," Garth assured Shane. "I got this."

The second SUV swung out around the first and accelerated, pulling up next to the Defender. The rear passenger window was down and a man leaned out, assault rifle in hand, aiming low, at the tires.

Garth glanced left and slammed on the brakes. The side SUV shot past before the man could fire. The one behind hit with more than a tap and both vehicles skidded, broke apart, and then Garth expertly spun the wheel hard right and accelerated onto a narrow dirt road into the marshy low country.

This gained them about fifty yards before the first SUV back-tracked to get on the dirt to continue the pursuit.

"Tell me you know where you're going," Shane said to Garth.

The young man was focused on the road ahead, the Defender bumping over ruts. They splashed through a low section, mud flying. Palmetto branches scraped along the side of the Rover and mud flew, but the four-wheel drive was solid. The dirt road split, an even narrower trail, almost overgrown, to the right, and, of course, that's the way Garth turned.

The SUVs were closing, churning through dirt and mud, knocking branches aside.

An old wood bridge, sagging in the middle, spanning dark, flat water, appeared ahead. Definitely not up to Agnes' sturdy standards.

"Garth?" Shane said.

But the young man ignored him and gunned the Defender over it.

The bridge held and Garth slowed down and looked in the rearview mirror. The first SUV slammed on its brakes just short of the bridge.

"Good job," Shane said, but his compliment was premature as the SUV crept forward, across the rotting wood.

"Dang," Garth said. "Usually scares folks and they back up."

"Does this road go anywhere?" Shane asked.

In response, Garth hit the gas.

The first SUV was gaining once more and Shane caught a glimpse of the second crossing the bridge through the high grass, palmettos and occasional oak festooned with Spanish Moss.

Garth leaned on the horn, blasting it three times.

"Garth?" Shane asked.

They raced into an oak tree encircled clearing of higher ground in the midst of the wetlands. Garth brought the Defender to a sliding halt in an encampment. It was in the middle of a shell ring, which was composed of tens of thousands of oyster, clam and mussel shells deposited in a two-foot-high circle one-hundred-and-fifty feet across. These types of ancient rings dotted the low-country, most lost to development, and dated back thousands of years. They were attributed to the Native Americans who'd populated the areas and put the empty shells around their village. However, the current occupants were modern.

Three large hunting tents were set up inside the ring, stove pipe chimneys poking out of their tops, smoke wafting out of them. Fifteen men in assorted camouflage that actually mirrored the terrain or stained coveralls dirty enough to match, were waiting, rifles and shotguns in hand in a way that indicated they knew how to use them. A half dozen pickups, vehicles of choice in these parts, including one with monster truck size tires, were parked on the far side of the clearing.

"Uncle Jack!" Garth shouted, opening his door.

The SUVs skidded to a stop as soon as they entered the open area, door flying open and men piling out until there were seven gunmen dressed in identical black, with body armor and automatic rifles, facing the swamp men.

Shane and Vicente stood together while the Bishop cowered in the Defender.

"Jack, this is Shane," Garth said, apparently more concerned about introductions to his uncle than the standoff.

"The guy you been telling me about?" the leader of the swamp creatures asked. He was short and thin, ferret-like. He had a shotgun in his hands, a top-of-the-line model Shane recognized as semi-automatic with an extended magazine.

"Yeah," Garth said.

"And who are these fuckers?" Jack said in a loud voice as his men spread out in a semi-circle.

Vicente stepped toward the intruders. "Guillermo," he said to the man in the middle of the group.

"We want the Bishop," Guillermo said in a Spanish accented voice. He was a large man, over six and a half feet tall, older, grey haired, with a short, pointed white beard. "We do not want any trouble."

"Too late for that, dick-wad," Jack said.

"Who is in the back seat?" Vicente asked, indicating the trail SUV, where the silhouette of a person could be seen. "Your exiled bitch?"

"Show some respect," Guillermo responded.

"She lost that long ago," Vicente said. "As did you."

"The Bishop," Guillermo said. "Now."

"That isn't going to happen," Vicente said.

"Where is Lucien?" Guillermo asked. "I'd hoped to see him."

"You don't want to meet him again," Vicente responded.

Shane stepped forward. "The decision is on the side of the heavier weaponry and the home team. Get in your trucks and leave."

Guillermo looked at him, then the swamp dwellers. He addressed Jack. "Whoever you are, you're going to fight for strangers?"

Jack answered. "Garth's my nephew. We fight for family. We're going to kill all of you and feed you to the gators. You're on our land. We're standing our ground so we're within our rights by the law."

Guillermo was re-assessing when the Bishop exited the Defender, hands held high. "Enough! I will sacrifice myself and go with them to end this dangerous charade and save all of you."

"Get back in the truck, your Excellency," Vicente ordered.

"No, no, no," the Bishop hurriedly said. "No need for anyone to get hurt over a misunderstanding. I was afraid of something like this and warned the Duke repeatedly. We can resolve these differences when cooler heads prevail. In Andova."

"Bishop!" Vicente yelled.

But the cleric scurried away, short steps limited by his cassock, straight to the trail SUV.

Guillermo nodded his head and his men backed up, weapons at the ready. The Bishop entered the back of the SUV.

Shane waited on Vicente's response, but the soldier wasn't ready to initiate what would be a bloody and devastating exchange of fire. Jack, on the other hand, was vibrating in place, his finger caressing the trigger of the shotgun, probably wanting to check out its shot pattern with what would be a legal shooting.

"Easy," Shane said.

Jack gave him a sidelong glance with bloodshot eyes. "Fuck you, too. I seen you around in that thing," he indicated the Defender. "You shot up the family place a while back."

"Not exactly," Shane said. "It was just pepper balls."

Jack wasn't placated. "You and your uncle working Garth when he should be helping family."

"Uncle Jack," Garth said, "he's my friend."

The doors slammed on the SUV. They comically tried to turn around in the small patch of muddy clearing, scraping against each other once and the palmettos a number of times. Shane winced as one of them ran into the shell ring, crunching a section that had been here long before Europeans ever came to this part of the world. They disappeared down the trail.

"Thanks, Uncle Jack," Garth said.

But Uncle Jack was staring at Vicente. "Who's he? Another friend? Who were those guys? And the priest? What the fuck, Garth? Why'd you bring them *here*? You know better."

"I apologize for the intrusion," Shane said. Staring into Jack's eyes he saw the redness, the pupils and the sheen of crazy. "We'll leave you be. Forget we were ever here. Hell, I don't even know where Garth turned."

"Bullshit," Jack said.

"Hey, Uncle," Garth pleaded, taking the older man by the elbow and leading him away.

Shane grimaced as Garth pulled a wad of bills out of his pocket and gave them to Jack. That mollified the old man and Garth hurried back, indicating they should get in the truck. As soon as the doors shut, Garth expertly turned and drove off.

"Shouldn't have done that," Shane said.

"We needed to get out of there," Garth said. "They're making moonshine and don't rightly like being interrupted."

Shane wondered if Garth was deliberately lying or if he really thought his relatives were actually making moonshine. "Why are you carrying a roll of cash?"

"Mister Joey told me a man always carries a 'nut', just in case he runs into trouble."

Shane remembered his uncle using the term. *Great*, Shane thought. Garth was getting advice from Joey, master of the back-room deal. Then it occurred to him that Joey had been *his* de facto father.

"Nobody in your family knows about the money, right?" Shane asked, noting that Vicente had his cell phone out in the back seat and was engaged in a hushed, but urgent conversation.

"Nope," Garth said.

"They know something now," Shane pointed out.

Garth sighed. "We needed to get out of there, Mister Shane," he repeated. "Uncle Jack can get kind of excitable and he really wants to use his new gun."

"You're right," Shane said, working on the theory that getting out alive trumped whatever would spill over from the encounter later on. "Thank you. You did a great job."

Garth blushed as he turned them onto the paved road toward Two Rivers.

Shane took his phone out and quickly texted Carpenter a brief summary of what had happened.

PHOEBE'S secure phone buzzed and she saw Carpenter's identifier.

"Yes, sir?"

Carpenter quickly updated her on what had happened at Two Rivers and what was pending. Phoebe listened without comment, then hung up. Phoebe grabbed the laptop, which was linked to the NSA's secure internet and began typing. She was so engrossed, she didn't even realize when they reached the airfield.

SHANE'S WORDS OF WISDOM #6

When in doubt mumble.
When in trouble, delegate.
Shane's Addendum: A key principle of leadership.

That is all.

FRIDAY EVENING

LL

Lisa Livia bumped into the door swinging out of the kitchen and the plates she'd been carrying went flying. They crashed to the barn floor, as Joey cursed.

"To the right, always to the right," Joey scolded Lisa Livia. "Geez, where's Garth?"

Lisa Livia knelt, muttering a few curses of her own under her breath, but then Lucien was there with a broom and trash bin, scooping up broken plates. "Let me help, m'lady. Are you all right?"

"Thank you," Lisa Livia said. "I'm fine."

"The meal was excellent," Lucien said to Joey. "As usual. Someday, I'd like to try your famous gumbo."

Joey forgot about the accident as quickly as it had happened. "I'll bring some later this evening for the party."

Lucien flashed a smile at Lisa Livia as they both stood. Joey headed to the tables to finish cleaning up after dinner.

"What kind of party does Joey have lined up for the Duke?" Lisa Livia asked Lucien.

"I'm not certain but it appears it will involve alcohol and food," Lucien said.

"Women?" Lisa Livia asked as they walked into the kitchen.

"You are the only woman I'm aware of here at Two Rivers," Lucien said.

"The Duchess," Lisa Livia reminded him.

Lucien laughed. "It's strange, but I don't think of her as a woman. She's always been the Duchess."

I don't think of her as human, Lisa Livia thought. "I meant is Joey bringing in women? Or a woman? It's kind of a tradition for some bachelor parties."

"No," Lucien said and there was no humor in that. "No outsiders. I was very clear on that issue." He softened. "Besides, that would be inappropriate for the Duke."

Lisa Livia nodded as she turned on the water for the large steel sink to soak the dishes. She added some soap. "That's good." She reached into the water and began to wipe them off before putting them in the industrial dishwasher.

Lucien came up behind her, very close, but not quite touching her. She felt the intimate warmth of his breath on her neck. "Shall I assist?" He reached around her and now he was touching, his hands running down her bare arms into the soapy water. His fingers intertwined with hers and she forgot about the dishes.

"Who knew cleaning up could be so nice?" Lucien said.

"The getting dirty part is even better," Lisa Livia said, but then Lucien's cell phone chimed and she silently swore if it was the Duchess, there was truly only going to be one woman left alive at Two Rivers.

"Excuse me," Lucien said, extracting his hands and hurriedly drying them. He walked a few steps away. "Yes?"

Lisa Livia stopped doing the dishes and turned to watch him. Her anger at the Duchess dissipated as she saw the look on his face.

"Anyone hurt?" Lucien asked. He saw her watching him, but didn't turn away. He nodded. "Good. And the Bishop?" He listened, then: "No doubt it was Guillermo? Damn him. Was *she* there?" Pause. "Do you know where they took the Bishop?" The answer didn't seem to please Lucien. "I will see you shortly." He punched the off.

"What's wrong?" Lisa Livia asked.

"There was trouble bringing the Bishop from the airport and he's been taken." Lucien shook his head. "I feared something, but not this."

"What kind of trouble? Taken? By who? Is everyone all right?"

"Everyone is fine." But Lucien was thinking ahead. "The marriage must happen tomorrow. The Great Charter is—" he stopped himself. "I am sorry. I ruined the moment. But I must speak to the Duke and Duchess immediately."

CARPENTER READ the abbreviated text from Shane about the confrontation in the Low Country. It ended with a promise to call when able to discuss the situation. The ghost on his shoulder was tapping its foot and clearing his throat, but Carpenter shrugged that off.

Carpenter left his office and walked down the hallway to the elevator. He got on and pressed his finger against the pad. The scan approved, the panel lit up and he hit the button for the lowest level.

Wilson, his predecessor, had made it a rule never to go to anyone else's office; everyone came to him. Carpenter viewed that as a flaw since seeing someone in their environment indicated things about them. Also, showing up unexpectedly, rather than giving people the chance to prepare before knocking on the vault door, yielded insights.

He strolled into Technical Support, not surprised that no one reacted as the analysts were absorbed by the screens in their little pools of light. He'd suggested to Fromm that they brighten the place up, but Fromm had told him that the dimness gave focus. Personally, Carpenter didn't agree, but since he was relatively new, he didn't see it as a point worth arguing at this time.

Carpenter stopped to let his eyes adjust. It was a testament to his time in the field and nerves of steel that he wasn't startled when Fromm suddenly appeared next to him.

"Sir. To what do I owe the honor?"

The tone was one Carpenter, who was experienced in nuances, found hard to decipher. Part deference, part real question, part WTF are you doing here?

"Operation Glacier," Carpenter said. "How many people have access to it?"

"Myself and three shifts at a single station," Fromm said. "And your operatives. The cleaners only have what they need." He paused. "Of course, *you* know that."

Carpenter filed that one in the WTF category because throughout the Organization there was wonderment on why Carpenter had been bumped up to a position well above his previous job. Department heads such as Fromm were not pleased. Carpenter pointed. "Let's talk in your office."

"Certainly," Fromm said, as if he were granting a favor.

Fromm sat behind his desk, leaving Carpenter standing because there were no other chairs in the office which spoke volumes. Carpenter sat on the corner of the desk, on the chair side, looming over Fromm, who scooted back a few inches and had to crane his neck.

"How did we get the Glacier tasking?"

"The NSA intercepted the communications. We were copied on it and—"

"Who else was copied?" Carpenter asked.

"The usual agencies," Fromm said.

"Why'd we get the tasking then?" Carpenter asked. "Seems more the bailiwick of the FBI."

"Well. Uh." Fromm blinked as his brain smacked into a question he didn't readily have the answer to. Fromm was forced to move his chair back in place to access his keyboard. He hunched over and tapped in and stared at the screen with that pause that indicated the result wasn't something he wanted to pass on.

"Go on," Carpenter prompted.

"We got tasked by the NCA," Fromm said, referring to the National Command Authority.

"I never saw the tasking."

Fromm indicated the screen as if doing so abdicated him of any responsibility, but Carpenter kept his focus on the man and added. "I didn't sign off on it."

"No, sir," Fromm agreed. "But we took it because we were designated."

"Who. Is. We?"

"The Organization."

Carpenter folded his arms and waited.

Fromm acted stupid, which incensed Carpenter. "How? Who did it?" he finally demanded.

Fromm focused on the computer screen as he typed the inquiry. Once more the pause before answering was too long. "This department, sir."

"You?"

"No, sir."

"Be more specific."

"I can't, sir," Fromm admitted. "Someone in this office saw the tasking and accepted it. Improper procedure, certainly."

"This department doesn't have that authority. If it wasn't you, who did it?"

"It doesn't say."

Carpenter indicated the work area. "Who out there did it?"

"It doesn't have an originator tag, just the receiving terminal."

Carpenter leaned over and put a finger under Fromm's chin, forcing him to look up. "I'm not a dentist. I don't sit around pulling teeth one at a time. I am losing patience. Which terminal?"

"Six."

They both looked out the window at the 6 hanging from the ceiling. Above Lou's workspace.

"Three shifts?" Carpenter asked.

"Yes."

"According to the date/time stamp, who was on duty at the time?"

Fromm checked his computer. "Louise Wingo."

"Call her in," Carpenter ordered.

SHANE LISTENED as Vicente briefly reported to Lucien. Shane didn't ask any questions because he knew Vicente wouldn't answer them. That would be up to the Duke and Duchess.

He didn't call Carpenter with a follow-up yet to discuss because he was trying to sort this out and he didn't want to do it in front of Lucien. There were too many loose ends, but he could begin to see a common thread.

Garth drove to Two Rivers and parked the Defender. Shane exited and looked at the mansion, where the windows were dark and the sky behind it cloudy with a hint of an evening thunderstorm as lightning flashed in the clouds. Rhett wasn't on the porch, most likely following his habit of going inside through the dog door when it got dark and curling up in his bed in the corner of the kitchen.

"Go home, Garth," Shane said. "You did a great job today."

Vicente added: "Thank you. That was fast thinking and excellent driving."

Garth flushed red under his tan and nodded in appreciation. He headed to his Camaro.

Shane walked toward the barn, steps behind Vicente. The two guards were in position at the gazebo, torches flickering in the dusk.

The Duke and Duchess were holding court at the long table. They were seated at one end with the Field Marshal to their right and Lucien to the left. There were six Andovan soldiers, which meant, minus the two in ceremonial gear at the gazebo, that three were elsewhere on the grounds, providing security, or resting for a shift later tonight. The six weren't in their suits, but dressed in black pants and shirts. They had combat vests on, pistols in holsters, extra magazines and other paraphernalia, including their radios, in the appropriate pockets. They hadn't broken out the automatic rifles yet, so Shane figured they weren't expecting an imminent assault.

Vicente marched to the table, snapped to attention and saluted.

The Field Marshal returned it, without getting up. "Lucien briefed us on what you told him."

"I can take some men and find where they are holding the Bishop," Vicente offered.

The Duke shook his head. "If he's with Guillermo, that will mean a fight."

"It is treason, your Grace," Vicente said. "The Bishop didn't have to go with Guillermo. We had them outgunned."

Lucien raised an eyebrow. "How so?"

Vicente indicated Shane. "His driver had friends. They were armed. But the Bishop went willingly, despite any protests he might make."

"I can well imagine that he wasn't protesting," the Duke said. "We will deal with him later. We have more immediate concerns."

"Hope I'm not bothering you people," Shane said, "but I just had weapons pointed at me. And I'm standing here. Who is Guillermo?"

The Duke made a gesture to the Field Marshal, who dismissed the men, leaving the Duke, Duchess and Lucien at the table.

"Join us," the Duke said to Shane. "You too, Vicente."

Shane sat down opposite the Duke and Duchess and waited.

The Duke spoke, "You know the backstory of the two families.

Guillermo used to hold Lucien's position as Captain of the Guard. He was in line to be the next Field Marshal."

He paused and Shane prompted: "Until?"

The Duke glanced at the Duchess, then proceeded. "Until he joined forces with my ex-wife."

"That's a delicate way of phrasing treason, adultery and assorted high crimes, my dear," the Duchess said.

A flicker of anger crossed the Duke's face and Shane finally understood another piece of this royal puzzle.

"Are they here to stop the marriage?" Shane asked.

"To stop more than the marriage," the Duke said.

"I warned you," the Duchess said to the Duke. "I told you she would act."

"The Bishop was likely to renege on his own," the Duke said. "They just incentivized him. Let us hope that's the end of it."

"Life doesn't run on hope," the Duchess said. She turned to Vicente. "Was *she* there?"

Vicente cleared his throat. "I believe so, your Grace. There was someone who remained inside one of the vehicles. My sense is that it was her."

"Who were the other men?" the Field Marshal asked him.

"I recognized several," Vicente said. "Former members of the Guard who left when Guillermo did. A few who departed the service before then for private ventures. The others were strangers."

"They were former military," Shane confirmed.

Lucien nodded. "Guillermo would have recruited those he knew from his time in the Guard and *La Unidad*. He has ample funds to pay. There are many former soldiers more than willing to work for hire. And since ETA laid down their arms, they haven't had an enemy."

"There were seven armed men," Shane said. "A lot just to get the Bishop. Will they stop at that?"

"They've ruined the ceremony," the Field Marshal said. "There's no reason for them to do anything further."

"Can we have a wedding without the Bishop?" Lucien asked,

looking to the Duke and Duchess. "I have all the required paperwork."

"The Bishop is tradition," the Duchess said, "but so is holding the ceremony in the Chapel of St. Ingrid. We are breaking many traditions, we can break a few more as long as we abide by the letter of the law of the Great Charter until it is no more." She pointed a long finger adorned with a sparkling ring at Shane. "Do you have, what do you call it here, a Justice of the Peace?"

"We could find someone," Shane said. He wondered if Agnes had penciled in a backup in the binder. The local cleric had been tossed out by Agnes at Palmer and Maria's wedding and had kept his vow never to return. The other wedding parties had always brought their preferred officiator to perform the ceremony.

"It must be a Catholic priest," the Duke said. "The wedding must be done within the bounds of the church."

"The wedding must be done, period," the Duchess said.

The Duke shook his head. "Even if legal, it will cause even more trouble and give Drusilla standing to object."

Shane didn't care about their religious issues. "My concern is whether this Guillermo will ramp up the conflict when he figures out the wedding is still happening?"

"Yes," the Duchess said as the Duke said: "No."

"Guillermo would never—" the Duke began, but he was cut off.

"It's not about Guillermo," the Duchess said, staring at her intended. "It's about Drusilla. What will it take for you to see her true nature?"

"If she believes taking the Bishop will delay the wedding," the Duke said, "she will have achieved her goal. The Charter will remain in effect the rest of the cycle. Then she will try her next move to regain control of my family. She will fail in that."

The Duchess shook her head. "My dear, I know it is difficult for you to see the evil in people. Ostensibly, this is about her regaining her position. That is what Guillermo and those in Andova who support her believe. But the divorce and exile shattered her core. Her very sense of self. This is about vengeance. She will not be satisfied until we are destroyed."

A silence settled over the barn.

The Duke stirred and looked to the right. "Field Marshal? Your opinion?"

"Why not fly back to Andova and do this the traditional way?" the Field Marshal suggested.

"I am not putting anyone else in danger," the Duchess insisted. "Besides, we don't have time."

"Not to revoke the Great Charter this year, your Grace," the Field Marshal agreed, "but you can still get married. Revoke it in a year."

"We won't survive the next cycle," the Duchess said. "We must act now."

"Hold on," Shane said. "What's all this about the Charter?"

"There are stipulations on certain dates and times during the year," the Field Marshal said. "Legal matters."

Lucien stepped in. "If the Duke and Duchess do not marry by six in the evening Andovan time tomorrow, they cannot revoke the Charter."

Shane did the math of plus one and minus five time zones transforming six in the afternoon on Sunday in Andova to local time. "High noon."

"Excuse me?" the Duke said.

"Six in Andova is noon here," Shane explained.

"If we do not marry by then," the Duchess said, "despite the divorce, Drusilla will attempt to take command next week instead of the Duke when power transfers to the Navarro family, and she has some legal basis based on the fact divorce is not recognized by the church and thus the Charter. Worse, hypocritically, because of the divorce which the Duke instigated, she will attempt to have him removed and rule alone. It will lead to a confrontation and be a disaster for our people."

"You brought a load of shit here, didn't you?" Shane said. "What about Lisa Livia? And Garth? And Joey? Who are we? Nobodies?"

"I *am* sorry," the Duke said. "I truly did not believe there would be trouble if we left Andova."

"Bullshit," Shane said. He pointed at Lucien. "You were reconning to prepare defensive plans, weren't you?" Then at the Duke. "You know more about me than you've let on. You came here for more than Agnes' cooking." He considered the information about Montana, but he needed to check in with Carpenter about that before bringing it up because the strategic scenario was murky and something was definitely wrong in the Organization.

Lucien abruptly stood and went to the kitchen door, pulling it open to reveal Lisa Livia standing there. She made no attempt to pretend she hadn't been listening. She walked past Lucien to the table, binder in hand. She slammed the binder on the table and sat next to Shane. "You *really* needed to fill the questionnaire out completely. Because Agnes is really, *really* thorough." She found the correct tab and opened to the plastic sheathed page. "Page seven. And I quote: '*Are there any family issues that might potentially cause a problem at the wedding?*'. End quote. I wouldn't even think to ask that, even though my daughter's wedding had a few issues. I'd say crazy killers wanting to stop the marriage qualifies. I was joking when I told Shane I was falling on a grenade for Agnes, but if I really am gonna fall on a grenade, we deserve the truth."

"I don't—" the Duke began, but the Duchess cut him off.

"We thought Mister Shane would be capable of helping with trouble if need be."

The Duke was staring at the Duchess and Shane was staring at the Duke while Lisa Livia was staring at Lucien. The only ones spared were the Field Marshal and Vicente.

"Sounds like they know more about you than Agnes does," Lisa Livia said in a low voice to Shane.

Shane wasn't pleased. "You put me, and the people here, in the line of fire."

The Field Marshal objected. "No weapon has been fired. This will be resolved peacefully. I suggest we depart ASAP for the airport and return to Andova. Save these poor people any more trouble."

"Silence," the Duchess snapped at him. "We have no idea where Drusilla and Guillermo are with the Bishop." She leaned forward, taking command, and meeting Shane's glare. "Our intelligence service works with the intelligence agencies of western democracies on sensitive matters given our country is a nexus for considerable sums of money, which, at times, given the nature of our world, involves criminal and terrorist activities. When we inquired about relocating the ceremony overseas for security reasons, your name came up."

"By who?"

The Duchess looked to Lucien.

"We, uh, queried through our usual secure channel," he said.

"Who?" Shane demanded.

"The French," the Duchess said. "It seems you did something in France a few years ago that brought you the attention of *Direction générale de la sécurité extérieure.*"

"I did them a favor, actually," Shane said, "although they didn't see it that way at the time."

"They're still a bit sore," Lucien said. "The French would rather wash their own soiled undergarments than have a foreigner do it. But, in retrospect, they *are* grateful."

"They haven't told me," Shane said.

The Field Marshal had regrouped and tried again. "If we fly—"

This time the Duchess only had to raise a hand to quiet him.

"This isn't our fight," Shane said. Then another piece snapped into place. "Guillermo."

"What of him?" Lucien asked.

"He shot me," Shane said. "In Montana."

"Yet you are still alive," the Duchess said.

Lucien nodded. "The cracked body armor. What was he doing in Montana?"

"Buying weapons and demolitions," Shane said. "Seems he doesn't have the same diplomatic pouch you do."

"What were *you* doing in Montana?" Lucien asked.

"Guillermo would have had access to the same intel when he was in your job, wouldn't he?" Shane looked at the Duchess. "And, according to my sources, the armament they got has halberds, swords and armor, much like your guards at the gazebo are wearing. He didn't use that to snatch the Bishop. Why did he go through so much trouble to ship it to the States?"

"*Quelle folie*," the Duchess murmured. "That changes everything." She looked at the Duke. "Drusilla is going to invoke the *Lacessere*."

"'*Lacessere*'?" the Duke repeated. "That's never been done. It's archaic and—"

The Duchess cut him off. "So is the Great Charter, but here *we* are trying to end it. *Lacessere* is part of it. Ignored for centuries and never invoked, but it *is* there."

Lisa Livia hit a glass with a spoon. "English, please!"

Lucien explained. "*Lacessere* is Latin for challenge."

"Gee, that helps," Lisa Livia said. "A game of cards? Scrabble? What?"

The Duchess nodded in growing awareness. "I am wrong. It's actually quite ingenious. Crazy, but brilliant. That is why they took the Bishop.. If I remember rightly, the Bishop must be the witness and judge to *Lacessere*."

"To what?" Lisa Livia demanded, but Shane had a good idea where this was going.

Lucien answered. "There is a clause buried in the Great Charter. That if either family breaks the Charter, the other family can challenge them."

"Like in court?" Lisa Livia said.

"No," Lucien said.

"Then where?" Lisa Livia was trying to follow. "If it's the Bishop, then some sort of religious thing?"

"No, m'lady," Lucien said. "By force of arms. That determines the winner."

"That's stupid," Lisa Livia said.

"No," Shane said. "That's the very definition of war. Politics by other means."

"Von Clausewitz," Lucien said.

"Indeed," the Duchess said.

"But you have automatic weapons," Shane said. "So do they. Why are they bringing swords?"

The Field Marshal spoke up. "It's decreed in the Great Charter that *Lacessere* must be implemented using the weapons that existed when it was signed by both sides. Since the Charter was written in eight-oh-two, that means the arms of the time."

"'Eight-oh-two'?" Lisa Livia repeated.

"Anno domini," the Duchess confirmed. "Written by Charlemagne the Great."

"Rewrite it," Lisa Livia said. "Geez, it's been long enough."

"That's what we're doing," the Duchess pointed out. "But changing the course of history, and the traditions of institutions, is never easy."

"This is nuts," Lisa Livia said. She turned to Shane. "Right?"

"Sure," Shane said. "Tell me what's sane about war?"

"You men!" Lisa Livia exclaimed. "Notify the authorities."

The Duchess gave a mirthless laugh. "What authorities, my dear? Your local *gendarme*? He'd be brushed aside like a fly by Guillermo and his mercenaries. The government?" She sighed. "We are our government. And—" she paused and looked at Shane—"your government is aware at the highest level that we are here."

Shane felt the words settle on him with the inevitability he experienced when heading into a mission, knowing it was a go. He was involved, regardless of how he felt about it. He'd been committed when he went to Montana, but he had no clue how that had happened to circle around and lead to this.

"What does she mean?" Lisa Livia asked Shane. "Does Carpenter know?

It was the question that was at the forefront of Shane's mind. Because if his friend, his boss, did, it meant Shane had been kept in the dark. "I don't know." *Did he have a need to, Shane wondered? Hell, yeah at this point.*

The Field Marshal gave it one more try. "We can avoid trouble by going back to Andova."

The Duchess was having none of it. "We'd be moving the trouble to where many more will be involved. Perhaps ignite a civil war. Drusilla has a following there. And she has powerful foreign supporters."

"*None* of you have a following here," Lisa Livia said. "This ain't our problem."

The door to the barn swung open and Joey entered, carrying a pot of his famous gumbo, followed by Garth with a case of bottles. Joey looked at the serious faces. "No party?"

As the Duke, Duchess, Field Marshal and Lucien argued, Lisa Livia got up in disgust and went to the kitchen. Joey followed her, after dismissing Garth, although he did appropriate one of the bottles.

"What da' fuck?" Joey asked once the door swung shut. "Garth told me about the Bishop getting hijacked. What else?"

Lisa Livia gave him a brief summary. As she was doing so, Shane entered.

"Are they leaving?" Lisa Livia asked, torn between danger and excitement and realizing they were similar.

Shane shrugged as he grabbed a cup of coffee. "The Field Marshal is adamant they go back. The Duchess is pissed. The Duke is trying to be a peace maker."

"And Lucien?" Lisa Livia asked.

"He's deferring to the Field Marshal," Shane said, "but he agrees with the Duchess."

"What did she mean that the highest levels of our government know about it?" Lisa Livia demanded.

"I don't know," Shane said.

"But Carpenter would, wouldn't he?" she persisted.

"I don't know."

Lisa Livia wasn't having it. She pointed at Joey, then herself. "We're involved. Don't give me this 'I don't know' crap. Or 'need to know'. Or whatever. Did you have any clue who these people were and what could happen? The truth, Shane."

"I had no idea," Shane said. He tried some humor. "Told you, I didn't read the binder."

"Not funny," Lisa Livia said. "It's not just us. This place is Agnes' heart and now it looks like there might be a war here. You know what it would do to her if Two Rivers got destroyed?"

"I'll keep Two Rivers safe," Shane vowed.

"This is nuts," Lisa Livia said.

"We gonna hit the mattresses?" Joey asked, a tad too eagerly. "I remember when old man Fortunato—"

Lisa Livia cut him off. "I didn't sign up for this."

Shane's phone buzzed with a text message and he read it.

"Why didn't they fly to Vegas like other people?" Joey asked. "Drive through the little chapel and have Fake Elvis marry them?" But his mind veered back to the good old days of mob wars. He opened the bottle and poured. "Gonna need to get some guns."

"Kick 'em out," Lisa Livia said to Shane.

He put his phone away. "Too late for that. I was involved in this before they showed up. There's help on the way."

"Carpenter?" Lisa Livia asked.

Shane shook his head. "Carpenter is sending someone."

"Who?" Lisa Livia demanded.

"I'll know when they get here," Shane snapped, his own irritation rising. He took a breath. "Regardless of what they decide in there, LL, you need to get out of here." He nodded at Joey. "You too."

"This place is everything to Agnes," Lisa Livia said. "You have to —" she stopped as Lucien came into the kitchen.

"The Duke and Duchess would like to proceed tomorrow with the wedding," Lucien said. "We understand this puts you in an awkward position."

"'Awkward? Awkward'?" Lisa Livia repeated. Her voice rose. "*Awkward*?"

"I'm sorry, m'lady," Lucien said to her, "but—"

"Don't give me that m'lady crap," Lisa Livia said. She folded her arms. "I'm not going anywhere. I made a promise to Agnes. I stand by my word."

Lucien bowed to her. "I respect that." He straightened and turned to Shane. "Sir?"

"Let's make it through the night, first, okay?"

"But if we are here tomorrow, we might as well do it?" Lucien asked. "Do you know someone who could officiate the ceremony?"

Shane hesitated, but Lisa Livia jumped in. "There's someone I can call. And I think he should be here anyway."

Lucien bowed again. "It would be greatly appreciated."

"Yeah, whatever," Lisa Livia said.

"The Duke and Duchess are indebted to you," Lucien added, indicating all of them.

Lisa Livia snorted, giving the Duchess a run for her money.

In the distance, Rhett gave a muted, lonely bark back at Two Rivers.

CARPENTER DIDN'T WASTE time on a preamble. "Why did you take the Operation Glacier tasking?" he asked Louise.

He and Fromm were at Louise's workstation. She was in the chair between them.

"It was tasked to the Organization, sir," Lou responded.

"It didn't come to me," Carpenter said.

Louise indicated her computer. "May I, sir?"

Carpenter nodded. He found a nearby seat and confiscated it. He rolled up behind and to the side of Louise. Fromm stood to her other side. Louise signed in, verified her password, fingerprint and retina. She scrolled back in her message log.

Carpenter's burner phone vibrated. He pulled it out knowing it had to be either Shane or Lisa Livia. "Excuse me," he said, pushing the chair back and walking away, out of earshot.

"What's going on?" he asked as he answered the phone.

"Hello to you, too," Lisa Livia said.

"Sorry, I'm in the middle of something."

"You're always in the middle of something." Lisa Livia didn't dwell on it. "How about *I'm* in the middle of something? That ever occur to you?" She didn't wait for an answer. "We need a preacher here tomorrow. Can you make it?"

"What?" Carpenter was confused. "Is Shane there?"

"Standing right next to me."

Carpenter waited for Shane to speak but there was silence. "Hello?"

"Do you want to speak to him?" Lisa Livia asked. "Or am I to assume that? Why do you have to talk to him? I asked you for a favor. Can you do it or not?"

Carpenter looked over at Station 6. Fromm was pointing at Louise's screen. The two were arguing.

"Could I please talk to Shane?" Carpenter said. "There's a lot going on."

"Did you know?" Lisa Livia asked.

"'Know'?" Carpenter said.

"About the Duke? The Duchess? The fucking Great Charter? Did you know what was coming to Agnes' Two Rivers?"

"I did not," Carpenter said.

"But you sent Shane to Montana."

"There was no connection that we knew of at the time."

"Are you coming tomorrow?" Lisa Livia pressed.

Carpenter was distracted as Fromm raised his voice. "But it's not there!" He tapped one of the monitor screens hard enough to shake it. "You're lying!"

Carpenter spoke into the phone, slowly and carefully. "Lisa Livia. I know you are upset. You can yell at me about it at another time. Right now, I need to talk to Shane."

"Whatever."

The ghost on Carpenter's shoulder started tap-dancing with glee, as it did every time Lisa Livia said that word in that tone. He clenched the phone tight.

Lisa Livia continued: "But if I don't see you here tomorrow, don't ever bother trying to explain anything to me. Ever. Whatever friendship we have is over."

There was a tense moment of silence, then Shane was on. "What's going on?"

"Tell Lisa Livia I'm sorry," Carpenter said, "but I'm trying to figure out how we ended up with Operation Glacier."

"That would be nice to know," Shane said, "because it's a tremendous coincidence I got tagged with the mission, given the fact the target of that group is here at Two Rivers, which *isn't* a coincidence. They knew about me and France. They picked this place because of me. *And* they say our government approved."

"I'm trying to get to the bottom of that," Carpenter said. "Is everyone safe?"

"For the moment, but it looks like we're facing a confrontation tomorrow." Shane was silent for a moment. "It's a bit complicated."

"Has Phoebe arrived?"

"She'll be here tonight."

"Okay," Carpenter said, watching Fromm hit the monitor again. Louise had her hand up in protest. "I've got to untangle this knot here. Talk to you soon. Out." He hung up.

Louise and Fromm were arguing and Carpenter cut that off.

"Silence." They both turned to him. He pointed at Fromm. "What's the problem?"

"The original tasking is gone," Fromm said. He nodded toward Louise. "She deleted it to cover her tracks."

"I did not!" Louise insisted.

"Tracks to where?" Carpenter said. "That makes no sense." As Fromm opened his mouth to speak, Carpenter held up a single finger, silencing him. "What happened to the tasking?" he asked Louise.

"Sir, I swear there was an NCA tasking to us on Operation Glacier," Louise said. She shook her head in frustration. "I don't know what happened to it." She indicated the screen. "It should be right here, between these two messages. I remember it exactly. But it's gone."

"She's lying," Fromm said.

"Is it there?" Carpenter asked him.

"No, but—"

"Then what is she lying about?"

"About what happened to it," Fromm said. "She deleted it to cover her tracks."

"You keep saying tracks," Carpenter said, "but I'm not seeing a destination. How do you know she deleted it?"

"Because only two people could have," Fromm said. "Her or me. And I know for certain it wasn't me."

"I didn't, sir," Louise said. "I swear."

Carpenter looked from one to the other. He reached out and put a hand on the back of a chair to steady himself. He closed his eyes, visualizing the pieces, from here, to Montana, to Two Rivers, to Andova and back, adding in Shane's latest tidbit.

"The mission operative ranking list," Carpenter said. "How does the computer come up with it?"

Fromm blinked. "It's an algorithm that was developed to optimize assignments."

"Can it be manipulated?" Carpenter asked.

"Of course not," Fromm said, but Carpenter saw a frown cross Louise's face.

"What?" he said to her. "You disagree?"

"It's a program that's internal to the Organization," Louise said. "Everyone here in Technical Support has access to it. It could be manipulated by adjusting some of the mission variables. But why would someone want to do that?"

Why indeed, Carpenter wondered.

"She was Wilson's favorite," Fromm said, pointing at Louise. "The two of them were thick as thieves."

"That's a lie," Louise exclaimed. "I do my job."

"Yes, but he called her up to his office," Fromm said. "A lot."

"Is that true?" Carpenter asked.

Louise appeared flustered. "He called me in a few times. But it was questions about tech. Always."

"One can collaborate without express knowledge that one is doing wrong," Fromm said. "But I think it went further than that."

"Do you have any proof?" Carpenter demanded.

"You have Wilson's visitor logs," Fromm said. "He was very anal about keeping those. For all we know, he might have even recorded everything in his office."

Carpenter hadn't seen any files of recordings, but Wilson would have buried it deep.

His secure phone buzzed as Fromm and Louise began arguing.

"Shut up." He pointed at Fromm. "Sit down and stay silent. I'm using your office."

Carpenter went up the steps into Fromm's office and shut the door as he checked the phone. He'd only seen the identifier once before. He sat down behind the desk and stared at the phone. Then he put the phone to his ear, answering, while glancing out the window at Fromm and Louise, who were glaring at each other, but, thankfully, not saying anything.

"Carpenter."

A mechanical voice responded: "Stay on the line."

There was no irritating music or even an indication the line was still open. Carpenter waited.

After twenty seconds, there was a click and a woman spoke: "Come see me."

SHANE'S WORDS OF WISDOM #7

Don't get in a pissing contest with a man on a balcony.
Shane's Addendum: This is a corollary to the maxim that shit rolls
downhill.

Either way, you end up dirty and smelly and you've lost.

FRIDAY LATE EVENING

Shane put a bowl of food in front of Rhett, who was snoring in a bed in his favorite corner in the kitchen. Joey carried the bottle as Shane led him and Lisa Livia to the basement, through the tunnel and into the bunker.

Joey whistled when he saw the weapons and gear. "I'd have loved this back in the day. Frankie didn't have nothing like this in the place." He picked up a revolver, popped out the cylinder and spun it, checking the chambers.

"I don't like it down here," Lisa Livia said.

"It's safe," Shane said.

Lisa Livia tapped the cracked armor plate. "What's this? Is this what caused your bruises?"

Joey put the gun down. "What bruises?"

"Were you shot?" Lisa Livia demanded. "When? How? Where? You said Montana. How was it connected to this?"

"LL, you're staying down here tonight." Shane indicated his sleeping pad. "It's not the most comfortable, but you'll be safe."

"No way," Lisa Livia said. "Never. I don't even want to be here now."

"You sent Garth home," Joey said.

"He's safer in the swamp with his family," Shane said.

"You're gonna need mattresses," Joey said. "I remember—" he began but was brushed aside by Lisa Livia.

"You've been sleeping here?" Lisa Livia asked.

"Since Agnes left."

"Since I found the guns," Lisa Livia realized. "That's why you kicked me out of here the other night, isn't it?"

"I still don't know what's going on," Shane admitted. "Carpenter has sent another operative to help."

"Is Carpenter coming tomorrow?" Lisa Livia asked.

"I don't know," Shane said. "He was in the middle of something."

"He's always in the middle of something," Lisa Livia said.

"*Nipote*," Joey said, in his rarely used serious voice. "This ain't your fight."

"It *is* my fight," Shane said. "For two reasons. One it's my job. Somehow I got sucked into this before these people showed up." He briefly explained what had happened in Montana. "And now that it's here, I've got to see it through to protect Two Rivers."

Lisa Livia cut to the heart of the matter. "This is here because *you're* here. The Duchess was full of shit about loving Agnes' cooking. They prefer your guns," she added, indicating the weaponry.

"The Duchess don't eat much," Joey confirmed, but he was still on the topic of who to put one's life on the line for. "I never understood why you went to fight for the government. Especially now, after what happened with that Wilson fellow. You fight for family."

"You mean like my uncle Don Fortunato?" Shane shot back. "Who killed my father? His own brother? That the family you're talking about? The old blood is thicker than water bullshit? C'mon uncle. Let's get real. Hell, you killed the Don. So much for family."

"What?" Lisa Livia said, having been unaware of that additional bloodshed on the day of Maria's wedding.

A lonely bark from Rhett echoed down the tunnel, filtered by the kitchen door.

"And speaking of family," Shane said to her, "what about your mother? In prison now for trying to kill Agnes? That the kind of family we're talking about?"

Joey and Lisa Livia stared at him in shock.

"*Nipote*," Joey said, shaking his head.

Before anyone could say more, the lights in the tunnel flickered on. Shane grabbed a rifle. "Who's there?"

"Lucien."

Shane put the rifle back.

Lucien entered, dressed in black, a sword on one side, a pistol on the other. He nodded toward Lisa Livia, but there was none of the usual banter. "What do you have planned?" he asked Shane.

"I don't have anything planned," Shane said. "Right now, I want to keep Lisa Livia and Joey safe. This is the place for that."

"No mattresses," Joey muttered.

"There won't be trouble tonight," Lucien said. "*Lacessere* doesn't involve an ambush or surprises. It must take place at the determined time and with the Bishop's blessing."

"He wave a flag or something?" Joey asked, intrigued.

Lucien replied: "It will happen tomorrow morning."

"You really trust these people to follow rules?" Shane asked Lucien. "They've already killed."

"What?" Lisa Livia said. "Who?"

"The man who sold them weapons," Shane said. "And they tried to kill me." He realized something. "You came in early not just to recon, but to check me out, didn't you?"

"We need to focus on the future," Lucien said. "My men have the perimeter secure. Both landward and via water."

"I have some help coming," Shane said.

"Who?" Lucien asked.

"An operative named Phoebe."

"'Phoebe'?" Joey and Lisa Livia said at the same time.

"She's inbound but I don't have an exact ETA," Shane said.

"I'll alert my men," Lucien said.

"You have a challenge and password?" Shane asked.

"No," Lucien said. "Don't worry. We'll be careful."

"Right," Shane said. "You really going to fight it out with these people with swords if it comes to it?"

Joey paused in his perusal of the gun collection to pay attention.

"Yes," Lucien said.

"It's stupid," Lisa Livia said.

"On one level, it would be considered that," Lucien agreed. "But it is the law."

"Stupid law," Lisa Livia noted.

"It's kept our country out of wars for over twelve hundred years," Lucien said. "That's more than most countries can attest to."

Lisa Livia had nothing to say to that.

"It is also about honor," Lucien continued.

"What good is honor if you're dead?" Lisa Livia asked.

"What good is living without honor?" Lucien replied.

"He got a point," Joey said.

Lisa Livia scoffed but it wouldn't have ranked a 1 on the Duchess' scale.

"You have a history with Guillermo?" Shane asked.

"I do."

"Kill him for me," Shane said. "I don't like getting shot."

"I will endeavor to do my best," Lucien said.

"Gotta do better than endeavor," Joey muttered.

"You guys are driving me nuts," Lisa Livia said. "I need to get out of here."

"Do you trust Guillermo to play by the rules?" Shane asked.

"No," Lucien admitted. "But with the Bishop accompanying, he will. The Bishop would not lie."

Lisa Livia didn't buy that. "You don't know the priests I grew up around."

"How will the Bishop know which side won?" Joey asked. "How does this Lacrosse thing end?"

"One side wins and one side loses," Lucien said.

"How?" Shane asked.

Lucien met his gaze straight on. "There is no quarter."

"That don't sound good," Lisa Livia said. "What does it mean?"

"One side doesn't get out alive," Shane said.

"We're gonna need some mattresses," Joey said.

Rhett barked in the muted distance.

"I'm getting out of here," Lisa Livia said and she exited the bunker.

CARPENTER WALKED down the street at Fort Meade to answer his summons, accompanied by the ghost which was whispering urgent recriminations. The post is one of the most secure places in the country because it's home to the National Security Agency. Despite being very early on a weekend morning, it hummed with activity, since intelligence gathering never takes time off. The nine-story building he approached was the apparent pinnacle of security on the post. The outside of the building was lined with special glass that deflected electronic eavesdropping. He flashed his badge to get in the front door, then passed through two more security checkpoints.

The guards at those positions thought the Ninth Floor was the peak of the security apparatus, where their leadership worked. But Carpenter wasn't going to the Ninth Floor. He went past the bank of elevators and down a narrow corridor. At the end, an elderly man sat behind a desk reading a paperback he held in one hand. The other wasn't visible. He peered up over reading glasses. There was an elevator door behind him.

"Identification, please."

Carpenter showed it.

"I remember you," the old man said, even though Carpenter had only been here once, many months ago when he was given command of the Organization. "You ever listen to Bob Dylan?"

Carpenter didn't understand why the question was being asked. "At times."

"Know his song *Gotta Serve Somebody*?"

"I vaguely remember it."

"Coming here this time of night means you were summoned," the guard said. "I don't know where you work or what you do, but the last lines of the song apply to any late-night summons: '*It may be the devil or it may be the Lord. But you're gonna have to serve somebody*'."

The ghost on his shoulder applauded and Carpenter ran a calming mantra through his consciousness. The guard put the book down and pressed something under the desk. The elevator doors opened. His other hand still remained out of sight and Carpenter had no doubt it held a weapon. Carpenter glanced at the cover of the book. A shirtless man with a shaved chest cradled a woman in a gown with one arm and the other held a sword.

Foreshadowing? Carpenter wondered. "Was that tip official or doing me a favor?"

The guard smiled. "Don't worry about a button. It'll take you where you're going."

Carpenter entered the elevator. As soon as the doors shut, it dropped fast, which might be the answer to the last line of the Dylan song. Much deeper than one floor. The halt was abrupt enough to cause him to flex his knees. The doors separated, revealing a long narrow corridor. The far end was a stainless-steel vault door, much nicer than the one in the bunker under Two Rivers. In front of it, a gray, government issue desk. A frumpy, white-haired woman sat behind it. There was nothing on the top.

"Step out of the elevator, please," she called out.

The doors shut behind Carpenter

"Walk on the white line, stop at the red," the woman ordered in a neutral voice.

Carpenter halted halfway to the desk.

"Weapons and any electronic devices in the alcove to your right."

Carpenter put his secure phone and personal burner in the alcove.

"Come forward along the white line and stop at the green. I will notify Hannah you are here."

The first time he'd been ushered in immediately. He wasn't sure if the wait was deliberate. Since he had the time, Carpenter inspected the walls and ceiling. They appeared perfectly smooth but he had no doubt the secretary controlled some sort of defensive device. At best incapacitating gas, at worst, explosives. Both her hands were out of sight, below desktop level; one on a trigger and the other typing a message to the person who had summoned him. Then she sat up straight and stared at him through thick glasses.

One minute stretched to two, an interminable amount of time to be standing on a line. Carpenter hadn't felt like this since eighth grade, when he'd been called to the principal's office for some unknown reason. He'd sat in the waiting area, sweating and scared, with a handful of known troublemakers, pondering his recent actions to determine if he'd unknowingly committed a transgression. The voice in his head had practically swooned in delight. It had turned out to be a scholarship offer to a prestigious private high school. At this moment he didn't think a scholarship was in the offing.

Physically, and literally, deeper than the Organization, this was the Cellar. Which, of course, caused Carpenter to wonder if there was something even more secret than the Cellar. Sort of like an endless layer cake or, more appropriately, an Escher painting, looping back on itself. The ghost on his shoulder was whispering, but Carpenter tuned it out.

The large metal door behind the secretary slowly opened via hydraulic hinges. The space beyond was dimly lit.

"Hannah will see you now," the secretary said.

Carpenter entered the vault. A silver-haired woman sat behind a large desk. Her face was attractive but the crows feet around her eyes and a tightness in the facial muscles and stress lines indicated a life laced with tough decisions. She had a pair of reading glasses perched on top of her head, forgotten for the moment.

A tape ticker clattered on one side of the desk and she ran the tape through her fingers while watching him. There was an in-box on one corner of the desk and an out-box on the other. Both were empty. There was a secure hard-wired phone to one side.

Like his own office, there were no pictures or plaques on the wall. Gray, bland, concrete walls, part of a bunker that could survive the building above being completely destroyed.

"Sit, please," Hannah said.

Carpenter sat in a hard, wooden chair facing the desk. The chair in the principal's waiting room had been softer even though it had been plastic.

Hannah indicated the tape. "My predecessor, Nero, was blind. He used this to read intelligence transmitted from the floors above. Braille. I learned it because getting the intelligence via a different sense is intriguing and often gives me a different perspective."

A blind one? Carpenter thought, but he understood the concept. He occasionally had the computer read him case files.

"And," Hannah continued, tapping the glasses on top of her head, "I hate using these. A reminder of time going by. I used to have perfect vision."

Better lighting would help, Carpenter thought, but did not say.

Hannah continued. "We met briefly when you took the mantle of the Organization." She put the tape down and touched something under her desk to stop the machine. "Presence gives a different perspective from a dossier." She held up her left hand. A gold band adorned her ring finger. "I had a husband once. He betrayed me, along with the country. But the very fact I was married to him indicates a lack on my part. It was a mistake. I wear the ring to remind me. I didn't trust my instincts when I was younger with that decision. I vowed always to trust them after coming into this office. I trusted them with you."

Definitely no scholarship coming.

She leaned back in her high-backed chair. "Shane was being groomed to take over the Organization by Wilson. He declined. Do you wonder why you were offered the position, given it meant leaping over a number of people with more experience who certainly believe they should be in charge?"

"Of course."

"And?"

"It is what it is."

Hannah chuckled. "What an interesting non-answer. I went from housewife to head of the Cellar. I served an apprenticeship under Nero for years, but he plucked me straight out of the suburbs. There was a test, of course. One I barely survived. But he saw in me something which he knew was the essential ingredient for this position. The rest, he knew I was smart enough to learn."

"And that was?"

"I can make decisions without my ego getting involved. Without any other factor dominating other than the Cellar's mandate."

"Is that why I was chosen?" Carpenter asked. "I know I wasn't high on Wilson's list."

"I chose you," Hannah allowed. "As to why? That you'll have to figure out on your own. Did you receive the Bob Dylan spiel?"

"Yes."

"And your first thought was who I served, wasn't it?"

"It occurred to me."

"Did you hear of the Cellar before you came here?"

"Rumors."

"What kind?"

"That you didn't want the Cellar coming after you."

"I work under a Presidential mandate established at the end of World War II, not a person," Hannah said. "The Cellar polices the world of covert operations. I could give the history, but you could imagine it just as well. The key is that this position is a permanent National Command Authority, not answerable to those who hold that power temporarily. My mandate is for life and it will be for life for my successor, as it was for Nero before me. He was the first."

"Am I being policed?" Carpenter asked.

"Your predecessor, Wilson, was corrupt. Was he the only one?"

"I don't think so."

"Why?"

"One of my current operations seems to be infected."

"'Seems to be'?"

"It is. You know that. It's why you called me in. The timing wasn't coincidence."

"Tell me why *you* think you have an infection?"

Carpenter summarized the strange tasking, then Shane and Phoebe's ambushes. The Andova connection between Montana and Two Rivers.

"I gave the Operation Glacier tasking to the Organization," Hannah said, "but not via the normal path."

"Why?"

"It needed to be done and to see what would happen."

"You were testing me?"

"No. That's a waste of resources. I used an opportunity to accomplish more than what was immediately apparent."

"Why are we involved in this Andova situation?" Carpenter asked.

Hannah leaned back in her chair. "You seem to forget, I summoned you."

Carpenter folded his hands in his lap and waited as the ghost mocked him.

"How do you feel about the mission algorithm Wilson instituted?" Hannah asked.

Carpenter didn't know where this was headed or what Hannah was fishing for, so he went to his standby: honesty. "I don't like it."

"Why not?"

"It's lacking."

"More specific."

"If we're going to let computers make decisions, then why have humans responsible?" Carpenter asked. "Computers can't factor in the unquantifiable. They're only as good as the people who program them."

"Yet you made decisions based on the algorithms," Hannah said. "Did it ever occur to you that the data were manipulated?"

"Of course, it occurred to me," Carpenter said. "Did *you* manipulate the data?"

"No. That came from your infection. I sent the mission tasking. It's intriguing that Shane was tapped for it, given subsequent events."

"Shane was specifically chosen for the original mission," Carpenter said, "because the target of the weapons exchange was eventually Two Rivers. They wanted to get him out of the picture from the start. Get the weapons and wipe out a potential threat. Smart."

"Which means they, whoever they are, was, and perhaps still is, in contact with your infection. Didn't you think it odd that Shane was picked as the optimum choice for what appeared to be a rather mundane task?"

The question was a reprimand because Carpenter had not questioned the tasking and the Ghost was cheering. As if reading his mind, Hannah spoke.

"You feel comfortable with Shane on an operation because you know he's competent. It's one less thing for you to worry about." It was not phrased as a question. "Why did you send Phoebe as backup?"

"The algorithm picked her," Carpenter said. "It's SOP to have backup on standby. Was Phoebe chosen by the infection?"

"No. I picked Phoebe for backup."

Carpenter blinked. "Why?"

"You'll see."

"Do you know who the infection is if you manipulated the computer?"

"That's not my job," Hannah said. "Let me rephrase: Not my job, *yet*. You don't want it to become my job. I'm giving you a chance to take care of it in-house. If not, it will become a Sanction."

"'Sanction'?"

"We police the world of covert ops," Hannah said. "My operatives are judge, jury and executioner."

"We'll take care of it," Carpenter said.

"I fear the infection might have affected more than just Operation Glacier. Keep your eyes wide open, Carpenter."

"Yes, ma'am."

"Regarding Shane. He was distracted while on an operation. He received a text from a person outside the Organization."

It was not a question so Carpenter didn't reply.

Hannah briefly pointed behind her. "There's a door in the wall. I live there. This is my life. The entirety. Where is your heart, Carpenter?"

"Excuse me?"

"We live in a world most people can't fathom. A world where our decisions, on a daily basis, mean not only life and death for others, but control a balance of power that can have world-changing ramifications. Is that not worthy of committing to?"

Before Carpenter could answer, Hannah pushed on. "To answer your question, the stability of Andova is important to world order. Andova has been a calm spot in the swirl of history for over twelve centuries. Such places are valuable and extremely rare and deserving of protection.

"They have a long record of supplying confidential data to Interpol and other security agencies on large financial transactions that certain parties believe are safe from prying eyes. After all, money makes the world go around, including the world of terrorism. In my time in this office, eight terrorist plots have been cut off before they could get traction because of Andovan intelligence. We are supporting this marriage and the dissolving of the Great Charter because Drusilla Navarro poses a threat to that. She is not only mentally unstable, but, more importantly, is supported by certain dark factions that we cannot allow to wield power in Andova."

"Why did they bring the wedding here?" Carpenter asked.

"There are many traditionalists in Andova who want things to stay the same, no matter how out of date or unwieldy or dangerous. The Duke and Duchess are trying to change the Great Charter which has been in existence since eight-oh-two. Can you imagine how people here would react if someone tried to change the Constitution and that's been around a fraction of the Charter."

"I think—" Carpenter began but Hannah silenced him with a slight lift of one finger.

"Are you up to date on events in South Carolina? The *Lacessere*?"

"Yes."

"And the Operative? Phoebe? Is she up to speed?"

"Yes." A lightbulb went on. "Phoebe is an expert with the blade. Is that why—"

Another finger lift silenced the observation.

Carpenter shifted. "The information about Andova would have —" Carpenter began but got cut off again.

"No. It wouldn't have changed a thing. Shane's mission was straightforward."

"I almost got him killed," Carpenter said.

"That's the nature of the job," Hannah said.

"How much latitude do I have to deal with this matter?" Carpenter asked.

"Are you inquiring if you have weapons free?" Hannah asked.

The ghost on Carpenter's shoulder cackled.

Hannah had made her point. "As much as you discern is needed to bring the results we desire without destabilizing Andova."

"Yes, ma'am."

"Do you believe in free will?" Hannah asked.

"Yes."

"Then Shane chose to be in Montana. You chose to be where you are and I chose to be here. We are responsible for the choices we make and the results. But we must commit to one thing." Hannah put both hands on the desk as she leaned forward. "To put it in simpler terms, Carpenter, you must decide whether you want to put a ring on it."

Several seconds of silence ticked away.

"Now," Hannah said, in a tone that indicated the meeting was over. "Go excise your infection and then officiate a wedding for your friend if you desire. Then make a decision."

. . .

Lisa Livia had told Shane in no uncertain terms that she was not spending the night in the vault even if Joey managed to wrestle a mattress down here, which she doubted. Since Shane wasn't going to take advantage of the king-sized bed and down comforter in the top floor master bedroom, then she was going to. If she was going to die in the next day or so, she wanted to be as comfortable as possible in the meanwhile. In fact, she'd decided if she was gonna die, she wanted it to be up there, nice and comfy with a high thread count.

As she pulled her overnight bag from her car, she noted a slender figure standing on the corner of the porch, looking toward the Intracoastal. Against her better self-interest, Lisa Livia left her bag at the kitchen door and walked to the Duchess.

"I love the moon off the water here," Lisa Livia said. "It's different than where I live in the islands."

A brief red glow illuminated the Duchess' face as she inhaled the thinnest cigarette Lisa Livia had ever seen. She wondered if they were specially made for the Duchess to match her frame.

"I gave these up years ago," the Duchess said. "Mostly. There are times, though, when I succumb to my base instincts. I had a feeling there might be a need on this trip." She extended a gold case toward Lisa Livia. "Would you like one?"

"I don't want to get started again," Lisa Livia said. "My self-control isn't that great."

The Duchess nodded. "I am sorry about your mother taking your money. I assume that was a truth?"

"It is true," Lisa Livia said. "I'm sorry your husband passed away."

"Don't be." The Duchess glanced at her in the moonlight. "Does that surprise you?"

"Nah," Lisa Livia said. "Not all marriages are great. One or two have been known to be lousy."

"There are some good ones," the Duchess noted.

"Sure, but not my parents. My father split town for twenty-five years and probably didn't give my mother a second thought. I know she didn't miss him. She got married again, and the new guy wasn't that much better, but he had money and that's all she cared about. I sometimes think she wacked him."

"Killed him?"

Lisa Livia shrugged. "You can kill someone without directly doing it. They said it was a heart attack, but my mother could make a saint's life hard and my step-father was no saint. I think his heart did the rest of him a favor and just gave up. What was wrong with your husband?"

"He was angry," the Duchess said. "Always angry. I thought when he got sick, after the diagnosis, that finally, things would change. That the specter of death would temper the anger. But it got worse. The last months were terrible." She turned her head away. "I was so relieved when he died. Does that make me a horrible person?"

"I'm glad my mom is in prison for the rest of her life. Why'd you marry him?"

"It was arranged, because that is the role in the life I was born into. The way our families have done things for centuries. What the Duke and I are trying to put an end to. Sometimes under the old system, one, how do you say, lucks out? Sometimes you don't. I had hope and I tried. God knows, I tried. I held off as long as possible and married late in life. Too late, according to my mother. Finally, I had no choice given the political circumstances."

"You married for your country," Lisa Livia said. "More than most people can say. And you're doing it again. Why'd the flowers upset you?"

There was just a glowing stub left of the cigarette. The Duchess surprised Lisa Livia by pressing it out against her palm and putting the remains in the gold case. "I learned to do that so my father wouldn't catch me. Strange how some habits last decades and we feel our parent's disapproval even after they're long gone." She put the case inside a pocket of her coat. "I love the arrangements. It's just that, given the businesslike approach we've taken to this wedding, it's a surprising digression into sentimentality." She took a deep breath. "It's why I love the Duke. He is thoughtful and kind and always thinking of my feelings. The flowers in those arrangements are from the high glades in the mountains. Where we spent time together when we were young. There's a small meadow by a stream. A beautiful, secluded spot. Where we first kissed." She sighed. "We exchanged rings."

"You were engaged?"

The Duchess nodded. "Known only to the two of us. The rings were special. Family heirlooms of which only eight were forged." She reached up and pulled a chain out. Two exquisite, narrow rings were on it. "Over a thousand years old. During a time when the families tried to unite and do away with the Charter and failed. Strands of gold and silver intwined."

"What happened?" Lisa Livia asked.

"A thousand years ago or more recently?"

"More recently. You and the Duke."

"When we dared tell our respective families we were met with a furious response. Marc had to return the ring to me. I hid them away, no matter how much father railed at me to return them to rest in the vault with the others. I've kept them all these years, waiting for the day we could exchange them again."

"Ring exchanging," Lisa Livia said. "Very romantic."

"The glade was, is, special to us. It was where we also, as you say, made hay while the sun was shining."

Lisa Livia noticed a dark figure talking to the two guards who were in the torch light, watching the statue. Lucien making his rounds. She didn't know what to say in response to the last revelation.

"Are you still desiring to make hay with Lucien?" the Duchess asked.

"It's a lower priority," Lisa Livia admitted. "Besides, if we get the justice of the peace I requested, it would get a little awkward."

"Another field you reaped?" the Duchess asked. She hurriedly added: "Don't take that the wrong way."

"I don't. You could say that."

"But not someone you feel anchored to?"

"Interesting choice of words."

"Committed, then?"

"Carpenter's a good man," Lisa Livia said. She sighed. "I don't even know his real name. I don't think that's it or whether it's a first name or a last name or a job description. So, I guess that means, no, no commitment or anchor. We ended it a while ago. But don't we need an anchor sometimes?"

"If it's a peaceful harbor and there's a storm brewing, yes." The Duchess saw where Lisa Livia was looking. "Lucien did speak of you."

Lisa Livia felt a thrill. "What did he say?" She immediately thought: *What am I, in high school?*

"He finds you intriguing and unlike most other women he has met."

Lisa Livia noted she said 'met' and not known. The Duchess seemed to be a woman who chose her words carefully.

"How so?"

The Duchess shrugged. "You would need to ask him."

They stood in silence for several moments.

"Remember the story I told you about Saint Ingrid?" the Duchess asked.

"Yes."

"Lucien served in the Foreign Legion," the Duchess said. "It's customary for our soldiers since we have never had an armed conflict. They gain experience. He was deployed to a country in Africa on a peacekeeping mission. The man that Drusilla has leading her mercenaries, Guillermo, was in *La Unidad*, but attached to the Legion on the same deployment. The two units have a working arrangement, brokered years ago by our country.

"I am not certain of the exact circumstances, but after their convoy was ambushed and several men wounded, Guillermo sought vengeance on the local villagers. He was preparing to gun down innocent women and children when Lucien faced him down."

She passed into silence and Lisa Livia waited. "What happened?"

"Oh, I thought you liked the Blood River versions," the Duchess said. "The Legion is full of hard men. Most wouldn't have cared one way or the other if Guillermo shot the villagers. In fact, I imagine most supported him. But Lucien put himself in the line of fire and when Guillermo shot him, that changed things. A Legionnaire does not harm one of their own. His comrades sided with him and against Guillermo. He was drummed out of *La Unidad*. Lucien saved those people."

"So, he's like a saint?" Lisa Livia asked.

"He's a good man," the Duchess said. Several seconds of silence played out. The Duchess retrieved the case, opened it, and lit a thin cigarette, all with practiced and smooth movements. "You asked if Lucien is married. Have you asked him?"

"No."

"If you did, he would say he was," the Duchess said. "He and his wife exchanged a set of the eight rings."

Lisa Livia felt a rush of stupid, but wasn't allowed to fully experience it as the Duchess spoke.

"His wife died eight years ago. They had a true marriage. Of choice. She was a commoner, which happens, since we need to keep, how shall I say, the gene pool from becoming murky?"

"Don't want two-headed kids," Lisa Livia said.

"Indeed. They had a child. Lucien's son has only one head and it is focused on art. He will not follow in his father's footsteps." She paused and stared off to the Low Country. "That will make it all worthwhile. That Jean-Paul's future is his own. He will not have to go into the Legion. Not have to serve in the Guard."

"Yeah," Lisa Livia said. "That's a positive."

"I think—" the Duchess began but stopped.

"What?" Lisa Livia asked, wondering why the Duchess was being so open.

"That the issue of Jean-Paul and the Legion is what started the Duke and I to take the path we have chosen. We'd discussed ending the Charter several times. But when Jean-Paul came of age, it suddenly became more pertinent. Especially given that Lucien's wife died while he was deployed. It most likely would not have happened had he been home."

Lisa Livia wanted more than the Blood River version but she was hesitant to interrupt the Duchess's stream of consciousness.

The Duchess' pale face was illuminated by the red tip of the cigarette as she inhaled. "You remind me of Zara. Even the Duke has remarked on it."

"I look like her?" Lisa-Livia asked.

"Not at all. It's your aura. Funny how that word is the same in French and English. And you are irreverent, as she was." She sighed and put the cigarette out. "I know you are wondering why I am being so loquacious. It is because we're most likely going to die tomorrow. I have no doubt that Drusilla will break the rules. She's proven it by cheating on the Duke with Guillermo and Lord knows who else. The Duke cannot accept that reality. He believes the best in people even if it is only a gnarled withered husk of who they pretended to be to get what they wanted. You should leave. Go someplace safe. It is not your fight."

"This is my friend's home," Lisa Livia said. "I'm staying."

The Duchess nodded. "Yes. That is very much like Zara. There is something else you should know about Lucien."

Lisa Livia waited.

"Despite his time in the Legion, he has never taken a life. If, by some wild chance, we prevail tomorrow, I am afraid what effect doing so will have on him. He is not as hard as he appears on the outside. I would not want him to change toward the darkness. Thus, regardless of how things turn out, it will not be good."

SHANE HAD EAVESDROPPED on Lisa Livia and the Duchess without any regrets from a dark shadow around the corner of the porch. He was dressed in black fatigues and had his combat vest on. He'd moved his dagger to a more readily accessible position on the right shoulder. The .45 was in a thigh holster. Night vision goggles, twin to the one Phoebe had used, were on his forehead.

Hearing the two women move toward the kitchen, he left the porch and stayed to the shadows. He spotted one of the soldiers lying in the high grass just above the sea wall, not far from the dock. The man wore night vision goggles and was watching the water. He had one of the rifles from the case next to him. Shane hoped Xavier didn't decide to do any late-night snooping.

Shane looped around and went into the gully that made Two Rivers an island at high tide and connected the Intracoastal with the Blood River. He made his way cautiously and as quietly as possible through the fluffer mud. There was about three feet of water in the center of the gully. As far as he could see ahead, there was no sign of security on or around the bridge, forty feet ahead, which he found curious. They had to have—

Shane spun about, but froze as sharp steel pressed against his neck. When it didn't slice flesh, he slowly turned his head to look at the man holding the sabre. "Lucien."

Lucien's free hand lifted a single finger to his lips. "Shh," he whispered. He was covered in mud once again and Shane realized he'd walked right past him where Lucien had been hidden on the side of the gully. Lucien pulled the sabre back and pointed to the right and indicated for Shane to follow him.

Lucien moved along the side of the gully. Shane followed.

Lucien paused thirty feet from the bridge. Shane crawled next to him, their bodies pressing against each other. Lucien pointed. There was a small red glow under the bridge. As his eyes adjusted, Shane saw a man in camouflage, wearing a red lensed headlamp. He was leaning on one of the heavy beams that angled up to the center, supporting the bridge. Shane couldn't make out details but he knew exactly what the man was doing: wiring demolitions.

Lucien pointed at himself, then the man, indicating the target was his. Then at Shane and up to the right, landward. Shane nodded. As Lucien resumed his low crawl, Shane drew his pistol and went to the other side, where any security covering the bomber would be positioned.

As he slithered ahead, he glanced to the left at Lucien heading to the bottom of the gully where a log was in a deep pool. Lucien was edging toward it, probably to use as cover.

Shane rolled down the gully, body tight, until he ran into Lucien who let out a startled grunt. Shane shoved his hand over Lucien's mouth, then pointed at the log. He leaned close.

"Alligator."

Lucien's eyes grew wide. Shane indicated for Lucien to go around. He resumed his way as Lucien gave the big gator a wide berth.

As Shane reached the lip of the gully, he heard a surprised yell, a brief scuffle and then silence. Shane scanned the trees and saw nothing out of the ordinary. He waited, then slid down. Lucien had the tip of his sabre pressed against the man's throat.

"Do you have support?" Lucien demanded.

The man didn't respond. He was dressed in dark camouflage, his face smeared with camo paint.

Lucien glanced at Shane. "Cuff ties in my belt."

As Shane reached for the black plastic ties looped through the back of Lucien's belt, the man made a break for it, slapping away the sword and scrambling up the side of the gully.

Lucien slashed, cutting through the man's left Achilles. Losing use of that leg, the man tumbled down, landing face first, Shane and Lucien rushed after him.

Lucien had his sword at the ready as the man rolled, bringing his gun up. But Lucien hesitated to strike. Shane shoved Lucien as the man fired the suppressed weapon. Shane returned fire. The roar of the forty-five reverberated underneath the bridge. The big round hit the man in the forehead, splattering brains and bones into the mud.

Shane remained still, breathing hard. Lucien was next to him, staring at the body. Then Shane quickly checked to make sure the alligator wasn't coming with the scent of blood, but it was moving away from the excitement, being smarter than the infiltrator.

"We need to check if he has backup," Shane said.

Lucien didn't respond.

Shane pointed up. "There might be a car out there," Shane said. "If there is backup, they heard my shot." Shane put an edge in his voice. "Let's go. I'll take the right, you take the left." Shane turned on the goggles and lowered them.

Lucien nodded.

They sprang up out of the ditch in tandem and ran into the trees. Shane's eyes tracked the muzzle of the pistol as he moved quickly through the trees. The time for stealth was over. If there was someone else as backup, then speed and force were the key.

Shane sprinted from tree to tree. After fifteen minutes he reached the main, coastal road where the drive to Two Rivers connected. He went along the road for a quarter mile, then returned to the drive. Nothing.

He looked to the left and after a minute, Lucien appeared.

"Clear," Shane said.

"Clear," Lucien echoed. Without another word he headed down the drive. Two of his men, armed with rifles were on top of the bridge, weapons at the ready.

"Maintain security," Lucien ordered the men.

Shane and Lucien slid into the draw.

"Light," Lucien warned and Shane turned off his goggles and pulled them up.

Lucien turned on the headlamp he'd taken from the intruder. Shane looked up as Lucien played the light along the beams, exposing lines of det-cord.

"We got him before he placed the charges," Lucien said, indicating a pack perched on one of the crossbeams.

Shane checked the contents. Plastic explosive and a detonator that would be attached to the det cord. He held up a small metal box. "Receiver for remote detonation." He stuffed it back in the pack.

"There's not enough demo here to blow this bridge. Damage it, but not take it out."

"They might have been working off old intelligence regarding the previous bridge," Lucien said. He was looking over the body. "I don't recognize him."

Shane checked the corpse crumpled in the bottom; half submerged in the incoming tidal water. There was nothing in the pockets. He pulled off the man's shirt and checked for tattoos. He pointed at one on the arm. "GSG9."

Lucien nodded. "German."

Shane searched further and found a swastika on the man's chest. "They've been purging the neo-Nazis from the military. The world won't miss him."

"Not surprising that Guillermo would recruit such."

"You faced down Guillermo once before, didn't you?" Shane asked.

Lucien looked at him over the body. "Who told you?"

"The Duchess was talking to Lisa Livia. I overheard."

Lucien cocked his head. "Interesting that she would divulge that."

"Yeah," Shane said.

"Ms. Lisa Livia seems quite the woman," Lucien said.

That was a different type of ambush Shane didn't want to wade into. "What do you want to do with the body?"

"We have body bags in our gear. We'll take care of it."

Who the hell packed body bags for a wedding? Shane thought and the answer was obvious. "I saw your man by the dock. Where are the others?"

"The QRF is above," Lucien said, referring to the Quick Reaction Force. Lucien told him the position of two more men, one of whom was over-watching them with a sniper rifle with thermal sight along the length of the gully and had radioed the intruder to Lucien.

"Is this within the rules?" Shane asked. "They have det-cord and C-4 back in eight-oh-two?"

Lucien indicated the bridge. "I suspect this was a way of isolating the field of combat. Guillermo wouldn't want the *Lacessere* to be interrupted by local law enforcement."

"Agnes will be really pissed if anything happens to this bridge," Shane said.

"She also sounds like quite a woman," Lucien said.

"She is." Shane looked back toward Two Rivers and noted that the lights were on in the top floor, the master bedroom. But it was Lisa Livia up there, not Agnes, and the house seemed farther away than ever before when he was here.

Vicente appeared, his case in hand. "Sir?" he said to Lucien.

Lucien indicated his right arm and Shane realized that he'd been hit by the man's bullet.

Vicente produced a pair of medical scissors and cut away the cloth. "Through and through," he announced.

The round had punched a small hole in Lucien's bicep, going from inside out.

"Why didn't you tell me you were wounded?" Shane asked.

"We needed to secure the area," Lucien said. He grimaced as Vicente cleaned the wound.

"How much blood have you lost?" Shane asked.

"Some. I'll be fine. It missed the bone."

Shane's secure phone vibrated. He checked the message from Carpenter.

WILL BE THERE LATE MORNING

"The preacher will be here for the wedding," Shane told Lucien. As he put the phone away, it buzzed again. A new number, which meant either a Cleaner or the incoming Operative. Shane checked it.

3 MINUTES OUT

He texted Phoebe back.

AT BRIDGE

MARKING WITH IR STROBE

"I've got help coming in," he told Lucien. "Three minutes."

THE REAR of the four-engine cargo plane opened, with the lower portion dropping level and the upper pulling up into the tail. As soon as the ramp was set, Phoebe walked forward, keeping an eye on the red light glowing up in the tail area of the cargo bay. She stopped at the edge. There were lights below and nothing but darkness stretching to the horizon on the right, the demarcation between land and water. Air swirled in with the strong smell of the fuel burning in the turboprop engines of the C-130. Beneath it, Phoebe picked up a faint odor which she recognized as salt water mixed with the unique smell of marshland. A mixture of life and death where the water met the land. The plane was at five thousand feet, flying above the Intracoastal.

She inhaled deeply, flexed her bad knee slightly, then shuffled forward until her toes were just over the end of the ramp. The cargo bay was big enough to hold 64 fully equipped paratroopers, over forty feet long, by ten wide and nine high. The loadmaster of the C-130 wore a monkey harness attached to a bolt in the floor and was watching her with interest. He had no idea who she was or how she'd been able to commandeer the cargo plane for herself. Nor did the pilots. Theirs was not to reason why.

He held up one finger, shouting the warning, which couldn't be heard over the sound of the engines and the wind as the plane slowed to one hundred and thirty-five knots.

Phoebe checked the phone and read the last message. She secured the phone inside a pocket on the vest. She turned on the strobe strapped to her shoulder, setting it to infrared. Her sword, hanging in the sheath on her belt, was strapped to her right thigh.

She checked the bad knee once more as if it had suddenly improved in the past minute.

The light turned green and Phoebe stepped off into darkness.

SHANE PULLED the goggles over his eyes and looked down the driveway toward the coastal road. No sign of headlights, which would appear like searchlights in the goggles, or an infrared strobe, invisible to the naked eye.

Lucien's two men had already shoved the body in a bag and carried it away.

"I'm not sure how much help another operative would be," Lucien said, "since the *Lacessere* will decide this and it is a private affair."

"You really plan on doing that?" Shane asked as he looked upward.

"We must," Lucien said. Vicente had bandaged the wound and concurred it wasn't critical or life-threatening.

A pulsing light was descending. He could make out the canopy above.

"*Now an angel from heaven appeared to Him*," Lucien muttered as the jumper descended, "*strengthening Him.*"

"Right, biblical," Shane said as Phoebe flared the chute, then touched down in the center of the bridge, stumbling slightly. "Didn't stick the landing." He turned off the goggles and pulled them up.

The parachute settled. Shane grabbed the apex and eight-rolled it up. The jumper unbuckled from the harness. Pulled off the helmet to reveal short, mussed reddish black hair and a pixie face.

"Truly an angel," Lucien said, as he gave a brief bow. "Welcome m'lady."

Phoebe gave a bow in return. "Sir."

"I am Lucien." He indicated Shane, who had the parachute in his hands. "And Shane."

"We've met," Phoebe said. "Although only briefly. Wedding's turning out to be a doozy, eh?"

Shane dumped the chute in a pile. "Did you get an update from Carpenter?"

Phoebe ripped the Velcro from around the sheath, freeing the wakizashi from her thigh. "Yep."

"May I?" Lucien asked, indicating her short sword.

Phoebe drew it, extending it hilt first to Lucien. He grimaced slightly as he took it. He angled the blade toward the moon, checking the edge.

"The *wakizashi* is considered a secondary armament for a samurai," Phoebe explained, "the primary being the *katana*. I find it sufficient."

"Excellent," Lucien said. He returned in the same manner.

Phoebe pointed at Lucien's sabre. "Ditto?"

Lucien handed over his sabre. Phoebe checked it approvingly, testing the balance. She gave the sabre back. She looked at Shane. "Care to share?"

"My dagger wouldn't measure up," Shane said.

Phoebe laughed. "Well, okay." She sniffed. "Blood. There's fresh blood. Gunpowder. Someone's been a bad boy."

Shane and Lucien exchanged a glance.

"We encountered an intruder trying to wire the bridge," Shane said.

Phoebe nodded. "To isolate the target. But the blood is really close and fresh."

Lucien indicated his bandaged arm. "I suffered a minor wound."

"It's never minor when it happens to you." Phoebe looked about. "The bad guys have observation on the place. Probably have for a while."

Lucien and Shane exchanged glances.

Phoebe explained: "They had the exchange site under surveillance. Before that, they had observation on the militia camp before the weapons exchange. Stands to reason they have eyes on this place since it's their target."

"She's right," Shane said.

"She is," Lucien agreed. "I'll do the honors and search it out."

Shane disagreed. "I know the area. You need to take it easy."

"I know exactly where they'd put someone," Phoebe offered.

"Yeah," Shane said, "but—"

Phoebe cut him off. "I studied the satellite imagery on the way here and know where I'd go to surveil. The island across the Intracoastal would be ideal, but there's people there. Easily compromised. There's a shoal off shore of the island on the other side of the Intracoastal. Tall grass. Perfect."

"I know it," Shane said. "It's about a quarter mile long. Almost completely under water at high tide."

Phoebe tapped the NVGs. "I also spotted a glow on the shoal while I was coming down. Someone smoking, but hidden from ground level view. I know the exact spot."

"Lead with the headline," Shane suggested.

"So, I lead?" Phoebe asked.

"That wasn't what I meant," Shane said.

Lucien's phone buzzed. He pulled it out. "It's the Bishop." He answered the phone while running toward the barn where the Duke and Duchess held court.

"The Bishop's with the bad guys, right?" Phoebe asked.

CARPENTER TOOK the elevator to Technical Support uncertain of how to proceed, the ghost on his shoulder repeating a number of Hannah's observations, but emphasizing how they indicated he had failed. The doors rolled open, revealing the small halos of light where each analyst worked. He went to Six, but it was unoccupied. Looking up, he didn't see Fromm in his office.

Carpenter went to the closest occupied cubicle. "Is Louise Wingo on duty?"

"Yes, sir."

"Where is she?"

The analyst craned his neck to check. "Not there, sir."

No shit, Carpenter thought. "What about Fromm? Has he been in?"

The analyst turned his seat. "Uh. He was. Saw him a little while ago."

Carpenter grabbed the secure land line phone on the man's desk. Punched in one. "Lock the building. Take into custody Louise Wingo and Fromm, head of Tech." Carpenter pointed at the analyst's screens. "Track their phones. ASAP!"

The man rapidly typed. "I've only got Wingo's. She's in the building." He pointed. "Down the hall. Fromm is dark. That's weird."

Carpenter sprinted to the hall leading to the break area and restrooms for Technical. The break room was empty. Carpenter shoved open the door to the ladies room. Louise was on the floor, her long blond hair cascaded around her head and haloed by a pool of glistening blood. There was a line of red on her right cheek where her face had been slashed.

Carpenter hit the red button on the intercom just inside the door. "Security and Medical to Technical."

A klaxon blared and red lights came on, urgently blinking. Carpenter knelt next to Louise, worried about the amount of blood. He put a hand on her throat, felt a faint pulse. Ripped off his shirt and gently pressed it against the gash in her scalp, afraid there might be a fracture beneath. Or worse, bleeding in the brain.

Louise stirred, which was an encouraging sign. She moaned and her eyes flickered, trying to blink out blood.

"Take it easy," Carpenter said. "You'll be fine. Medical is on the way."

"Fromm did it," Louise's voice was barely audible.

Carpenter kept the pressure with one hand, while he gripped her hand with the other. "You're going to be all right," he reassured.

Louise squeezed tight, distressed. "He's the infection. I broke the encryption for his private messages. That lawyer in New York. Money. Fromm sold us out for money. He must have had a tracer on his data, though, to alert him. I should have . . . ." her voice drifted off as her eyes rolled back.

"Damn it!" Carpenter yelled. "Where's medical?"

SHANE'S WORDS OF WISDOM #8

There is no we and they until they fuck up.
Shane's Addendum: We are always 'they'.

Self-explanatory.

SATURDAY EARLY MORNING

Shane and Phoebe hurried after Lucien to the barn.

"What's with the Snidely Whiplash mustache?" Phoebe asked. "He'd be cute without it."

"I'm told it's a long story," Shane said as he slid open the door and they entered the barn.

"Probably boring," Phoebe said.

Lucien had the phone on speaker and the Duke, Duchess and Field Marshal were gathered round it at the end of the table.

"I've pled with Guillermo," the Bishop was saying, "but he insists."

"I'm sure you were convincing in your sincerity," the Duchess said coldly. She glanced over at Shane, gave Phoebe a once-over, then focused on the phone.

"She really a Duchess?" Phoebe whispered to Shane.

"Doesn't she look like it?" Shane replied in a low voice.

"Yeah, in a starving, *Frozen* sorta way."

"You were the ones who left Andova contrary to tradition," the Bishop said. "We could have resolved this in Andova."

"No," the Duchess said, "we could not. Because Drusilla is mentally ill."

"There is no need—" the Bishop began, but a woman's harsh voice overrode him.

"I'll see you strung up on a gibbet, rotting, until the birds have plucked your eyes out and ripped every tiny morsel of flesh from your body."

"Ain't gonna be much with the Duchess," Phoebe whispered. "Looks like she keeps in shape."

If a stick is a shape, Shane thought.

"Ah, Drusilla," the Duchess said. "How unpleasant to hear your voice. Are you finding Guillermo as repulsive as he has always been?"

"You forget, I've been with the Duke," Drusilla responded. "I know what you'll be getting and it's not much."

"Women are the worst," Phoebe confided to Shane. "Sometimes in good ways, but not this time."

Drusilla went on: "But *you* already know what you are getting, don't you?" she pointed out. "Is he there? Your bastard?"

The Duke put a hand on the Duchess' forearm. "Easy," he whispered.

Shane and Phoebe exchanged a confused glance.

"You dare exile *me*?" Drusilla demanded. "Take a pedestal of moral high ground? After your sins? Your immorality? Your wantonness? I know what you truly desire. You speak of passing power to the people, but the truth is the opposite. You want to make Lucien a king! Your illegitimate bastard with the Duke!" By the end of her short diatribe, Drusilla was screeching.

"Your Graces," the Bishop pleaded, with some commotion in the background. "Please. Let's conduct ourselves with dignity."

"This is getting juicy," Phoebe whispered to Shane.

The Duke spoke up. "Get to the point, Bishop. What do you want?"

"I want peace," the Bishop said. "I want things to be as they were.

It is you and the Duchess who have upset the order of things and threaten the Great Charter. And now there are consequences. Terrible ones, but I bear no responsibility."

"Why are you calling?" the Duke pressed.

"The Duchess Drusilla Navarro is claiming her right under the Great Charter, to invoke *Lacessere*."

"It's *not* her right," the Duke said. "She has no rights as she is the *former* Duchess. I speak for my family."

"Divorce is not recognized by the Charter or by the church unless the marriage is nullified," the Bishop replied. "Which the church has *not* done, as you know. Thus, she is still legally Duchess according to the Church and the Great Charter. This wedding will be an abomination. And there is also the issue of Lucien."

"You do not dare speak of my son!" the Duchess snapped.

"Whoa," Phoebe muttered. "Momma Grizzly is pissed."

Shane stared at Lucien, who did not appear surprised at his mother's revelation or comment.

"This wedding *will* happen," the Duchess continued. "And Lucien has no bearing on this, other than as Captain of the Guard."

Guillermo spoke. "*Lacessere* will occur. Nine in the morning local time. We will be there. Then the wedding will no longer be an issue."

The line went dead.

"Some anger issues there all around," Phoebe's voice filled the void, which drew attention to her.

Shane quickly did the introductions. "Duke Navarro, Duchess Embrie, Field Marshal Ricard. This is Phoebe."

"Charmed," the Duchess said brusquely.

"M'lady," the Duke said with a smile and the Field Marshal spared a nod.

"How y'all doing?" Phoebe said. "Drusilla sounds like a real bitch."

The Duchess' lips twitched. "An appropriate observation."

"We killed an infiltrator," Lucien said. That got the Duke and Duchess' attention. "He was trying to wire the bridge for remote detonation."

"Why?" The Duchess asked. "Who killed him?"

"They were trying to isolate this area," Lucien said. "I assume to keep local authorities at bay and prevent anyone from escaping."

"Who killed him?" the Duchess repeated.

"I did," Shane said.

The Duchess nodded her thanks.

"Anyone we know?" the Field Marshal asked Lucien.

Lucien shook his head. "By his tattoos, he was German."

"What is wrong with your arm, Lucien?" the Duchess asked.

"A minor wound," Lucien said. "Vicente tended to it."

The Duchess turned to the Field Marshal. "Blood has been spilled. We are at war."

"No shit," Phoebe muttered to Shane. "Lead with the headline, people."

LISA LIVIA SLID naked under the down comforter reveling in the excellent sheets. Agnes had really done a great job with the place and splurged on the important things. Lisa Livia stared at the powder blue ceiling of the master bedroom on the top floor of Two Rivers. Agnes had always been good with color.

She heard Rhett snoring at the foot of the bed, in his own smaller doggie bed that matched the comforter. He'd followed her upstairs, laboring with the steps until she picked him up. The old dog's presence was a surprising solace.

She checked her phone for a message from Carpenter, but there was nothing so she put it back on the nightstand. She punched one of the many pillows, adjusting it. She remembered how much Agnes had talked about this room and her dream for it and Two Rivers. Lisa

Livia didn't think the dream had included a medieval fight to the death.

Rhett gave a semi-bark, more of irritation than alarm, then Lisa Livia heard people coming up the stairs. She hopped out of the big, king-sized bed and put on a long t-shirt, as there was a knock on the door.

"Lisa Livia?" Shane called out.

"Yeah?" She pulled the door open, then stepped back, because behind Shane was Lucien, dressed all in black and holding a very long gun with a bulky scope on it, and a small girl, actually a woman, dressed in a bulky black sweater and with a gun and a sword and this was just crazier and crazier. "What the fuck?"

Shane pointed toward a corner of the bedroom. "The ladder for the attic is there. We need to get on the roof to take a look see. This is Phoebe. She works with me. Carpenter sent her."

"Look see at what?" Lisa Livia demanded, but Shane had moved past and was shoving a chair under the cord hanging from the trap door. "Where's Carpenter?"

Lucien smiled at her, the corners of his mustache twitching up. "You look lovely this evening, m'lady."

"Geez," Phoebe muttered. "You guys are all the same. Eye on the ball, Snidely."

Lisa Livia felt exposed in the t-shirt, but Phoebe was already with Shane, who pulled the ladder down and clambered up. Phoebe was gone as quickly. But Lucien lingered. "I am sorry we have brought this trouble here."

"You should be," Lisa Livia said. "What's going on?"

"We believe there is an observer across the water. Miss Phoebe and Shane will be swimming out to neutralize it." He hefted the gun. "I'll provide security from the roof."

"That's a big gun," Lisa Livia said.

"It'll get the job done, if need be," Lucien acknowledged. Reluctantly he walked past, slung the rifle next to the pack on his back, and climbed up the ladder.

Only after he was gone did Lisa Livia realize that the night light behind her had silhouetted her inside the t-shirt.

"Damn right I look good," Lisa Livia said to herself as she pulled on a pair of sweatpants and grabbed one of Agnes' sweaters from the closet. Then she sat in the rocking chair in the other corner to wait. She didn't bother to check her phone.

"There." Phoebe pointed toward a low dark smudge across the Intracoastal. She wore her goggles and was lying with Shane and Lucien on the narrow widow's walk on top of Two Rivers. There was a brick chimney at either side of the walk. "On the north end, about two meters from the water."

"To the left of the slight hump?" Lucien asked.

"Yeah," Phoebe said.

"Got it," Lucien said. He extended the bipod for the rifle and settled it in place. "Let me check thermal." He switched on the bulky scope after removing the NVGs. He pressed his eye against the scope. "You're right," he finally said. "An image in the high grass."

"You know," Phoebe suggested, "we could just shoot whoever it is right now."

"Not very sporting," Lucien said.

"Sniping is excellent sporting," Phoebe said. "Remember, he can shoot back. Not like hunting."

"We want to take him alive," Shane said, "in order to interrogate."

"All right, all right," Phoebe said. "Don't get your tightey-whiteys in a bunch."

"I will shoot if either of you are threatened," Lucien promised.

"You sure?" Shane asked.

"I'm sure."

"Okey-dokey," Phoebe said.

Lucien pulled his eye back from the scope. "What is wrong with your leg?"

Shane had noted the hitch in Phoebe's step and the way she favored one leg climbing up the ladder. And the stumble on landing.

"Tweaked it," Phoebe said. "It's fine."

"We have a medic," Lucien said. "Perhaps have Vicente take a look at it?"

Phoebe sniffed the air. "It will be dawn in less than three hours. We need to get out there before then."

Shane wondered how she could tell time by smelling. He discreetly checked his watch, but she was right. There wasn't much room for error. "All right," he said to her. "You lead. I'll follow."

They made their way back to the ladder and descended. Lisa Livia was in the rocking chair.

"Nice bed," Phoebe commented as they climbed down the attic ladder to the master bedroom.

"Keep moving," Shane said.

"This your lair?" Phoebe asked Shane.

"Get out," Lisa Livia ordered from the rocking chair.

"Sorry," Shane said to her. He pointed to the stairs and watched the grimace on Phoebe's face as she hit the second step. He paused to grab his rubber soled water shoes from the closet.

"What's going on?" Lisa Livia said. "Where's Lucien?"

"He's covering us from the roof. Phoebe and I are going for a swim."

"How romantic," Lisa Livia said. "A moonlight swim."

Shane closed the door behind him.

They made it to ground level and stopped in the kitchen. Shane sat down and took off his boots and pulled on the water shoes. Phoebe stripped off the sweater, carefully placing it over a chair. She strapped the sword across her back and hung a pistol around her waist. Shane went with a belt holding his pistol and dagger.

"Ready for the prom?" Phoebe asked. "Got a corsage for me?"

"Flowers will be coming in a few hours," Shane said. "I hope you like red."

"I noticed the banners and other stuff," Phoebe said. "A red wedding? You're shitting me, right?"

"They don't have cable in Andova. Ready?" Shane asked Phoebe.

"Nothing but good times ahead."

$$\mathcal{LL}$$

Lisa Livia climbed the ladder to the attic, then the steps to the widow's walk. "Don't shoot," she called out before she pulled herself onto the roof.

Lucien was prone, rifle to shoulder, eye to scope. The pack was in front of him. He didn't look her way. "Be careful. It's a long way down."

"Mind if I join you?" Lisa Livia asked.

Several seconds of silence went by. "I have to keep my focus."

"I know. I'll be quiet. You won't even know I'm here."

"That is doubtful," Lucien murmured, but his focus was on the scope. "Please lie down so you're not outlined."

"What's wrong with your arm?" Lisa Livia asked.

"An injury."

"What kind of injury?" Lisa Livia asked.

"A bullet. But a very small one and the wound is clean and taken care of."

"'A very small one'?" Lisa Livia repeated as she lay next to Lucien, close, but not touching.

"Inconsequential," Lucien said.

"I don't believe you," Lisa Livia said. "How did you get shot? I heard a gun fired a while ago."

"An accident," Lucien said.

Picking up a definite 'do not disturb' sign about whatever had happened, Lisa Livia changed subjects. "Where are Shane and Phoebe?"

"Going into the water," Lucien said. He lifted the rifle and pulled the backpack out. "Put this in front of you. It's made of Kevlar."

"Don't you need to rest your rifle on it?"

"I have a bipod," Lucien said as he flipped that down.

THE WATER WAS WARM, which was a pleasant surprise. Phoebe crouched down and waded out as far as she could underneath the dock walkway, using it as concealment. She didn't bother to check if Shane was following. She'd picked out a particularly tall tree on the barrier island beyond the shoal as her navigation point and kept her focus there.

Before she got to the floating dock, she leaned forward and began a breast stroke across the Intracoastal. Her leg hurt but it worked. The problem she hadn't forethought was the ace bandage was now soaked and throwing off her stroke. She adjusted and filed that lesson-learned away.

It was three hundred meters to the shoal, and halfway across Phoebe rolled onto her back and shifted to arms folded on her chest and finning, but keeping the feet from breaking the surface. This slowed her down, but was covert. She noted that Shane mirrored her action.

The hardest part was having to turn her head every five kicks to stay oriented and on course.

"THEY'RE ALMOST THERE," Lucien said. "You know, you are a distraction."

"Oh," Lisa Livia said and began to get up. "I'm sorry."

"No, stay down, please. A pleasant one. You have that same smell. Intoxicating."

"I washed off the sunscreen."

"I know."

SHANE CAME up beside Phoebe who had turned over once more, holding position against the tide with her hands and toes in the mud, only the top of her head above water. They were twenty feet from the shoal, which had an embankment of millions of shells deposited by birds after being cracked open and the interior eaten.

Phoebe pointed to the left as she drew her sword. Shane edged that way, staying in the water. He pulled his dagger out, debated, then consigned himself to gripping it between his teeth as he needed his hands to stealthily negotiate the shells as he moved up on the shoal.

"THEY'RE THERE," Lucien said.

Lisa Livia became as still as possible, worried even a loud breath could disturb his concentration. She watched as Lucien's finger curled over the trigger.

A chill settled on her, not one that came and went, but persistent, as she realized that if Lucien pulled that sliver of metal, a person would die. A stranger, one who might mean her harm, true, but a human being.

For the first time she gained true insight into the way Carpenter acted. Why he always seemed preoccupied. He gave orders that led to this. And people like Shane and Phoebe executed them.

SHANE FELT EXPOSED as he crawled through the tall grass, knowing it gave no cover, just concealment.

That ended when he heard a yell, a man's, directly ahead. Shane jumped to his feet and sprinted forward. Phoebe was silhouetted in the darkness, kneeling over a man lying on his back, unable to get up, nor trying to. Because Phoebe's wakizashi was impaled in his right shoulder and her hands were holding it tight.

"Top of the morning," Phoebe said as Shane joined her. "Looks like it's gonna be a great day."

The man was draped in a ghillie suit and his face was smeared with camouflage paint. A .50 caliber Barrett sniper rifle lay next to him in a well-designed blind, facing Two Rivers. The rifle looked familiar to Shane.

Phoebe pointed at a small pile of white paper next to his head. "Smoking is bad for your health." She kept one hand on the hilt of the wakizashi while she crouched and looked through the Barrett's scope.

Shane pulled the radio off the man's vest, ripping the earpiece out. "How often do you make com checks?"

The man didn't respond. He glared at Shane.

"Hey," Phoebe said, getting his attention. "I'm the person with the sword in you. There are people working in our field who enjoy inflicting pain. Maybe you do. I can assure you, I do not. It is a tool of the job. Like a good blade or firearm. My pleasure derives from the acquisition of knowledge and mission accomplishment. So, you understand that the pain you are experiencing now, is an unnecessary byproduct of what we truly desire? Are you gonna make me happy?"

There was no response.

Phoebe sighed. "I'm going to wait for the beautiful sunrise while you think on it." She turned east, but in doing so twisted the hilt of the wakizashi.

The man bit back a scream and scrambled with his good hand and both feet to try and turn with the blade but he was painfully behind.

"Bet you get great sunrises here, don't you?" Phoebe said to Shane.

Lucien pulled back from the scope and turned it off. "Everyone is fine."

Lisa Livia took a deep breath. "That's good."

Lucien sat. "This is beautiful country. Very different from our mountains. Warmer. Lusher."

"I don't want anyone to die today," Lisa Livia said.

Lucien gave her a sharp glance and Lisa Livia thought: *Oh shit.* She stood and held out her hand. "Let's go downstairs."

· · ·

"IT JUST OCCURRED TO ME," Shane said, as the sniper writhed under Phoebe's blade, "that we don't have a way of taking a prisoner back with us."

"I thought of that before we left," Phoebe said. "I figured we'd just kill him and leave him here for the gators."

Shane had no idea if Phoebe knew alligators primarily stayed in fresh water or not, but he went along. "There'll be nothing left of him by noon. They're probably smelling the blood in the water already."

"I am just observation," the man said with a Spanish accent.

"That's what they all say until they pull the trigger," Phoebe said.

Shane lay down next to him and lifted the butt of the Barrett. It was definitely his from Montana, which pissed him off. He peered through the scope. It was aimed at Two Rivers. The thermal outlined two people on the top of the house. Shane blinked and checked. Definitely two, although one was hidden behind something. As he watched one stood, then the other and they disappeared into the house. "Damn it," he muttered. He got up. "What's your name?"

"Ronaldo."

Shane held up the radio. "How often do you do a com check, Ronaldo?"

"No com checks."

"None?" Shane demanded.

Phoebe turned to look down on him, the sword moving with her and he gasped. "Stop!"

"The man asked you a question," Phoebe said.

"Nothing. I swear."

"I don't believe him," Phoebe said.

"Doesn't matter," Shane said. "We don't have the gun at our backs. They don't have time to get someone else out here in broad daylight."

Phoebe twitched the hilt. "Are you really here for observation? Why do you have the rifle? Childhood insecurities?"

"Just in case."

"'Just in case' what?" Shane asked. "The *Lacessere* is bladed weapons."

Phoebe pressed a knee on Ronaldo's chest, one hand near the blade. She gave it a ping with her forefinger. "What does Guillermo have planned?"

"He will do *Lacessere*," Ronaldo said. "But . . ."

"But what?" Phoebe demanded.

"The queen bitch is crazy. She will not allow defeat. If things go wrong . . ."

"How many of you are there?" Shane asked.

Ronaldo closed his eyes. Phoebe made a clicking noise and he opened them.

"Twenty-two," Ronaldo said.

That's not good, Shane thought. Of course, that was minus two, so twenty. Lucien had his eleven men. The Duke. The Field Marshal. He looked down. And he and Phoebe. Still not optimal.

"So, I kill him?" Phoebe asked. She sniffed. "Motor."

Shane didn't hear anything, nor smell it, but the Intracoastal carried a fair amount of traffic. He looked up and down and then spotted the running lights of a familiar, sixteen-foot Boston Whaler trolling from the direction of Keyes in the lessening darkness of pre-dawn.

"Please, no," Ronaldo begged. "The Duchess, Drusilla, she forced me to fight. She threatened my family."

"Oh yeah, right," Phoebe said.

"I swear on Saint Ingrid," Ronaldo said.

"Who?" Phoebe said.

"He's probably serious," Shane said.

"I will depart," Ronaldo promised. "You will never see me again."

"You are gonna depart," Phoebe promised. "Who's inbound?" she asked Shane.

"An old acquaintance," Shane said, debating whether to lie down and hide from the detective or catch a ride back across to Two Rivers. The prisoner and the long rifle might take some explaining.

"Take your blade out and bandage him," Shane said to Phoebe. He appreciated it when she immediately followed through. Then he walked out of the blind toward the channel, shells crunching under his feet, and waved. A small searchlight came on and Xavier briefly ran it across Shane and the shoal before turning pointing it downward to provide indirect light without blinding anyone and allowing him some idea of what was ahead.

"Out for an early morning swim?" Xavier called out. "I'm always impressed with those who maintain physical fitness. I find it an admirable trait; that is one to be admired from a distance."

"Helping a stranded wayfarer," Shane said. He gestured and Phoebe got the sniper to his feet, his shoulder crudely bandaged.

"He doesn't appear dressed for a morning cavort with the dolphins," Xavier said, expertly stopping the boat just short of the shoal.

"It's complicated," Shane said.

"Isn't it always with you?" Xavier sighed. "You're going to ruin my weekend, aren't you? The young fellow in camouflage appears injured. Or would that be wounded, given the weapon on the young woman's back?"

"It's a long story," Shane said. "Could you give us a ride across to Two Rivers?"

Xavier waved for them to board. "It's not far enough of a journey to do this mystery justice."

As Shane helped Ronaldo wade to the boat, Phoebe gathered up the Barrett and radio.

"It's not the season for duck hunting," Xavier said. "And that's not a duck gun."

Shane lifted Ronaldo into the boat, then grabbed the Barrett from Phoebe. "We were zeroing in the scope."

"I heard no shots," Xavier said. "And your bleeding man got all dressed for the event," Xavier backed the boat out of the shallow water. "You know I'm not stupid, Shane. I'll ask you to pay me a modicum of respect on that front."

"It's a long story and don't you want to enjoy your weekend?" Shane asked.

"I suspect my weekend is already ruined. There's been odd goings-on. Besides this."

"Such as?"

"We had a pick-up truck stolen and then found on the side of the road between Two Rivers and the airport," Xavier started with.

"Between the airport and Keyes," Shane said. "What does that have to do with me?"

"Didn't say it did," Xavier said. "You asked. I answered. The pick-up was wiped clean of prints. Kids snatching a truck for a joy ride don't wipe it clean."

"So?"

"There's a private plane at the Keyes airport with the Roman Catholic church emblem on the tail," Xavier said. "Anything to do with your wedding?"

"The Bishop who will be officiating the wedding," Shane said.

"What kind of Bishop has his own plane?"

"This one."

"I'll rack that one on the odd shelf." Xavier pointed in the direction they were headed. "Hammond found a motorcycle a mile down the road from Two Rivers. Covered in brush. No plates. Ran the serial number. Stolen in Savannah two days ago. Also, no prints. Perhaps your wedding guests are doing some illegal joy-riding?"

"And?" Shane asked, realizing he and Lucien hadn't searched far enough for the bridge bomber's ride.

"I once inadvertently watched a horror movie," Xavier said, "and the plot was about a place that was the nexus of trouble." He nodded toward Two Rivers where a couple of torches flickered near the gazebo. "The center of the vortex."

"We're just having a wedding," Shane said. "We've done it before."

"Oh, yes," Xavier said. "I remember that. Definitely vortexy."

"We've had seven weddings since Maria's with no trouble. While you were gone. Maybe look in the mirror, Mrs. Fletcher."

"By the way," Xavier said as he slowed the boat and angled it toward the light on the end of the dock, "Hammond keeps asking if Maria is around."

"She isn't," Shane said. "You should advise him to give up on married women, given your experience."

Xavier shot Shane a hard look. "Don't poke me, son."

"Sorry," Shane said.

Xavier stopped the boat short of the dock. He turned to the others. "And you are?"

Phoebe smiled, dimple wrinkling. "I'm Phoebe. Friend of the family."

"Which family?" Xavier said.

"The bride's."

"And who might that be?" Xavier asked.

"The Duchess," Phoebe said.

"And you?" Xavier asked Ronaldo.

"I am with the groom's side. The Duke."

Xavier frowned. "I'm just a low brow American, but I watched *The Queen*. Something's not adding up."

"Did you do the Google search, I suggested?" Shane asked.

"I've been busy," Xavier said. "Detecting." He gestured at the .50 caliber Barrett. "Since when do wedding guests carry sniper rifles and spears and swords?"

"It's thematic," Shane said.

"Times of yore when deeds of derring-do were done?" Xavier asked. "Manly men doing manly things with other men? The sheep have to worry? The rifle mixes the motif, though." He sat and looked over his shoulder. "It's Saturday. It was my day off. I've only been back a week."

"You must be bad juju," Shane said. "Our very own Mrs. Fletcher."

"We're going to sit here until you tell me what's going on."

"You want the long or short version?" Shane asked.

"I want the one that keeps me from taking this boat to Keyes and having Hammond waiting at the dock with cuffs."

SHANE'S WORDS OF WISDOM #9

Fortune is generally on the side of superior firepower.
Shane's Addendum: Colt .45 beats four aces

Sometimes bigger is better.
Don't bring a knife to a gun fight.
Except . . . .

SATURDAY MORNING

LL

"Hope you're hungry," Joey said as Lisa Livia entered the kitchen of Two Rivers.

She'd woken tucked in and comfy, but to an empty bed. She had no memory of Lucien leaving. Then again, she'd collapsed utterly exhausted and completely content into a deep sleep only to be awoken by the irritating chirping of the alarm on her phone after not enough rest. There were things she did have memories of and she'd reveled in them for a few moments before reluctantly sliding out of bed and getting dressed. There was, however, a large blood stain on the sheets and she'd stripped the bed. The last thing she remembered was telling Lucien to see Vicente and get re-bandaged. She was afraid she'd over-exerted him, but didn't regret it at the time, although she felt a surge of guilt now.

Joey was working several pans and the smell of bacon filled the room despite the powerful exhaust running.

"What about the army?" Lisa Livia asked as she made a beeline to the coffee pot.

"That's why I'm cooking here," Joey said. "Don't want to waste the food. They ate army stuff—called them iron rations-- at the barn. Stuff in packets." Joey was appalled. "The Field Marshal told me they were on a war time footing and needed to act like it. Can you believe they packed rations for a wedding?"

"I can," Lisa Livia said as she poured the coffee. "They also brought guns and grenades." Although she doubted the Duchess had packed any in her luggage. She took a sip. It was obvious Joey had made it as she immediately perked up.

Joey was still on the food. "When we hit the mattresses, I ate some of the best food of my life. It's where I learned a lot of my recipes. Everyone took a shot at it, no pun intended, and there were a lot of great cooks among the fellows."

"Cooks among crooks," Lisa Livia noted.

"Lucien snuck out the front door a few minutes ago," Joey noted. "Like he was on some sort of super-secret mission. Or coming from one."

"He did?"

"He did. Guess he missed breakfast with the men."

"Where's Shane?"

Joey pointed toward the dock, visible in the first light of dawn. "Speak of the devil and he appears, bringing all sorts of folk with him. Guess I need to put more bacon on."

Lisa Livia looked out the window. Shane was coming down the walkway. Xavier next to him, along with a man draped in what looked like wet Spanish moss and Phoebe from the night before. Shane was carrying a rifle. "This will be interesting."

"Seems like your morning was already interesting," Joey noticed as he peeled off slices of bacon and dropped them on the grill.

"Remember, Joey, I'm a Fortunato," Lisa Livia said. "I can hurt you."

Joey laughed. "You're a Fortunato for sure."

"That's the biggest gun I've ever seen," Lisa Livia said as the group approached the house. "Why do men have to compensate so much?" Now that they were closer, she saw in daylight that Phoebe was a young woman with badly colored reddish-black, damp hair slicked back and dressed in a one-piece black outfit. With a sword on her back. "This is going to be really interesting. But not good interesting."

One of Lucien's men came running over. Xavier and Shane halted, along with the camouflaged man, who had a bloody shoulder and hands flex-cuffed behind his back. They were discussing something as Phoebe came up the steps and entered the kitchen.

She looked at the stove. "Breakfast is the most important meal of the day." She stuck her hand out. "We weren't properly introduced earlier. You must be Lisa Livia. I'm Phoebe. I'm a, uh, colleague of Shane's."

Lisa Livia automatically returned the handshake, noting that Phoebe had finely honed facial features and the muscles under the skin tight outfit rippled. The look in those deep blue eyes reminded her of someone, and then she realized it was the same as Carpenter's and Shane's and Joey at times.

Phoebe turned to the cook. "And you must be Joey. Love your book."

With that, Lisa Livia knew Joey would throw himself on a grenade for this stranger.

Xavier came in behind Phoebe. "Smells good."

"Who invited you?" Joey demanded.

"Circumstances," Xavier said.

"More like an ill wind blew your boat off course," Joey griped.

Lisa Livia noted that Lucien's soldier was pushing the wounded man in the direction of the barn, none too gently. She suddenly realized that was the person who would have died if Lucien had pulled the trigger. She shivered at the thought.

Shane entered. He put the rifle down on the far counter and Lisa Livia winced at the potential for scarring the top. Phoebe placed her short sword next to the rifle. Lisa Livia was glad Agnes wasn't here to see her counter top turned into an armory.

Shane's phone buzzed. "Excuse me," he said and stepped outside and walked out of earshot.

"You're from Carpenter?" Lisa Livia asked Phoebe who was helping herself to the coffee, pouring it into a Mob Food mug.

A line creased Phoebe's smooth forehead as if that was an inappropriate question. "Who?"

"Carpenter," Lisa Livia said. "Big guy. Black. Says 'stay centered' often. Runs some sort of super-secret group for the government. Worries a lot. Sound familiar?"

"I meet a lot of people in my line of work," Phoebe said. "And I'm bad with names."

"What line of work is that?" Lisa Livia asked.

"I paint houses," Phoebe said and Joey paused, looking at her. Phoebe graced him with a sweet smile and cold eyes.

Xavier had been behind Phoebe and poured himself a cup of coffee, then waved the empty pot. "Coffee's out."

"Make more," Lisa Livia snapped.

"Where're the grounds?" Xavier asked as he opened the top of the brewer to add water.

"You're a detective," Lisa Livia said. "Figure it out."

Shane spoke up from the doorway. "Be nice, Lisa Livia."

"Was that Carpenter?"

"Yeah."

"Is he coming?" Lisa Livia demanded.

"He'll be here in time for the wedding. There were some problems he had to deal with at work."

Lisa Livia tried to tamp down the surge of anger; that Carpenter would tell Shane but not let her know, despite what she'd said. Then she remembered Lucien and the anger dissipated.

Shane looked at Phoebe. "There was trouble last night in Technical, but we know who the infection is."

"Anyone else you want to invite in to discuss classified material in front of?" Phoebe asked Shane as she checked the frying bacon. "I like it crisp," she informed Joey.

"That's the way I make it," Joey said. "How do you want your eggs?"

"Surprise me," Phoebe said.

"My kind of gal," Joey said.

Phoebe shifted back to Shane. "What happened in Technical?"

"Louise was hurt," Shane informed Phoebe. Lisa Livia noted that name grabbed Phoebe's undivided attention.

"How bad?" Phoebe asked.

"She's in the hospital," Shane said, "but will be fine. Hit on the head, some blood, but nothing broken. Cut on the face. No internal injuries."

"Fromm," Phoebe said.

Shane nodded. "He set me up, set you up, and when Louise discovered it, he attacked her. Luckily, he's incompetent in that area. He's gone dark."

"I'll find him and kill him." Phoebe said it was such calm conviction that even Joey paused in his stove work once more. Then the old man nodded approvingly.

Lisa Livia figured he was probably thinking this was the daughter he'd never wanted but wouldn't mind having, then he flipped an omelet.

"I am an officer of the law," Xavier reminded them. Which everyone ignored.

"First things, first," Shane said. "Let's get through today."

"Roger that," Phoebe said. "One clusterfuck at a time." But her jaw was tight and she emanated raging cold as if the Duchess upset about sunburn was mixed with Joey in vengeance mode.

"I'm behind on a few things here," Lisa Livia said as she sat down at the table. The binder was in the center, but no one was paying attention to it. She gestured at the big rifle. "You got that over on the shoal?" And then she realized that the young man who'd had it could have as easily shot her or Lucien and she shivered. And *then* she realized that Lucien had given her his pack and put it in front of her as protection. Which meant he'd been exposed. She gripped the coffee mug tighter.

Joey tore off some paper towels and put them on a platter. Then began laying bacon on it.

"Don't worry about it," Shane said, preoccupied with the news from Carpenter.

Lisa Livia picked up the binder and threw it at him.

Shane was bringing his hands up to protect himself but Phoebe snatched it out of the air. "Breakfast always this much fun here?" She put it on the counter, out of range of Lisa Livia. She tapped it and Lisa Livia noticed that her fingernails were gnawed to the quick. "Hey, tabs. Cool. I love organization."

"Food," Joey announced putting the platter of bacon on the table and rapidly loading plates with omelets. "Chow down."

"Scooch over," Phoebe said to Lisa Livia as she slid onto the bench against the wall, next to her. "Better eat up. Big day ahead."

Lisa Livia gave way barely an inch but it was enough for Phoebe to fit.

Joey finished the plates and took one of the chairs and Shane took the other. Xavier grabbed a chair from the corner and dragged it over. Rhett, smelling bacon, ambled in and pushed his way through the legs to take his rightful place underneath the table.

"Want me to do the blessings?" Phoebe asked.

"What?" Joey asked.

Phoebe laughed. "Pulling your leg, old timer."

Lisa Livia could tell by the scowl on Joey's forehead that he was reconsidering *the daughter I never wanted but would like*, but then Phoebe tore into the food and the look disappeared.

Lisa Livia felt Rhett's nose push between her leg and Phoebe's.

"What's his name?" Phoebe asked.

"Rhett," Lisa Livia said.

Phoebe gave the dog a piece of bacon. *"Great balls of fire! It's Rhett'."*

"They don't quote that movie much in these parts," Lisa Livia said.

"I didn't name the dog," Phoebe said as she fed Rhett more bacon.

"What's going to happen?" Lisa Livia asked, addressing Shane. "Please tell me this has all been a bad dream." *Not all bad*, she reminded herself.

"I'm afraid not," the Duchess said from the kitchen door. The Duke was behind her. While she wore her long red coat over an ornate red dress, the Duke was dressed in red breeches and a red, puffy sleeved shirt. He had not donned his armor yet, but had a foil at his side, the blade exposed. Lisa Livia noted that the Field Marshal and Lucien remained on the porch, both dressed in the ceremonial outfit, sans armor, but plus swords. A new, thicker bandage, decorated Lucien's upper right arm. Lisa Livia felt a surge of guilt, but not regret.

"Want some hot chow?" Joey asked, pushing back his seat and hurrying to the stove.

"We ate with the men," the Duke said as they came in. "But a cup of tea would be wonderful."

That threw Joey off. "'Tea'?"

"I'll make it," the Duchess said which threw Lisa Livia off even more. The Duchess went to the stove, took the tea pot and filled it, then set it back on the stove and fired up the burner.

"Thank you, my dear." The Duke glanced over his shoulder. "Lucien? Would you like some food? You missed the Field Marshall's iron rations this morning."

"I'm fine," Lucien said.

"I'm sure you are," the Duchess said, glancing at Lisa Livia who met her gaze.

The Duke nodded at Shane and Phoebe. "Thank you for securing the back door. Ronaldo is a misguided youth and Drusilla has exerted dangerous influence on his family. I am glad you spared him. He is redeemable."

Phoebe snorted, but it was more a lazy *yeah, right*, than anything that would rate on the Duchess disdain scale.

"You still think they're going to follow the law of the *Lacessere*?" Shane asked. "So far they've tried to mine the bridge and positioned a sniper. That's not exactly covered in the Great Charter, is it?"

"Wait!" Lisa Livia said. "The bridge? Agnes loves that bridge."

"Don't worry," Shane said.

"It's all she talked about on the phone for like a month," Lisa Livia continued. "About drove me crazy. I learned more about trusses and spanners than I ever wanted or needed to. It was like she was building the Golden Gate."

"Don't worry," Shane repeated. "We stopped him."

"Who stopped him?" Lisa Livia asked. "Stopped who? How? Is that how Lucien got shot?"

Shane exchanged a look with Phoebe as the tea kettle began to whistle. The Duchess busied herself putting tea bags in two cups and pouring the hot water, while no one answered Lisa Livia's question.

"You gonna eat that bacon?" Phoebe asked her.

Lisa Livia eyed the knives and the hanging frying pans, deciding which would be the most convenient weapon.

"Can we speak outside?" the Duke asked Shane, now that the Duchess had her tea.

"Sure," he said. He walked outside with the royalty.

Xavier was leaning back in his seat, watching and listening carefully, but not commenting.

"Can I have some more?" Phoebe asked Joey, holding up a plate that appeared licked clean to Lisa Livia. "Pretty please?"

"What did Ronaldo tell you?" the Duchess asked. "What are we facing?"

"If you think he's redeemable," Shane said, "you can ask him yourself."

"We did," Lucien said. "We want to see if it matches what he told you while there was a blade in his shoulder."

Shane relayed the brief amount of intelligence he and Phoebe had garnered.

"Twenty-two is also what he told us," the Field Marshal said when he was done. "The odds are not good."

"They can only use twelve for *Lacessere*," the Duke said. "He will field those who used to be in the Guard, not the mercenaries. Those who know the way of the blade."

"And it's only twenty now," Lucien added, "minus the man under the bridge and Ronaldo."

The Field Marshal wasn't dissuaded. "There is still time to negotiate. Remember, Ronaldo said that if it appears they might lose, Drusilla will not hesitate to break the rules."

"He's right about that last bit," Shane said. "You can't expect to win by sticking to the Charter."

"We must try," the Duke said.

"We have the perimeter covered with early warning devices," the Field Marshal said. "We will know if anyone attempts to approach in plenty of time to change from being prepared for *Lacessere* to a more modern assault."

"Where are you monitoring this?" Shane asked, wondering why any of them believed the other side would follow the rules.

"We're set up in the main area of the barn," Lucien said. "We've got motion sensors and video with thermal and visual."

"But you didn't know about the sniper," Shane pointed out.

"We'll be ready for any contingency," the Field Marshal said.

"We must be—" the Duchess began but Lucien held up his hand and pressed a finger against his ear, listening. "There's a truck at the bridge. A woman named Maisie is demanding admittance."

Shane tried to reorient. "Flowers."

"Ah," the Duke said. "The arrangements. They must be allowed."

The Duchess nodded at Lucien.

"I'll go with him," Shane said, "or Maisie will freak out." He paused and spoke to the trifecta of Duke, Duchess and Field Marshal. "Might want to figure out how you want to deal with this if it goes sideways. Which it's going to."

He headed down the driveway, Lucien at his side.

"How's the arm?" Shane asked.

"It will heal."

"Yeah, but how is it?" Shane asked. "Seriously."

"There is difficulty with certain movements," Lucien allowed.

"Torn muscle," Shane said. "It *will* heal, but it's going to take a while. And you shouldn't be using it."

"I don't have much choice."

"A misplaced sense of honor can get people killed," Shane said.

Lucien didn't respond.

"I understand the way these things work," Shane said. "My uncle Joey does also, in a different way. But this isn't Lisa Livia's thing. She was on the roof with you, wasn't she?"

"Yes. I saw you check through the scope. But she was safe. My Kevlar pack was in front of her."

"Which means you left yourself exposed."

"Yes."

"Why? That was foolish."

"Perhaps," Lucien said. "She came up and I did not think it was the proper time to have an argument. She is a very strong-minded woman."

Shane couldn't argue that point, since he'd seen Lisa Livia when she was adamant. As they got closer, he spotted Maisie standing next to a large rental truck arguing with one of the soldiers.

"Good morning," Shane said, not even trying to dredge up a 'welcome to Two Rivers' smile.

Maisie Shuttle had a permanent frown and Shane wasn't sure if she had a '*welcome to anything*' smile in her repertoire.

"I've got the arrangements," Maisie complained, "and I'm on a tight schedule. You're not the only wedding around here today, you know. And where's Agnes?"

"But I bet this is the one paying you the most," Shane pointed out.

Maisie dialed it down a notch. "The flowers from Europe didn't get in until late and I was up all night finishing. And then, there was the last-minute special request. Really, people think I have nothing better to do?"

Lucien stepped forward and gave a slight bow. "Excuse me, m'lady. What last minute special request?"

Maisie blushed. "He said he was a friend of the family. Stopped by the shop yesterday. He paid cash, which, really, I wished more people did. He was very specific and even brought the arrangement. He just asked to have it delivered."

"Who was this?" Lucien asked. "Did he leave a name?"

"No, no name. Like I said, he paid cash. A big man. Gray beard. Spoke foreign, like not from these parts. Maybe from up north?"

"Guillermo," Lucien said to Shane. He smiled at Maisie and indicated the truck. "May we take a look?"

"Well," Maisie said, not certain. "It would be easier if you just let me in and start laying things out."

"I'd prefer to check first," Lucien said. "The man you describe is known for tasteless pranks and I wouldn't want to upset the Duke."

"'The Duke'?" Maisie repeated. "There's a Duke? No one told me there would be a Duke. This have anything to do with what Xavier's going around town asking about? What's going on? Where's Agnes? A real Duke?"

"Could you open the back of the truck, please?" Shane asked.

"M'Lady?" Lucien smiled at her and that worked better.

Shane thought Lucien might make a better 'welcome to Two Rivers' greeter.

They walked to the back of the truck as Maisie continued complaining. "And I couldn't fit all this in my van. I had to rent this. It's on the bill, you know. I don't want to hear any complaining. Seriously. You pay for what you get."

"Absolutely," Shane said. He took a step back as Maisie threw the handle and opened the gate.

"There's really a Duke here?" Maisie asked. "Like one of those English folk?"

There was an overwhelming sea of red, marred only by a pink and gold arrangement shaped in a shield. Even Shane, no connoisseur of arrangements, recognized that it was both distinctive and clashed.

"That's the one the guy paid me to bring," Maisie said apologetically. "He paid cash," she repeated as if that negated taste. "I've never seen the pink blooms before, but the gold dahlia's are classic."

"*Cercis siliquastrum*," Lucien said. "The pink blooms are from the Judas Tree. The dahlia represents the color of Drusilla's family crest. It will not be displayed."

"Okey-dokey," Shane said. "Tell you what," he said to Maisie. "Why don't you wait here while we offload the arrangements? It won't take us long."

"But that's *my* job! You don't 'offload' them!"

"It can't be that hard to put some flowers out," Shane said, which caused Maisie to stagger back and grasp her chest. Lucien looked at him and shook his head.

"M'Lady," Lucien said, which Shane was beginning to think was the dude's all-around female charmer term, "we have someone who has trained in such things and has great experience. Although I'm sure not as proficiently as you. But at the moment, we are experiencing some discord in the wedding party and would prefer to keep it quiet."

That clicked with Maisie. "Oh, my. You should see some of the things I've seen. My goodness gracious. There was the time I did that Thibault wedding and they wanted an arrangement of Spanish Moss shaped like a gator except—"

Shane cut her off. "Are the keys in the truck?"

"Yes, but—"

Shane turned away and got in the driver's seat. Lucien entered the opposite side.

"I see charm is not part of your repertoire," Lucien observed. "I'll send one of the men with some treats and a gift from the Duchess to mollify her."

"Like the early settlers brought trinkets and beads for the natives?" Shane asked as he drove the truck across the bridge and turned toward the gazebo.

Lucien sighed, leaning his head back on the steel wall of the truck. "It might have been better to have Ms. Agnes here after all."

Shane slammed on the brakes and Lucien had to throw his hands out in front to keep from bouncing his forehead off the dash. He winced having to use his wounded arm.

Shane twisted in the seat and glared at Lucien. "You guys got Agnes that slot in Paris. To get her out of here."

Lucien straightened. "I am sorry I mentioned it. I'm tired and not thinking straight."

"You did, didn't you?"

"Of course," Lucien said. "The Duchess insisted that Ms. Agnes be removed from any possible danger."

Shane faced forward, chagrined he hadn't seen it. "Shit," he muttered. "What else have I overlooked?"

"We all miss things," Lucien said. "We didn't know how much you would be told about the scenario by your superiors so we kept things tight. The hope was everything would go smoothly."

"You know what they say about hope," Shane said.

"And that is?"

"Fuck, I don't know," Shane said. "But sometimes it's bad." He slammed a hand into the steering wheel. "I'm getting soft. Not discerning things I should." He didn't add that the Duchess' attempt to keep Agnes safe had almost gotten him killed. They couldn't have foreseen that. He also couldn't let Lucien in on the fact that the Organization had an infection.

"You put Lisa Livia, Joey and Garth in harm's way," Shane said.

"We did not know Ms. Agnes would bring someone in to take her place," Lucien said. "We assumed you would be the only occupant of Two Rivers."

"You thought I was going to put on a wedding by myself?"

"It's the reason most of the questionnaire was left blank," Lucien weakly explained. "It was noted it would be very simple. It was implied that we would be taking care of everything."

"Agnes doesn't do implied." Shane would have laughed if he hadn't killed someone this morning and more death was looming on the near horizon.

"It was not handled well," Lucien admitted.

"Lisa Livia was on the roof next to you this morning," Shane reminded him. "You seem to like her. I saw the way she looked at you at breakfast."

"I regret having her there," Lucien said, "but it was a spur of the moment thing on her part and I didn't want to get into an argument. As I said, I gave her my backpack as cover. It's Kevlar." He added, "I wasn't thinking straight."

"We better get our act together," Shane said.

Lucien agreed. "And quickly."

But Shane was already thinking deeper into the situation, trying to understand how they'd ended up here. "I know the Duchess said there'd be trouble if you held the wedding in Andova, but you guys haven't had a war in what, twelve centuries? Yet you're getting ready to have one here. Why? Wouldn't you have been better off on your home turf?"

"The wedding *was* scheduled for tomorrow at the Cathedral of Saint Ingrid," Lucien said. "But our intelligence network, and that of your country and others in Europe, picked up disturbing data. The Duchess is focused on Drusilla, but the Duke understands the larger picture. There are powerful players in the shadows who see Drusilla as a useful pawn they can put in charge of Andova. They're the ones who have given her the financial backing. They've been manipulating social media in our country to foment dissent. They are also paying off certain nefarious factions to cause trouble. The blunt assessment became that any attempt to hold the wedding in Andova would result in riots, if not worse. We'd planned this venue as a secret back up. The decision to go with it was made just hours before we took flight. It was why Ms. Agnes got her notification of the slot in Paris at the last minute."

"You have an infection," Shane said.

"Excuse me?"

"Drusilla and her people were prepared to operate here at least a week ago. They shipped the traditional weapons to Canada, then hired someone to bring them across the border and supply them with modern weaponry, including the demo we found at the bridge. They knew before you did that you'd be coming here."

It was Lucien's turn to realize he'd missed the obvious. "But the decision was made last minute."

"By who?"

"The Duke and Duchess, of course, with the input of the Field Marshal. Guillermo must have known of our contingency and planned his own."

"How did he know of the contingency?" Shane asked. "And he acted *before* the decision was made."

"I don't know," Lucien admitted. "But we must deal with the immediate problem of what will happen today."

Shane didn't want to argue the point. "Do you have a spare radio? So I can be on the net? You know. Stay informed."

"We'll get one at the gazebo from the guards."

Shane took his foot off the brake and drove to the gazebo. Several of Lucien's men were there, halberds and armor stacked nearby. They quickly off-loaded the arrangements, leaving Drusilla's insult in the truck. Lucien gave Shane one of the radios and he put the earpiece in. Then stepped back to admire the set up.

It was a hell of a lot of red. Indeed, the gazebo was a lone white tower in the midst of a scarlet sea.

"You really haven't seen *Game of Thrones*?" Shane asked Lucien.

LISA LIVIA HELPED Joey clean up in the kitchen while Phoebe checked Agnes' knives, clearly impressed. Xavier had excused himself, saying he needed a walk after such a fine breakfast which meant he was snooping.

Phoebe lightly touched one of the edges. "Well maintained. Do you know where the sharpening stones are?"

Lisa Livia shrugged. "Feel free to look."

Phoebe opened the drawer underneath the block holding Agnes' best set of knives. She removed two stones. She took them and her sword onto the deck. Rhett waddled after her to his outside bed.

"Traitor," Lisa Livia muttered.

"I like her," Joey said.

"That's because she can eat everything in sight," Lisa Livia said. "And paints houses. I heard that term bandied about growing up. I know what it means."

The phone on the wall rang and both Lisa Livia and Joey looked at it with suspicion. The mechanical voice intoned: '*GARTH THEEBOT*', mangling the last name.

Joey laughed.

Lisa Livia picked up the receiver. "Yes, Garth?"

"Miss Lisa Livia?" Garth asked.

"Yes, Garth. Where are you?"

"I'm at the airport. But it's really early. But Mister Joey, he told me to come straight here. I'm sorry, but I forgot the eye-pad for the names. The one I forgot the other day. That's cause it's in the kitchen desk. And I've got time to come back and get it. So, I was wondering if—"

"No. Absolutely not. Just stay there."

"Everything okay?" Garth asked. "I'm sorry I forgot the eye-pad. But—"

"Garth. Do not come back here until you call me and I tell you it's safe." Lisa Livia winced as she said the last word. "Until I tell you everything is set for the wedding is what I mean. Do you understand?"

A silence for several seconds. "Sure, Miss Lisa Livia. I understand."

"Good. We'll see you later, right?"

"Sure, Miss Lisa Livia."

The phone clicked off.

"You scared the boy," Joey said. "No need to yell at him."

"I didn't yell."

Joey laughed. "Now you sound like your mother when she was ripping your dad a new one."

"Joey. Do not ever compare me to my mother."

"*Now* you really sound like her."

Rather than snatch a frying pan, Lisa Livia grabbed a fresh cup of coffee and went onto the deck. Phoebe was in one of the wicker chairs, rhythmically working the edge of the sword with one of the stones. Her back was to the wall, something Carpenter did every time they sat down to eat, so smoothly it had taken Lisa Livia a while to figure it out.

"You can do the rest of the knives in the kitchen if you feel like it," Lisa Livia said as she took the chair next to Rhett.

"They're fine," Phoebe said. "Agnes maintains her tools."

"Is that your tool?" Lisa Livia asked.

Phoebe glanced up at her, her hands never stopping. "One of them."

"How'd you end up working for Carpenter?"

"I'm not at liberty to discuss that," Phoebe said.

"Need to know and all that bullshit, right?"

Phoebe nodded. "All that bullshit."

"Aren't we here because of that?" Lisa Livia asked.

"I don't know how all this came about," Phoebe said. "It's not my concern."

"Something that can get you killed isn't your concern?"

Phoebe stopped sharpening. "You got something going on with Carpenter and—"

Lisa Livia cut her off. "*Had* something. Long over."

"'Had something'," Phoebe amended. "That makes sense."

"How so?" Lisa Livia asked.

"I saw the way you looked at Lucien."

Lisa Livia didn't think she'd looked at Lucien any particular way in his brief appearance outside the kitchen door. Hell, he hadn't even come in, nor had he looked at her.

"It seems you like dangerous men," Phoebe said. She put a dab of oil on the blade and selected a different stone. She angled the wakizashi and focused on the edge. "It can be fun for a little while."

Lisa Livia wasn't sure if she was talking about dangerous men or sharpening the blade.

Phoebe secured her sword, sliding it in the scabbard over her shoulder without looking, which Lisa Livia grudgingly found impressive.

"Carpenter is a good man," Lisa Livia said, more out of reflex than trying to make a point.

Phoebe shrugged. "He's my boss. That's the only context I know him in. I'm here because he ordered me to be here. People like us? We're not in the bell curve and I very much doubt we're on the positive side of it. I'm not saying we're bad. Hell, we man the walls against the bad people. Honestly, I don't know what we are." She cocked her head staring off into the brightening dawn over the Low Country. "I like to think we're the good people." Phoebe sniffed. "Not much longer now. It's pretty here."

SHANE AND LUCIEN had driven the truck back to a completely nonplussed Maisie whose attempts to engage the guards in conversation had gone nowhere, but was offset by a small handbag that had been brought to her as a sign of appreciation from the Duchess for her extra diligence in working 'all night' on the arrangements. Shane had no idea how a woman could swoon over a handbag, but that's pretty much what Maisie did. They'd piled her into the rental and she'd driven away, the happiest person in a several mile radius.

Then Lucien had gone to join his army while Shane gathered the Two Rivers contingent to figure out their next steps. He was with Phoebe, Xavier, Joey and Lisa Livia on the porch of Two Rivers. Rhett was on guard duty, snoring nearby.

"Let me call the authorities," Xavier suggested for the third time.

"Get on your boat and go home," Shane said as he checked his watch.

"Ain't you the authorities?" Joey muttered.

"And miss the fun?" Xavier answered Shane, ignoring Joey. "I enjoy fishing, but this promises to be quite the show. Like one of those Renaissance dinner theaters."

"I ain't serving no food," Joey said. "Shoulda ate more at breakfast. Now it's time to serve up some lead." He had a revolver tucked in his belt and looked several years younger with the prospect of danger pumping the adrenaline.

"Isn't the concept that modern weapons not be used?" Xavier pointed out. "As far as I've been able to gather."

"They ain't been playing by the rules," Joey said, indicating the Barrett which Shane had brought outside and was next to Rhett's bed.

"Where is Garth?" Shane asked Joey.

"I had him take the limo and he's waiting at the airport for the Spanish and French embassy reps. He won't be back until just before the wedding based on their arrival time."

Shane was relieved at least one person would be out of the line of fire. "Good," Shane said. "Lisa Livia, you should go to the vault until this is over. Even better, if Xavier would be so kind, you two could take his boat and go to Keyes."

"Yeah, sure," Lisa Livia said. "Hide down there and not know what's going on and wait until someone comes down there to either tell me all okay or slice me into pieces? Or go with this old coot on his leaky boat?"

Phoebe laughed.

"My boat does not leak," Xavier said.

"Why not show her?" Shane suggested. "Hell, you guys can cruise to Savannah. Have some drinks on the riverfront."

One of the soldiers approached, fully kitted out in red, with gleaming armor, sword on the side, halberd in hand, red plumed helmet. He also carried an old-styled black leather medical bag. Shane recognized Vicente as he got closer.

"Gentlemen," Vicente said, touching a finger to the brim of his helmet. "M'ladies," he added to Lisa Livia and Phoebe. He went to the latter. "I was just relieved of duty at the gazebo. My captain said you are having trouble with your knee?"

"It works," Phoebe said.

"One hundred percent, then?" Vicente asked as he put the kit down but didn't open it.

Phoebe glanced at Shane. "Well. Maybe ninety. I've got full range of movement. An occasional twinge."

Vicente ran his hands over Phoebe's leg, his fingers splayed around her knee. "It is not torn. No permanent damage. A strain."

"Break out the big needle," Phoebe suggested.

Vicente smiled. "No need for that. You're a strong woman. Time will heal it, but for now? Here." His fingers tightened down, there was a crunching noise, and Phoebe let out an involuntary gasp as everyone within hearing winced.

"Whoa!" she said. She flexed it. "Cool. I need your number." She indicated the bag. "What kind of pills you have? I always liked the yellow ones."

Vicente stood. "No need for that."

"How is Lucien's arm?" Shane asked him.

"That is a bit more difficult," Vicente said. "It will take time to heal."

"Is he combat effective?" Shane asked.

Vicente considered the question. He didn't equivocate. "No."

The earpiece in Shane's ear had been nothing but normal radio traffic. Guards in various positions checking in. Change of duty at the gazebo. The Field Marshal giving time hacks to *Lacessere*. But that changed.

"Vicente!" The Field Marshal sounded out of sorts and Shane glanced toward the bridge, but there was no sign of an approaching enemy. "Return to base."

"I am needed," Vicente said to them and headed toward the barn.

Shane checked his watch once more. "We don't have much time. Joey, you take Lisa Livia and guard her in the bunker."

Joey wasn't pleased but he nodded. "Yeah. Hate to miss the show though."

Lisa Livia opened her mouth to protest but Shane cut her off.

"Please, LL? I need to focus and I can't be worried about you being in danger."

"This is screwed up," Lisa Livia groused, but she went into the house with Joey.

"Take Rhett!" Shane called after them. Joey reappeared and scooped up the old hound in his bed and carried him inside.

"The guards at the gazebo are gone," Phoebe said.

Shane had already noticed that. "They are. They're consolidating at the barn." He turned to Xavier. "Your boat?"

Xavier tried to stall. "Son, this is going to go bad."

"It's already bad," Shane said.

"Why don't you go with Joey and Miss Lisa Livia?" Xavier asked. "Why are you going to fight a battle that isn't yours?"

"You sound like Joey," Shane said. "I'm not going to fight unless forced. They said the Charter mandates it be twelve on twelve. I'm just going to be insurance that it doesn't go out of bounds. The bad guys have brought more than twelve men. Guys who know modern weapons but not swords and spears. I don't think they're going to watch this on cable. They'll be somewhere close by. I got to protect Two Rivers." He pointed. "How about helping? Go out on your boat and guard the approach from the water. The Field Marshal has been pulling his men in and no one's protecting that approach."

"In other words, get out of the way."

"You must be excellent during interviews with suspects. You pick up on the key stuff right away."

Xavier bowed to the inevitable and headed for the dock.

"Shall we?" Phoebe said, indicating the walkway to the barn.

Shane waited a moment to make sure Xavier was really going.

"Ladies first," he said to Phoebe.

Phoebe snorted. "Guys in the battalion used to say that to me after we put the breaching charge on the door prior to entry to kill the bad guys. Nothing noble about it."

But she led the way.

JOEY HAD LOCKED the kitchen stair door behind them, then swung the heavy vault door almost closed. "We're safe from a nuclear blast now," he boasted. "I remember when Frankie put it in. We did it at night so—"

"Please!" Lisa Livia said. "Do not talk of my father and the crazy things he did. Not now."

Joey was puzzled. "Geez. What's wrong?"

"'What's wrong'?" Lisa Livia stared at him. "Seriously?"

"Your cousin Shane can take care of himself," Joey said as he went over to the weapons rack. He grabbed a double-barreled shotgun and broke it open. "A classic." He found shells, on the shelf directly below the weapon and loaded it. He offered it, as if making peace, to Lisa Livia. "You just point and pull the trigger. It'll clear a mess up pretty quick."

She didn't take it. "You mean make one."

"That too."

"I don't like it in here, Joey."

"It ain't the most comfortable place," Joey allowed. "There was a time we hit the mattresses in Brooklyn after Little Benny Lazy Eye, not to be confused with Big Benny Lazy Eye, ratted on—"

"Joey!" The edge in Lisa Livia's voice stopped the memory.

"What's wrong?"

"Did you know my mother used to lock me in a closet when I was little?"

Joey blinked. "What?"

"Yeah," Lisa Livia said. "When she didn't want to be bothered with me. Or when a man was over. You know. While my father was on the lam, leaving me with her. She'd put me in that old closet on the second floor, the one with the skeleton key, and lock it. Leaving the key in so there was no light. Not even the keyhole." She was talking faster and faster, which flustered Joey. "Just her clothes which smelled like that shit perfume she wore all the time. I hated that fucking perfume."

"Calm down," Joey said.

"Do not tell me to calm down!"

"Okay," Joey said. He looked about in desperation. "Would holding Rhett help?"

SHANE HEARD the problem before he saw it. The sound of men violently retching.

He and Phoebe walked in on a nauseating scene. Almost all of the guard were sick. The Duchess was holding the Duke, steadying him. He had his arms on either side of a trash can as he threw up. The Duke's face was pale with a sheen of sweat. The Duchess, however, seemed fine.

Vicente was working on one of the soldiers while Lucien was helping another.

"Is anyone on security?" Phoebe demanded.

Lucien indicated a bank of monitors lined up on a table. The barn had shifted from a wedding venue to a war room overnight. "We've got sensors and imagery."

"Don't help if no one's watching," Phoebe said as she went over.

Shane followed her. Each monitor displayed an image of a piece of Two Rivers' perimeter. Shane spotted Xavier in his Boston Whaler, slowly circling near the deep-water dock. Another display looked from the bridge along the drive from the coast road. There was no sign of Drusilla's contingent. Yet.

The Duchess joined them along with Lucien and the Field Marshal, who seemed fine. Shane checked the time: 0851.

"What's going on?" Shane asked.

"Food poisoning, best we can tell," Lucien said.

Before anyone could respond, Phoebe drew her sword and had the point under the chin of the Field Marshal. "Iron rations? What was in them?"

The Duchess took a step back in shock while Shane and Lucien locked eyes, then both turned to the Field Marshal as they realized her logic.

"Answer her, sir," Lucien ordered.

"What is going on?" the Duchess demanded. Then she also had her moment of enlightenment. Her voice dripped ice as she turned on the old man. "Ricard. Tell me it isn't true."

The Field Marshal was the most stunned of all at Phoebe's instant deduction. "What? What are you saying?"

"I didn't eat the rations and am not sick," the Duchess said. "Lucien didn't eat and he is not sick. I noted you didn't partake. Vicente was on duty at the gazebo and didn't eat and he is not sick. But every man who did, is violently ill. Will they die?"

To emphasize the Duchess' question, Phoebe pressed the tip of her wakizashi deeper into the chin flab.

"No!" the Field Marshal bleated. "No. They'll be fine in a few hours."

Shane checked his watch. They had less than eight minutes. He had a feeling Drusilla and Guillermo were going to be punctual.

"Should I kill him?" Phoebe asked the Duchess.

The Duchess shook her head. "Stand down, please."

Phoebe was disappointed. She removed the blade from the Field Marshal's chin, but kept it unsheathed.

"Why?" the Duchess asked. "Why did you do it?"

"To prevent bloodshed," the Field Marshal said.

Lucien was more to the immediate problem. "Is there an antidote? What did you put in the rations?"

"They'll be fine in a few hours," the Field Marshal said. "Their systems will clear out naturally. It's not reversible except by time."

"I vote for killing him," Phoebe said. "That's the penalty for treason."

"Andova is not yet a complete democracy," the Duchess said. "And you're not Andovan."

"We're not in Andova," Phoebe pointed out.

The Field Marshal faced the Duchess. "I did it for you, your Grace. I did it for Andova. I took an oath to the Great Charter. To maintain it at all cost. Unto death."

"See?" Phoebe said. "He agrees with me. Let me kill him."

The Duchess ignored her.

Shane was listening, but he was crunching the manpower numbers and he didn't like the math. None of the affected men could stand on their feet without holding onto something. That left Lucien, Vicente with the other guard from the gazebo, Phoebe and him. And Lucien wasn't combat effective according to Vicente.

Seeing that the Duchess wasn't impressed with his reasoning, the Field Marshal turned to Lucien and offered the blue baton. Now that he was closer and it was daylight, Shane could see that the baton had eagles on them and an inscription in Latin.

"If they destroy the Charter, you'll never wield this," the Field Marshal told him.

"I don't want to wield it," Lucien said. "You're talking out both sides of your mouth. You have betrayed the Duke and Duchess. And you have violated the Great Charter."

"They're *destroying* the Great Charter!" the Field Marshal cried out.

"We don't have time for this," Shane said. He held up his watch. "Clock's ticking."

The Duchess snatched the baton from the Field Marshal's hand. "You will not wield it ever again."

Shane was more interested in the line of black SUVs approaching the bridge along the drive on the monitor. "They're here."

The vehicles came to a halt at the edge of the bridge, effectively blocking it. A dozen men piled out, sporting gleaming armor, swords and halberds. As did the Bishop. The soldiers wore gold-colored garments underneath the shining metal. A woman dressed in a gold gown with a long black cape stood next to the Bishop. Her hair was platinum blonde and piled high on her head.

"Nice entrance," Phoebe muttered.

"Drusilla," the Duchess hissed, with so much contempt even Phoebe took half a step away. "Damn her black heart." The Duchess abruptly left them, taking the interior stairs to the balcony and disappearing into one of the rooms.

"Whoa," Phoebe said. "Some cold hate there."

XAVIER

XAVIER IDLED the engine and floated in the Intracoastal, binoculars to his eyes, scanning Two Rivers. There was no movement at all. No guards at the gazebo. No one on the porch of the big house. No sign of life. The barn was hidden among the old oaks and he'd seen Shane and Phoebe hurrying towards it.

He'd contemplated calling this in, but to whom? Hammond and the three other officers in the Keyes Police Department would be lambs led to the slaughter. And Shane? He was some sort of highly connected government spook, of that Xavier had no doubt.

He wished he'd stayed in the mountains.

Xavier didn't like being shuttled off to the sidelines. He lowered the glasses. He frowned as he saw a trail of bubbles in the water forty feet to starboard. After a moment the trail indicated a direction: toward the point of land on which Two Rivers was perched.

Xavier engaged the electric trolling motor and slowly edged the boat parallel to the bubbles. Then he grabbed a gaff and went to the side. He looked down and spotted the diver finning hard toward shore. Xavier jabbed down, hooking the man.

The diver thrashed about, but then a hand came out of the water holding a pistol and fired wildly.

Xavier wasn't in the mood for it. He lashed the gaffe to a cleat and engaged the engine. He accelerated along the Intracoastal, then spun the wheel hard, while releasing the gaff. The diver, gaff attached, was propelled into a live oyster bed.

Xavier glanced over his shoulder as he piloted his boat away. The diver was on the surface, cursing in a foreign language. He tried to stand.

"Don't do that," Xavier said to himself.

The man screamed as the shells lacerated his feet, cutting through his wet suit. He collapsed in the shallow water.

He wouldn't be going anywhere until someone lifted him out of that bed of razor-sharp shells.

"CAN YOU CALL THIS OFF?" Shane asked Lucien with little hope. He was watching the monitor. Guillermo wore armor and had his eleven men lined up, preparing to move forward. They had swords at their sides and halberds in hand. Behind them, a half-dozen men with modern weaponry were scattered around the SUVs. Shane did the math and one was still unaccounted for.

Drusilla and the Bishop were engaged in conversation, probably trying to figure out how many body bags they'd need, Shane thought.

"I would like nothing better," Lucien said. He was on Shane's left, also watching. Phoebe was to the right. Vicente was doing the best he could for the sick men, but it was apparent the Field Marshal's prediction was true. The vomiting wasn't making them better; only time would do that. The Duke was suffering the most. He was in a chair, pale, a sheen of sweat on his face. He kept trying to get up, despite Vicente insisting he remain seated.

"Whoa," Phoebe said, looking up.

The Duchess was coming down the stairs. She'd exchanged the dress for red pantaloons and tunic under bright red armor with her family crest on the breastplate. She had a sword in hand. Her hair was down, flowing over her narrow shoulders in a silver wave.

"Definitely a theme," Phoebe said. She dropped her voice so only Shane could hear: "And I don't like it. We're really far down the Red Wedding path now."

"No!" the Duke cried out as he tried to stand, but crumpled back into the chair.

The Duchess went to him and leaned over and whispered to him. She placed a hand on his forehead.

"That'll cool him off," Phoebe muttered as Lucien joined his parents.

Shane was more concerned with the activity on the monitor. Guillermo was consulting with the Bishop and Drusilla. Then the huddle broke up and Guillermo took lead, his eleven men following in single file onto Two Rivers. As he took point, Shane could see that Guillermo wore more armor than the others: greaves on his lower legs up to the knees, gauntlets that extended to the elbow, and he carried a helm with visor under one arm. The sword at his side looked large on him, which meant it was huge.

"The Mountain," Phoebe whispered. "Cool."

"What?" Shane asked.

"Nothing."

Drusilla and the Bishop followed Guillermo. The other mercenaries remained on the bridge.

"Time's up," Shane called out.

"I GOTTA GET OUT OF HERE," Lisa Livia said.

"Take it easy," Joey said.

Lisa Livia gritted her teeth. "Do *not* tell me to take it easy. Give me the shotgun."

"I don't think that's a good idea right now," Joey said.

"Changed your mind, have you?" Lisa Livia looked about. "Plenty of others to choose from."

While Lisa Livia armed herself, Joey pulled the vault door completely shut and spun the wheel.

Rhett barked and Lisa Livia whirled about. "What did you just do?"

"Got to keep you safe," Joey said, folding his arms across his chest.

"You idiot! It's broken. You never spin the wheel. Why do you think Shane is using the hasp lock instead of the wheel? My damn father couldn't do anything right. Now, we're trapped!"

"YOU GOT something bigger than that itty-bitty knife?" Phoebe asked as they followed the Duchess, Lucien, Vicente and other guard who'd been on duty at the gazebo. The Field Marshal was duct-taped to a chair, a gag in his mouth. The Duke and the others were as comfortable as possible. There'd been several valiant, but futile attempts by the men to follow the Duchess. Whatever the Field Marshal had given them was nasty.

Gonna have a front seat to a massacre, Shane thought. He'd considered grabbing a halberd or sword, but figured that would only hasten his demise if he got embroiled in a blade melee. He was bringing a knife to a sword fight, but he also had guns, which made this thing murky.

As they cleared the trees, Shane saw that Guillermo had his men arrayed in a line, spaced three feet apart, in front of the gazebo and the statue of Saint Ingrid. The men were at a form of 'at ease', the staffs of their halberds on the ground, the arm forward angling the blade. Guillermo, Drusilla and the Bishop stood behind them, on the steps of the gazebo. Guillermo was a striking figure in his suit of gold armor.

"This is nuts," Shane muttered.

"This is cool," Phoebe said.

"We need a delay," the Duchess said.

"I am not an expert, but I believe the decision rests with the Bishop," Lucien said.

"He isn't exactly on our side, is he?" Shane said.

"Have any of you guys actually read this Charter thing?" Phoebe asked.

"Of course," Lucien said.

The Duchess stopped twenty feet from Drusilla.

"Where is the Duke?" the Bishop inquired.

"Ask Drusilla," the Duchess said. "She suborned the Field Marshal. He poisoned my Duke and our men."

The Bishop didn't seem surprised. "Will he recover?"

"He will," the Duchess said, "and that is why I am requesting a delay for *Lacessere* until he does."

"That is unprecedented," the Bishop said.

"The poisoning?" the Duchess asked.

"A delay," the Bishop replied.

"*Lacessere* is unprecedented," the Duchess pointed out.

"Yack, yack, yack," Phoebe muttered.

Shane glanced over his shoulder toward the bridge. The soldiers he could see were armed with automatic weapons and milling about. *No one gets out of here alive*, he thought.

"I'm afraid I can't authorize that," the Bishop said.

Drusilla couldn't hold back. "You whore, and that shadow of a man you are consorting with, are tearing up the Great Charter, which has withstood the travails of history for thirteen centuries, because of your petty love for each other and your bastard son."

"That is not true," the Duchess said, "but it would be an excellent reason, would it not? To do something for love? A matter you know nothing of."

Drusilla took a step forward, but Guillermo put an arm out, keeping her from leaving the gazebo, whispering to her urgently.

"Women are the worst," Phoebe said to Shane.

"The *Lacessere* will proceed," the Bishop intoned.

The Duchess looked at Lucien. He nodded grimly. "We will follow your orders, your Grace."

"Geez," Phoebe said. She pushed forward, between the Duchess and Lucien and spoke to them in a low voice. "Did either of you really read the Charter? Like, all of it? I did on the flight here." She held up a hand and addressed the Bishop. "We invoke trial by battle."

"Who is this girl?" Drusilla demanded.

"Isn't that what we're doing?" Shane asked Phoebe as he moved forward next to her.

"Hush," Phoebe said. She turned to the Duchess. "Demand trial by battle."

The Duchess lowered her voice. "What are you speaking of? *Lacessere* is trial by battle."

"Nobody reads the footnotes anymore," Phoebe complained. She addressed the Bishop; and everyone else. "The Great Charter was written by Charlemagne the Great in Eight-Oh-Two."

"Shut up girl," Drusilla snapped.

"Is that not a fact?" Phoebe asked.

"Every Andovan knows that," Guillermo said. "Get this foreigner out of here, Duchess. This is between families."

Phoebe continued, undeterred. "The Great Charter is law, but by its own letter, it is subordinate to Charlemagne's law. Part of his law was *Lex Alamannorum*. Under that, any legal dispute can be settled by trial by battle. One on one. Each side picks a champion and they fight until death. The one still standing is legally in the right. Quaint, but charming in its own way."

"They're stalling," Drusilla shouted. "I want to taste the bitch's blood. I want to grind her bones under my heel."

"Anger issues much?" Phoebe said.

But the Duchess was watching the Bishop. Shane could see the slightest crack in the solid line of steel in front of Drusilla. More a sense, what Vicente would call an aura, that those in the line who weren't psychopaths, wouldn't mind this turning out other than blade on blade. *Their* blades, at least.

"Bishop?" Duchess pressed.

"There is some validity to that," the Bishop allowed. "The Great Charter is part of Charlemagne's law. Even though his kingdom no longer exists, we live under his law via the Great Charter."

Phoebe pressed home her legal argument. "And *Lex Alamannorum*?"

"Is trial by combat," the Bishop ceded. "One on one."

Drusilla wheeled, faster than the Bishop could react, slapping him across the face with a hand bedecked with jeweled rings. The Bishop staggered from the blow and blood flowed from a cut on his cheek. Guillermo stepped between the two. The men in the line of gold soldiers glanced over their shoulders, then at each other.

"We demand *Lex Alamannorum*!" the Duchess shouted. "It is our right by law." She drew her sword. "I will fight the cheating bitch who dares to challenge my rule."

"You go, girl," Phoebe muttered. "As if."

Guillermo had one arm out, keeping Drusilla from tearing the Bishop apart, but both heard the Duchess. Drusilla pivoted while reaching for Guillermo's sword. "I will cut you in half!"

"Won't be hard," Phoebe noted.

The Bishop was urgently talking to both of them but Shane and the others couldn't hear what was said.

Guillermo was able to keep Drusilla from getting the weapon, not that she could have drawn the great sword. Whatever the Bishop said had the desired effect and she took her hand off the hilt and nodded. Guillermo turned toward them.

"Trial by combat," Guillermo said, "dictates that each side chooses a champion."

Drusilla pulled a gold tie from her cloak and wrapped it around the armor on his massive upper right arm. "My champion!"

Guillermo drew his great sword. "I will battle Lucien!" The blade was four feet long, double-edged and heavy. The hilt was a foot long and required two hands, and strength, to wield.

Lucien took a step forward, hand on the hilt of his sabre.

Shane looked at Phoebe. "Can you?"

"Sure," she said, her eyes on Guillermo.

"He's got a big sword," Shane noted. "And armor."

"No shit," Phoebe said.

"You sure?"

"Abso-fucking-lutely," Phoebe said. "Can I borrow your dagger?"

"I thought it was too small," Shane said. "I believe you called it 'itty-bitty'?"

"Pretty please?" Phoebe said.

Shane slid it out of the sheath and passed it to her. She tucked it in her harness.

The Duchess listened to the exchange between Shane and Phoebe without comment. Shane and Phoebe huddled with her, Vicente, and Lucien.

"Listen to me," Shane said. Certain he had their attention, he continued. "Lucien. You took a round from Guillermo in Africa, right?"

Lucien nodded.

"But he's here, now. You've never killed, have you?"

"He is Captain of the Guard," the Duchess said. "He is the one who must—"

Shane cut her off. "You need someone who will finish this."

"I will finish it," Lucien said.

"No," Shane said. "You're wounded. Vicente says you are combat ineffective."

Lucien shot a hard look at the medic.

Shane pressed his case. "This is my land. My place. These people have invaded it. You brought this here, you owe me to let me finish it. I pick the champion."

"It is not your right," the Duchess said.

"You are not skilled enough with the blade," Lucien protested. "Guillermo is renowned for his expertise with the great sword."

Shane noted that the Duchess said nothing.

"Not me," Shane said. He nodded at Phoebe.

"You jest," Lucien said, but his heart wasn't in the objection.

Vicente spoke for the first time. "She is the one, your Grace." He reached out and put a hand on Lucien's good shoulder. "You do not have it in you and your arm will not help. You will, if you must. But she? She has it in her. We must have faith."

"You want me to stake the future of my country on a stranger?" the Duchess asked. "A girl at that?"

"I can hear you," Phoebe said. "I'm standing right here. I trained under a master of the blade. I have a fourth-degree black belt in *Sha-Ki-Toledo*."

"And that is?" the Duchess asked.

"The wakizashi." Phoebe winked at Shane, which the others didn't see.

"IT WON'T OPEN," Joey said, a trickle of sweat on his forehead as he tried to turn the wheel once more.

"No shit," Lisa Livia said. She pulled back the slide on a semi-automatic and chambered a round. "You need to get me out of here."

"I'm trying," Joey said.

Lisa Livia took a deep breath. "Joey, I'm not joking. I can't stay in this place. You gotta get me out of here. I don't give a shit if there's a million people with swords up there waiting to hack us to death. Get me out!"

"HE'S PRETTY BIG," Shane said.

"More of a target," Phoebe said.

"Do you want my armor?" the Duchess asked Phoebe.

"Nah," Phoebe said. "It'll just slow me down." She turned to Shane and spoke so only he could hear. "If I lose? Shoot him."

"You got it," Shane assured her.

"Maybe do it slowly?" she asked as she rolled her head, loosening her shoulders.

"If he beats you, I'd have to be lucky to beat him," Shane said.

Phoebe nodded. "Thanks."

Lucien made a final protest. "It is my duty."

"I'm better at it," Phoebe said. "Killing, that is."

"Did you see the Red Viper versus the Mountain in Game of Thrones?" Vicente asked.

"So, one of you *did* see Game of Thrones," Phoebe said. "I was beginning to wonder."

"Didn't the small guy lose?" Shane asked, not quite sure.

"That's because he got stupid," Phoebe said. "I don't plan on doing stupid."

Lucien offered some belated and obvious advice. "You will have speed. But Guillermo is undefeated. His strength, quite bluntly, is his strength. No one can survive a direct strike from the great sword."

Phoebe stepped forward. "Duchess? Make the introduction."

"Are you certain?" the Duchess asked, staring into Phoebe's eyes.

"Abso-fucking-lutely."

The Duchess pulled a red sash off her sword arm and tied it around Phoebe's, where it immediately slid down to her elbow. "This is our champion."

"You jest," Guillermo said.

"Let me kill her," Drusilla demanded.

The Bishop was confused. "But Lucien is Captain of the Guard."

"The champion is whomever I choose," the Duchess replied.

The Bishop opened his mouth to reply but his brain refused to supply any words.

"Let me finish the girl and then we can get on with things," Guillermo said, lifting his great sword with both hands and pointing it at Phoebe.

"So be it," the Bishop said. "I will bless the battle with an invocation to Saint—"

"Shut up," Drusilla snapped at him. "Crush her," she said to Guillermo.

Guillermo stomped down the steps and through his rank of soldiers to the open ground between the two groups. He put on the gold helmet and lowered the visor. Shane was really glad Agnes wasn't here to see this.

Guillermo went to an on-guard position, the long sword angled across his body, glaring at Phoebe. She turned and began walking toward the waterfront.

"Where are you going?" Guillermo demanded; his voice muffled by the visor.

"I don't want to fight right there," Phoebe said over her shoulder. "I don't like the *feng shui*."

"The what?" Guillermo said.

Guillermo glanced at the Bishop and Drusilla, confused, then followed. Bereft of their leader, Drusilla's soldiers remained in place, but when she came down off the gazebo, they gathered round her.

"Six of you, stay here and guard the statue," Drusilla ordered. "The rest, with me."

Shane, the Duchess, Lucien, Vicente and the other soldier also followed Phoebe and Guillermo, staying parallel to Drusilla's party. Phoebe didn't head onto the dock, which Shane knew would have been a tactical error, channeling her. He wasn't quite sure what her plan was. She continued along the shoreline, just above the low sea wall, Guillermo clanking in pursuit.

Twenty feet from the woods surrounding the barn, Phoebe abruptly turned and charged Guillermo, her wakizashi raised. Guillermo went on guard and easily parried her slash. He shifted into position to strike back.

Phoebe backed up, out of reach of his sword and nodded. Then ran into the woods.

"Stop and fight!" Guillermo shouted. "You coward." He turned to those following. "Duchess, your champion runs away. This is a sham. You're wasting time."

"You in a rush to die?" Shane asked him. "No one said anything about where the fight had to take place." He indicated the forest. "She's waiting for you."

Guillermo growled in disgust, but went into the woods.

"What is she doing?" the Duchess whispered to Shane.

"She has a plan," Shane said. At least he hoped she did.

PHOEBE WENT thirty feet in the forest, then turned. Guillermo was a towering figure in gold as he lumbered toward her. She charged him. He brought his great sword up at the ready.

Phoebe executed a compound attack, thrusting, then slashing, then thrusting again.

Guillermo blocked all three, two with the long blade, one with the double-handed hilt, then counter-attacked. Phoebe deflected his swing, but the heavy sword and the power behind it sent a shiver from her blade up her arm and through her body. If he landed a direct blow, she'd be done for from blunt force trauma, never mind the blade. She gave ground quickly and Guillermo hurried after her, a human tank.

"Stand and hold your ground!" Guillermo yelled.

"You need some oil," Phoebe shouted back.

Phoebe darted among the trees, forcing Guillermo to constantly change direction.

Shane glanced at Lucien, who nodded in understanding as Phoebe's tactics began to make sense.

Guillermo halted and faced those following him. "Bishop! This is ridiculous. This is not combat. This is making a mockery of it."

Drusilla turned on the Bishop, who was breathing hard and dabbing blood off his cheek with a handkerchief stained red.

"*Lacessere*," Drusilla said. "Not this nonsense. The Duchess makes fools of us, hoping to gain time."

"You are the one who violated *Lacessere*," the Duchess yelled back. "By suborning the Field Marshal and poisoning the Duke and his men. You have no credibility."

Shane looked back the way they'd come. Drusilla's six men were around the gazebo, but relaxed. The others were barely visible through the trees at the bridge.

Phoebe heard the arguing but her focus was on Guillermo. She headed landward, Guillermo in pursuit, although he couldn't run in his armor. She reached the edge of the gully, the bridge seventy-five yards to her right, the Blood River twenty yards to the left, the barn to her right rear. She turned. Guillermo caught up and smiled as he brought his heavy sword up to the ready. Phoebe drew the dagger with her off hand. And moved sideways until they were both parallel to the gully.

"Nowhere to go, girl!"

Phoebe charged and they exchanged a half dozen thrust and parries. Faster, Phoebe avoided the great sword.

On her third attack she managed to strike Guillermo on the chest with the wakizashi, but all she achieved was a scratch in the armor. Nevertheless, she pressed the charge, inside the range of the great sword, her wakizashi bouncing off his armor and sliding along it on the right side. With her other hand, she blindly jabbed upward with the dagger, the tip hitting armor on his side and skittering along it into Guillermo's armpit. As Guillermo prepared a counter-strike, she tucked and rolled over the edge and into the gully.

The tide was coming in and there was four feet of sluggish swamp water in the bottom of the gully. Phoebe landed with a splash. She struggled to her feet, her boots sinking into the fluffer mud. Her knee almost buckled, but held. The water was well above her waist.

Guillermo appeared above her. "Damn you! If you cross, then this is over. We will wipe all of your people out."

"It's nice down here," Phoebe yelled back. "Come join me. What? Are you afraid?"

Guillermo, however, refused to be baited into entering the gully. Phoebe had figured he wouldn't fall for it, but it had been worth a try.

"I know what you're trying to do," Guillermo said. He indicated the water. "Besides the obvious. You want to wear me down. But you will not. I can play this game all day."

"No," Phoebe said, "you can't." She held up her dagger, the tip red with blood. "You're already dead. But the reality hasn't gotten through that armor on your head yet."

SHANE AND COMPANY arrived behind Guillermo in time to hear the last exchange. Drusilla, the Bishop, who appeared on the verge of a heart attack, and her soldiers stood close to Guillermo, who was staring down at Phoebe.

"What?" Guillermo's voice was muted by the visor. He shoved it up. "What did you say?"

"Dead man walking," Phoebe said. She cocked her head and sniffed. "Something's coming."

A few seconds later, everyone turned as the sound of approaching loud mufflers rumbled across the Low Country. Guillermo removed his helmet and then dropped the gauntlet from one hand. He reached into his armpit, then pulled his hand back. It was coated in blood.

"ON THREE," Joey said. "Use your legs."

Lisa Livia was next to him on the ladder leading to the emergency entrance from the bunker in the floor of the gazebo. He'd unlatched the dogs on the hatch but it hadn't budged when he'd tried to push it up.

"One," Joey said. "Two. Three."

Together, they flexed their legs and the hatch grudgingly gave way. Then it swung wide open as they heard a loud crash. Lisa Livia, like a drowning sailor escaping a sinking ship, clambered up, pushing Joey to the side. She stood in the center of the gazebo, the broken statue of Saint Ingrid in front of her and six men armed with halberds and swords, wearing gold armor, staring at her in surprise.

Joey scrambled up to her side and leveled a pump action shotgun at them. "Drop the . . . " he sputtered, not quite sure, "weapons."

"Fuck you," one of the men shouted back.

Joey fired and the solid shot hit the guy in the chest, punched through the armor, and dropped him like a stone. Joey racked in a new round as Lisa Livia drew the big pistol she'd settled on.

The remaining five dropped their halberds.

PHOEBE SAW the comprehension come over Guillermo's face. The big man ripped off his other gauntlet and then, to Phoebe's surprise and admiration, he leapt toward her, the great sword high above his head.

She scrambled away as he landed in the bottom of the dish, a cascade of water around him. He brought the great sword down in a mighty sweep and the tip missed her by less than an inch and sliced into the water, deep into the mud.

Guillermo struggled to pull it out as Phoebe worked to put distance between her and the big man. Both were slowed by the mud which grabbed at blade and feet. By the time Guillermo jerked the great sword free, Phoebe was ten feet away. She watched, backing up, as he came after her in his heavy armor, one ponderous step at a time. The water around him was tinged with red from blood spurting out of the axillary artery she'd punctured in his armpit. Phoebe spared a glance up at the audience: Drusilla and the Bishop and her men and then Shane, the Duchess, Lucien and the other two.

THE SOUND of mufflers and engines was growing louder but Shane couldn't see anything on the incoming road. He heard the blast of a shotgun from the vicinity of the gazebo and knew Joey was involved somehow, but he couldn't leave the Duchess and Phoebe.

Drusilla gasped as Guillermo dropped to his knees in the dark water. Shane realized she hadn't known he was wounded as the majority of the blood had flowed inside his armor and down his leg.

"It is over," the Duchess said, which was bad timing in Shane's opinion.

Drusilla had had enough. She snatched a sword from one of her men. She charged the Duchess screaming incoherently. Shane drew his forty-five, but hesitated, given that they were within range of the armed men on the bridge.

The Duchess easily parried Drusilla's wild thrust and stepped to the side. Drusilla stumbled, then fell into the gully, landing with a loud splash and a flurry of curses in Spanish. She managed to get to her feet, dripping mud and water. Her hair was a mess.

"Kill them!" She screamed toward the armed men at the bridge.

Which is when Uncle Jack's monster truck rumbled down the road and without slowing, ran right over the SUV blocking the bridge, crushing the roof and shattering the windows. Other pickup trucks skidded to a halt and over a dozen men from the swamp, Jack and Garth among them, piled out, weapons at the ready.

"SURRENDER," the Duchess called to Drusilla.

"It is to the death!" Drusilla yelled back. She was pushing through the water to the side of the gully.

Which is when Guillermo, struggling to get to his feet, keeled over and died, disappearing under the murky, reddish water.

"Good timing," Phoebe whispered.

"Never!" Drusilla screamed. "I am going to kill you and—"

The fourteen-foot alligator exploded out of the water and

snatched her in its jaws before anyone could react. Then it was rolling with Drusilla into the deep-water pool.

"Your gun!" Lucien held his hand out to Shane.

Instead, Shane holstered it. He slid halfway down the embankment, extending his hand to Phoebe. He helped her out of the gully.

"You all right?" he asked.

"Peachy," Phoebe said. "Is that what they say round these parts?"

"That's Georgia," Shane said. "'*Sha-Ki-Toledo*'? Never heard of it."

"Neither have I," Phoebe said. "Best I could come up with at the moment."

Shane turned away from the sounds of the end of Drusilla. "We better make sure Joey and Lisa Livia are okay."

As they walked out of the woods, a Blackhawk helicopter swooped overhead and a fast rope was tossed out each side. Carpenter was the first one on the ground, followed by Delta Force operators.

"A smidge late," Phoebe said to Shane.

"But he's early for the wedding. Priorities."

SHANE'S WORDS OF WISDOM #10

Revenge is a dish best served when they least expect it.

Don't let 'em know you're coming.

SATURDAY NOON

LL

Carpenter had swapped out his combat gear for a black suit and stood alone on the raised platform of the gazebo. The soldiers who'd come with him had policed up Drusilla and Guillermo's bodies and her men, living, wounded and dead, and flown them out on the helicopters, including a man sliced up on an oyster bed. Lisa Livia didn't want to know where they were taking them.

The Duke and others had recovered, although they were shaky on their feet. The Spanish and French embassy staff representatives were stranded at the airport given Garth's quick trip to the swamp to get reinforcements. The Duchess had said it was fine with her that they could just go back to their embassies. There was nothing here for them. Lisa Livia knew she was talking about the big picture, not just the wedding.

The armor had been taken off, it was just too much, and everyone was gathered round the gazebo, sitting in the chairs Garth and his relatives had quickly arrayed in front of it. They were staying too, at the specific request of the Duchess, in thanks for their assistance. The lure of a royal wedding wasn't much of a factor for Jack and his men, but the promise of free booze afterward, was. Joey had made a quick run back to the diner and returned with all the liquor he'd previously liberated from the bunker.

Lisa Livia stood next to Shane in the front row of seats with Lucien flanking her. Phoebe was on the other side of Shane.

"I'm really, really sorry about the statue," Lisa Livia said for the fourth time.

Lucien reassured her for the fourth time. "Of all that happened, that is the smallest problem. There are craftsmen in Andova who will be thrilled to rebuild it."

"Better than they did Humpty-Dumpty?" Phoebe asked.

"Hush," Lisa Livia said. "But it was so old and expensive. All the jewels."

Ah," Lucien said. He lowered his voice. "Regrettably, it is an imitation. The true statue was stolen a week ago. We believe by Drusilla's people. I have no doubt we should be able to track it down now."

"Always have doubt," Phoebe muttered.

A ripple of excitement ran through the crowd. Lisa Livia looked over her shoulder and they all turned as the Duke and Duchess came out from the trees. The Duchess had swapped armor for her red dress, but her hair was still down over her shoulders. It was amazing how that softened her, Lisa Livia thought. The Duke had his arm linked through the Duchess's and they walked slowly, but steadily forward.

"Excuse me," Lucien said, joining the honor guard lined up in two rows in the opening between the seats.

Lisa Livia looked past Shane at Phoebe. "I heard what you did. Thank you."

"No problemo," Phoebe said. "Part of the job."

"Thank you, anyway."

The Andovan honor guard snapped to attention and saluted, hilts of their swords to their chins, blades angled into the air. Even Uncle Jack and clan quieted down as the royal couple walked between the guard and joined Carpenter on the platform. Xavier was seated across the aisle from the Thibaults, eyeballing them, cataloguing how many times he'd arrested each.

Carpenter looked a bit confused for a moment as the honor guard dropped the salute and retook their positions.

"A best man? A maid of honor?" Carpenter asked, and Lisa Livia realized she hadn't gotten him up to speed on the scaled down ceremony. Not that there had been time, given the policing up of bodies and prisoners. The not-usual pre-wedding stuff. Lisa Livia didn't think she'd tell Agnes to add that to the questionnaire.

She was about to clarify about the wedding party, when the Duke cleared his throat. "Lucien? Would you stand by my side as best man?"

Lucien stepped up onto the platform, next to the Duke.

"Making the bastard legit," Phoebe whispered. "That's cool."

Lisa Livia was startled, though, when the Duchess beckoned to her. "Would you do me the honor of standing by my side, Miss Lisa Livia Fortunato?"

Lisa Livia swallowed hard and nodded. She joined them in the gazebo.

Carpenter glanced between her and Lucien and nodded at her with a sad smile. Then he turned to those assembled.

"Welcome friends of Duke Marc Navarro and Duchess Margaurite Embrie. To be here, after the events of this morning, shows your love and dedication for this couple."

One of the Thibault clan snickered, but Lisa Livia heard Garth snarl an admonition and there was nothing further from that crowd.

"Do you promise to live together in contentment with the past, happiness in the present, and hope for the future?" Carpenter asked.

"Yes, I do," the Duke said.

The Duchess glanced at Lisa Livia, then over her shoulder at Shane and Phoebe. She smiled at Phoebe, a real smile, one that dropped years from her face. "To quote the bravest warrior I have ever seen, 'abso-fucking-lutely'."

"Whoa," Phoebe whispered.

Duchess whispered something to Carpenter and he nodded. "You may now exchange rings."

The Duchess pulled the chain out of the collar of her dress. She unclasped it and handed both rings to the Duke.

"It's been so long," the Duke said as he held them up to the sunlight. The silver and gold flashed. "My love," he said as he slid one on the Duchess' hand. Then he handed her the other and she returned the favor.

"Then I now pronounce you, man and wife," Carpenter said.

The Duke swept the Duchess into his arms and kissed her. Lisa Livia looked past them at Lucien, while Carpenter stepped back, then left the gazebo via the rear steps.

The Duke finally released his bride, while whispering something to her. The Duchess nodded, then faced everyone. "Let us join hands." She and the Duke held up their hands, clasped together, bound by the ancient rings and their vows.

Behind them, Lucien gave Lisa Livia a questioning look, and she nodded. "The no was conditional," she said.

He took her hand and raised it, his fingers warm and tight around hers.

"Our houses are joined and the Great Charter is dissolved," the Duke called out. "*Virtus Unita Fortior!*"

The Andovans gave a cheer, the swamp rats eyed the booze and Lisa Livia turned to Lucien. "What does this make you? A junior duke or something?"

"It makes me Lucien. Just Lucien."

THE ANDOVAN SOLDIERS were having a blast, given they no longer faced *Lacessere* and the Duke and Duchess were hitched and they were taking turns driving Uncle Jack's monster truck around. Shane figured they didn't have such in the mountains of Andova. Joey's liquor supply also helped.

Shane had just completed a brief after-action-report to Carpenter, whose helicopter was waiting.

"Phoebe finished it?" Carpenter asked, not surprised.

"Yeah," Shane said. "She's good. Better than—"

Carpenter raised a hand, trying to cut him off, but Shane wasn't having it.

"—better than me."

"She's inexperienced," Carpenter said.

"Everyone is at the start."

Carpenter had no answer to that.

"I'm done," Shane replied. "Got to drop me from the rolls, my friend. Please."

Carpenter nodded. "I understand." He looked to the right, at Lisa Livia and Lucien sitting at a table with the Duke and Duchess. "Change is a necessary part of the evolution of life."

"What are you going to do?" Shane asked.

"My profession."

Shane nodded. He indicated Phoebe, who was talking to Vicente, probably still trying to wheedle some happy pills off him. "You'll have good help."

Carpenter extended his hand and Shane took it, but then his boss wrapped him in his arms for a big hug. "Stay centered, my friend."

"You too," Shane replied.

"I HATE TO INTERRUPT," Carpenter said to Phoebe and Vicente, "but my ride is waiting." He indicated the Blackhawk helicopter parked as far away from the gazebo as possible, without being in the trees.

"Certainly," Vicente said. He gave a slight bow toward Phoebe, then headed toward the outdoor dinner that Joey was serving.

"We need to hire him," Phoebe said. "He's out of a job anyway, as they're disbanding the army. He's a great medic. Fixed my knee, pretty much with just his hands."

"I'll look into it," Carpenter said.

"What about Fromm?"

"He took something with him."

"What?"

"The latest encryption program used by the NSA," Carpenter said. "It's worth a lot on the dark market."

"Any idea where he is?"

"We don't have a line on him, yet," Carpenter said.

"He's a computer geek," Phoebe said. "He'll go online eventually. He won't be able to stop himself."

"He's an expert at it," Carpenter said. "He'll conceal any trace."

"Lou will find him," Phoebe said. "And when she does, I'll go to wherever he is and kill him."

"Yes," Carpenter allowed. "You will." *If the Cellar doesn't get to him first*, he thought.

He reached inside his coat and produced a thick brown envelope. "This is yours."

Phoebe took it without questioning the contents.

Carpenter walked toward the chopper. The pilot, seeing him approach, started the engines. By the time he reached it, the blades were beginning to turn. Just before he stepped on board, Carpenter turned and looked.

The Duke and Duchess had gone to the seawall and were staring out over the water. Lisa Livia was with Lucien near the gazebo, talking to Garth. Shane stood in front of Two Rivers, looking at the house, Rhett sitting at his side. He was the most relaxed Carpenter had ever seen him.

Carpenter suddenly realized something. He cocked his head, but there was no whispering, no foot tapping, no mocking on his shoulder. The ghost was gone.

Carpenter got in the chopper and put on a headset. "Go."

As the helicopter lifted, he saw Phoebe standing at the end of the dock and saluted her.

PHOEBE OPENED THE BROWN ENVELOPE, revealing three blue medal boxes and a couple of sheets of folded paper. She slid them out and arrayed them on the wood plank on top of the railing. She opened each lid. A Distinguished Service Cross and two Silver Stars. A citation was inside. She read each one, remembering blood, fear, the adrenaline rush of combat. Comrades lost or wounded.

She looked up as the Blackhawk swooped by, heading north. She touched a single finger to her forehead in salute, returning Carpenter's.

She unfolded the pages and smiled when she read the heading on the first page: *Shane's Words of Wisdom.*

"Can't hurt," she murmured, folding them back up and slipping them inside a pocket.

Her secure phone buzzed and she pulled it out. She frowned when she didn't recognize the number. This wasn't a phone that got car warranty spam calls.

She pushed the on and put it to her ear, but didn't say anything.

"Phoebe, Phoebe, Phoebe," Fromm said. "I know you're listening. I'm surprised you're still alive. I'd have thought you'd have gone down in a blaze of glory by now."

Phoebe looked at the medals in front of her, but didn't respond.

"Phoebe, are you giving me the silent treatment? How's your friend, Louise?"

Phoebe stared at the water, taking slow and measured breaths. She put the phone on the railing next to the medals.

"I didn't kill her on purpose," Fromm said. "I did mark her face, though, so every time you look at her, you remember me." Fromm chuckled, an ugly sound echoing out of the phone's speaker. "You, and Carpenter, and all the rest of them, think you're so smart. You've been behind the entire time and you're even further behind now. You have no idea who I am and the things I've done, but you'll learn. Too late, of course, but you'll learn."

Phoebe silently recited a calming mantra.

"I know you're listening," Fromm said. "You can't help yourself. You have to. It's who you are. Don't you understand? I know every move you're going to make. None of you have free will. You're programed. Except your hardware and software are cheap and weak. Old-fashioned. It's so easy to project out your possible courses of action and know which you'll choose. *Everyone* has been so easy to predict."

Phoebe spotted a bird and followed its path.

"Come on, Phoebe," Fromm taunted. "Aren't you going to threaten me? Issue dire warnings?"

Phoebe bit back the retort that his boast raised. She snapped shut the covers on the medal cases.

"What was that?" Fromm asked.

She tossed the medals off the dock. They bobbed on the surface for a few moments, before sinking out of sight. She drew the wakizashi and raised it over her head. She heard Fromm say something but couldn't make it out. There would be time enough to say something to him when she met him face to face.

The blade flashed down but Phoebe stopped it a fraction of an inch from destroying the phone. She took a deep breath. The phone was a link to Fromm. One she, and Lou, would pull on until she could look right into his beady little eyeballs and her face would be the last thing he ever saw.

SHANE'S WORDS OF WISDOM #11

"You can find a quote about anything."

Really. What do I know?
I'm just a guy, who loves a woman who gets cranky once in a while,
and lives in a big house surrounded by water.
You'll figure out your own way and it will probably be better.

TUESDAY

S hane stood on the approved side of security, like the rest of those waiting to greet arrivals since he no longer carried the various I.D. cards that would allow him to do otherwise.

He had a small box, a gift from the Duchess. It contained a set of special rings like the wedding bands that she and the Duke had exchanged. Lisa Livia had explained their significance, and that only eight existed, and Shane was humbled by their trust when the bands arrived by courier from Andova. Phoebe had muttered something about dwarves and elves and the reign of man ending in response, but Shane had ignored her. He loved them and he hoped Agnes would too.

He spotted Agnes striding through the terminal and his heart leapt in his chest. *I have a great woman and a great home and a great life,* he thought.

He wrapped Agnes in his arms before she had a chance to say anything, holding her tight.

"I need to go away more often," Agnes said as he finally released her.

She took a step back when Shane went to one knee, attention getting behavior, and held up the box containing the rings. "Contentment with the past, happiness in the present and hope for the future. All three by your side. Will you have me?"

THE END

Thanks for the read!
If you enjoyed the book, please leave a review as they are very important.
Of course, Phoebe won the battle, but not the war.
Fromm is out there. And she goes after him in:
PHOEBE AND THE TRAITOR

An excerpt from
PHOEBE AND THE TRAITOR
follows.
And exciting news. Bob and Jenny Crusie are back with the exciting Liz Danger series with the following titles:
Lavender's Blue
https://amzn.to/46P1Yd4

Rest in Pink
https://amzn.to/43MlFQD

One in Vermillion
https://amzn.to/45NRlqJ

and **Rocky Start** in 2024

https://amzn.to/3LtcWMi

Sign up for Bob's newsletter for more news:
http://goo.gl/XnSgtB

For a book in this same vein, perhaps a bit more serious, check out:
BODYGUARD OF LIES
It's the story of how Hannah became the head of the Cellar. With the
assistance of Neeley, an assassin with an interesting history of
her own.

AUTHOR INFORMATION

Bob is a NY Times Bestselling author, graduate of West Point and former Green Beret. He's had over 80 books published including the #1 series The Green Berets, The Cellar, Area 51, Shadow Warriors, Atlantis, and the Time Patrol. Born in the Bronx, having traveled the world (usually not tourist spots), he now lives peacefully with his wife and dogs.

For information on all his books, please get a free copy of the *Reader's Guide*. You can download it in mobi (Amazon) ePub (iBooks, Nook, Kobo) or PDF, from his home page at www.bobmayer.com
For free eBooks, short stories and audio short stories, please go to
http://bobmayer.com/freebies/
The page includes free and discounted book constantly updated.
There are also free shorts stories and free audiobook stories.

Questions, comments, suggestions: Bob@BobMayer.com

Blog: http://bobmayer.com/blog/
Twitter: https://twitter.com/Bob_Mayer
Facebook: https://www.facebook.com/authorbobmayer
Subscribe to his newsletter for the latest news, free eBooks, audio, etc.

All fiction is here: **Bob Mayer's Fiction**
All nonfiction is here: **Bob Mayer's Nonfiction**

Thanks to Beta readers: Melanie Jayne, Jackie Brooks, Kendra Delugar, Pearson Moore, Laurie Anderson and L.G. O'Connor

EXCERPT PHOEBE AND THE TRAITOR

S hane's Words of Wisdom #1
Murphy's Law: What can go wrong, will go wrong.
Shane's addendum: And it will always be worse than you can imagine.

No one knows who Murphy was.

Phoebe's Observations #1
Murphy was a guy.
Enough said.

Chapter 1

"*FIE, FOH AND FUM*," Louise said from the hospital bed as Phoebe entered the room. "Of the three, my favorite is thee, Phoe."

"You always go with Shakespeare," Phoebe said, placing a small pewter figurine on the empty food tray. "I prefer *Jack and the Beanstalk*. *'Fee-fi-fum. I smell the blood of an Englishman. Be he alive, or be he dead. I'll grind his bones to make my bread'.*" She paused in thought. "I think Fromm sounds English. I'm gonna crush him."

"Oh, Phoe," Louise said with a shake of her head and a smile. "Fromm is Germanic."

"Whatever," Phoebe said. "I don't care where his ancestors came from, I know his future. The traitor's gonna die for doing this to you."

Louise's lovely halo of long golden hair was piled on the pillow, imperfect because of the bandage over the wound Fromm had given her before escaping the Organization and stealing the highly classified Orion encryption program and proving he was a traitor. She frowned at the figurine. "Gollum? I don't like him."

"But now you have all the hobbits," Phoebe pointed out. She loved listening to Louise speak in her deep Kathleen Turner voice and while she'd enjoy sitting and listening, work was calling. Plus, Phoebe hated hospitals. They were always full of sick people, which was logical but that didn't mean she had to like it.

"Was Fromm our Gollum at the Organization?" Louise asked as she sat up. Her left cheek was covered by a white bandage over the cut Fromm had inflicted. Her right arm ended just above the elbow, a disability she'd been born with.

"No," Phoebe said. "Gollum served a purpose. Fromm is worse than worthless. He betrayed us and he's still out there. But we'll find him."

They were on the fifth floor of the Fort Meade post hospital and it was time for Louise to check out. Phoebe, at five-four, much shorter than Louise, had rolled in a wheel chair for the event. She was in her late twenties and petite, with a wiry body, muscles rippling like whipcord under a black body suit. She wore a red blazer over that, the inside lined with various weapons. Her favorite, a Japanese short sword called a wakizashi, was hidden inside the coat in the center of her back, like an external spine of steel with the handle just under the collar. If someone looked for it, of course they'd spot the outline of the sword, but who is going to question a woman carrying a sword? Best to be silent and move on.

Phoebe's short black hair, with a bad red dye job mixing it up, was spiked, pointing in different directions indicating an indifference to style or perhaps an unwillingness to spend the time organizing it. Given it was Phoebe, it was a combination. Her eyes were icy blue and tiny lines of worry, too many for someone her age were emerging at the edges.

Phoebe indicated the already packed small bag. "That's everything?"

Louise nodded. "I don't need the wheelchair."

"Hospital rules."

"Since when do you worry about rules?" Louise asked.

"When it involves getting you out of here," Phoebe responded. "Some of these nurses scare me."

"Nobody scares you, Phoebe," Louise said as she swiveled in the bed and put her feet on the ground.

That gave Phoebe pause. "You did. When I heard you were hurt, it made me feel—" she shook her head unable to finish the thought, or, more appropriately, delve into the emotion behind the thought.

"Hey," Louise said, reaching out.

Phoebe took her hand and then hugged her, careful not to touch the bandage on Louise's head as she pulled her to her chest. The two remained like that for a long ten seconds, before Phoebe stirred.

"We best be going," Phoebe said.

"Yes. We should." Louise took the figurine and made the transfer from bed to chair. She'd been ready to leave for hours. She was dressed in a flowery sundress, which Phoebe had brought to her the previous evening. It was Phoebe's favorite for Louise although she would be hard-pressed to remember the last time she had worn a dress herself.

"Let us go forth then," Louise said.

Phoebe put the bag on Louise's lap and pushed her into the corridor. Nurses, doctors, patients and visitors bustled back and forth. The air held the stench of sickness and death; at least that's what Phoebe thought. She swallowed down some bile, so extreme was her reaction. This was a woman who was capable of killing with a wide array of weapons and her bare hands.

"What about the paperwork?" Louise asked.

"We don't do paperwork," Phoebe said. "We're the Organization. As far as these people are concerned, you no longer exist."

"That's not as comforting as you think it is," Louise pointed out.

Phoebe rolled Louise into the elevator, turning as she did, so Louise faced the doors. A man in over-sized scrubs, walking with a limp, hustled to catch a ride before the doors closed.

He pushed his way in, bumping against Louise's wheelchair, and moved to the rear, next to Phoebe. The elevator began descending.

Phoebe sniffed. "Fee, fi, fum. Fresh blood."

The man glanced at Phoebe. She smiled at him, her cold eyes belying the gesture, then hit him with a knuckle strike to the throat. He gasped in pain as his hands scrambled to retrieve the gun holstered inside the scrubs.

Phoebe followed up her first strike with four more in rapid succession: throat once more, solar plexus twice and a knee to the groin. As the man collapsed to the floor, she reached down and retrieved the pistol. She hit the stop button. The elevator lurched to a halt between floors.

"Phoe?" Louise was looking over her shoulder in shock. "What the Dickens?"

Phoebe pulled up the cuff of the scrubs, revealing a blood-stained bandaged stump at the ankle and an artificial foot crudely attached. Phoebe knelt on his chest as he gasped for breath. "Looking for your foot? Forensic support has it."

"Fuck you," the man finally managed, with a foreign accent.

"I wish people would get more original with their protestations,"

Phoebe said. "Lou, this is the guy whose foot I cut off at that lawyer's place you found for me. Got to give him credit for staying on the task, even though Drusilla, his boss, is dead." As she said that, Phoebe caught a flicker in the man's eyes. "Then again, *was* it Drusilla you were working for when you were cleaning up the tracks? Interesting." She nodded in growing awareness. "You were working for Fromm, weren't you? Still are."

The man grimaced, his jaw clenching.

"No, you don't!" Phoebe exclaimed, pressing against either side of his jaw to open his mouth, but she was too late. He was dead in seconds, inert on the floor, white foam bubbling over his lips.

"Oops," Phoebe whispered to herself.

"Did he just kill himself?" Louise asked.

"Yep," Phoebe said.

"Who does that?" Louise wondered in shock. "Why would he do that?"

"He came in here missing a foot and bleeding to kill us," Phoebe said. "I'd say there was considerable pressure being put on him by Fromm. Who knows what Fromm threatened?"

She took her phone out and snapped a picture of the man's face, then turned the head to take a profile shot. She noted a small fish-hook scar or brand behind the right ear and took a picture of that. Then she stood.

"There's a dead body," Louise pointed out the obvious. "What are we going to do?"

"We walk away," Phoebe said, pressing the stop once more and the elevator continued its descent.

"But ..."

"It's easier than you think," Phoebe said as they arrived at the ground floor. "Allow me, my dear." The doors opened and Phoebe briskly pushed the wheelchair out of the elevator and through the lobby toward the front doors. It was twelve seconds before someone shouted in alarm upon finding the body in the elevator. Phoebe and Louise were outside as a cluster of people were trying to make sense of the dead man in scrubs with a missing foot and froth around his mouth.

They were in the Cleaner's van before the first security guard was on scene in the elevator. Phoebe assisted Louise out of the wheelchair and into the back.

"There's a body in the elevator that needs to be policed," Phoebe informed the Cleaner, a dull looking man dressed in a cheap suit. He was one of the Support personnel from the Organization who assisted Operators on their missions, even if it was a simple trip to the hospital. Because, as had happened, even a simple trip can turn hinky. Since he was stationed here at Fort Meade it meant he probably wasn't the sharpest knife in the Organization's drawer, but even those were good enough.

The Cleaner, showing no surprise, nodded in acknowledgement and murmured something into a handheld device, getting the gears of the Organization working to clean up this mess as he put the van in drive.

"That went well," Phoebe said, "although I wish we could have taken him alive." She shut the door and the van drove off.

Louise stared at her in disbelief. "A man just died."

"Better him than us," Phoebe said. "The troubling part is that Fromm is still coming after us."

"Maybe because we're coming after him?" Louise noted.

"A valid point," Phoebe allowed. "So, let's get him."

"Where do we start?" Louise asked as the van pulled up to a nondescript building housing the Organization. It was a small, two-story concrete building with no windows. A faded, rusting sign in front bemoaned that it was *Facilities Maintenance*. The condition of the sign did not bode well for the facility, but it was a lie. The bulk of the Organization was underground and the facility was the entire country. There were three more buildings like it spread out across a field, the others over-grown with vegetation, abandoned remnants from when a Nike missile battery was stationed at Fort Meade early in the Cold War to defend Washington DC from intercontinental ballistic missiles. From a more optimistic time when it was thought a nuclear onslaught could be stopped. This particular building, though, was much more than it appeared.

"Fromm isn't just coming for us," Phoebe noted. "He's wiping out anyone who was involved in the whole Andovan thing. Even though that guy didn't kill us, he killed himself which erases another link."

"Who is left?" Louise asked as the Cleaner opened the door and Phoebe helped her out.

"The Hacker who sold the lawyer the classified encryption program that was used to set up the weapons deal that started all of this," Phoebe said. "The Feds picked him up after I got his list of clients. We'll find out where they stashed him. I never got a chance to interrogate him when we met." She paused, staring at the steel doors. "Who is *foh* and *fum*?" Phoebe suddenly asked.

Louise was confused. "What?"

"You said that I was your favorite among *Fie, foh and fum.* I want to know who my competition is."

"Oh, Phoe. You'll never have competition. You're an original. My one and only."

Lisa Livia Fortunato stood on the top floor of the Eiffel Tower feeling as if she could conquer the world, or at least a small enough portion of it for her to be happy, which was an earth-shattering concept for her. Her lover, Lucien's, arms were wrapped around her from behind, his solidly built body warm against her back. Her hands cradled a hot cup of coffee in a cardboard container. The combination of warm arms and hot nectar of the Gods offset the early morning chill and she thought for a moment: *really, could it get any better?*

Lisa Livia had dark hair that tumbled over her shoulders and olive skin, giving her an exotic, Mediterranean look which fit in here in Paris. Her New Jersey accent didn't.

There was no one else on this level as the Tower didn't open to the general public for another couple of hours. Dawn was breaking to the east over Paris and she swore that even at this altitude, she could smell freshly baked baguettes from the shops that were swinging open their shutters in the streets. The weather was warm, the trees were budding with the first green of spring, and it promised to be a beautiful day.

Paris. Lisa Livia could hardly believe she was here.

"I know we got in late last night," Lucien said, "but I wanted you to see this. I love watching the sun come up over the city. Paris is called the City of Light and most enjoy the evening, but I prefer the early morning. The quiet. The promise of the day ahead." He let go of her with one hand and pointed. "There is where we spent the night. The house on Rue St. Charles has been in our family for over a millennium."

"It's worth getting up for," Lisa Livia said, although it had been from a seriously comfortable, canopied, bigger than king-sized feather bed, the likes of which Lisa Livia had never known existed. Plus, there'd been the naked presence of Lucien, so it had been with great difficulty that he'd been able to entice her to get dressed and accompany him on the pre-dawn walk to the Tower. Vicente, one of Lucien's soldiers and friends, had been waiting to unlock the entrance for them and with the most thoughtful cup of coffee.

It had been a wonderful night with very little sleep. Lucien's arm wound had bled a little from his exertions, but Lisa Livia respected a man who could take a little pain for his pleasure with her. Lucien sported a handlebar mustache that was the trademark of the soldiers in the Andovan Army; all twelve of them. Somehow, they pulled it off without looking like fools, but rather manly men. Dark-haired, ruggedly built, Lucien sported the wound in his arm from the recent kerfuffle at Two Rivers in South Carolina involving Lucien, Shane, and primarily Phoebe defeating usurpers to the Andovan throne. That wound was added to the scar from an old bullet wound absorbed on a peace-keeping mission in Africa years ago.

"So, M'lady," Lucien asked as he held her tight once more, "what do you think of Paris so far?"

"Not too bad," Lisa Livia understated. "How'd Vicente wrangle the early opening?"

"There are perks to being in a royal family," Lucien allowed. "The French have always been partial to my mother's side, the Embrie's, considering our lineage and affiliation with France. We exchange favors. It was not difficult."

"Beats the mob in New Jersey," Lisa Livia said. "At best, you can get a free sausage at the local butcher. But didn't the French chop the heads off their royals?"

"Some," Lucien allowed. "There was a difficult period of time. But Andova was far from that not just geographically, but in temperament. We have always been very stable because of the Great Charter. We have never had a king to get his head chopped off. Just the Duke and Duchess, alternating every year for hundreds of years. No heads lost."

Lisa Livia was trying to downplay her happiness because a life of heartbreak and betrayal, especially by one's mother, isn't easily let go of in less than twenty-four hours of bliss with a good man in Paris who was granted favors because he was part of a royal family. She was content and happy and thus, not surprised when a voice spoke up from the shadows behind them.

"No sudden moves or you both die."

"Just fucking great," Lisa Livia muttered.

Lucien slowly removed his arms and they both turned. A man dressed in black, his face covered by a balaclava, held a very big gun, with a suppressor on the end of the barrel, aimed at them. He wore a climbing harness with a short loop of rope dangling from it and several carabiners.

"Pardon, but my contract is only for the man," the assassin said, in a French accent that to this point Lisa Livia had only associated with great sex, excellent food and love. "Please step apart, let me do my job, and I'll be on my way."

Lisa Livia hated the prospect of re-evaluating her affection for the French accent.

"Drusilla is dead," Lucien said, referring to the now defunct other side of the royalty in his home country of Andova. "There is no need for this. It's over and the Great Charter has been revoked."

"I do not know this Drusilla or what you speak of." The assassin shrugged, which did not alter the aim of the gun in the slightest. "I get paid. I do not worry about; how do you say? Why's and where-fores. I could have shot both, one round through, and saved myself time and a bullet, but I am a professional. Collateral damage is for amateurs."

"Did you just call me collateral?" Lisa Livia demanded.

"You will not get away with this," Lucien said.

"It will not matter to you, my friend, since you will be dead."

"But I won't be," Lisa Livia snapped. "I was having a special moment here and *you* ruined it." She indicated Lucien and asked: "You know who he is, but do you know who I am?"

"I know you are not the target," the assassin said. "You may leave. It would be best."

"I'm not going anywhere." Lisa Livia said. "My name is Lisa Livia Fortunato. If you got any experience at all as a button man, you've heard of the Fortunato's. I don't care if we are in France. Anybody whose anybody has heard of my family. You think you can whack my man here and we won't track you down wherever you go? You don't think my family can put a contract on you that will follow you around the world?" She was bluffing because her tie to the Fortunato syndi-cate other than the last name, was a father who'd betrayed it decades ago, while also abandoning her and her mother.

"Ah, American organized crime." His tone was dismissive. "Good television. Real life? Not so much to talk about." He cocked his head in momentary thought. "Ah. Fortunato's. Might have heard of them. New Jersey. But not the Sopranos. I liked them. But he did die at the end. The head of the family. Tony. Cut to black, just like what will happen now."

Great, Lisa Livia thought. *A Sopranos' fan is gonna kill me.*

The assassin shifted his aim slightly, but paused as Lisa Livia stepped in front of Lucien.

"LL, please move," Lucien whispered harshly. "This does not involve you."

"Bullshit," Lisa Livia said. "We've got a full day in Paris before we go to your home. I prefer not to spend it alone."

"Thoughtful and most practical, my dear, as always," Lucien said and Lisa Livia, once more, realized how much she loved this man.

The assassin shrugged. "Then, regrettably, it must be both of you."

"You were wrong," Lisa Livia said to him.

"Excuse?" the Assassin replied.

"Earlier. You wouldn't have saved a bullet by shooting through both of us. You're still going to use one."

"Ah. You are right, but it does not matter now, does it?"

"That's a mistake," Lisa Livia said. "I bet you've made another one."

"You talk too much," the Assassin said.

Lisa Livia hunched her shoulders, resisting Lucien's attempt to move her aside. "Who put out the contract?" she demanded.

The assassin laughed. "If I tell you, then I certainly cannot let you leave here alive. You know that, Ms. Fortunato. Nevertheless, I do not know, nor do I need to know. It is just a contract. Business. That is the beauty of our system and also why I am not worried about your threats of reprisal."

"What system?" Lisa Livia asked.

He brought the gun up and Lisa Livia was surprised at how large the black hole pointing directly between her eyes appeared. She abruptly threw the cup at the assassin. It hit him in the chest and hot coffee exploded on his body armor.

The assassin cursed in French, which despite the circumstances, still sounded somewhat sexy. And fatal.

Lisa Livia tensed, waiting for the bullet, but the assassin's gun arm dropped abruptly, then he went to his knees and keeled over, hitting the metal deck with a solid thud. *That must have hurt*, Lisa Livia thought as the man's head bounced off the deck with a sickening noise. A tall, familiar figure stood behind the body and fired once more from a suppressed pistol into the assassin's head.

"I apologize that I was not here sooner," Vicente said, sounding, indeed, very apologetic. He knelt and checked the body. "Unfortunately, I had to kill him, as I did not see another option." He didn't sound as sorry about that.

Lucien grabbed Lisa Livia and spun her about, wrapping his arms around her tightly. "Don't ever do that again!" he pled.

"Waste coffee?" Lisa Livia allowed herself the luxury of his embrace for a few seconds before objecting, speaking into his shoulder. "I had to gain us time. I knew Vicente would get here."

"You know what I mean," Lucien said.

"How about let's try not to be in that situation again," Lisa Livia suggested.

Vicente finished checking that the corpse was exactly that and looking for any sort of ID without success. He turned the head and frowned. "Curious."

"What?" Lucien asked.

"There is a very small mark behind the right ear." He ran his fingers over it. "It's a brand." He looked up. "I've seen it before."

"Where?" Lucien asked as he reluctantly let go of Lisa Livia.

"Ronaldo," Vicente said. "When I treated him at Two Rivers, I noticed it because it was not an old wound. It was a brand."

"Who is Ronaldo?" Lisa Livia asked, trying to sort through her memory of the hectic events at Agnes' home.

"The man who had the sniper rifle across the water from Two Rivers," Lucien said, which reminded Lisa Livia of their first time together, in Agnes' master bedroom. Right after Shane and Phoebe had swum across the Intracoastal to disarm the sniper who she now knew was named Ronaldo. It had been a strange, but inspiring night.

"That makes no sense," Lucien said. "Ronaldo worked for Drusilla."

"I wonder," Vicente said as he took a picture using his phone.

Lucien turned his attention to more immediate matters. "What took you so long, Vicente?"

"M'lady requested privacy before you got on the elevator." Blood was pooled around the man's head. It was the darkest blood Lisa Livia had ever seen and glistened in the early morning sun.

"Why in Heaven's name would you do that?" Lucien asked her.

"It's not quite the mile high club," Lisa Livia said, "but it would have been pretty special, you gotta admit."

"You never cease to amaze me," Lucien said.

"Let's hope so," she said. "Ignore me next time," Lisa Livia suggested to Vicente.

"I do not think I would be able to do that," Vicente said, "but I will do better in my duty."

"How did he get by you?" Lucien asked.

"I was waiting at the second level." Vicente indicated the framework of the Tower, then at the harness the dead man wore. "I suspect he climbed past me via the exterior, exclusive of the stairs and elevator."

"How did you know to come up now?" Lucien wanted to know.

"I sensed something was wrong." He was a lanky, dark-skinned man of French and Algerian parents. He sported the same mustache as Lucien, plus a beard shaded with grey. He was a soldier and trained medic, who had spent time in India studying holistic medicine. He exhibited the type of calm that soothed those around him.

"Good sense," Lisa Livia said. "Always trust your gut."

"We'll discuss this in more detail later," Lucien said to Vicente. "Are you sure he was alone?"

"I believe so, my Lord."

"We must leave and go to Andova immediately," Lucien said. "What of that?" he indicated the body.

"I will get in touch with our contact at *Direction générale de la sécurité extérieure*," Vicente said. "But first I will secure the body from sight and clean up as the Tower must open on time." He looked about at the city. "For it not to open, would be a travesty to culture and the city."

FROMM LEANED back in his chair, which was much better than the government issued one he'd had in his office in the Organization, and watched the Andovan bodyguard police up the body at the top of the Eiffel Tower. Fromm had hacked into the Tower's CCTV system and hijacked the signal to watch the assassin complete his mission and block any recording.

Fromm's computations had projected a greater probability of failure than success, so he wasn't upset. In fact, being right about the projection brought more satisfaction in some ways than Lucien's death would have. Plus, there were times when a failure brought results as worthwhile as a success. The reaction of Lucien with the woman who'd been at Two Rivers caught Fromm's interest.

He shifted his attention to another body being picked up. This one via the security camera in the elevator in the hospital at Fort Meade. That attempt had had a very slight chance of success so it had been no surprise when Phoebe, dear little Phoebe, had handled the gunman so easily. Fromm's focus, though, hadn't been on Phoebe, but rather Louise. He'd hacked into the smart TV in her hospital room and watched her, off and on, for the past twenty-four hours.

He used the mouse to bring up a clip of Louise from last month. Taken from a surveillance camera he'd had installed in her house by NSA operatives a year ago. It amused him how easy it was to get worker bees of clandestine services to do things, even illegal things, with a simple electronic order that had the right encryption and classification. They had no idea why they were doing what they did, nor who ordered it. Theirs was not to question why. It had been a mundane task, one of dozens they did every year. The fact it was illegal meant nothing as that was the reason they were a covert unit, used to doing such things.

This feed was from Louise's bedroom. She was disrobing in preparation to take a shower. Fromm relished the clip for a few moments, but he was drawn back to the screen showing the body in the elevator being placed on a gurney, a strange juxtaposition.

Phoebe? Fromm envisioned her as a cat. Lucky and skillful, but sooner or later the former would run out and the second would be trumped. In fact, he'd enjoyed running the projections. There was a whiteboard in the room labeled PHOEBE. On it he had the progressive odds of her surviving deadly encounters, in the order in which he had planned for her. He crossed through the first one, but the second loomed if the pieces on the board moved in the way he had projected. Which, of course, he knew they would. It no longer surprised him how easy it was to know what people would do once you gathered enough data on them. Facebook had proved that at a pervasive level in terms of marketing, but Fromm had taken it to a much higher level, where life and death were the stakes.

There were a number of whiteboards in the room. They were covered with nodes and arrows and probabilities. While he preferred the screens, the whiteboards allowed him to see the big picture of all the games he had in play at one time.

He was in the lair he'd been preparing for many years. He liked that word: lair. The primary definition of it is *a place where a wild animal, especially a fierce or dangerous one, lives.* It was a long sliver of room encased in steel reinforced concrete. Forty feet long by twelve wide. One end was slightly narrower than the other, a concession to the old plan of the facility he was hidden inside of. He knew that because the first time he'd entered it, he'd sensed the difference. He'd used a laser measuring tool to confirm his suspicions. It bothered him because he was attuned to things in his environment. He'd compensated by lining up the bank of high-speed computers to offset the deviation. But he knew it was there.

He glanced over at a terminal that was different than the others. The monitor had a teal blue fringe. The mainframe, larger than any other in the room, was the same color. It was currently in sleep mode. Next to it, numerous power couplings attached to nothing, poked out of the floor. They were awaiting the last piece. The draw of electricity would be tremendous once he installed the quantum computer he needed, but that would not be a problem given where the lair was located.

After all, he was the ghost in the machine.

And then he received the alert he had been anticipating.

CARPENTER, the head of the Organization, waited for Phoebe and Louise in front of the elevator in the bland entryway in the surface building, where hidden, automated weapons were trained on them as facial recognition technology checked to determine who they were.

"Really?" Carpenter said to Phoebe. "You killed someone in the post hospital?"

He was a tall black man in his forties, dressed in a well cut, dark suit. His bald head was scrolled with scars from old missions when he'd been in the field. Despite the wounds and various near-death experiences, he missed those days. It beat being the boss in more ways than he could have anticipated before he was unexpectedly promoted. He spoke precisely and in a calm, deep tone. No one in the Organization had ever heard him raise his voice, which he was well aware of because it was one of his personal rules.

"Discretionary latitude?" Phoebe suggested. "Doesn't that kick in when someone is trying to kill you? Besides, I found the owner of that foot I brought back from the last mission, so you can consider it a continuation. We now have the complete body. Maybe Support can identify him now? Besides, I didn't kill him. He did us that favor."

Carpenter sighed as they walked to the steel elevator doors. He held his card against the scanner, then his hand print, and leaned forward and had his retina scanned. They slid open. They boarded to descend into the bowels of the Organization. "Are you all right, Louise?"

"Yes, sir," she replied.

"I'm okay, too," Phoebe said. "My knuckle is a little sore from—"

Carpenter raised a hand and she stopped. "Why?"

Phoebe didn't need more than that. "Fromm was the one cutting away the links, not Drusilla. I should have realized that earlier. That guy worked for Fromm. I'm thinking Fromm has his fingers in a lot of stuff and they all stink. The whole Andova thing might be a subset of something bigger."

"You didn't know Fromm was a traitor earlier," Carpenter pointed out as the elevator dropped. "None of us did. And that's not good."

"It's a big oops," Phoebe agreed.

"Anything new turn up on Fromm, sir?" Louise asked.

"Not yet," Carpenter said.

The elevator doors slid open to a depressing vista that Carpenter had high on his list of things that should be changed; but he also knew that decision would have to be someone else's. He led Phoebe and Louise into the work area. Technical had a low ceiling with indirect lighting along the edges. The walls were painted drab, government contract to the lowest bidder, off white. Cubicled work areas were marked by small glowing pools where analysts stared at their screens doing analyzing things. It had once been where the crews for the Nike Hercules missiles worked, supposedly safe from a nuclear attack. Which, if it happened, meant their Nike missiles hadn't succeeded in stopping the enemy's missiles from hitting the nation's capitol.

"You could brighten this place up," Carpenter suggested to Louise.

"It's like the crypt of the undead," Phoebe contributed. "No offense," she added to Louise.

Louise was confused by Carpenter's statement. "What?"

"Now that Fromm is gone," Carpenter said, "you're in charge."

"Cool beans, babe," Phoebe said. "You deserve it."

Carpenter pointed to the raised office with glass windows at the far end of the room. "That's yours now. I recommend better lighting."

"The lighting is useful for the work we do," Louise said. "What we need are better screens. The ones we have are old. Not good for the eyes."

"That's your call," Carpenter said as he led her and Phoebe across the room.

"What about the budget, sir?" Louise, ever the practical one, asked.

Carpenter sighed, reminded of why he missed being the field, even at the risk of death. "Send the requisition to Mrs. Finch in purchasing. She handles that stuff."

"Have you ever seen Mrs. Finch smile?" Phoebe asked. "She's like this grim reaper sort. She grilled me over the motorcycle I crashed in Montana, as if I did it on purpose. The fact I almost died didn't seem to matter. She acted like she personally bought it and wanted to know why we didn't recover it. So, she could sell it for parts, I guess."

"All good accountants are like that," Carpenter said, his mind on more important matters as the three went into the office.

Phoebe sniffed. "Get some scented candles. This smells of old, soon-to-be-dead, traitor. I think he farted a lot too. He always looked constipated."

"TMI, Phoebe," Louise said.

As Louise sat down behind the desk, Carpenter turned to Phoebe.

"Any idea how you're going to find Fromm?"

"The Hacker I got the information about the lawyer from is still alive," Phoebe said. "I'm willing to bet a spare foot he got the encryption program he was selling from Fromm."

"I won't take that bet," Carpenter said.

"I'll find out what he knows about Fromm," Phoebe said, "because they most likely didn't do their transaction via Fromm's Organization computer. They had to have a connection. Where did the Feds stash him?"

"Technically, we're the Feds," Carpenter reminded her. "But in this case, there were some very perturbed people in the NSA and CIA about the Hacker selling their encryption program. The latter organization spirited him away to their stateside black site, which means no one can talk to him."

"Wait," Louise said. "What do you mean 'stateside', sir? That's illegal."

"The ones overseas aren't exactly legal either," Phoebe pointed out.

"That's the problem," Carpenter said. "The one in the States is very hush-hush. No one goes there."

"Not even us, the Feds?" Phoebe said.

"The CIA says such a site doesn't exist," Carpenter said. "If they allowed anyone in, that would mean it did exist."

"So, it's a Schrodinger's prison thing?" Phoebe asked.

"It's an illegal thing, as Louise pointed out," Carpenter said, "but the Organization doesn't have the moral high ground to quibble."

"We're a step above the CIA, aren't we?" Phoebe asked.

"We're kind of sideways from them," Carpenter said. "We're allowed to act domestically."

"We're sort of the FBI and CIA smushed together," Phoebe summarizesd, "but with the same pay scale and no publicity."

"The prison is domestic," Phoebe pointed out. "And the CIA isn't."

"That's the problem with them running a black site here," Carpenter said.

"Can I get in?" Phoebe asked.

"Not unless I pull in a big favor," Carpenter said, "which I only have so many of."

"Don't worry," Phoebe said. "I'll figure out a way to get to him."

"He's in a secret super-max," Carpenter warned. "The place is automated to keep the number of people working there to a minimum. Just a handful of caretakers of the computers and machines. It's the way everything is going now."

"That's good news," Louise said. "Since it relies on computers to run things, we can work with that."

"Probably easier to get in than out of," Phoebe said.

"True," Carpenter agreed, "but you still have to get out."

"I'll leave a trail of bread crumbs," Phoebe said.

"I'll make a call," Carpenter promised, afraid Phoebe's bread crumbs, might be bodies.

"Appreciate it." Phoebe turned to Louise. "How do you like your new set up?"

"Thank you," Louise said to Carpenter. "Not just for the job, but all of this." She indicated the old-style keyboard that had been at her old work station. She put on the special glasses that worked as a mouse to compensate for her missing arm.

"One of your techs tried accessing Fromm's computer," Carpenter said, "but no luck. I'm hoping you'll do better."

"Does it call for a pass code?" Louise asked as she turned it on.

"No," Carpenter said. "The screen just stays black."

"Did you unplug and plug it back in?" Phoebe asked, which Carpenter and Louise saw fit to ignore.

Louise waved her access card, then did the palm print and retina scan.

The screen flickered and came on, blank white.

"That's a better result than we had," Carpenter said.

"I don't think so," Phoebe said. "It means Fromm knew I'd try. I'm afraid—" She stopped as the power went out, encasing the entire floor in pitch black.

"Oops," Phoebe said.

"This isn't good," Louise said.

Emergency lights came on near the exit.

"Fromm left us something," Louise said as she typed to no avail.

The screen flickered and an image appeared.

Phoebe glanced out at the work area. All the screens displayed the same.

Fromm's voice echoed out of the small speakers on the side of the display, but not on the computers outside the office. "There was an eighty-six percent chance you'd be standing there right now, Carpenter. Looking over Louise Wingo's shoulder, exactly like you are."

Louise pointed at the small dot on top of the monitor and mouthed '*Cover?*' to Carpenter. Carpenter heard a small whisper from the ghost on his shoulder. The voice he thought he'd finally banished, was back. His late father's voice of guilt and recrimination. The shrink had advised him to externalize the voice, but that hadn't silenced it.

He shook his head to Louise. "How about letting us see you?" Carpenter said to Fromm. "It's only fair."

"'Fair'?" Fromm gargled something that might have been a laugh. "When has that ever been a standard for action by the Organization?" He didn't wait for answer. "You don't control this, Carpenter. Not at all, in case you haven't been paying attention. On the other hand, I see so much more than you can imagine. It's the World Wide Web, after all. Did you know that when ARPERNET first came on line in 1969 a very prescient man predicted it would be the end of secrecy? No one listened, of course. They never listen to geniuses. And, ever since, we've been in this battle to encrypt, trying to stay one step ahead of the enemy who are trying to decrypt. A fun game I've devoted most of my life to. Wherever the Internet goes, so can I. And there are few places left it hasn't spread its tentacles to. I can travel almost anywhere in the world right from here."

Carpenter noted Phoebe rolling her eyes. "Where is here?" he asked.

Fromm ignored the question. "I'm not surprised that Louise is in my office. I was certain you'd give her my position, Carpenter. And she's even the right choice. If you're playing a game of checkers, that is. But she's in way over her head. You too, Carpenter." There was a short pause. "I don't see her, but is our damaged angel of death, Phoebe, there? Did she tell you I called her after the pyrrhic victory in South Carolina? She's a good little Girl Scout, so I imagine she did. And I know for certain she's vowed to come after me with all sort of dire proclamations. Little does she know what I have in store for her. For all of you. What a sad, pathetic little group you all are."

Phoebe crossed her arms over her chest but didn't say anything to indicate she was in the office.

"Why was South Carolina pyrrhic?" Carpenter asked.

Out of sight of the camera, Louise's hand was typing, working. Carpenter knew she was trying to track Fromm down. He also knew, as she probably did too, that it was a fruitless task.

"Because the war isn't over," Fromm said. "Come on, Carpenter. You know history. And you're not a stupid man. Not a genius, but not stupid. I still wonder, though, why you were promoted to be in charge. Especially, since I was so much more capable."

"Perhaps because you're a traitor," Carpenter said.

"Traitor to who?" Fromm said. "To what? A corrupt country?"

"Your oath," Carpenter said. "Your word."

"You're a fool. This is just beginning."

"You've already failed," Carpenter said. "The Great Charter was dissolved. Andova has an elected government and is stable."

"Was it? Is it?" Fromm asked, but Carpenter knew he wasn't really asking.

"What do you want?" Carpenter demanded.

"What do I want?" Fromm mused. "Funny how no one asked me that when I sat in that office. No one cared what I wanted then."

Phoebe couldn't help herself. "Whiner."

"Ah, we finally hear from the cheap seats," Fromm said. His sigh was clearly audible from the speakers. "Phoebe, Phoebe, Phoebe."

"You're repeating yourself," Phoebe said. "Sounds like your brain is broken."

"I'm multitasking," Fromm said. "Surely you don't think this is the only game I'm involved in. Life would be unbearably boring if that were so. Ever watch a Grandmaster playing multiple boards at the same time? Defeating so many aspiring masters? And the Grandmaster always wins, remember that. But for you, Phoebe, I have something special lined up for you. You've only just begun to walk the course I've laid out especially for you."

Phoebe rolled her eyes once more. "You got a repetition thing going." She walked around and stood behind Louise's other shoulder. "Really, Fromm. Why are you hiding? Your bald spot getting bigger? What are you afraid of? You one of those guys who tapes over his computer camera while he jerks off?"

The skull and swords disappeared, but only on this computer, and was replaced by black, then Fromm appeared. He was facing the camera, his head and shoulders visible. Behind him was a dull grey wall. "Happy?" He was a late middle-aged man with pale skin and a receding hairline. Unremarkable at best. His eyes were noticeable though, with a slight sheen of crazy covering the dead soul behind them.

"My heart has skipped a beat," Phoebe said, dripping sarcasm. "Where are you? Save me some time tracking you down."

Fromm scoffed. "I said you had no idea of the depth of what you've waded into. You'll learn, bit by bit, but always at least one step behind. Usually more than one. Always too late. That is, of course, dependent on how long you survive. My data suggests an exponential possibility of failure based on encounters. With failure equating to your death."

"What is the mean of the exponential?" Louise asked.

Phoebe had no idea what the question meant.

"Three point seven," Fromm said. "Which is impressive but indicates that ultimately our dear, dear Phoebe, will die."

"Blah, blah, blah," Phoebe said. "You really like the sound of your own voice, don't you?"

"Now who is repeating themselves?" Fromm asked. "Andova is anything but stable, Carpenter. The Duke and Duchess proclaiming it so during their little ceremony in South Carolina isn't holding much weight back home. And killing the Duchess Navarro? Some people are not happy about that at all. And not just in Andova."

"She killed herself," Phoebe said, "by frolicking in the mud with an alligator."

"That's your version," Fromm said. "I'm playing a different version in Andova that has more traction. Remember, *who controls the past, controls the future. Who controls the present controls the past*."

"You're no George Orwell," Carpenter said.

"I'm better," Fromm said. "Orwell was just a scribbler of words. And that wasn't even his real name. Just as Fromm isn't the name I was born with."

Carpenter felt an uneasy stirring. "You were thoroughly vetted." But the voice on Carpenter's shoulder was already whispering.

Fromm laughed. "Who do you think gets *that* job? Vetting for security clearances? Not the best and the brightest, I assure you. The ones no one wants on their team doing real world ops. The people crossing off days on their calendar, waiting for that magic date when they can get their federal pension and retire, to mark off days on their calendar doing nothing until they die. Besides, my vetting was decades ago, Carpenter. Do you know how easy it was back then to invent an identity and backstop it with enough validity that it would pass a security check by the rubes doing it?"

"Who are you, then?" Carpenter asked, regretting the question as soon as he said it.

"I am the end of you," Fromm said. "All of you. I control the internet and thus control the present. I can reshape the past in whatever way I desire. I can influence events to achieve the future I desire. Do you not think it odd that people have access to more information than ever before but know less? They only seek out that which supports what they already think. The key is to find those people and amplify and then adjust the message, whether it is true or not."

Phoebe leaned forward, putting her fists on Louise's desk. "Thanks for the TED talk, Fromm. Why don't you just tell me where you are so we can end this? Keep running and you're just going to die tired."

"I'm not running," Fromm said. "Not at all. I'm very comfortable actually. You're the one who will get tired of chasing ghosts."

"I have a lot of energy," Phoebe said.

"It won't help you," Fromm said. "You're going to be the one running, Phoebe. But eventually, you'll get caught."

"Who is going to be chasing me?" Phoebe asked.

"It's already started," Fromm said.

"And you're losing," Phoebe said.

"Exponential," Fromm repeated.

"So far we seem to be winning," Phoebe said. "We stopped you in South Carolina and just now. Your one-footed man failed. Really, is that the best you can do?"

"Doesn't matter. It was a win either way. You did my work for me. One less loose end to concern myself with. I'd have been happier, though, if he'd removed you from the board, but alas, there was an eighty-two percent possibility he would not succeed, so I wasn't surprised. But, remember. Exponential. Sooner or later, you will lose, Phoebe."

"Why'd he kill himself?" Louise asked. "What did you threaten him with?"

"He had a code," Fromm said.

Louise spoke up. "Sort of a 'On my shield or with it' code?"

"Something like that," Fromm said.

Phoebe was skeptical. "You trusted a code? When you violated your own oath?"

"Not really," Fromm admitted. "He was already a walking dead man."

"What do you mean?" Carpenter asked.

Fromm gave a sly smile. "You see, Carpenter? So much you don't know."

"You're babbling, Fromm," Carpenter said.

"I was being nice," Fromm said. "Humoring you. But I can see that's wasted. You want to know what I want, Carpenter? Chaos. Because only out of chaos can order begin anew."

"You're crazy," Carpenter said.

"They say that about all geniuses," Fromm said. "Those who can't understand what they can't comprehend." There was a noise in his background. A voice. He glanced over his shoulder. "Patience, my dear. I'll be done with these pests shortly."

Carpenter exchanged a glance with Phoebe, then Louise, wondering who Fromm was speaking too. According to his file, Fromm was single without any social life.

"Talking to a mirror, Fromm?" Phoebe asked.

"Why do you think you're humorous, Phoebe?" Fromm asked. "You use humor to cover up your pain. Could it be because you have no clue who your mother is?"

Carpenter jumped in. "You're not even making sense, Fromm. What the hell do you want?"

Before Fromm could answer, a woman entered the frame, behind Fromm's right shoulder, out of focus. In side silhouette was a thin short-haired, tall blond dressed in black turtleneck and black slacks. "Stop wasting time with these people." Her voice was reminiscent of Katherine Hepburn at the height of her haughty.

Phoebe couldn't hold back. "What online bride order site did you get her off of, Fromm? We know your charm had nothing to do with it, since you don't have any."

Fromm nodded his head. "Lilith, meet Carpenter, Louise and Phoebe. I spent many years of my life working amidst their ignorance."

"What a waste of brilliance," Lilith said, turning to face the camera and shaking her head.

"I'll be with you in a minute, dear," Fromm said.

Carpenter looked at Louise and then Phoebe as they clearly saw the woman's face for the first time. She was Louise's twin in facial structure and body, but had both arms intact. Her hair was much shorter but the same color. The eyes were also a match.

"What the fuck?" Phoebe exclaimed.

"You like?" Fromm said. "You would, wouldn't you, Phoebe? Given how you feel about Louise." He turned in the seat. "Give us some space, dear."

Lilith frowned and moved out of sight.

"I had decades to prepare," Fromm said. "You've had hours. By now, those outside of the Organization are aware that your system is infected. Which they were figuring out anyway. I'm always far ahead and your counter-moves play right into my hands." The skull and swords disappeared and a CCTV image from the camera on the front of the building displayed a number of black SUVs pulling up and armed guards establishing a perimeter.

"I predict you'll get a call in a few minutes, Carpenter," Fromm promised. "From that woman, Hannah, whom you know nothing about, who heads a unit you know even less about. She runs the Cellar which is even more secret than the Organization. She will not be happy. Because all you see right now is the smoke. But the fire? It's burns hot and deep. Think long and hard before your next move. And remember, it doesn't matter, it will always be the wrong one." He smiled. "Welcome to the game, Phoebe. And remember this. I want you to see your end coming. No easy out for you. I want you to experience that exquisite pain of knowing you failed and I won before it all goes black. In that last lingering moment before final oblivion, think of me."

The screen went blank and silence reigned for a few seconds.

"What an asshole," Phoebe said. "Can't believe you had to work for him," she said to Louise.

None of them spoke about Lilith, each trying to process what they had seen.

Carpenter's secure phone rang and the ghost on his shoulder cackled.

"Excuse me," Carpenter said, nodding toward the door.

Phoebe and Louise exited, shutting the door.

He took the call standing up. "Carpenter."

Unlike the last time, there was no wait as a woman's voice spoke: "I'd have you come see me, but the NSA has locked down your facility."

"The infection left a Trojan Horse in our system," Carpenter told Hannah, the head of the Cellar.

"Oh, Mister Carpenter, it's worse than that. Much worse. Your infection, and let's call him by name, Fromm, if that is his real name, did considerably more. He took Orion, our latest cipher, with him and has put it on the open market. The deep, black market, that is. Final bids are due in four days, with the program going to the winner. The baseline is two hundred million dollars and it's already been met on the dark net."

"I'll be—"

Hannah cut him off. "The NSA has shut down the Organization indefinitely until it's determined whether Fromm acted alone. We don't know who we can trust. Fromm's infected your computer system so the NSA has isolated you since they control those lines. They're checking now to see if the virus infested their systems. If it has . . . ." She left the remainder unsaid

Carpenter had nothing to say to that.

"Fromm is only part of this," Hannah said. "Your predecessor, Wilson, was corrupt. Who knows how far the cancer has spread in the Organization." It was not a question; more a threat. "I'll keep this line open for you, Carpenter. I'm sure you'll have questions that need answers. I have resources that are, shall we say, unique."

Carpenter pondered the implications. Asking Hannah about things was also potentially targeting the subject of those questions.

"Do you understand?" Hannah asked.

"Yes."

"The entire Organization is on the line," Hannah said. "Similar corrupt entities in the past have been eradicated."

Carpenter envisioned a great white shark swallowing everyone in this place.

"I'm going to give you a chance to make this right," Hannah said. "You have until the end of the auction. If you fail to stop it, secure Orion, and terminate Fromm, I will be forced to take action."

Carpenter didn't say anything.

Hannah continued. "You need to get your operative on Fromm's trail. It's Phoebe, right?"

"Yes."

"She'll need help. Bring her in and put us on speaker."

Carpenter looked out the glass and pointed at Phoebe. She and Louise were in an intense discussion, no doubt over the confusing issue of Lilith. He crooked his finger and she came in. He pointed at the phone. "Hannah wants to speak with us."

Phoebe mouthed '*Hannah*' with a questioning look.

In response, Carpenter mouthed '*Cellar*'. Then he announced. "Phoebe's here."

Hannah spoke: "As your boss will tell you, the Organization is locked down by the NSA. I'm sure you are ingenious enough to slip out. When you do, there's someone you should go to who might be of help."

"'Might'?" Phoebe said.

"She's peculiar," Hannah said.

Phoebe raised an eyebrow at Carpenter. "Meaning?"

"She's a former operative," Hannah said. "She has considerable experience and contacts. She could be of great assistance."

"You keep qualifying it," Phoebe pointed out.

"She's eccentric," Hannah said.

"Peculiar and eccentric," Phoebe noted. "Sounds like my kind of gal." She winked at Carpenter who wondered if Phoebe understood the danger of the Cellar.

Hannah must have felt the same because her sigh was audible. "Young woman, tread lightly in the darkness."

"Yes, ma'am," Phoebe said. "How do I find this person?"

"Go to *The Dog's Balls*," Hannah said.

"Excuse me?" Phoebe said.

"It's a bar. You'll find it," Hannah assured her.

"Who do I ask for?" Phoebe said.

"Just go there. She'll find you."

"Right," Phoebe said.

"Carpenter," Hannah said. "I'll contact you when we learn more." The line went dead.

"She's kind of touchy," Phoebe said.

"She runs the Cellar," Carpenter said. "Her operatives are judge, jury and executioner for anyone she targets. Her mandate is to police the ranks of covert operations. That means us."

"Sort of like discretionary latitude," Phoebe said. "Except on a bigger scale, right?"

Carpenter shook his head and waved Louise into the office. He updated her on what Hannah had said. When he was done, Phoebe asked: "I guess that means you can't make a call to get me in to see the Hacker at the super-max?"

"Did you hear what Hannah said?" Carpenter said, putting an edge in his voice. "I doubt I can get you out of here."

Phoebe exchanged a look with Louise, then addressed Carpenter. "I can get out."

Carpenter stared at her, then nodded, accepting that Hannah knew more about his own unit than he did. "All right."

"How the heck is he going to get paid two hundred million?" Phoebe asked. "In small bills in a briefcase?"

"It will likely go much higher than that," Carpenter said.

"Andova," Louise interjected.

That clicked with Carpenter. "If he had a favorable regime there, he could process a lot of money through their banks."

"But he doesn't," Phoebe pointed out.

"At the moment," Louise said. "It's obvious he worked with Drusilla and Guillermo to wipe out the Embries and put them in charge. And now he's working with people in Andova to push the Embrie family out. Fromm liked to boast, but there was always something of substance behind what he said. If he says control of Andova is uncertain, then it is. This is why he was involved from the start."

"It was a distraction," Carpenter said.

Both women turned to him, wondering what he was talking about.

"The woman," Carpenter said. "The one with Fromm. An actress most likely. He found someone who looked like you," he said to Louise, "and had her show her face to confuse us."

Surprisingly, Louise laughed. "It wasn't real."

It was Carpenter's turn to be confused. "What?"

"The woman," Louise said. "It was a hologram. Projected. Something Fromm conjured. The way it moved. Like a videogame. Almost perfectly human in image but not quite. He was always a bit weak in that area of programming."

"Asshole," Phoebe said.

"Let's forget about the distraction," Carpenter said. "Keep our eye on the main issue. Finding Fromm and getting the encryption program off the market."

Both women nodded in agreement.

"You're going to need help," Carpenter said. "Besides this contact from Hannah."

"I want Sam the Cleaner," Phoebe said, referring to the man she'd worked with in Montana.

"You have my authorization to get Sam."

Louise spoke up. "I'll use a secure, private link separate from the Organization's system to stay in contact with Phoebe until I can cleanse Fromm's infection."

"Why did you make a separate line?" Carpenter asked Louise. "Doesn't that violate security?"

Louise couldn't meet his gaze. "Just a contingency, sir."

Phoebe jumped in to the defense. "It's not a security risk if no one knows about it and it's never been used."

"Did you know about it?" Carpenter asked her.

"Not until recently," Phoebe said, "which is why I'm certain no one other than Louise knew."

"Which means it's secure from Fromm," Louise added.

"And this way you have out of here?" Carpenter pressed Phoebe.

"We found that together," Phoebe admitted. "I had Louise dig up the old blueprints for this place. They were in the National Archives in DC. You know what year thing was built?"

"Nineteen-fifty-three," Carpenter said. "When the first Nike Ajax missile battery was emplaced here to defend the capitol. It was abandoned and then repurposed for the Organization."

Phoebe blinked, recognizing she'd asked the wrong man a historical question. "Right. Okay. Well, Lou found the original blueprints and we saw a small line on the paper and it turned out to be a service tunnel that was sealed off."

"You unsealed it?" Carpenter asked and something in his tone must have alerted Phoebe because she became defensive and proper.

"Not yet, sir. We just know where it is and that it's accessible and exits on the surface a distance away. I'm sure I can get through. The people guarding us are NSA. I mean how many of those dudes ever did a real on-the-ground op? You call them to fix your laptop, but not stop an operator."

"Don't kill any of them," Carpenter ordered.

"I won't, sir," Phoebe promised.

"Or maim," Carpenter added.

Phoebe appeared disappointed.

The voice on Carpenter's shoulder was whispering doubts. Could he trust Phoebe and Louise? As significant a take was whether he could trust Phoebe or Louise. They might or might not be working in concert. To what end if they were?

Carpenter folded his arms. "Why did you do this?" he asked both of them.

Phoebe and Louise exchanged another look, with Phoebe nodding toward Louise, whose turn it was to get nervous. "I didn't trust Fromm, sir."

"Why?" Carpenter asked.

Phoebe answered, *the other half of frick and frack*, the voice on Carpenter's shoulder whispered.

"He stunk," Phoebe said. "Besides literally. There was something off about him. You must have noticed."

Carpenter had and he suspected that was the reason his father's voice was back. He'd never felt right about Fromm, but when he was unexpectedly elevated to take over the Organization less than a year ago, he didn't feel he had the experience or the solid footing to relieve a department head whom he'd leapfrogged.

The ghost on his shoulder was cackling at what that had resulted in.

"So, there's really a Cellar?" Phoebe mused. "I've heard rumors."

"There's really a Cellar and you just talked to the head of it," Carpenter confirmed.

"Hannah?" Phoebe said. "That's what she's called? Just Hannah?"

"Yes."

"She'd probably be pretty cool to meet," Phoebe said.

Carpenter stopped that one in its tracks. "She isn't. The Cellar's mandate is to take out rogue operatives. That's Fromm. But I'm afraid that might expand to the entire Organization if we don't show that we can handle our own mess."

"So, this contact she gave might be a setup," Phoebe said.

Carpenter nodded. "It's a possibility. Go in with your eyes open."

"I always try to," Phoebe said. "Even if I'm treading carefully in the dark."

"It would be advantageous if you got to Fromm before the Cellar does," Carpenter said.

"If I hook up with this contact of Hannah," Phoebe observed, "I'll be getting to Fromm at the same time as the Cellar."

"She didn't say the contact was a former Cellar operative," Carpenter pointed out. "Just an operative."

"You're thinking Hannah has her own people after Fromm?" Phoebe asked.

"It's likely," Carpenter said.

"Then why does she care about what I do?" Phoebe wondered.

Carpenter had no answer to that.

"This is a big mess," Louise said. "If an enemy gets their hand on Orion, all our secure networks will be breached."

"Won't they just go to the next cipher, whatever it is?" Phoebe asked.

"If the NSA has one, they certainly will," Louise agreed. "But it means all our old traffic can be deciphered. Everyone is constantly tapping into comms and recording each other. Lots of covers and operations will be exposed. It would be a crippling blow to the intelligence community and the country. We can't go back and change what's already been sent."

"And the clock is ticking," Carpenter said. "How long will it take to cleanse our computer system and get us back on-line?"

Louise shook her head. "I need to dive into it and get an idea of what Fromm did before I can give an estimate."

Carpenter's secure phone buzzed and he glanced down. Lisa Livia. He'd gotten rid of the burner they talked on after the first wedding at Two Rivers when they'd met last year. He'd given her his official number with strict instructions that it was only to be used in emergency.

Phoebe and Louise were staring at him, waiting.

Reluctantly, knowing it would not be good news, Carpenter picked it up.

"Lisa Livia, what's going on?"

She led with the headline. "Someone just tried to kill Lucien. On the Eiffel Tower. Ruined a perfectly wonderful morning." She went on to tell him what had occurred.

"Are you safe?" Carpenter asked when she was done.

"Yeah. We're in the car on the way to the airport. We're flying to Andova."

"Have Lucien's people send us what they have on the assassin," Carpenter said. He gestured to Louise. *Secure email?* He mouthed.

Louise wrote on a pad and showed him. "Have them use this address," he said to Lisa Livia.

"I'm all right, by the way," Lisa Livia said.

"I assumed that," Carpenter said, wincing as he said it.

"That was always the problem," Lisa Livia's voice held that red tinge of anger which he knew better than to reply to. "You assuming. You assumed your way right away from me."

"Lisa Livia," Carpenter said, but that was the extent of his reply because what else was there to say?

"Yeah, yeah," Lisa Livia. "I know. You have something going on. Just letting you know what's happening in my life. Assassins on the Eiffel Tower and all that. Since it seems I'm still connected to your problems somehow." The phone went dead.

Carpenter informed Phoebe and Louise of the attempted assassination. Concluding with: "Fromm is behind it. He said the situation in Andova wasn't settled. But that's not our priority right now. We've got to get Fromm." He looked at Phoebe. "You best move out. Louise? Give her everything we have on the CIA supermax in West Virginia."

PHOEBE AND THE TRAITOR

SHANE AND THE HITWOMAN

ISBN
ebook: 9781621253662
Trade paperback: 978-1621253679
Hardcover: 978-1621253686

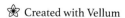 Created with Vellum